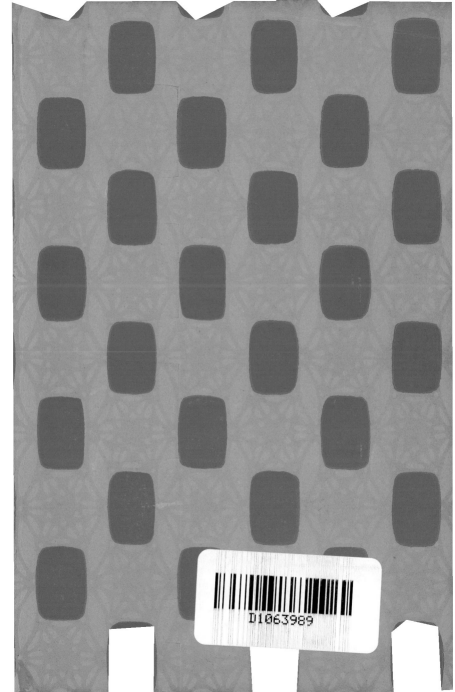

THE THREE
BLACK PENNYS

Joseph Hergesheimer

NOVELS

The Lay Anthony, 1914
Mountain Blood, 1915
The Three Black Pennys, 1917
Java Head, 1918
Linda Condon, 1919
Cytherea, 1922
The Bright Shawl, 1922
Balisand, 1924

SHORTER STORIES

Wild Oranges, 1918
Tubal Cain, 1918
The Dark Fleece, 1918
The Happy End, 1919

TRAVEL

San Cristobal de la Habana, 1920

AUTOBIOGRAPHY

The Presbyterian Child, 1923
From An Old House, 1925

JOSEPH
HERGESHEIMER

THE THREE
BLACK PENNYS

A NOVEL

ALFRED·A·KNOPF
NEW YORK
1925

A DEDICATION

Dear John Hemphill.

   This is a record and act of memory
of you at Dower House — of June
nights on the porch, with the foliage
of the willow tree powdered against
the stars; the white-panelled hearth
of the yellow room in smouldering
winter dusks; dinner with the candles
wavering in tepid April airs; and
the blue envelopment of late September noons.   A quiet reach like the old
grey house and green fields, the little
valleys filled with trees and placid
town beyond the hill, where the calen-
dar of our days and companionship is
set.

                Joseph Hergesheimer

CONTENTS

I THE FURNACE

I

A TWILIGHT like blue dust sifted into the
shallow fold of the thickly wooded hills.
It was early October, but a crisping frost
had already stamped the maple trees with gold, the
Spanish oaks were hung with patches of wine red,
the sumach was brilliant in the darkening underbrush. A pattern of wild geese, flying low and unconcerned above the hills, wavered against the serene,
ashen evening. Howat Penny, standing in the comparative clearing of a road, decided that the shifting, regular flight would not come close enough for
a shot. He dropped the butt of his gun to the
ground. Then he raised it again, examining the
hammer; the flint was loose, unsatisfactory. There
was a probability that it would miss firing.

He had no intention of hunting the geese. With
the drooping of day his keenness had evaporated; an
habitual indifference strengthened, permeating him.
He turned his dark, young face toward the trans-

3

parent, green afterglow; the firm eyebrows drawn up at the temples, sombre eyes set, too, at a slight angle, a straight nose, impatient mouth and projecting chin. Below him, and to the left, a heavy, dark flame and silvery smoke were rolling from the stack of Shadrach Furnace. Figures were moving obscurely over the way that led from the coal house, set on the hill, to the top and opening of the furnace; finishing, Howat Penny knew, the charge of charcoal, limestone and iron ore.

Shadrach Furnace had been freshly set in blast; it was on that account he was there, to represent, in a way, his father, who owned a half interest in the Furnace. However, he had paid little attention to the formality; his indifference was especially centred on the tedious processes of iron making, which had, at the same time, made his family. He had gone far out from the Furnace tract into an utterly uninhabited and virginal region, where he had shot at, and missed, an impressive buck and killed a small bear. Now, that he had returned, his apathy once more flooded him; but he had eaten nothing since morning, and he was hungry.

He could go home, over the nine miles of road that bound the Furnace to Myrtle Forge and the Penny dwelling; there certain of whatever supper he would elect. But, he decided, he preferred something now, less formal. There were visitors at Myrtle Forge, Abner Forsythe, who owned the other half of Shadrach, his son David, newly back from

4

England and the study of metallurgy, and a Mr. Winscombe, come out to the Provinces in connection with the Maryland boundary dispute, accompanied by his wife. All this Howat Penny regarded with profound distaste; necessary social and conversational forms repelled him. And it annoyed his father when he sat, apparently morose, against the wall, or retired solitary to his room.

He would get supper here; they would be glad to have him at the house of Peter Heydrick, the manager of the Furnace. Half turning, he could see the dwelling at his back — a small, grey stone rectangle with a narrow portico on its solid face and a pale glimmer of candles in the lower windows. The ground immediately about it was cleared of brush and little trees, affording Peter Heydrick a necessary, unobstructed view of the Furnace stack while sitting in his house or when aroused at night. The dwelling was inviting, at once slipping into the dusk and emerging by reason of the warm glow within. Mrs. Heydrick, too, was an excellent cook; there would be plenty of venison, roast partridge, okra soup. Afterwards, under a late moon, he could go back to Myrtle Forge; or he might stay at the Heydricks all night, and to-morrow kill such a buck as he had lost.

The twilight darkened beneath the trees, the surrounding hills lost their forms, in the east the distance merged into the oncoming night, but the west was still translucent, green. There was a faint movement in the leaves by the roadside, and a grey fox crossed, flattened on the ground, and disappeared. Howat Penny could see the liquid gleam of its eyes as it watched him. From the hill by the coal house came the heavy beating of wild turkeys' wings.

He could go to Peter Heydrick's, where the venison would be excellent, and Mrs. Heydrick was celebrated for her guinea pickle with cucumbers; but . . . the Heydricks had no daughter, and the Gilkans had. Thomas Gilkan was only a founderman; his house had one room below and a partition above; and Mrs. Gilkan's casual fare could not be compared to Mrs. Heydrick's inviting amplitude. Yet there was Fanny Gilkan, erect and flaming haired, who could walk as far as he could himself, and carry her father's clumsy gun all the way.

His thoughts, deflected by Fanny Gilkan, left the immediate present of supper, and rested upon the fact that his — his appreciation of her was becoming known at the Furnace; while Dan Hesa must be circulating it, with biting comments, among the charcoal burners. Dan Hesa, although younger than Howat, was already contracting for charcoal, a forward young German; and, Fanny had said with a giggle, he was paying her serious attention. Howat Penny had lately seen a new moroseness among the charcoal burners that could only have come from the association of the son of Gilbert Penny and the potential owner of Myrtle Forge with the founder-

6

man's daughter. Charcoal burners were lawless men, fugitive in character, often escaped from terms of indenture; Dan Hesa was, he knew, well liked by them; and the hazard created by his attraction to Fanny Gilkan drew Howat Penny irresistibly away from the superior merits of the Heydrick table.

That was his character: denial as a child had filled him with slow-accumulating rage; later discipline at school had found him utterly intractable. Something deep and instinctive within him resisted every effort to make him a part of any social organization, however admirable; he never formed any personal bonds with humanity in particular. He had grown into a solitary being within whom were immovably locked all the confidences, the spontaneous expressions of self, that bind men into a solidarity of common failings and hopes. He never offered, nor, apparently, required, any marks of sympathy; as a fact, he rarely expressed anything except an occasional irrepressible scorn lashing out at individuals or acts that conspicuously displeased him. This had occurred more than once at Myrtle Forge, when assemblymen or members of the Provincial Council had been seated at dinner.

It was after such a scene that his mother had witnessed perhaps his only attempt at self-explanation. "I am sorry you were disturbed," he had pronounced, after standing and regarding her for a silent, frowning space; " but for me there is something unendurable in men herding like cattle, pro-

7

tecting their fat with warning boards and fences. I can't manage the fiddling lies that keep up the whole silly pretence of the stuffy show. If it gets much thicker," he had threatened, waving vaguely toward the west, " I'll go out to the Ohio, or the French forts."

That this was not merely a passive but an active state of mind was amply expressed by his resolute movement toward Thomas Gilkan's house. He had, ordinarily, an unusual liking for the charcoal burners, and had spent many nights in their huts, built, like the charring stacks, of mud and branches. But, organized by Dan Hesa into an opposition, a criticism of his choice of way, they offered an epitome of the conditions he derided and assailed.

His feeling for Fanny Gilkan was in the greater part understood, measured; there was a certain amount of inchoate, youthful response to her sheer physical well being, a vague blur of pleasant sensation at her proximity; but beyond that he felt no attraction except a careless admiration for her endurance and dexterity in the woods, a certain relief in the freedom of her companionship. He had never considered her concretely as a possible source of physical pleasure. He was not easily excited sexually, and had had few adventures with women; something of his contempt, his indifference, removed him from that, too. His emotions were deep, vital; and hid beneath a shyness of habit that had grown into a suspicious reserve. All bonds were irksome

8

to him, and instinctively he avoided the greater with the lesser; instinctively he realized that the admission of cloying influences, of the entanglements of sex, would more definitely bind him than any generality of society.

It had, he thought, grown dark with amazing rapidity. He could now see a feeble light at the Gilkans, ahead and on the right. At the same moment a brighter, flickering radiance fell upon the road, the thick foliage of the trees. The blast was gathering at Shadrach Furnace. A clear, almost smokeless flame rose from the stack against the night-blue sky. It illuminated the rectangular, stone structure of the coal-house on the hill, and showed the wet and blackened roof of the casting shed below. The flame dwindled and then mounted, hanging like a fabulous oriflamme on a stillness in which Howat Penny could hear the blast forced through the Furnace by the great leather bellows.

He turned in, over the littered ground before the Gilkan house. Fanny was standing in the doorway, her straight, vigorous body sharp against the glow inside. "Here's Mr. Howat Penny," she called over her shoulder. "Is everything off the table? There's not much," she turned to him, "but the end of the pork barrel." A meagre fire was burning in the large, untidy hearth; battered tin ovens had been drawn aside, and a pair of wood-soled shoes were drying. The rough slab of the table, pushed back against a long seat made of a partly hewed

9

and pegged log, was empty but for some dull scarred
pewter and scraps of salt meat. On the narrow
stair that led above, a small, touselled form was
sleeping — one of the cast boys at the Furnace.

A thin, peering woman in a hickory-dyed wool
dress moved forward obsequiously. " Mr. Penny! "
she echoed the girl's announcement; " and here I
haven't got a thing fit for you. Thomas Gilkan has
been too busy to get out, and Fanny she'll fetch
nothing unless the mood's on her. If I only had a
fish I could turn over." She brushed the end of the
table with a frayed sleeve. " You might just take
a seat, and I'll look around."

Fanny Gilkan listened to her mother with a comprehending smile. Fanny's face was gaunt, but her
grey eyes were wide and compelling, her mouth was
firm and bright; and her hair, her father often said,
resembled the fire at the top of Shadrach. Howat
knew that she was as impersonal, as essentially un-
stirred, as himself; but he had a clear doubt of Mrs.
Gilkan. The latter was too anxious to welcome him
to their unpretending home; she obviously moved to
throw Fanny and himself together, and to disparage
such suits as honest Dan Hesa's. He wondered if
the older woman thought he might marry her daughter. And wondering he came to the conclusion that
the other thing would please the mother almost as
well. She had given him to understand that at
Fanny's age she would know how to please any Mr.
Howat Penny that chance fortune might bring her.

10

That some such worldly advice had been poured into Fanny's ears he could not doubt; and he admired the girl's obvious scorn of such wiles and surrenders. She sat frankly beside him now, as he finished a wretched supper, and asked about the country in regions to which she had not penetrated. "It's a three days' trip," he finished a recital of an excursion of his own.

"I'd like to go," she returned; "but I suppose I couldn't find it alone."

He was considering the possibility of such a journey with her — it would be pleasant in the extreme — when her mother interrupted them from the foot of the stair.

"A sensible girl," she declared, "would think about seeing the sights of a city, and of a cherry-derry dress with ribbons, instead of all this about tramping off through the woods with a ragged skirt about your naked knees."

Fanny Gilkan's face darkened, and she glanced swiftly at Howat Penny. He was filling a pipe, unmoved. Such a trip as he had outlined, with Fanny, was fastening upon his thoughts. It would at once express his entire attitude toward the world, opinion, and the resentful charcoal burners.

"You wouldn't really go," he said aloud, half consciously.

The girl frowned in an effort of concentration, gazing into the thin light of the dying fire and two watery tallow dips. Her coarsely spun dress, col-

11

oured with sassafras bark and darker than the yellow hickory stain, drew about her fine shoulders and full, plastic breast. "I'd like it," she repeated; "but afterward. There is father —"

She had said father, but Howat Penny determined that she was thinking of Dan Hesa; Dan was as strong as himself, if heavier; a personable young man. He would make a good husband. But that, he added, was in the future; Dan Hesa apparently didn't want to marry Fanny to-morrow, that week. Meanwhile a trip with him to the headwaters of a creek would not injure her in the least. His contempt of a world petty and iron-bound in endless pretence, fanning his smouldering and sullen resentment in general, flamed out in a determination to take her with him if possible. It would conclusively define, state, his attitude toward "men herding like cattle." He did not stop to consider what it might define for Fanny Gilkan. In the stir of his rebellious self there was no pause for vicarious approximations. If he thought of her at all it was in the indirect opinion that she was better without such a noodle as Dan Hesa threatened to become.

"I'd get two horses from the Forge," he continued, apparently to his mildly speculative self; "a few things, not much would be necessary. That gun you carry," he addressed Fanny indirectly, "is too heavy. I'll get you a lighter, bound in brass."

She repeated sombrely, leaning with elbows on the table, her chin in her hands, "And afterwards —"

12

"I thought you were free of that," he observed; "it sounds like the town women, the barnyard crowd. I thought you were an independent person. Certainly," he went on coldly, "you can't mistake my attitude. I like you, but I am not in the least interested in any way that — that your mother might appreciate. I am neither a seducer nor the type that marries."

"I understand that, Howat," she assured him; "and I think, I'm not sure but I think, that what you mean wouldn't bother me either. Anyhow it shouldn't spoil the fun of our trip. But no one else in the world would believe that simple truth. If you could stay there, in those splendid woods or a world like them, why, it would be heaven. But you have to come back, you have to live on, perhaps for a great while, in the world of Shadrach and Myrtle Forge. I'm not sure that I'd refuse if you asked me to go, Howat. I just don't know if a woman can stand alone, for that's what it would come to afterward, against a whole lifeful of misjudgment. It might be better in the end, for everybody, if she continued home, made the best of things with the others."

"You may possibly be right," he told her with a sudden resumption of indifference. After all, it was unimportant whether or not Fanny Gilkan went with him to the source of the stream he had discovered. Every one, it became more and more evident, was alike, monotonous. He wondered again, lounging

13

back against the wall, about the French forts, outposts in a vast wilderness. There was an increasing friction between the Province and France, the legacy of King George's War, but Howat Penny's allegiance to place was as conspicuous by its absence as the other communal traits. Beside that, beyond Kaskaskia, at St. Xavier and the North, there was little thought of French or English; the sheer problem of existence there drowned other considerations. He would, he thought, go out in the spring . . . leave Myrtle Forge with its droning anvil, the endless, unvaried turning of water wheel, and the facile, trivial chatter in and about the house. David Forsythe, back from England in the capacity of master of fluxing metals, might acquire his, Howat's, interest in the Penny iron.

Fanny Gilkan said, " You'll burn a hole in your coat with that pipe." He roused himself, and she moved across the room and pinched the smoking wicks. The embers on the hearth had expired, and the fireplace was a sooty, black cavern. Fanny, at the candles, was the only thing clearly visible; the thin radiance slid over the turn of her cheek; her hovering hand was like a cut-paper silhouette. It was growing late; Thomas Gilkan would soon be back from the Furnace; he must go. Howat had no will to avoid Gilkan, but the thought of the necessary conversational exchange wearied him.

The sound of footsteps approached the house from without; it was, he thought, slightly annoyed,

14

THE FURNACE

the founderman; but the progress deflected by the
door, circled to a window at the side. A voice
called low and urgent, " Seemy! Seemy!" It was
repeated, and there was an answering mutter from
the stair, a thick murmur and a deep sigh.

The cast boy slipped crumpled and silent in bare
feet across the floor. " Yes," he called back, rapidly waking.

The voice from without continued, " They're going to start up the Oley."

" What is it? " Fanny demanded.

" The raccoon dogs," the boy paused at the door.
" A lot of the furnacemen and woodcutters from
round about are hunting."

Fanny Gilkan leaned across the table to Howat,
her face glowing with interest. " Come ahead," she
urged; " we can do this anyhow. I like to hear the
dogs yelping, and follow them through the night.
You can bring your gun, I'll leave mine back, and
perhaps we'll get something really big."

Howat himself responded thoroughly to such an
expedition; to the mystery of the primitive woods,
doubly withdrawn in the dark; the calls of the others, near or far, or completely lost in a silence of
stars; the still immensity of a land unguessed, myth-
ical — endless trees, endless mountains, endless riv-
ers with their headwaters buried in arctic countries
beyond human experience, and emptying into the
miraculous blue and gilded seas of the tropics.

Fanny Gilkan would follow the dogs closely, too,

15

with infinite swing and zest. She knew the country better than himself, better almost than any one else at the Furnace. He stirred at her urgency, and she caught his arm, dragging him from behind the table. She tied a linsey-woolsey jacket by its arms about her waist, and put out the candles. Outside the blast was steadily in progress at the stack; the clear glow of the flame shifted over the near-by walls, glinted on the new yellow of more distant foliage, fell in sharp or blurred traceries against the surrounding night.

They could hear the short, impatient yelps of the dogs; but, before they reached them, the hunt was away. A lantern flickered far ahead, a minute blur vanishing through files of trees. Fanny turned to the right, mounting an abrupt slope thickly wooded toward the crown. A late moon, past full, shed an unsteady light through interlaced boughs, matted grape vines, creepers flung from tree to tree; it shone on a hurrying rill, a bright thread drawn through the brush. Fanny Gilkan jumped lightly from bank to bank. She made her way with lithe ease through apparently unbroken tangles. It was Fanny who went ahead, who waited for Howat to follow across a fallen trunk higher than his waist. She even mocked him gaily, declared that, through his slowness, they were hopelessly losing the hunt.

However, the persistent barking of the dogs contrived to draw them on. They easily passed the stragglers, left a group gathered about a lantern

16

and a black bottle. They caught up to the body of men, but preferred to follow a little outside of the breathless comments and main, stumbling progress. They stirred great areas of pigeons and countless indifferent coveys of partridges barely moved to avoid the swiftly falling feet. But no deer crossed near them, and the crashing of a heavy animal through the bushes diminished into such a steep gulley that they relinquished thought of pursuit. The chase continued for an unusual distance; the moon sank into the far, unbroken forest; the stars brightened through the darkest hour of the night.

Fanny Gilkan and Howat proceeded more slowly now, but still they went directly, without hesitation, in the direction they chose. They crossed a log felled over a shallow, hurrying creek; the course grew steeper, more densely wooded. "Ruscomb Manor," Fanny pronounced over her shoulder. "Since a long way back," he agreed. Finally a sharper, stationary clamour announced that the object of the hunt had been achieved, and a raccoon treed. They made their way to the dim illumination cast on moving forms and a ring of dogs throwing themselves upward at the trunk of a tree. There was a concerted cry for "Ebo," and a wizened, grey negro in a threadbare drugget coat with a scarlet handkerchief about his throat came forward and, kicking aside the dogs, commenced the ascent of the smooth trunk that swept up to the obscure foliage above. There was a short delay, then a violent agi-

17

tation of branches. A clawing shape shot to the
ground, struggled to its feet, but the raccoon was
instantly smothered in a snarling pyramid of dogs.

Howat Penny was overwhelmingly weary. He
had tramped all day, since before morning; while
now another dawn was approaching, and the hunters
were at least ten miles from the Furnace. He would
have liked to stay, sleep, where he was; but the
labour of preparing a proper resting place would
be as great as returning to Shadrach. Besides,
Fanny Gilkan was with him, with her new, cautious
regard for the world's opinion. They stood silent
for a moment, under a fleet dejection born of the
hour and a cold, seeping mist of which he became
suddenly conscious. The barrel of his gun was
wet, and instinctively he wiped off the lock. Two
men passing brushed heavily against him and
stopped. "Who is it," one demanded, "John Ra-
jennas? By God, it's a long way back to old Shadrach with splintering shoes." A face drew near
Howat, and then retreated. "Oh, Mr. Penny! I
didn't know you were up on the hunt." It was, he
recognized, one of the coaling men who worked for
Dan Hesa. The other discovered Fanny Gilkan.
"And Fanny, too," the voice grew inimical. The
men drew away, and a sharp whispering fluctuated
out of the darkness.

"Come," Howat Penny said sharply; "we must
get back or stay out here for the rest of the night.
I don't mind admitting I'd like to be where I could

18

sleep." She moved forward, now tacitly taking a place behind him, and he led the return, tramping doggedly in the shortest direction possible.

The hollows and stream beds were filled with the ghostly mist, and bitterly chill; the night paled slightly, diluted with grey; there was a distant clamour of crows. They entered the Furnace tract by a path at the base of the rise from where they had started. On the left, at a crossing of roads, one leading to Myrtle Forge, the other a track for the charcoal sleds, a blacksmith's open shed held a faint smoulder on the hearth. The blast from Shadrach Furnace rose perpendicular in the still air.

Fanny Gilkan slipped away with a murmur. Howat abandoned all thought of returning to Myrtle Forge that night. But it was, he corrected the conclusion, morning. The light was palpable; he could see individual trees, the bulk of the cast-house, built directly against the Furnace; in the illusive radiance the coal house on the hill seemed poised on top of the other structures. A lantern made a reddish blur in the cast-house; it was warm in there when a blast was in progress, and he determined to sleep at once.

Thomas Gilkan, with a fitful light, was testing the sealing clay on the face of the Furnace hearth; two men were rolling out the sand for the cast over the floor of the single, high interior, and another was hammering on a wood form used for stamping the pig moulds. The interior was soothing; the lights,

19

blurred voices, the hammering, seemed to retreat, to mingle with the subdued, smooth clatter of the turning wheel without, the rhythmic collapse of the bellows. Howat Penny was losing consciousness when an apparently endless, stuttering blast arose close by. He cursed splenetically. It was the horn, calling the Furnace hands for the day; and he knew that it would continue for five minutes.

Others had entered; a little group gathered about Thomas Gilkan's waning lantern. Far above them a window glimmered against the sooty wall. Howat saw that Dan Hesa was talking to Gilkan, driving in his words by a fist smiting a broad, hard palm. The group shifted, and the countenance of the man who had recognized Howat Penny in the woods swam into the pale radiance. His lassitude swiftly deserted him, receding before the instant resentment always lying at the back of his sullen intolerance — they were discussing him, mouthing some foul imputation about the past night. Hesa left the casthouse abruptly, followed by the charcoal burner; and Howat rose, the length of his rifle thrust forward under his arm, and walked deliberately forward.

The daylight was increasing rapidly; and, as he approached, Thomas Gilkan extinguished the flame of the lantern. He was a small man, with a face parched by the heat of the furnace, and a narrowed, reddened vision without eyebrows or lashes. He was, Howat had heard, an unexcelled founder, a position of the greatest importance to the quality of metal

20

run. There was a perceptible consciousness of this
in the manner in which Gilkan moved forward to
meet Gilbert Penny's son.

"I don't want to give offence," the founderman
said, "but, Mr. Penny, sir —" he stopped, commenced again without the involuntary mark of respect. "Mr. Penny, stay away from my house.
There is more that I could say but I won't. That
is all — keep out of my place. No names, please."

Howat Penny's resentment swelled in a fiery anger
at the stupidity that had driven Thomas Gilkan into
making his request. A sense of humiliation contributed to an actual fury, the bitterer for the
reason that he could make no satisfactory reply.
Gilkan was a freedman; while he was occupying a
dwelling at Shadrach Furnace it was his to conduct
as he liked. Howat's face darkened — the meagre
fool! He would see that there was another head
founder here within a week.

But there were many positions in the Province
for a man of Gilkan's ability, there were few workmen of his sensitive skill with the charge and blast.
Not only Howat's father, but Abner Forsythe as
well, would search to the end all cause for the founderman's leaving. And, in consequence of that, any
detestable misunderstanding must increase. He determined, with an effort unaccustomed and arduous,
to ignore the other; after all Gilkan was but an insignificant mouthpiece for the familiar ineptitude of
the world at large. Thomas Gilkan might continue

21

at the Furnace without interference from him; Fanny marry her stupid labourer. Howat had seen symptoms of that last night. He would no longer complicate her existence with avenues of escape from a monotony which she patently elected.

"Very well, Gilkan," he agreed shortly, choking on his wrath. He turned and tramped shortly from the interior. A sudden, lengthening sunlight bathed the open and a sullen group of charcoal burners about Dan Hesa. Their faces seemed ebonized by the grinding in of particles of blackened wood. Some women, even, in gay, primitive clothes, stood back of the men. As Howat passed, a low, hostile murmur rose. He halted, and met them with a dark, contemptuous countenance, and the murmur died in a shuffling of feet in the dry grass. He turned again, and walked slowly away, when a broken piece of rough casting hurtled by his head. In an overpowering rage he whirled about, throwing his rifle to his shoulder. A man detached from the group was lowering his arm; and, holding the sights hard on the other's metal-buttoned, twill jacket, Howat pulled the trigger. There was only an answering dull, ineffectual click.

The rifle slid to the ground, and Howat stared, fascinated, at the man he had attempted to kill. The charcoal burners were stationary before the momentary abandon of Howat Penny's temper. "Right at me," the man articulated who had been so nearly shot into oblivion. "— saw the hammer

22

fall." A tremendous desire to escape possessed
Howat; a violent chill overtook him; his knees
threatened the loss of all power to hold him up.
He stepped backward, his gun stock trailing over
the inequalities of the ground; then he swung about,
and, in an unbroken silence, stumbled away.

He was not running from anything the charcoal
burner might say, do, but from a terrifying spectacle of himself; from the vision of a body shot
through the breast, huddled in the sere underbrush.
He was aghast at the unsuspected possibility revealed, as it were, out of a profound dark by the
searing flash of his anger, cold at the thought of
such absolute self-betrayal. Howat saw in fancy
the bald triumph of a society to which his act consummated would have delivered him; a society that,
as his peer, would have judged, condemned, him.
Hundreds of faces — faces mean, insignificant, or
pock-marked — merged into one huge, dominant
countenance; hundreds of bodies, unwashed or foul
with disease, or meticulously clean, joined in one
body, clothed in the black robe of delegated authority, and loomed above him, gigantic and absurd and
powerful, and brought him to death. Deeper than
his horror, than any fear of physical consequences,
lay the instinctive shrinking from the obliteration of
his individual being, the loss of personal freedom.

23

II

HE was possessed by an unaccustomed desire to be at Myrtle Forge; usually it was the contrary case, and he was escaping from the complicated civilisation of his home; but now the well-ordered house, the serenity of his room, appeared astonishingly inviting. Howat progressed rapidly past the smithy, and turned to the right, about the Furnace dam, a placid and irregular reach of water holding the reflection of the trees on a mirror still dulled by a vanishing trace of mist, above which the leaves hung in the motionless air, in the aureate wash of the early sun, as if they had been pressed from gold foil. Beyond the dam the path — he had left the road that connected Forge and Furnace for a more direct way — followed the broad, rippling course of the Canary, the stream that supplied the life of Myrtle Forge. He automatically avoided the breaks in the rough trail; his mind, a dark and confused chamber, still lighted by appalling flashes of memory. A thing as slight, as incalculable, as a loose flint had been all that prevented . . . He wondered if Fanny and Thomas Gilkan were right in their shared conviction; Fanny half persuaded, but the elder with a finality stamped with an accent of the heroic. Whether or not they were right didn't concern him, he decided; his only problem was to keep outside all such entanglements. And at present he wanted to sleep.

The path left the creek and joined the road that swept about the face of the dwelling at Myrtle Forge. The lawn, squarely raised from the public way by a low brick terrace, showed the length of house behind the dipping, horizontal branches, the beginning, pale gold, of a widespread beech. It was a long structure of but two stories, built solidly out of a dark, flinty stone with an indefinite pinkish glow against the lush sod and sombre, flat greenery of a young English ivy about a narrow, stiff portico.

Howat crossed the lawn above the house, where a low wing, holding the kitchen and pantries, extended at right angles from the dwelling's length. A shed with a flagging of broad stones lay inside the angle, where a robust girl with an ozenbrigs skirt caught up on bare legs and feet thrust into wooden clogs was scrubbing a steaming line of iron pots. He quickly entered the centre hall from a rear door, and mounted, as he hoped, without interruption to his room. That interior was singularly restful, pleasant, after the confused and dishevelling night.

The sanded floor, patterned with a broom, held no carpet, nor were the walls covered, but white and bare save for a number of small, framed engravings — a view of Boston Harbour, Queene Anne's Tomb, and some black line satirical portrait prints. A stone fireplace, ready for lighting, had iron dogs and

25

fender, and a screen lacquered in flowery wreaths on a slender black stem. At one side stood a hinge-bound chest, its oak panels glassy with age; on the other, an English set of drawers held a mirror stand and scattered trifles — razors and gold sleeve-buttons, a Barcelona handkerchief, candlesticks and flint, a twist of common, pig-tail tobacco; while from a drawer knob hung a banian of bright orange Chinese silk with a dark blue cord.

By the side of his curled black walnut bed, without drapery, and set, like a French couch, low on three pairs of spiral legs, was a deep cushioned chair into which he sank and dragged off his sodden buckskin breeches. The room wavered and blurred in his weary vision — squat, rush-bottomed Dutch chairs seemed to revolve about a table with apparently a hundred legs, a bearskin floated across the floor . . . He secured the banian; and, swathing himself in its cool, sibilant folds, he fell, his face hid in an angle of his arm, into an immediate profound slumber.

The shadows of late afternoon were once more gathering when he woke. He lay, with hands clasped behind his head, watching a roseate glow disperse from the room. From without came the faint, clear voice of Marta Appletofft, across the road at the farm, calling the chickens; and he could hear the querulous whistling of the partridges that invariably deserted the fringes of forest to join the domesticated flocks at feed time. A sense of well-being flooded him; the project of St. Xavier, the French

26

forts, drew far away; never before had he found
Myrtle Forge so desirable. He was, he thought,
growing definitely older. He was twenty-five.

A light knock fell on his door, and he answered
comfortably, thinking that it was his mother. But
it was Caroline, his oldest sister. " How you have
slept," she observed, closing the door at her back;
" it was hardly nine when you came in, and here it
is five. Mother heard you." Caroline Penny was
a warm, unbeautiful girl with a fine, slender body,
two years younger than himself. Her colouring was
far lighter than Howat's; she had sympathetic hazel
eyes, an inviting mouth, an illusive depression in one
cheek that alone saved her from positive ugliness,
and tobacco brown hair worn low with a long, turned
strand. She had on a pewter-coloured, informal
wrap over a black silk petticoat, lacking hoops, with
a cut border of violet and silver brocade; and above
low, green kid stays with coral tulip blossoms
worked on the dark velvet of foliage were glimpses of
webby linen and frank, young flesh.

She came to the edge of the bed, where she sat with
a yellow morocco slipper swinging from a silk
clocked, narrow foot. He liked Caroline, Howat
lazily thought. Although she did not in the least
resemble their mother in appearance — she could not
pretend to such distinction of being — Caroline unmistakably possessed something of the other's personality, far more than did Myrtle. She said generally, patently only delaying for the moment com-

munications of much greater interest than himself, " Where were you last night? " He told her, and she plunged at once into a rich store of information.

" Did you know that Mr. and Mrs. Winscombe are staying on? It's so, because of the fever in the city. David and his father stopped all night, too, and only left after breakfast. He's insane about London, but I could see that he's glad to get back to the Province. Mr. Forsythe is very abrupt, but ridiculously proud of him —"

" These Winscombes," Howat interrupted, " what about them? The Forsythes are a common occurrence."

" David's been gone more than three years," she replied. " And you should hear him talk; he's got a coat with wired tails in his box he's dying to wear, but is afraid of his father. Oh, the Winscombes! Well, he's rather sweet, sixty or sixty-five years old; very straight up the back, and wears the loveliest wigs. His servant fixes them on a stand — he turns the curls about little rolls of clay, ties them with paper, and then bakes it in the oven like a pudding. The servant is an Italian with a long duck's bill of a nose and quick little black eyes. He makes our negro women giggle like anything. It's evident he is fearfully impertinent. And, what do you think? — he hooks Mrs. Winscombe into her stays! Mother says that that isn't anything, really; Mrs. Winscombe is a lady of the court, and the most extraordinary happenings go on there. You see,

28

mother knows a lot about her family, and it's very good; she's part Polish and part English, and her name's Ludowika. She's ages younger than her husband.

"Myrtle doesn't like her,—" she stopped midway in her torrent of information. "I came in to talk to you about Myrtle," she went on in a different voice; "that is, partly about Myrtle, but more of myself and of —"

"How long are the others going to stay?" he cut in heedlessly.

"I don't know," she again repressed her own desire; "perhaps they will have to go back to Annapolis — don't ask me why — but they hope to sail from Philadelphia in a week or so. She has marvellous clothes, and I asked her if she would send me some babies from London. You know what they are, Howat — little wooden dolls to show off the fashion; but she made a harrowing joke, right in front of father and Mrs. Forsythe. The things she says are just beyond description; it seems that it's all right to talk anyway now if you call it classic. And she has fans with pictures and rhymes on, honestly —" words apparently failed her.

Howat laughed. "Little Innocence," he said. He fell silent, thinking of their mother. The court, he knew, had been her right, too, by birth; and he wondered if, with the reminder of Mrs. Winscombe and her reflections of St. James, she regretted her marriage and removal to the Province. She was essentially lady, while Gilbert Penny had been the son of a small country squire. He had seen a profile of his father as a young man, at the time he had first met Isabel Kingsfrere Howat. It was a handsome profile, perhaps a shade heavy, but admirably balanced and stamped with decisive power. He had characteristically invested almost his last shilling in a tract of eight hundred acres in Pennsylvania and the passage of himself and his bride to the Province.

It was natural for men so to adventure, but Howat thought of Isabel Penny with, perhaps, the only marked admiration he felt for any being. There had been a period, short but strenuous, of material difficulties, in which the girl — she had been hardly a woman in years — entirely unprepared for such a different activity, had been finely competent and courageous. This had not endured long because Gilbert Penny had been successful almost from the first day of his landing in a new world. Chance letters had enlisted the confidence of David Forsythe, a Quaker merchant of property and increasing importance; the latter became a part owner of an iron furnace situated not far from the Penny holding; he assisted Gilbert in the erection of a forge; and in less than twenty years Gilbert Penny had grown to be a half proprietor in the Furnace, with —

"Howat," Caroline broke in on his thoughts sharply, "I came in, as I said, to talk about something very important to me, and I intend to do it."

Even after that decided announcement she hesitated, a deeper colour stained her clear cheeks. "You mustn't laugh at me," she warned him; "or think I'm horrid. I can talk to you like this because you seem a — a little outside of things, as if you were looking on at a rather poorly done play; and you are entirely honest yourself."

He nodded condescendingly, his interest at last retrieved from the contemplation of his mother as a young woman.

"It's about David," Caroline stated almost defiantly. "Howat, I think I'm very fond of David. No, you mustn't interrupt me. When he went away I liked him a lot; but now that he is back, and quite grown up, it's more than liking . . . Howat. His father brought him out here right away he returned, and for a special reason. He was very direct about it; he wants David to marry — Myrtle. I heard father — yes, I listened — and him talking it over, and our old darling was pleased to death. It's natural, Mr. Forsythe is one of the most influential men in the city; and father adores Myrtle more than anything else in the world." She paused, and he studied her in a growing wonder; suddenly she seemed older, her mouth was drawn in a hard line: a new Caroline. "You know Myrtle," she added.

He did, and considered the youngest Penny with a new objectivity. Myrtle was an extremely pretty, even a beautiful girl. "You know Myrtle," she repeated; "and why father is so blind is more than

31

I can understand. She doesn't care a ribbon for truth, she never thinks of anything but her own comfort and clothes, and — and she'd make David miserable. Myrtle simply can't fancy anybody but herself. That's very different from me, Howat; or yourself. You would be a burning lover." He laughed incredulously. " And I, well, I know what I feel.

" It's practically made up for David to marry Myrtle, that is, to urge it all that's possible; and she will never care for him, while all he thinks of now is how good looking she is. I want David, terribly," she said, sitting erect with shut hands; " and I will be expected to step aside, to keep out of the way while Myrtle poses at him. Oh, I know all about it. I see her rehearsing before the glass. Or I will be expected to act as a contrast, a plain background, for Myrtle's beauty.

" You see, there is no one I can talk to but yourself. Even mother wouldn't understand, completely; and she couldn't be honest about Myrtle. The best of mothers, after all, are women; and, Howat, there is always a curious formality between women, a little stiffness."

" Well," he demanded, " what do you want me to say, or what did you think I might do? "

" I don't know," she admitted, her eyes bright with unshed tears. " I suppose I just wanted a little support, or even some encouragement. I don't propose to let Myrtle walk off with David and not

32

turn my hand. Of course I am not a beauty, but then I'm not a ninny, either. And I have a prettier figure; that is, it will still be pretty in ten or fifteen years; Myrtle's soft."

"Good heavens," he exclaimed, half serious, "what Indians you all are!"

"I'm quite shameless," she admitted, "and this is really what I thought — you can, perhaps, help me sometimes, I don't know how, but he will be out here a lot, men talk together —"

"And I can tell him that Myrtle is an utterly untrustworthy person who would make him ultimately miserable. I'll remind him that her beauty is no deeper than he sees it. But that Caroline there, admirable girl, seething with affection in a figure warranted against time or accident —" her expression brought his banter to an end. He studied her seriously, revolved what she had said. She was right about Myrtle, who was undoubtedly a vain and silly little fish. His father's immoderate admiration for her had puzzled him as well as the elder sister. He remembered that never had he heard their mother express a direct opinion of Myrtle; but neither had Isabel Penny shown the slightest question of her husband's high regard for their youngest child. She was, he realized with a warming of his admiration, beautifully cultivated in the wisdom of the world.

Caroline was vastly preferable to Myrtle, he felt that instinctively; and he was inclined to give her whatever assistance he could. But this would be negligible, and he said so. " You will have to do the trick by yourself," he advised her. " I wouldn't pretend to tell you how. As you said, you're not a ninny. And Myrtle's none too clever, although she will manage to seem so. It's wonderful how she'll pick up a hint or two and make a show. You see — she will be talking iron to David as if she had been raised in a furnace."

" Men are so senseless! " Caroline exclaimed viciously. She rose. " It's been a help only to talk to you, Howat. I knew you'd understand. Supper will be along soon. Make yourself into a charmer for Mrs. Winscombe. I'm certain she thinks the men out here are frightful hobs." The light had dimmed rapidly in the room, and he moved over to the chest of drawers, where he lit the candles, settling over them their tall, carved glass cylinders.

III

HE dressed slowly, all that Caroline had said, and he thought, tangling and disentangling deliberately in his mind. Mrs. Winscombe . . . thinking there were no presentable men in the Provinces. His hand strayed in the direction of a quince-coloured satin coat; but he chose instead a commonplace, dun affair with pewter buttons, and carelessly settled his shoulders in an unremarkable waistcoat. Then, although he could hear a concerted stir of voices below that announced impending supper, he slipped into a chair for half a pipe. He was indifferent, not diffident, and there was no hesitation in the manner in which he finally approached the company seated at supper. His place was, as usual, at his mother's side; but opposite him where Myrtle usually sat was a rigid, high shouldered man in mulberry and silver, jewelled buckles, and a full, powdered wig. He had thin, dark cheeks, a heavy nose above a firm mouth with a satirical droop, and small, unpleasantly penetrating eyes. An expression of general malice was, however, corrected by a high and serene brow.

"Mr. Winscombe," Howat Penny's mother said, "my son." The former bowed with formal civility, but gave a baffling effect of mockery which, Howat discovered, enveloped practically every movement and speech. He was, he said, enchanted to meet Mr. Penny; and that extravagant expression, delivered in a slightly harsh, negligent voice, heightened the impression of a personality strong and cold; a being as obdurate as an iron bar masquerading in coloured satin and formulating pretty phrases like the sheen on the surface of a deep November pool. Gilbert Penny echoed the introduction at the other end of the table.

Howat saw, in the yellow candlelight, a woman not, he decided, any better looking than Caroline, in an extremely low cut gown of scarlet, with a rigid girdle of saffron brocade, a fluted tulle ruff tied with a scarlet string about a long, slim neck, and a cap of sheer cambric with a knot of black ribbons. Her eyes were widely opened and dark, her nose short, and her mouth full and petulant. She, too, was conventionally adequate; but her insincerity was clearer than her husband's, it was pronounced quickly, in an impertinent and musical voice, without the slightest pretence of the injection of any interest. Howat Penny felt, in a manner which he was unable to place, that she vaguely resembled himself; perhaps it lay in her eyebrows slanting slightly toward the temples; but it was vaguer, more elusive, than that.

He considered it idly, through the course of supper. At intervals he heard her voice, a little, high-pitched laugh with a curious, underlying flatness: not of tone, her modulations were delicate and exact; but deeper. Again he was dimly conscious of an aspect of her which eluded every effort to fix and define. He could not even comprehend his dwelling upon the immaterial traits of a strange and indifferent woman; he was at a loss to understand how such inquiries assailed him. He grew, finally, annoyed, and shut his mind to any further consideration of her.

Mrs. Penny was talking with charming earnestness to the man on her other hand. The amber radiance flickered over the beautiful curves of her shoulders and cast a warm shadow at the base of her throat. She smiled at her son; and her face, in spite of its present gaiety, held a definite reminder of her years, almost fifty; but when she turned again her profile, with slightly tilted nose and delightfully fresh lips and chin, was that of a girl no older than Caroline. Howat had often noticed this. It was amazing — with that slight movement she would seem to lose at once all the years that had accumulated since she was newly married. In a second she would appear to leave them all, her mature children, the heavy, palpably aging presence of Gilbert Penny, the house and obligations that had grown about her, and be remotely young, a stranger to the irrefutable proof that her youth had gone. At such moments he was almost reluctant to claim her attention, to bring her again, as it were, into the present, with so much spent, lapsed: at times he almost thought, in that connection, wasted.

She had, in adition to her profile, a spirit of youth that had remained undimmed; as if there were within her a reserve warmth, a priceless gift, which life had never claimed; and it was the contemplation of that which gave Howat the impression that Isabel Penny's life had not fully flowered. He had never known her to express a regret of the way she had taken; he had never even surprised her in a perceptible retrospective dejection; but the conviction remained. Gilbert Penny had been an almost faultless husband, tender and firm and successful; but his wife had come from other blood and necessities than domestic felicities; she had been a part of a super-cultivation, a world of such niceties as the flawless courtesy of Mr. Winscombe discussing with her the unhappy passion of the Princess Caroline for Lord Hervey.

Howat Penny thought sombrely of love, of the emotion that had brought — or betrayed? — Isabel Howat so far away from her birthright. It had gripped his sister no less tyrannically; stripping them, he considered, of their essential liberty. The thing was clear enough in his mind — nothing more than an animal instinct, humiliating to the human individual, to breed. It was the mere repetition of nature through the working of an automatic law. No such obscure fate, he determined, should overtake, obliterate, him. Yet it had involved his mother, a person of the first superiority. A slight chill, as if a breath of imminent winter had touched him, communicated itself to his heart.

A trivial conversation was in progress across the table between Mrs. Winscombe and Myrtle. The latter was an embodiment of the familiar Saxon type of beauty; her hair was fair, infinitely pale gold, her complexion a delicately mingled crimson and white, her eyes as candidly blue as flowers. Her features were finely moulded, and her shoulders, slipping out from azure lutestring, were like smooth handfuls of meringue. Her voice was always formal, and it sounded stilted, forced, in comparison with Mrs. Winscombe's easy periods.

The supper ended, and the company trailed into a drawing room at the opposite end of the house from the kitchen wing. Howat delayed, and Caroline, urged forward by Mr. Winscombe's sardonically ubiquitous bow, half lingered to cast back a glance of private understanding at her brother. When he decided reluctantly to follow he was kept back by the sound of a familiar explanation in his father's decisive, full tones.

" Howat," he pronounced, obviously addressing the elder Winscombe, " is a black Penny. That is what we call them in our family. You see, the Pennys, some hundreds of years back, acquired a strong Welsh strain. I take it you are familiar with the Welsh — a solitary-living, dark lot. Unamenable to influence, reflect their country, I suppose; but lovers of music. I have a touch of that. Now any one would think that such a blood, so long ago, would have spread out, been diluted, in a thick English stock like the Pennys; or at least that we would all have had a little, here and there. But nothing of the sort; it sinks entirely out of sight for two or three and sometimes four generations; and then appears solid, in one individual, as unslacked as the pure, original thing. The last one was burned as a heretic in Mary's day; although I believe he would have equally stayed Catholic if the affair had been the other way around. Opposition's their breath. This boy —"

"You must not figure to yourself, Mr. Winscombe," Mrs. Penny's even voice admirably cut in, "that the black is a word of reproach. I think we are both at times at a loss with Howat, he is so different from us, from the girls; but he is truly remarkable. I have an unusual affection for him; really, his honesty is extraordinary."

He ought, he knew, either follow the others into the drawing room or move farther away. His father's explanation repelled him; but his mother's capital defence — it amounted to that — made it evident to him that he should, by his presence, give her what support he could.

At the fireplace Gilbert Penny was lost in conversational depths with Mr. Winscombe. About the opening, now closed for the introduction of a hearth stove, were tiles picturing in gay glazes the pastoral

40

history of Ruth, and above the mantel a long, clear mirror held a similitude of brilliant colour — the scarlet of Mrs. Winscombe's gown, Myrtle's azure lutestring on a petticoat of ruffled citron spreading over her hoops and little white kid slippers with gilt heels, Caroline's flowered Chinese silk. The room was large and square, with a Turkey floor carpet, and walls hung with paper printed in lavender and black perspectives from copper plates. A great many candles had been lighted, on tables and mantel, and in lacquer stands. One of the latter, at Mrs. Winscombe's side, showed her features clearly.

Howat Penny saw that while she was actually no prettier than Caroline she was infinitely more vivid and compelling. Her face held an extraordinary potency; her bare arms and shoulders were more insistent than his sister's; there was about her a consciousness of the allurement of body, frankness in its employment. She made no effort to mask her feeling, which at present was one of complete indifference to her surroundings; and, not talking, a shadow had settled on her vision. Caroline was seated on a little sofa across from the fireplace, and she moved her voluminous skirt aside, made a place for him.

" Almost nothing of Annapolis," Mrs. Winscombe replied to a query of what she had seen in Maryland. " We were there hardly two weeks, and I hadn't recovered from the trip across the sea. When I think of returning God knows I'd almost stay here. You wouldn't suppose one person could vent so much. I believe Felix went to a Jockey Club, there were balls and farces; but I kept in bed." Mrs. Penny asked, " And London — how are you amused there now? " The other retied the bow of a garter. " Fireworks, Roman candles to Mr. Handel's music, and Italian parties, Villeggiatura. Covent Garden with paper lanterns among the trees, seductions —"

Gilbert Penny smote his hands on the chair arms. " This hectoring of our commerce will have to rest somewhere! " he declared; " taking the duty from pig iron, and then restricting its market to London, is no conspicuous improvement. It is those enactments that provide our currency with Spanish pieces instead of English pounds. The West Indies are too convenient to be overlooked." Mr. Winscombe replied stiffly, " The Government is prepared to meet infractions of its law." Mr. Penny muttered a period about Germany in England, with a more distant echo of Hanoverian whores and deformed firebrands. His guest sat with a harsh, implacable countenance framed in the long shadows of his elaborate wig, his ornate coat tails falling stiffly on either side of his chair.

Howat, bred in the comparative simplicity of the Province, found the foppery of the aging man slightly ridiculous; yet he was aware that Mr. Winscombe's essential character had no expression in his satin and powder; his will was as rugged and virile as that of any adventuring frontiersman clad in untanned hides. He was, Howat decided, at little disadvantage with his young wife. He wondered if any deep bond bound the two. Their personal feelings were carefully concealed, and in this they resembled Isabel Howat, rather than Gilbert, her husband. The latter had a habit of expressing publicly his affectionate domestic relations. And Howat Penny decided that he vastly preferred the others' reserve.

An awkward silence had developed on top of the brief political acerbities. There was no sound but the singing of the wood in the open stove. Myrtle had an absent, speculative gaze; Caroline was biting her lip; Mrs. Winscombe yawned in the face of the assembly. Gilbert Penny suggested cards, but there was no reply. Howat left the room by a door that opened on a rock threshold set in the lawn. The night was immaculate, still and cold, with stars brightening in the advance of winter. He walked about the house. The counting room of the forge was a separate stone structure back of the kitchen; and to the right, and farther away, was a second small building. The ground fell rapidly down to the Forge on the water power below. He could barely discern the towering bulk of the water wheel and roofs of the sheds.

He felt uneasy, obscurely and emotionally disturbed. Already Fanny Gilkan seemed far away, to have dropped out of his life. He would give some gold to the charcoal burner he had attempted to shoot. Mrs. Winscombe annoyed him by her atti-

tude toward Myrtle Forge, her unvarnished air of
condescension. How old was she? A few years
more than himself, he decided. The Italian hooked
her into her stays. A picture of this formed in his
thoughts and dissolved, leaving behind a faint stinging of his nerves. He recalled her bare — naked —
arms . . . the old man, her husband.

She had spoken of Italian parties; he had seen a
picture on a fan labelled Villeggiatura — a simper-
ing exquisite in a lascivious embrace with a frail
beauty on the bank of a stream, and a garland of
stripped loves reeling about a slim, diapered Har-
lequin. It was a different scene, a different world,
from the Province; and its intrusion in the person of
Mrs. Winscombe was like an orris-scented air moving
across the face of great trees sweeping their virginal
foliage into the region of strong and pure winds.

He was dimly conscious of the awakening in him
of undivined pressures, the stirring of attenuated yet
persisting influences. He was saturated in the space,
the sheer, immense simplicity of the wild, hardly
touched by the narrow strip of inhabited coast. He
had given his existence to the woods, to hunting cunning beasts, the stoical endurance of blinding fa-
tigue; he had scorned the, to him, sophistications of
bricks and civilization. But now, in the length of
an evening, something invidious and far different had
become sentient in his being. Italian parties, and
Covent Garden with lanterns among the trees . . .

44

Trees clipped and pruned, and gravel walks; seductions.

A falling meteor flashed a brilliant arc across the black horizon, dropping into what illimitable wilderness? Fireworks set to the shrill scraping of violins. One mingled with the other in his blood, fretting him, spoiling the serene and sure vigour of youth, binding his feet to the obscure past. Yet colouring all was the other, the black Welsh blood of the Pennys. Ever since his boyhood he had heard the fact of his peculiar inheritance explained, accepted. In the past he had been what he was without thought, self-appraisal. But now he recognized an essential difference from his family; it came over him in a feeling of loneliness, of removal from the facile business of living in general.

For the first time he wondered about his future. It was unguarded by the placid and safe engagements of the majority of lives. He would, he knew, untimately possess Myrtle Forge, a part of Shadrach, and a considerable fortune. That was his obvious inheritance. But, suddenly, the material thing, the actual, grew immaterial, and the visionary assumed a dark and enigmatic reality.

Howat abruptly quitted the night of the lawn, his sombre questioning, for the house. The candles had been extinguished in the drawing room. A square, glass lamp hung at the foot of the stairs; and there he encountered a man in a scratch wig, with a long

nose flattened at the end. He bowed obsequiously
— a posturing figure in shirtsleeves with a green
cloth waistcoat and black legs. The Italian servant,
Howat concluded. He passed noiselessly, leaving a
reek of pomatum and the memory of a servile smile.
Howat Penny experienced a strong sense of distaste,
almost depression, at the other's silent proximity.
It followed him to his room, contaminated his sleep
with unintelligible whispering, oily and disturbing
gestures, and fled only at the widening glimmer of
dawn.

IV

THE sun had almost reached the zenith before Mrs. Winscombe appeared from her room. And at the same moment David Forsythe arrived on a spent grey mare. He had come over the forty rough miles which separated Myrtle Forge from the city in less than five hours. He was a year older than Howat, but he appeared actually younger — a candid youth with high colour and light, simply tied hair. He had, he told Howat, important messages from his father to Mr. Winscombe. The latter and Gilbert Penny were conversing amicably in the lower room at the right of the stairway — a chamber with a bed that, nevertheless, was used for informal assemblage. Mr. Winscombe wore an enveloping banian of russet brocade with deep furred cuffs, and a turban of vermilion silk comfortably replacing a wigged formality. Under that brilliant colour his face was as yellow as an orange.

The written messages were delivered, and David returned to the lawn. The day was superb — a crystal cold through which the sun's rays filtered with a faintly perceptible glow. Caroline was standing at Howat's side, and she gave his hand a rapid pressure as David Forsythe approached. " Where's

47

Myrtle?" the latter asked apparently negligently. Howat replied, "Still in the agony of fixing her hair — for dinner; she'll be at it again before supper." David whistled a vague tune. Caroline added, "You've got fearfully dressy yourself, since London." He replied appropriately, and then became more serious. "I wish," he told them, "that we belonged to the church of England; you know the Penns have gone back. It's pretty heavy at home after — after some other things. The Quakers didn't use to be so infernally solemn. You should see the swells about the Court; the greatest fun. And old George with a face like a plum —"

"Don't you find anything here that pleases you?" Caroline demanded with asperity.

"Myrtle's all right," he admitted; "not many of them are as pretty."

"I'll tell her you've come," Caroline promptly volunteered; "she won't keep you waiting. There she is! No, it's Mrs. Winscombe."

She was swathed in a ruffled lilac cloak quilted with a dull gold embroidery; satin slippers were buckled into high pattens of black polished wood; and her head, relatively small with tight-drawn hair, was uncovered. She was not as compelling under the sun as in candle light, he observed. Her face, unpainted, was pale, an expression of petulance discernible. Yet she was more potent than any other woman he had encountered. "Isn't that the garden?" she asked, waving beyond the end of

48

the house. " I like gardens." She moved off in
the direction indicated; and — as he felt she expected, demanded — he followed slightly behind.

A short, steep terrace descended to a formally
planted plot, now flowerless, enclosed by low privet
hedges. There were walks of rolled bark, and,
against a lower, denser barrier, a long, white bench.
The ground still fell away beyond; and there was a
sturdy orchard, cleared of underbrush, with crimson
apples among the grey limbs. Beyond, across a
low, tangled wild, an amphitheatre of hills rose
against the sky, drawn from the extreme right about
the façade of the dwelling. They seemed to enclose
Myrtle Forge in a natural domain of its own; and,
actually, Gilbert Penny owned most of the acreage
within that immediate circle.

Mrs. Winscombe sank on the garden bench, where
she sat with a hand resting on either side of her.
Above them a column of smoke rose from the kitchen
against the blue. A second, heavier cloud rolled up
from the Forge below. " They have been repairing
the forebay," Howat explained; " the Forge has been
closed. I'm supposed to be in the counting house."

" You work? " she demanded surprised.

" At the ledger, put things down — what the men
are paid, mostly in tobacco and shoes, ozenbrigs
and molasses and rum; or garters and handkerchiefs
for the women. Then I enter the pig hauled from
Shadrach, and the carriage of the blooms."

" I don't understand any of that," she announced.

49

" It probably wouldn't interest you; the pig's the
iron cast at the furnace. It's worked in the forges,
and hammered into blooms and anconies, chunks or
stout bars of wrought iron. We do better than two
tons a week." The sound of a short, jarring blow
rose from the Forge, it was repeated, became a continuous part of the serene noon. " That's the hammer now," he explained. " It goes usually all day
and most nights. We're used to it, don't hear it;
but strangers complain."

" Mr. Forsythe said your father was an Ironmaster, one of the biggest in the Province, and I
suppose you'll become that too." She gazed about
at the hills, sheeted in scarlet and yellow, at the wide
sunny hollow that held Myrtle Forge. " Here,"
she added in a totally unexpected accent of feeling,
" it is very beautiful, very big. I thought all the
world was like St. James or Versailles. I've never
been to Poland, my mother's family came from there
to Paris, but I'm told they have forests and such
things, too. This is different from Annapolis, that
is only an echo of London, but here —" she gazed
far beyond him into the profound noon.

He recovered slowly from the surprise of her un-
looked for speech, attitude. Howat studied her
frankly, leaning forward with his elbows on his knees.
Her discontent was paramount. It was deeper than
he had supposed; like his there were disturbing qualities in her blood, qualities at a variance with the

50

obvious part of her being. A sense of profound intimacy with her pervaded him.

" This," she continued, " is like a cure at a Bath, a great bath of air and light. I should like to stay, I think . . . Are you content? "

" It always seemed crowded to me," he admitted. " Usually I get as far away as possible, into the woods, the real wilderness. But you heard my father last night — I'm a black Penny, a solitary, dark lot. You couldn't judge from what I might feel."

" Your father and you are not sympathetic," she judged acutely. " He is practical, solid; but it isn't easy to say, even with an explanation, what you are. In London — but I'm sick of London. Myrtle Forge. It's appalling at night. I'd like to go into the real wilderness, leave off my hoops and stays, and bathe in a stream; a water nymph and you . . . but that's only Watteau again, with a cicisbeo holding my shift and stockings. In London you'd be that, a lady's servant of love; but, in the Province, I wonder? "

He sat half comprehending her words mingling in his brain with the pounding of the trip hammer at the Forge, one familiar and one unfamiliar yet not strange sound. Above them, on the lawn, he could see Myrtle — through the middle of the day the sun had increased its warmth — with skirts like the petals of a fabulous tea rose. The sun glinted on the living gold of her hair and bathed an arm white as snow. David was there no doubt. His thoughts dwelt for a moment on Caroline, then returned to Mrs. Winscombe, to himself. His entire attitude toward her, his observations, had been upset, disarmed, by her unexpected air of soft melancholy. In her lavender wrap she resembled a drooping branch of flowering lilac. She seemed very young; her air of sophistication, her sensuality of being, had vanished. Traces of her illness on shipboard still lingered darkly under her eyes. Asleep, he suddenly thought, her face would be very innocent, purified. This came to him involuntarily; there was none of the stinging of the senses she had evoked in him the night before. His instinct for preservation from any entanglements with life lay dormant before her surrender to influences that left her crumpled, without the slightest interest in any exterior fact.

A sententious black servant in maroon livery and a bright worsted waistcoat announced dinner from the foot of the terrace, and they moved slowly toward the house. There was a concerted interest in the faces they found already about the table. Howat took his seat at his mother's side, Gilbert Penny assisted Mrs. Winscombe. David was placed between Caroline and Myrtle. Mr. Winscombe, again formally wigged and coated, was absorbed in thought. He said to his hostess, "It's the uncertainty that puts me in doubt. Ogle thought the thing thoroughly reviewed, when now Hamilton comes out with his

52

damned Indians and Maryland rum. Forsythe suggests my presence in Council to-morrow, and it's barely possible that there will be a return to Annapolis. While Ludowika —"

" I can't travel another ell over the atrocities they call roads here," Mrs. Winscombe declared. " I expect to die returning to England as it is, and I won't put up with any more preliminary torment. You'll have to leave me."

" At Myrtle Forge," Gilbert Penny added at once; " at Myrtle Forge as long as you like. Unless," he added with a smile, " you prefer the gaiety at Abner Forsythe's." A hot colour suffused David's cheeks.

Mr. Winscombe bowed over the table, " I am inclined to take advantage of that. Ludowika would be the better without even Quaker gaiety for a little." He stopped, turned toward her. " I'd like it immensely," she replied simply. " I am sure it would give me back all that I've lost in passage. Perhaps," she leaned forward, smiling at Howat, " I could see something of what's behind those hills, go into the real Arcadia."

" Out there," said Mr. Penny, " are the Endless Mountains."

The faint, involuntary chill again invaded Howat; suddenly an unfamiliar imagery attached to the commonplace phrase uttered by his father — the Endless Mountains! It brought back his doubt, his questioning, of life. It was the inconceivable term endless, without any finality of ultimate rest, without even the arbitrary peace of death, that appalled him. He thought of life going on and on, with nothing consummated, nothing achieved nor final. He thought of the black Penny who had been burned as a heretic to ashes years before; yet Howat was conscious of the martyr's bitter stubbornness of soul, alive, still alive and unquenched, in himself. He wondered about the heritage to come. There was a further belief that it followed exclusively the male line. The Pennys, like many another comparatively obscure name, went far back into the primeval soil of civilization. If he had no issue the endlessness might be confounded; a fatality in his long, dangerous excursions would have vanquished the ineradicable Welsh blood. He might have no children; yesterday he would have made such a decision; but now he was less sure of himself, of his power to will. He was dimly conscious of vast exterior forces and traitorous factors within. It was as if momentarily he had been lifted to a cloud beyond time, from which he saw the entire, stumbling progress of humanity, its beginning hid in humid mist, moving into a nocturnal shadow like a thunder bank.

He sat with chin on breast and sombre eyes until his mother laid her hand on his shoulder. "Howat," she protested, "you are too glum for the comfort of any one near you. I think you must make a pose of being black. I'd almost called one of the servants to fiddle in your ear."

Howat smiled at her; he returned slowly to the actual, the particular. Mr. Winscombe had pushed back his chair, excusing himself in the pressure of necessary preparations. His wife disappeared with him, leaving behind the echo of a discussion about Cecco, the Italian servant. The women followed, with David at Myrtle's shoulder, leaving Howat and Gilbert Penny.

The latter was still a handsome man, with his own hair silvered on a ruddy countenance, and a careful taste in clothes. His nose was predominant, with a wide-cleft mouth above a square chin. "I had thought," he said deliberately, "that you were employed in the counting house, but Schwar tells me that it has been a week since you were seen there." He raised a broad hand to silence Howat's reply. "While I can afford to keep you merely at hunting, the result to the table is so meagre that I'm not justified. There is no St. James here, in Pennsylvania, no gentlemen supported by the Crown for the purpose of amusement. You will have to sail for England if you expect that sort of thing." He rose, "You owe an intelligent interest in Myrtle Forge, to your sisters and mother, toward all that I have accomplished. It's a rich property, and it's growing bigger. Already young Forsythe has a list of improvements to be instituted at the Furnace — clerks and a manager and new system for carrying on the blast."

"I'm not an iron man," Howat Penny told him,

" I'm not a clerk. David can take all that over for you, particularly if he marries one of the girls."

" What are you? " the elder demanded sharply.

" You ought to know. You explained it fully enough to the Winscombes."

" If it wasn't for that you'd have been dumping slag five years ago. What I hoped was that with maturity some sense of obligation would be born into you. What is this pretended affection for your mother worth if you are unwilling to conserve, make safe, her future, in case I die? " All that his father said was logical, just; but it only brought him a renewed sense of his impotence before very old and implacable inner forces.

" I'll try again," he briefly agreed. " But I warn you, it will do little good. There is no pretence in the affection you spoke of, but — but something stronger —" he gave up as hopeless the effort to explain all that had swept through his mind.

Gilbert Penny abruptly left the room.

It transpired that the Italian servant was to be left at Myrtle Forge; he was now assisting the servants in strapping a box behind the chaise that was to carry Mr. Winscombe and David to the city. Howat pictured the long, supple hands of the Italian hooking Mrs. Winscombe into her clothes, and a sudden, hot revulsion clouded his brain. When the carriage had gone, and he stood in the contracted space of the counting room, before a long, narrow forge book open on a high desk, he was still conscious of

56

a strong repulsion. It was idiotic to let such an insignificant fact as the Winscombes' man persistently annoy him. But, in a manner entirely unaccountable, this Cecco had become a symbol of much that was dark, potentially threatening, in his conjectures.

The hammer fell with a full reiteration through the afternoon; the sun, at a small window, shifted a dusty bar across inkpots and quills and desk to a higher corner. He could hear the dull turning of the wheel and the thin, irregular splash of falling water. Other sounds rose at intervals — the tramping of mules dragging pig iron from Shadrach, the rumble of its deposit by the Forge. Emanuel Schwar entered with a piece of paper in his hand. " Eleven hundred weight of number two," he read; " at six pounds, and a load of charcoal. Jonas Rupp charged with three pairs of woollen stockings, and shoes for Minnie, four shillings more."

Howat mechanically entered the enumerated items, his distaste for such a petty occupation mounting until it resembled a concrete power forcing him outside into the mellow end of the day. A figure darkened the doorway; it was Caroline. " I hardly saw him," she declared hotly. " Myrtle hung like a sickly flower in his buttonhole." Her hoops flattened as she made her way through the narrow entrance. " There's one thing about Myrtle," she continued, " she's frightfully proper in her narrow little ideas. Myrtle's a prude. And I promise you I won't be if I get a chance at David." She stood with vivid, parted lips, bright eyes; almost, Howat thought, charming. Such a spirit in Caroline amazed him; he hadn't conceived of its presence. He recognized a phase of his own contempt for customary paths, accepted limitations and proprieties. "Remember David's Quaker training," he told her in his habitual air of jest. "David's been to London," she replied. "I saw him pinch the Appletofft girl at the farm."

Again in his room, he changed into more formal clothes than on the evening previous; he did this without a definite, conscious purpose; it was as if his attitude of mind required a greater suavity of exterior. He wore a London waistcoat, a gift from his mother, of magenta worked with black petals and black stone buttons; his breeches were without a wrinkle, and the tails of his coat, even if they were not wired like those David was said to have brought from England, had a not unsatisfactory swing.

At supper Mrs. Winscombe sat at his left, Caroline and Myrtle had taken their customary places opposite, the elders had not been disturbed. Mrs. Winscombe had resumed the animation vanished at noon. She wore green and white, with plum-coloured ribbons, and a flat shirred cap tied under her chin. The fluted, clear lawn of her elbow sleeves was like a scented mist. He was again conscious of the warm seduction, the rare finish, of her body, like a flushed marble under wide hoops and dyed silk. She was talking to Myrtle about the Court. "I am in waiting with the Princess Amelia Sophia," she explained; " I have her stockings. There is a frightful racket of music and parrots and German, with old Handel bellowing and the King eternally clinking one piece of gold on another."

Gilbert Penny listened with a tightening of his well shaped lips. " It's into that chamber pot we pour our sweat and iron," he asserted. Ludowika Winscombe studied him. " In England," she said, " the American provinces are supposed to lie hardly beyond the Channel, but here England seems to be at the other end of the world." Myrtle added, " I'd like it immensely."

And Howat thought of Ludowika — he thought of her tentatively as Ludowika — in the brilliant setting of tropical silks and birds.

He considered the change that had overtaken his father, English born, in the quarter century he had lived in America; the strong allegiance formed to ideas fundamentally different from those held at St. James; and he wondered if such a transformation would operate in Ludowika if she could remain in the Province. It was a fantastic query, and he impatiently dismissed it, returning to the contemplation of his mother's problematic happiness. He determined to question the latter if a permissible occasion arose; suddenly his interest had sharpened toward her mental situation. He compared the two women, what he could conjecture about Isabel Howat and Ludowika Winscombe; but something within him, automatic and certain, whispered that no comparison was possible. His mother possessed a quality of spirit that he had never found elsewhere; he could see, in spite of their resemblance of blood and position, that the elder could never have been merely provocative. Such distinctions, he divined, were the result of qualities mysterious and deeply concealed. Love, that he had once dismissed as the principle of blind procreation, became more complex, enigmatic. He had no increased desire to experience it, with the inevitable loss of personal liberty; but he began to be conscious of new depths, unexpected complications, in human relationship.

He was not so sure of himself.

They had moved to the less formal of the rooms used as places of gathering. The bed in a corner was hung in blue shalloon over ruffled white muslin, and there was blue at the windows. Against the wall a clavichord, set aside as obsolete, raised its dusky red ebony box on grooved legs. Myrtle was seated at it picking out an air from Belshazzar. She held each note in a silvery vibration that had the fragility of old age. Ludowika was by the fire, quartered across a corner; there was no stove, and the wood burning in the opening sent out frequent, pungent waves of smoke. She coughed and cursed. "Positively," she declared, "I'll turn salt like a smoked herring."

She rose, her gaze resting on Howat. "I must go out," she continued; "breathe." He was strangely reluctant to accompany her, his feet were leaden.

60

Nevertheless, in a few moments he found himself at her side on the lawn. Her sophistication had again disappeared, beneath the stars drawn across the hills, over Myrtle Forge. There was a pause in the hammering below. " Take me down there," she commanded.

He led the way on a beaten path that dropped sharply to a bridge of hewn logs crossing the spent water. The Forge, a long shed following the stream, was open on the opposite side; an enclosure of ruddy, vaporous gloom with pools of molten colour, clangorous sounds. The bubbling, white cores of three raised and hooded hearths were incessantly agitated with long rods by blackened and glistening shapes. At intervals a flushing rod was withdrawn from a fire and plunged in a trough of water; a cloud of ghostly steam arose, a forgeman's visage momentarily illuminated like a copper mask. A grimy lantern was hung above the anvil, its thin light falling on the ponderous head of the trip hammer suspended at right angles from a turning cogged shaft projection through the wall.

The hearths, set in a row beyond the anvil, had at their back an obscure, mechanical stir, accompanied by the audible suction of squat, drum bellows. The labour was halted at a fire; half naked anatomies, herculean shoulders and incredible arms, gathered about its mouth with hooked bars. An incandescent mass was lifted, born, rayed in an intolerable white heat, into the air. A hammer was swung upon

61

it; and, as if the metal were sentient, a violet radiance scintillated where the blow had fallen. The pasty iron was carried to the anvil, the hooks dropped for wide-jawed tongs; the trip hammer moved up and fell. The hardening metal darkened to a carnation from which chips scattered like gorgeous petals. The carnation faded under ringing blows; the petals, heaping in the penumbra under foot, were as vividly blue as gentians. The colour vanished from the solidifying bloom . . . It was ashen, black. The hammering continued.

A sense of the vast and antique simplicity of the forging, a feeling of hammering the earth itself into the superior purposes of man, enveloped Howat. He forgot for the moment his companion, lost in a swelling pride of Myrtle Forge, of his father's fibre — the iron of his character like the iron he successfully wrought. He could grasp Gilbert Penny's accomplishment here, take fire at its heroic quality; a thing he found impossible in the counting room above, recording such trivial details as wool stockings for Jonas Rupp. He could be a forgeman, he thought, but never a clerk; and in that limitation he realized that he was inferior to his father. There were aspects of himself beyond such discipline and control.

Ludowika Winscombe grasped his arm. " Come away," she begged; " it's — it's savage, like Vulcan and dreadful, early legends." She hurried him, clinging to his arm, over the ascent to the orderly lawn, the tranquil shine of candle-lit windows. There, with her hood fallen from her head, she sat on a stone step.

"You frighten me, a little," she confessed. "Are you at all like — like that below inside of you? I have a feeling that you might be. If you were one of the men about Vauxhall you'd be kissing me now . . . if I liked you. But, although I do like you, I wouldn't kiss you for an emerald buckle." He recognized that she spoke seriously; her voice bore no connective suggestion. Kisses, it appeared, were no more to her than little flowers which she dealt out casually where she pleased. Yet the idea, with its intimate sensual implications, stayed in his thoughts. He considered kissing her, holding her mouth against his; and he was conscious of a sharp return of his stinging sense of her bodily seductiveness.

At the same time an obscure uneasiness, rebellion, possessed him; it was the old, familiar feeling of revolt, of distaste for imprisoning circumstance. It came to him acutely, almost as if a voice had whispered in his ear, warning him, urging him into the wild, to escape threatening catastrophe. He determined to leave Myrtle Forge in the morning, to return to the stream he had followed into the serene heart of the woods. There he would stay until — until Ludowika Winscombe had gone. Howat had no especial sense of danger from her; only for the moment she typified the entire world of trivial artifice. He gazed at her with a conscious detachment

63

possible because of the rarity in his existence of such figures as hers.

She had risen, and her cloak fallen upon the grass. Howat could see her face beneath hair faintly powdered with silver dust and the ruffled patch of white tied pertly under her chin. Her smoothly turning shoulders, filmed in lawn, and low bodice crowned an extravagant circumference of ruffled silk and rosettes. Against the night of the Province, the invisible but felt presence of immutable hills, she was like a puppet, a grotesque figure of comedy. He regarded her sombrely from the step, his chin cupped in a hand.

But, again, she surprised him, speaking entirely out of the character he had assigned her, in a spirit that seemed utterly incongruous, but which was yet warm with conviction. " I want to explain a great deal to you," she said, " that really isn't explainable. It isn't sensible, and yet it is the strongest feeling I remember. It's about here and you and me. You can't picture my life, and so you don't know how strange this is, how different from all I've ever lived.

" I think I told you I was born in Paris — you see some of us came to France when Louis took a Polish princess, and there my mother married an English gentleman. Well, it was always the Court, in France and in England. Always the Court — do you know what that means? It's a place where women are pretty pink and white candies that men

64

are always picking over. It's a great bed with a rose silk counterpane and closed draperies. Champagne and music and scent and masques. Little plays with the intrigue in the audience; favours behind green hedges. I was in it when I was fourteen, and I had a lover the first year. He showed me how to make pleasure. Don't think that I was indifferent to this," she added directly; "that I wanted to escape it. I wasn't; I didn't. Only beneath everything I had a feeling of not being completely satisfied; I wanted — oh, not very strongly — something else, for an hour. At times the air seemed choking; and inside of me, but not in my body, I seemed choking too. I used to think about the Polish forests, and that would help a little."

She resumed the place at his side, with her silk billowing against his knee. "This is it," she declared, her face set against the illimitable, still dark. "I recongized it only a little while ago. I think unconsciously I came to America hoping to find it; there was nothing at Annapolis, but here —" she drew a breath as deep, he noted, as her stays would permit. "It includes you, somehow," she continued; "as if you were the voice. What I said coming away from the Forge, about dreading you, was only momentary. I have another feeling, premonition —" she broke off, her manner changed. "All the Court believes in signs: Protestantism and vampires.

"It seems unreal here; I mean St. James and all

that was so tremendously important; incredibly stupid — the Princess Amelia's stockings. But you can't imagine the jealousy. Every bit of it shall go out of my thoughts. You'll help me, a harmless magic. I'll be as simple as that girl across the road, with the red cheeks, in a single slip. You must call me Ludowika; Ludowika and Howat. I'm not so terribly old, only twenty-nine."

" I am going away to-morrow," he informed her; " I won't be back before you leave."

A slight frown gathered about her eyes. Her face was very close to his. " But I don't like that either," she replied. " You were to be a part of it, its voice; excursions in the woods. Is it necessary, your absence? "

He knew that it was not; and suddenly he was seized with the conviction that he would not go. It was as if, again, a voice outside him had informed him of the fact. But if there were no reason for his going there was as little for his remaining at Myrtle Forge; that was, so far as Ludowika Winscombe was concerned. He had been untouched by all that she had said; untouched except for a faint involuntary shiver as she had spoken of premonition. And that had vanished instantaneously. There was his duty in the counting house. But he was forced to admit to himself the insufficiency of that reason; it was too palpably false.

He had not been moved by the intent of what she had said, but his imagination had been stirred, as if

66

by the touch of delicate, pointed fingers, at her description of Court — a bed with a silk counterpane . . . behind clipped greenery. He recalled the fan with its painted Villeggiatura, the naked, wanton loves. " Something different," she half repeated, with a sigh, an accent, of longing. Howat heard her with impatience; it was absurb to try to picture her tramping in the wilderness, breaking her way hour after hour through thorned underbrush, like Fanny Gilkan. She wouldn't progress a hundred yards in her unsteady pattens and fragile clothes.

Suddenly the Italian servant appeared absolutely noiselessly at her side, speaking a ridiculous, oily gibberish. " At once," she replied. She turned to Howat. " My bed has been prepared. Are you going to-morrow? "

" No," he answered awkwardly. She turned and left without further words. The servant walked behind her, resembling an unnatural shadow.

The metallic clamour at the anvil rose and fell, diminished by the interposed bulk of the dwellings, ceaselessly forging the Penny iron, the Penny gold. He thought of himself as metal under the hammer; or rather ore at the furnace: he hadn't run clear in the casting; there were bubbles, bubbles and slag. Endless refinements — first the furnace and then the forge and then the metal. A contempt for the lesser degrees possessed him, for a flawed or clumsy forging, for weakness of the flesh, the fatality of easy surrender. An overwhelming, passionate emotion

67

swept him to his feet, clenched his hands, filled him with a numbing desire to reach the last purification.

The mood sank into an inexplicable nostalgia; he dragged the back of a hand impatiently across his vision. His persistent indifference, the inhibition that held him in a contemptuous isolation, again possessed him, Howat, a black Penny. A last trace of his emotion, caught in the flood of his paramount disdain, vanished like a breath of warm mist. He entered the house and mounted to his room; the stairs creaked but that was the only sound audible within. His candles burned without their protecting glasses in smooth, unwavering flames. When they were extinguished the darkness flowed in and blotted out familiar objects, folded him in a cloak of invisibility, obliterated him in sleep. As he lost consciousness he heard the trip hammer dully beating out Penny iron, Penny gold; beating out, too, the Penny men . . . Slag and metal and ruffled muslin, roman candles and stars.

V

THERE came to him in the counting house, the following afternoon, rumours and echoes of the day's happenings. David Forsythe had arrived after dinner, and there had been word from Mr. Winscombe; he would be obliged to return to Maryland, and trusted that Ludowika would not be an onerous charge. David was to take Myrtle and Caroline back with him to the city, for an exemplary Quaker party. "There's no good asking you," he told Howat, lounging in the door of the counting room. David was flushed, his sleeve coated with dust. "Caroline," he exclaimed, "is as strong as a forgeman; she upset me on the grass as quickly as you please, hooked her knee behind me, and there I was. She picked me up, too, and laughed at me," he stopped, lost in thought. "Myrtle's really beautiful," he said again; "Caroline's not a thing to look at, and yet, do you know, a — a man looks at her. She is wonderfully graceful."

Howat gave Caroline the vigorous stamp of his brotherly approval. "She understands a lot, for a girl," he admitted. "Of course Myrtle's a particular peach, but I'd never go to her if a buckle —" he stopped abruptly as Myrtle appeared at David's side. "Isn't he industrious?" she said indifferently. "You'd never guess how father's at him. Have you heard, Howat — Mrs. Winscombe will be here perhaps a month. It's a wonder you haven't gone away, you are so frightfully annoyed by people. Last night you were with her over an hour on the lawn. I could see that father thought it queer; but I explained to him that court women never thought of little things like, well, husbands."

Howat gazed at her coldly, for the first time conscious that he actually disliked Myrtle. He made up his mind, definitely, to assist Caroline as far as possible. She was absurd, criticizing Mrs. Winscombe. "Where," he demanded, "did you get all that about courts? And your sudden, tender interest in husbands? That's new, too. You're not thinking of one for yourself, are you? He'd never see you down in the morning."

A bright, angry colour flooded her cheeks. "You are as coarse as possible," she declared. "I'm sure I wish you'd stay away altogether from Myrtle Forge; you've never been anything but a bother." She left abruptly. "Sweet disposition." Howat grinned. "You are seeing family life as it's actually lived." Later his thoughts returned to what she had said about Ludowika Winscombe; he recalled the latter's speech, seated on the doorstep; some stuff about a premonition. Myrtle had suggested that he was interested in her. What ridiculous nonsense! If his father said anything on that score

70

the other would discover that he was no longer a boy. Besides, such insinuations were a breach of hospitality. How Mrs. Winscombe would laugh at them if she suspected Myrtle's cheap folly.

She had asked him to call her Ludowika. He decided that he would; really he couldn't get out of it now. It would do no harm. Ludowika! It was a nice name; undoubtedly Polish. He thought again about what she had said of Polish forests, the dissatisfaction that had followed her for so many years. A lover at fourteen. A surprising sentence formed of itself in his brain.— She had never had a chance. That pasty court life had spoiled her. It had no significance for himself; he was simply revolving a slightly melancholy fact.

Felix Winscombe was a sere figure, yet he was extraordinarily full of a polished virility, rapier-like. Howat could see the dark, satirical face shadowed by the elaborate wig, the rigid figure in precise, foppish dress. He heard Winscombe's slightly harsh, dominant voice. His position in England was, he knew, secure, high. Ludowika had been very sensible in marrying him. That was the way, Howat Penny told himself, that marriage should be consummated. He would never marry. David Schwar appeared with a sheaf of papers, which he himself proceeded to docket, and Howat left the counting room.

He met Ludowika almost immediately; she advanced more simply dressed than he had ever seen her before. She pointed downward to the water flashing over the great, turning wheel. " Couldn't we walk along the rill? There's a path, and it's beautiful in the shadow." The stream poured solid and green through the narrow, masoned course of the forebay, sweeping in a lucent arc over the lip of the fall. An earthen path followed the artificial channel through a dense grove of young maples, seeming to hold the sun in their flame-coloured foliage. Myrtle Forge was lost, the leaves shut out the sky; underfoot some were already dead. The wilderness marched up to the edges of the meagre clearings.

Ludowika walked ahead, without speech; irregular patches of ruddy light slid over her flared skirt. Suddenly she stopped with an exclamation; the trees opened before them on the broad Canary sweeping between flat rocks, banks bluely green. Above, the course was broken, swift; but where they stood it was tranquil again, and crystal clear. Yellow rays plunging through the unwrinkled surface gilded the pebbles on the shallower bottom. A rock, broad and flat, extended into the stream by the partial, diagonal dam that turned the water into Myrtle Forge; and Ludowika found a seat with her slippers just above the current. Howat Penny sat beside her, then dropped back on the rocks, his hands clasped behind his head.

A silence intensified by the whispering stream enveloped them. He watched a hawk, diminutive on the pale immensity above. "Heavens," Ludowika finally spoke, "how wonderful . . . just to sit, not to be bothered by — by things. Just to hear the water. Far away," she said dreamily; "girl."

From where he lay he could see her arms, beautiful and bare, lost in soft Holland above the elbows; he could see the roundness of her body above the lowest of stays. Suddenly she fascinated him; he visualized her sharply, as though for the first time — a warm, intoxicating entity. He was profoundly disturbed, and sat erect; the stream, the woods, blurred in his vision. He felt as if his heart had been turned completely over in his body; the palms of his hands were wet. He had a momentary, absurd impulse to run, beyond Shadrach Furnace, beyond any distance he had yet explored, farther even than St. Xavier. Ludowika Winscombe gazed in serene, unconscious happiness before her. He felt that his face was crimson, and he rose, moved to the water's edge, his back toward her. He was infuriated at a trembling that passed over him, damned it in a savage and inaudible whisper.

What particularly appalled him was the fact that his overmastering sensation came without the slightest volition of his own. He had had nothing to do with it, his will was powerless. He was betrayed like a fortified city whose gate had been thrown open by an unsuspected, a concealed, traitor inside. In an instant he had been invaded, his being levelled, his peculiar pride overthrown. He thought even that he heard a dull crash, as if something paramount had irremediably fallen, something that should have been maintained at any cost, until the end of life.

Howat felt a sudden hatred of his companion; but that quickly evaporated; he discovered that she had spread, like a drop of carmine in a goblet of water, through his every nerve. By God, but she had become himself! In the space of a breath she was in his blood, in his brain; calling his hands about her, toward her smooth, beautiful arms. She was the scent in his nostrils, the sound a breeze newly sprung up stirred out of the leaves. A profound melancholy spread over him, a deep sadness, a conviction of loss. Ludowika was singing softly:

> "Last Sunday at St. James's prayers
> — dressed in all my whalebone airs."

He had come on disaster. The realization flashed through his consciousness and was engulfed in the submerging of his being in the overwhelming, stinging blood that had swept him from his old security. Yet he had been so detached from the merging influences about him, his organization had been so complete in its isolation, his egotism so developed, that a last trace of his entity lingered sentient, viewing as if from a careened but still tenable deck the general submergence. His thoughts returned to the automatic operation of the consummation obliterating his person, the inexorable blind movement of the thing in which he had been caught, dragged into the

74

maw of a supreme purpose. It was, of course, the
law of mere procreation which he had before contemptuously recognized and dismissed; a law for animals; but he was no longer entirely an animal. Already he had considered the possibility of an additional force in the directing of human passion,
founded on something beyond the thirst of flesh,
founded perhaps on soaring companionships, on —
on— The condition, the term, he was searching for
evaded him.

He thought of the word love; and he was struck
by the vast inaccuracy of that large phrase. It
meant, Howat told himself, literally nothing: what
complex feeling Isabel Penny might have for her
husband, Caroline's frank desire for David Forsythe, Myrtle's meagre emotion, Fanny Gilkan's
sense of Hesa and life's necessary compromises, his
own collapse — all were alike called love. It was
not only a useless word but a dangerous falsity.
It had without question cloaked immense harm, pretence; it had perpetuated old lies, brought them
plausibly, as if in a distinguished and reputable company, out of past superstitions and credulity; the
real and the meaningless, the good and the evil, hopelessly confused.

They were seated at supper, four of them only;
Isabel and Gilbert Penny, and, opposite him, Ludowika. Occasionally he would glance at her, surreptitiously; his wrists would pound with an irregular, sultry circulation; longing would harass him like

the beating of a club. She, it seemed to him, grew gayer, younger, more simple, every hour. Happiness, peace, radiated in her gaze, the gestures of her hands. Howat wondered at what moment he would destroy it. Reprehensible. A moment must come — soon — when emotion would level his failing reserve, his falling defences. He thrilled at the thought of the inevitable disclosure. Would she fight against it, deny, satirize his tumult; or surrender? He couldn't see clearly into that; he didn't care. Then he wondered about the premonition of which she had spoken, deciding to ask her to be more explicit.

An opportunity occurred later. Gilbert Penny had gone down to the Forge store, his wife had disappeared. Ludowika Winscombe and Howat were seated in the drawing room. Only a stand of candles was lit at her elbow; her face floated like a pale and lovely wafer against the billowing shadows of the chamber. The wood on the iron hearth was charring without flame. He questioned her bluntly, suddenly, out of a protracted silence. She regarded him speculatively, delaying answer. Then, " I couldn't tell you like this, now; it would be too silly; you would laugh at me. I hadn't meant to say even what I did. I'd prefer to ignore it."

" What did you mean, what premonition came to you? " he insisted crudely.

She seemed to draw away from him, increase in years and an attitude of tolerant amusement. Only an immediate reply would save them, he realized. He leaned forward unsteadily, with clenched hands. " I warned you," she proceeded lightly; " and if you do laugh my pride will suffer." In spite of her obvious determination to speak indifferently her voice grew serious. " I had a feeling that you mustn't kiss me, that this — America, the Province, Myrtle Forge, you, were for something different. You see, I had always longed for a peculiar experience, release, and when it came, miraculously, I thought, it must not be spoiled, turned into the old, old thing. That was all. It was in my spirit," she added almost defiantly, as if that claim might too be susceptible of derision.

He settled back into his chair, turning upon her a gloomy vision. Whatever penalty threatened them, he knew, must fall. Nothing existing could keep him from it. He felt a fleet sorrow for her in the inevitable destruction of the release for which she had so long searched, her new peace, so soon to be smashed. All sorrow for himself had gone under. Isabel Penny returned to the drawing room, and moved about, her flowered silk at once gay and obscure in the semidarkness. " The fire, Howat," she directed; " it's all but out." He stirred the logs into a renewed blaze.

A warm gilding flickered over Ludowika; she smiled at him, relaxed, content. He was surprised that she could not see the tumultuous feeling overpowering him. He had heard that women were im-

77

mediately aware of such emotion. But he realized that she had been lulled into a false sense of security, of present immunity from "the old, old thing," by her own placidity. He did not know when his mother left the room. He wondered continuously when it would happen, when the bolt would fall, what she would do. Howat was hot and cold, and possessed by a subtle sense of improbity, a feeling resembling that of a doubtful advance through the dark, for a questionable end. This was the least part of him, insignificant; his passion grew constantly stronger, more brutal. In a last, vanishing trace of his superior consciousness he recognized that the thing must have happened to him as it did; it was the price of his more erect pride, his greater contempt, his solitary and unspent state.

She rose suddenly and announced that she was about to retire. It saved them for the moment, for that day; he muttered something incomprehensible and she was gone.

Isabel Penny returned and took Mrs. Winscombe's place before the fire. She spoke trivially, at random intervals. A great longing swept over him to tell his mother everything, try to find an escape in her wise counsel; but his emotion seemed so ugly that he could not lay it before her. Besides, he had a conviction that it would be hopeless: he was gone. She was discussing Ludowika now. "Really," she said, "they seem very well matched, a good arrangement." She was referring, he realized, to the Winscombes' experience. He never thought of Felix Winscombe as married, Ludowika's husband; he had ceased to think of him at all. The present moment banished everything else. " She has a quality usually destroyed by life about a Court," the leisurely voice went on; " she seems quite happy here, for a little, in a way simple. But, curiously enough, she disturbs your father. He can't laugh with her as he usually does with attractive women."

It was natural, Howat thought, that Gilbert Penny should be uneasy before such a direct reminder of the setting from which he had taken Isabel Howat. It was a life, memories, in which the elder had no part; that consciousness dictated a part of his father's bitterness toward St. James, the Royal Government. But Gilbert Penny had never had serious reason to dread it. His wife had left it all behind, permanently, without, apparently, a regret. He had a sudden, astonishing community of feeling with the older man; a momentary dislike of St. James, Versailles, the entire, treacherous, silk mob. A lover at fourteen! Howat damned such a betrayal with a bitterness whose base lay deeply buried in sex jealousy.

" I am glad," the other continued, " that you are not susceptible; I suppose you'll be off hunting in a day or more; Mrs. Winscombe is bright wine for a young man. Women like her play at sensation, like eating figs." He thought contemptuously what nonsense was talked in connection with feminine in-

79

tuition; it was nothing more than a polite chimera, like all the other famous morals and inhibitions supposed to serve and direct mankind.

He wondered once more about his mother, what the course of her life had been — happily occupied, filled, or merely self-contained, hiding much in a deep, even flow? Her head was turned away from him, and he could see the girlish profile, the astonishing illusion of youth renewed. Howat wanted to ask her how she had experienced, well — love, since there was no other word. It had come to her quickly, he knew; her affair with Gilbert Penny had been headlong, or else it would not have been at all; yet he felt she had not been the victim of such a tyranny as mastered himself. But, perhaps, after all, secretly, every one was — just animal-like. He repudiated this firmly, at once. He himself had felt that he was not entirely animal.

"The girls," Isabel Penny said, "will be gallopading now. Myrtle has a new dress, her father gave it to her, an apricot mantua."

"He's really idiotic about Myrtle," Howat declared irritably. His mother glanced swiftly at him. She made no comment. "Now Caroline! It's Caroline who ought to marry David Forsythe."

"Such things must fall out as they will."

God, that was true enough, terribly true! He rose and strode into the farther darkness of the drawing room, returning to the fireplace, marching away again. He saw the white glimmer of Ludowika's arms; he had a vision of her tying the broad ribbon about her rounded, silken knee. ". . . a man now," his mother's voice was distant, blurred. "Responsibilities; your father —" He had heard this before without being moved; but suddenly the words had a new actuality; he was a man now, that was to say he stood finally, irrevocably, alone, beyond assistance, advice. He had never heeded them; he had gone a high-handed, independent way, but the others had been there; unconsciously he had been aware of them, even counted on them. Now they had vanished.

Caroline and Myrtle, bringing David with them again, returned on the following morning. It seemed to Howat that the former was almost lovely; she had a gayer sparkle, a clearer colour, than he had ever seen her possess before. On the other hand, Myrtle was dull; the dress, it seemed, had not been the un-qualified success she had hoped for. Something newer had arrived in the meantime from London. Ludowika, it developed, had one of the later sacques in her boxes; but that, she said indifferently, must be quite dead now. It seemed to Howat that she too regarded Myrtle without enthusiasm. Ludowika and Myrtle had had very little to say to each other; Myrtle studied Mrs. Winscombe's apparel with a keen, even belligerent, eye; the other patronized the girl in a species of half absent instruction.

The sky was flawless, leaden blue; the sunlight fell in an enveloping flood over the countryside, but it was pale, without warmth. There was no wind, not a leaf turned on the trees — a sinuous sheeting of the country-side like red-gold armour. But Howat knew that at the first stir of air the leaves would be in stricken flight, the autumn accomplished. Caroline dragged him impetuously down into the garden, among the brown, varnished stems of the withered roses, the sere, dead ranks of scarlet sage. " He hugged me," she told him; " I was quite breathless. It was in a hall, dark; but he didn't say anything. What do you think? " There was nothing definite that he might express; and he patted her shoulder. He had a new kinship with Caroline; Howat now understood her tempest of feeling, concealed beneath her commonplace daily aspect.

Myrtle and David joined them, and he left, resumed his place at the high desk in the counting house. Strangely his energy of being communicated itself to the prosaic work before him. It was, he suddenly felt, important for him to master the processes of Myrtle Forge; it would not do for him to remain merely irresponsible, a juvenile appendage to the Penny iron. He would need all the position, the weight, he could assume; and money of his own. He found a savage pleasure in recording every detail put before him. He compared the value of pig metal, the cost of charcoal, wages, with the return of the blooms and anconies they shipped to England. Howat experienced his father's indignation at the manner in which London limited the Province's industries. For the first time he was conscious of an actual interest in the success of Myrtle Forge, a personal concern in its output. He had always visualized it as automatically prosperous, a cause of large, inexact pride; but now it was all near to him; he considered the competition rapidly increasing here, and the jealous menace over seas.

His final trace of careless youth had gone; he felt the advent of the constant apprehension that underlies all maturity, a sense of the proximity of blind accident, evil chance, disaster. At last he was opposed to life itself, with an immense stake to gain, to hold; in the midst of a seething, treacherous conflict arbitrarily ended by death. There was no cringing, absolutely no cowardice, in him. He was glad that it was all immediately about him; he was arrogant in pressing forward to take what he wanted from existence. He forgot all premonitions, doubt was behind him; he no longer gauged the value of his desire for Ludowika Winscombe. She was something he would, had to, have.

David Forsythe sat across the back of a chair in Howat's room as the latter dressed in the rapidly failing light. David had smuggled his London coat with the wired tails out to Myrtle Forge, and had the stiffened portion now spread smoothly out on either side. His cheerful, freshly-coloured face was troubled; he seemed constantly on the point of breaking into speech without actually becoming audible. Howat was thinking of Ludowika. It would happen to-night, he knew. He was at once apprehensive and glad.

"You knew," David ventured finally, "that I'm supposed to ask Myrtle to marry me. That is, your father and mine hoped I would. Well," he drew a deep breath, "I don't think I shall. Of course, she is one of the prettiest girls any one ever saw, and she's quite bright — it's wonderful what she has picked up about the Furnace, but yet —" his speech suddenly ran out. With an effort Howat brought himself back from his own vastly more important concern. "Yes?" he queried, pausing with his fingers in the buttonholes of a mulberry damask coat. "I have decided to choose, to act, for myself," David announced; "this is a thing where every man must be absolutely free.— Caroline can have me if she likes."

Howat could not avoid a momentary, inward flicker of amusement at David Forsythe's absolute freedom of choice. He felt infinitely older than the other, wiser in the circuitous mysteries of being. He pounded David on the back, exclaimed, "Good!"

"I don't know whether to speak to Abner," the other proceeded unfilially, "or the great Penny first. I don't care too much for either job. It would be pleasanter to go to Caroline. I have an idea she doesn't exactly dislike me."

"Perhaps I oughtn't to tell you," Howat replied gravely; "but Caroline thinks a lot of you. She has admitted it to me —"

84

David Forsythe danced agilely about the more serious figure; he kicked Howat gaily from behind, ironically patted his cheek. " Hell's buttons! " he cried. " Why didn't you tell me that before? You cast iron ass! I'll marry Caroline if I have to take her to a charcoal burner's hut. She would go, too."

Howat Penny gripped the other's shoulder, faced him with grim determination. " Do you fully realize that Myrtle Forge, Shadrach, will be us? They will be ours and our wives' and childrens'. We must stand together, David, whatever happens, whatever we may, personally, think. The iron is big now, but it is going to be great. We mustn't fail, fall apart. We'll need each other; there's going to be trouble, I think."

David put out his hand. " I didn't know you felt like that, Howat," he replied, the effervescent youth vanished from him too. " It's splendid. We'll hammer out some good blooms together. And for the other, nothing shall ever make a breach between us."

VI

THEY went down to the supper table silently, absorbed in thought. David was placed where Mr. Winscombe had been seated, on Mrs. Penny's right, and next to Myrtle. Gilbert Penny maintained a flow of high spirits; he rallied every one at the table with the exception of, Howat noted, Ludowika. Her hair was simply arranged and undecorated, she wore primrose with gauze like smoke, an apparently guileless bodice with blurred, warm suggestions of her fragrant body. Howat was conscious of every detail of her appearance; she was stamped, as she was that evening, indelibly on his inner being. He turned toward her but little, addressed to her only the most perfunctory remarks; he was absorbed in the realization that the most fateful moment he had met was fast approaching. His father's cheerful voice continued seemingly interminably; now it was a London beauty to which he affected to believe David had given his heart. The latter replied stoutly:

"I brought that back safely enough; it's here the danger lies. Humiliating to cross the ocean and then be lost in Canary Creek."

Gilbert Penny shot an obvious, humorous glance

at Myrtle. She did not meet it, but sat with lowered gaze. Caroline made a daring " nose " at Howat; but he too failed to acknowledge her message. David's affair had sunk from his thoughts. The drawing room was brilliantly lighted: there was a constant stir of peacock silk, of yellow and apple green and coral lutestring, of white shoulders, in the gold radiance of candles like stiff rows of narcissi. Caroline drifted finally into the chamber back of the dining room, and they could hear the tenuous vibrations of the clavichord. Soon David had disappeared. The elder Penny discovered Myrtle seated sullenly at her mother's side; and, taking her arm, he escorted her in the direction of the suddenly silenced music.

Ludowika sat on a small couch away from the fireplace. She smiled at Howat as he moved closer to her. She never did things with her hands, he noticed, like the women of his family, embroidery or work on little heaps of white. She sat motionless, her arms at rest. His mother seemed far away. The pounding recommenced unsteadily at his wrists, the room wavered in his vision. Ludowika permeated him like a deep draught of intoxicating, yellow wine. He had a curious sensation of floating in air, of tea roses. It was clear that, folded in happy contentment, she still realized nothing. . . . She must know now, any minute. Howat saw that his mother had gone.

He rose and stood before Ludowika, leaning

slightly over her. She raised her gaze to his; her interrogation deepened. Then her expression changed, clouded, her lips parted; she half raised a hand. Her breast rose and fell, sharply, once. Howat picked her up by the shoulders and crushed her, silk and cool gauze and mouth, against him. Ludowika's skirts billowed about, half hid, him; a long silence, a long kiss.

Her head fell back with a sigh, she drooped again upon the sofa. She hadn't struggled, exclaimed; even now there was no revolt in her countenance, only a deep trouble. "Howat," she said softly, "you shouldn't have done that. It was brutal, selfish. You — you knew, after all that I told you; the premonition —" she broke off, anger shone brighter in her eyes. "How detestable men are!" She turned away from him, her profile against the brocade of the sofa. Unexpectedly he was almost cold, and self-contained; he saw the gilded angle of a frame on the wall, heard the hickory disintegrating on the hearth.

He had kissed her as a formal declaration; what must come would come. "I was an imbecile," she spoke in a voice at once listless and touched with bitterness; "Arcadia," she laughed. "I thought it was different here, that you were different; that feeling in my heart — but it's gone now, dead. I suppose I should thank you. But, do you know, I regret it; I would rather have stayed at St. James all my life and kept that single little delusion, longing.

The premonition was nonsense, too; nothing new, unexpected, can happen. Kisses are almost the oldest things in the world, kisses and their results. What is there to be afraid of? You see, I learned it all quite young.

"I am an imbecile; only it came so suddenly. You would laugh at me if you knew what I was thinking. I can even manage a smile at myself." She appeared older, the Mrs. Winscombe who had first come to Myrtle Forge; her mouth was flippant. "The eternal Suzanna," she remarked, "the monotonous elders or younger." He paid little heed to her words; the coldness, the indifference, were fast leaving him. His heart was like the trip hammer at the Forge. Yellow wine. He was still standing above her, and he took her hands in his. She put up her face with a movement of bravado, of mockery, which he ignored.

"I didn't choose it," he told her; "it's ruined all that I was. Now, I don't care; there is nothing else. One thing you are wrong about — if there had been another in your life like myself you wouldn't be here with — as you are. I'm certain of that. It's the only thing I do know. My feeling may be a terrible misfortune; I didn't make it; I can't see the end. There isn't any, I think." He pressed her hands to his throat with a gesture that half dragged her from the sofa. A deeper colour stained her cheeks, and her breath caught. "Endless," he repeated, losing the word on her lips. She wilted into a corner of the sofa, and he strode over to the fire, stood gazing blindly at the pulsating embers. Howat returned to her almost immediately, but she made no sign of his nearness. The bitterness had left her face, she appeared weary, pallid; she sat heedlessly crumpling her flounces, a hand bent back on its wrist.

"I think it is something in myself," she said presently; "something a little wrong that I'm dreadfully tired of. Always men. Out here a Howat Penny, just like any fribble about the Court. God, I'd like to be that girl across the road, in the barnyard." He was back at the fire again when Gilbert Penny entered the room. The latter dropped a palm on Howat's shoulder.

"Schwar says the last sow metal was faulty," he declared; "the Furnace'll need some attention with Abner Forsythe deeper in the Provincial affairs. Splendid thing David's back. Look for a lot from David." Howat hoped desperately that Ludowika would not leave, go to her room, while his father was talking. "David says you have an understanding, will do great things. I hope so. I hope so. I won't damn him as an example but he will do you no harm. That is, if he touches your confounded person at all. A black Penny, Mrs. Winscombe," he said, turning to the figure spread in pale silk on the sofa. "Fortunate for you to have no such confounded, stubborn lot on your hands. Although," he added laughingly, "Felix Winscombe's no broken reed. But this boy of mine — you might think he had been run out of Shadrach," he tapped a finger on Howat's back. " Not like those fellows about the Court, anyway. They tell me he'll go fifty miles through the woods in a day. Now if we could only keep that at the iron trade —"

His father went on insufferably, without end. Howat withdrew stiffly from the other's touch. Irresistibly he drifted back, back to Ludowika. She had not moved; her bent hand seemed dislocated. An immense tenderness for her overwhelmed him; his sheer passion vapourized into a poignant sweetness of solicitous feeling. He was protective; his jaw set rigidly, he enveloped her in an angry barrier from all the world. He had a sensation of standing at bay; in his mulberry damask, in brocade and silver buttons, he had an impression of himself stooped and savage, confronting a menacing dark with Ludowika flung behind him. Inexplicable tremors assailed him, vast fears. His father's deliberate voice destroyed the illusion; he saw the candles about him like white and yellow flowers, the suave interior. The others had returned. He heard Ludowika speaking; she laughed. His tension relaxed. Suddenly he was flooded with happiness, as if he had been drenched in sparkling, delightful water. He joined in the gay, trivial clamour that arose. Isabel Penny gazed at him speculatively.

There would, it appeared, be no other opportunity

that evening for him to declare himself to Ludowika. He was vaguely conscious of his mother's scrutiny; he must avoid exposing Ludowika to any uncomfortable surmising. His thoughts leaped forward to a revelation that he began to feel was inevitable; he got even now a tangible pleasure from the consideration of an announcement of his passion for Ludowika Winscombe, a sheer insistence upon it in the face of an antagonistic world. But for the present he must be careful. This, the greatest event that had befallen him, summed up all that he innately was; it expressed him, a black Penny, absolutely; Howat felt the distance between himself, his convictions, and the convictions of the world, immeasurably widening. His feeling for Ludowika symbolized his isolation from the interwoven fabric of the plane of society; it gave at last a tangible bulk to his scorn.

As he had feared, presently she rose and went to her room. Myrtle took her place on the sofa. Gilbert Penny vanished with a broad witticism at the well known preference of youth, in certain situations, for its own council. David Forsythe made a wry face at Howat. Caroline gaily laid her arm across her mother's shoulder and propelled her from the room. David stood awkwardly in the middle of the floor; and Howat, hardly less clumsy, took his departure. He found Caroline awaiting him in the shadow of his door; she followed him and stood silent while he made a light. Her face was serious, and her hands clasped tightly. "Howat," she said in a small voice, "it's — it's, that is, David loves me. Whatever do you suppose father and Myrtle will say?"

"What do you think David is saying to Myrtle now?" he asked drily. "I am glad, Caroline; everything worked out straight for you. David is a damned good Quaker. For some others life isn't so easy." She laid a warm hand on his shoulder. "I wish you were happy, Howat." A slight irritation seized him at the facile manner in which she radiated her satisfaction, and he moved away. "David's going back to-night. I wish he wouldn't," she said troubled. "That long, dark way. Anything might happen. But he has simply got to be at his father's office in the morning. He is going to speak to him first, see what will be given us at the Furnace."

"It should be quite a family party at breakfast," Howat predicted.

VII

HE was entirely right. Ludowika rarely appeared so early; Myrtle's face seemed wan and pinched, and her father rallied her on her indisposition after what should have been an entrancing evening. She declared suddenly, " I hate David Forsythe! " Gilbert Penny was obviously startled. Caroline half rose, as if she had finished breakfast; but she sat down again with an expression of determination. Howat looked about from his removed place of being. " I do! " Myrtle repeated. " At first he seemed to like — I mean I liked him, and then everything changed, got horrid. Some one interfered." Resentment, suspicion, dominated her, she grew shrill with anger. " I saw him making faces at Howat, as if he and Howat, as if Howat had, well —"

" Don't generalize," said Howat coolly; " be particular."

" As if you had deliberately spoiled any chance, yes," she declared defiantly, " any chance I had."

" That's ridiculous," Gilbert Penny declared. " What," he asked his wife, " are they all driving at? " She professed herself equally puzzled. " Howat would say nothing disadvantageous to young Forsythe. He knows what we all hope." Caroline suddenly leaned forward, speaking in a level voice: " This has nothing to do with Howat, but with me. I am going to tell you at once, so that you can all say what you wish, get as angry as you like, and then accept what — what had to be. David and I love each other; we are going to be married."

Gilbert Penny's surprise slowly gave place to a dark tide suffusing his countenance. " You and David," he half stuttered, " getting married — like that." Myrtle was rigid in an indignation that left her momentarily without speech. Mrs. Penny, Howat saw, drew into the slight remoteness from which she watched the conflicts of her family. " I know I'm fearfully bold, yes, indecent," Caroline went on, " and undutiful, impertinent. I'm sorry, truly, for that. Perhaps you'll forgive me, later. But I won't apologize for loving David."

" Incredible," her father pronounced. " A girl announcing, without the slightest warrant or authority, that she intends to marry. And trampling on her sister's heart in the bargain." Howat expostulated, " What does it matter which he marries? The main affair is to consolidate the families." The elder glared at him. " Be silent! " he commanded. Howat Penny's ever present resentment rose to the surface. " I am not a girl," he stated; " nor yet a nigger. And, personally, I think David was extremely wise."

95

"I was sure of it," Myrtle cried; "he — he has talked against me, helped Caroline behind my back." She sobbed thinly, with her arm across her eyes. "If I thought anything like that had occurred," their father asserted, "Howat would —" he paused, gazing heavily about at his family.

Howat's ill temper arose. "Yes —?" he demanded with a sharp inflection. "Be still, Howat," his mother said unexpectedly. "This is all very regrettable, Gilbert," she told her husband; "but it is an impossible subject of discussion." Gilbert Penny continued hotly, "He wouldn't stay about here." She replied equably, "On the contrary, Howat shall be at Myrtle Forge until he himself chooses to leave."

Howat was conscious of a surprise almost as moving as that pictured on his father's countenance. He had never heard Isabel Penny speak in that manner before; perhaps at last she would reveal what he had long speculated over — her true, inner situation. But he saw at once that he was to be again disappointed; the speaker was immediately enveloped in her detachment, the air that seemed almost one of a spectator in the Penny household. She smiled deprecatingly. How fine she was, Howat thought. Gilbert Penny did not readily recover from his consternation; his surprise had notably increased to that. His mouth was open, his face red and agitated. "Before the children, Isabel," he complained. "Don't know what to think. Surely,

96

surely, you don't uphold Howat? Outrageous conduct if it's true. And Myrtle so gentle, never hurt any one in her life." Myrtle circled the table, and found a place in his arms. "If they had only told me," she protested. "If Caroline —" He patted her flushed cheeks. "Don't give it another thought," he directed; "a girl as pretty as you! I'll take you to London, where you'll have a string of men, not Quakers, fine as peacocks." He bent his gaze on his son.

"Didn't I tell you last evening that the cast metal has been light?" he demanded. "Must I beg you to go to the Furnace? Or perhaps that too conflicts with your mother's fears for you. There are stumps in the road." There was a whisper of skirts at the door, and Ludowika Winscombe stood smiling at them. Myrtle turned her tear-swollen face upon her father's shoulder. Howat wondered if Ludowika had slept. He endeavoured in vain to discover from her serene countenance something of her thoughts of what had occurred. He had a sudden inspiration.

"I can go to Shadrach as soon as Adam saddles a horse," he told his father. "You were curious about the Furnace," he added to Ludowika, masking the keen anxiety he felt at what was to follow; "it's a sunny day, a pleasant ride." She answered without a trace of feeling other than a casual politeness. "Thank you, since it will be my only opportunity. I'll have to change." She was gazing, Howat dis-

97

covered, lightly at Isabel Penny. "I must get the figures from Schwar," his father said. Before he left the room he moved to his wife's side, rested his hand on her shoulder. She looked up at him with a reassuring nod. Howat saw that, whatever it might be, the bond between them was secure, stronger than any differences of prejudices or blood, more potent than time itself. The group, the strain, about the table, broke up.

The horses footed abreast over the road that crossed the hills and forded the watered swales between Myrtle Forge and the Furnace. Ludowika, riding astride, enveloped and hooded in bottle green, had her face muffled in a linen riding mask. He wondered vainly what expression she bore. Speech he found unexpectedly difficult. His passion mounted and mounted within him, all his being swept unresistingly in its tide. Howat said at last:

"Are you still so angry at life, at yourself?"

"No," she replied; "I slept that foolishness away. I must have sounded like a character in *The Lying Valet*." Her present mood obscurely troubled him; he infinitely preferred her in the pale crumpled silk and candle light of the evening before. "I wish I could tell you what I feel," he said moodily.

"Why not?" she replied. "It's the most amusing thing possible. You advance and I seem to retreat; you reach forward and grasp — my fan, a handful of petticoat; you protest and sulk —"

"Perhaps in Vauxhall," he interrupted her sav-

98

agely, " but not here, not like that, not with me.
This is not a gavotte. I didn't want it; I tried to
get away; but it, you, had me in a breath. At once
it was all over. God knows what it is. Call it love.
It isn't a thing under a hedge, I tell you that, for
an hour. It's stronger than anything else that will
ever touch me, it will last longer. . . . Like falling
into a river. Perhaps I'm different, a black Penny,
but what other men take like water, a woman, is
brandy for me. I'm — I'm not used to it. I
haven't wanted Kate here and Mary there; but only
you. I've got to have you," he said with a marked
simplicity. " I've got to, or there will be a bad
smash."

Ludowika rode silently, hid in her mask. He
urged his horse closer to her, and laid a hand on her
swaying shoulder. " I didn't choose this," he repeated; " the blame's somewhere else." He felt a
tremor run through her. " Why say blame? " she
finally answered. " I hate moralities and excuses
and tears. If you are set on being gloomy, and
talking to heaven about damnation, take it all
away from me." A shadow moved across the countryside, and he saw clouds rising out of the north.
A sudden wind swept through the still forest, and immediately the air was aflame with rushing autumn
leaves. They fell across Howat's face and eddied
about the horses' legs. The grey bank deepened in
space, the sun vanished; the wind was bleak. It
seemed to Howat Penny that the world had changed,

its gold stricken to dun and gaunt branches, in an instant. The road descended to the clustered stone houses about Shadrach Furnace.

The horses were left under the shed of the smithy at the primitive cross roads. Thomas Gilkan had gone to the river about a purchase of casting sand, but expected to be back for the evening run of metal. Fanny was away, Howat learned, visiting Dan Hesa's family. They would, of course, have dinner at the Heydricks; and the latter sent a boy home to prepare his wife. Ludowika and Howat aimlessly followed the turning road that mounted to the coal house. A levelled and beaten path, built up with stone, led out to the top of the stack, where a group of sooty figures were gathered about the clear, almost smokeless flame of the blast. Below they lingered on the grassy edge of the stream banked against the hillside and flooding smoothly to the clamorous fall and revolving wheel by the wood shed that covered the bellows. Pointed downward the latter spasmodically discharged a rush of air with a vast creasing of their dusty leather. A procession of men were wheeling and dumping slag into a dreary area beyond. There was a stir of constant life about the Furnace, voices calling, the ringing of metal on metal, the creak of barrows, dogs barking. The plaintive melody of a German song rose on the air.

Behind a blood red screen of sumach Howat again kissed Ludowika. Her arms tightened about his neck; she raised her face to him with an abandon that blinded him to the world about, and his entire being was drawn in an agony of desire to his lips. She sank limply into his rigid embrace, a warm sensuous burden with parted lips.

At the Heydricks he ate senselessly whatever was placed before him. The house, solidly built of grey stone traced with iron, had two rooms on the lower floor. The table was set before a fireplace that filled the length of the wall, its mantel a great, roughly squared log mortared into the stones on either side. Small windows opened through deep embrasures, a door bound with flowering, wrought hinges faced the road, and a narrow flight of stairs, with a polished rail and white post, led above. Mrs. Heydrick, a large woman in a capacious Holland apron and worsted shoes, moved about the table with steaming pewter trenchards while Heydrick and their guests dined.

Howat Penny's face burned as if from a violent fever; his veins, it seemed, were channels through which ran burning wine. He was deafened by the tumult within him. Heydrick's voice sounded flat and blurred. They were conscious at Shadrach of the thin quality of the last metal. The charge had been poorly made up; he, Heydrick, had said at once, when the cinders had come out black, that the lime had been short. His words fled through Howat's brain like racing birds; the latter's motions were unsteady, inexact.

101

The clouds had now widened in a sagging plain across the sky, some scattered rain pattered coldly on the fallen leaves. It was pleasant before the hickory burning in the deep fireplace; the Heydricks had taken for granted that they would wait there for Thomas Gilkan, and they protested when Howat and Ludowika moved toward the door. But Howat was restless beyond any possibility of patiently hearing Mrs. Heydrick's cheerful, trivial talk. He was so clumsy with Ludowika's cloak that she took it from him, and, with a careless, feminine scorn in common with Mrs. Heydrick, got into it without assistance. They stood for a while in the cast house, watching a keeper rolling and preparing the pig bed for the evening flow. They were pressed close together in a profound gloom of damp warmth rising from the wet sand and furnace. An obscure figure moved a heavy and faintly clanging pile of tamping bars. The sound of rain on the roof grew louder, continuous. A poignant and then strangling emotion clutched at Howat Penny's throat. Silently they turned from the murky interior.

A grey rain was plastering the leaves on the soggy ground; puddles accumulated in the scarred road; the smoke from the smithy hung low on the roof. At the left a small, stone house had a half opened door. Ludowika looked within. "For storing," Howat told her. Inside were piled sledges and cinder hooks, bars and moulds, and bales of tanned hides. Ludowika explored in the shadows. A sudden eddy of

102

wind slammed to the door through which they had entered. They drew together irresistibly, and stood for a long while, crushed in each other's arms; then Ludowika stepped back with her cloak sliding from her shoulders. She rested against precarious steps leading aloft through a square opening in the ceiling. "For storage," he said again. He thought his throat had closed, and that he must suffocate. A mechanical impulse to show her what was above set his foot upon the lower step, and he caught her waist. "You see," he muttered; "things for the store . . . the men, wool stockings, handkerchiefs . . . against their pay." The drumming rain was scarcely a foot above their heads; an acrid and musty odour rose from the boxes and canvas-sewed bales about the walls. "Ludowika," Howat said. He stopped — she had shut her eyes. All that was Howat Penny, that was individually sentient, left him with a pounding rush.

A faint sound, infinitely far removed, but insistent, penetrated his blurred senses. It grew louder; rain, rain beating on the roof. Voices, somewhere, outside. Ringing blows on an anvil, a blacksmith, and horses waiting. Myrtle Forge. Ludowika. Ludowika Winscombe. No, by God, never that last again!

He stood outside with his head bare and his face lifted to the cool shock of the rain. Ludowika was muffled in her cloak. Howat could see a renewed activity in the cast house; a group of men were gathered about the furnace hearth, in which he saw Thomas Gilkan. He moved forward to call the latter; but a tapping was in progress, and he was forced to wait. Gilkan swung a long bar against a low, clay face, and instantly the murky interior was ablaze with a crackling radiance against which the tense figures wavered in magnified silhouettes. The metal poured out of the furnace in a continuous, blinding white explosion hung with fans of sparkling gold; the channels of the pig bed rapidly filled with the fluid iron.

Finally Howat Penny lifted Ludowika to her saddle and swung himself up at her side. The rain had stopped; below the eastern rim of cloud an expanse showed serenely clear. Their horses soberly took the rise beyond Shadrach Furnace and merged into the gathering dusk of the forest road. A deep tranquillity had succeeded the tempest of Howat's emotions; it would not continue, he knew; already the pressure of immense, new difficulties gathered about him; but momentarily he ignored them. He searched his feelings curiously.

The fact that struck him most sharply was that he was utterly without remorse for what had occurred; it had been inevitable. He experienced none of the fears against which Ludowika had exclaimed. He lingered over no self-accusations, the reproach of adultery. He was absolutely unable then to think of Felix Winscombe except as a person generally unconcerned. If he repeated silently the term husband

104

it was without any sense of actuality; the satirical
individual in the full bottomed wig, now absent in
Maryland, had no importance in the passionate situation that had arisen between Ludowika and himself.
Felix Winscombe would of course have to be met,
dealt with; but so would a great many other exterior
conditions.

Ludowika, in her linen mask, was enigmatic, a
figure of mystery. A complete silence continued between them; at times they ambled with his hand on
her body; then the inequalities of the road forced
them apart. The clouds dissolved, the sky was immaculate, green, with dawning stars like dim white
flowers. A faint odour of the already mouldering
year rose from the wet earth. Suddenly Ludowika
dragged the mask from her face. Quivering with
intense feeling she cried:

"I'm glad, Howat! Howat, I'm glad!"

He contrived to put an arm about her, crush her
to him for a precarious moment. "We have had
an unforgettable day out of life," she continued rapidly; "that is something. It has been different,
strangely apart, from all the rest. The rain and
that musty little store house and the wonderful iron;
a memory to hold, carry away —"

"To carry where?" he interrupted. "You must
realize that I'll never let you go now. I will keep
you if we have to go beyond the Endless Mountains.
I will keep you in the face of any man or opposition
created."

105

A wistfulness settled upon her out of which grew a slight hope. "I am afraid of myself, Howat," she told him; "all that I have been, my life — against me. But, perhaps, here, with you, it might be different. Perhaps I would be constant. Perhaps all the while I have needed this. Howat, do you think so? Do you think I could forget so much, drop the past from me, be all new and happy?"

He reassured her, only half intent upon the burden of her words. He utterly disregarded anything provisional in their position; happiness or unhappiness were unconsidered in the overwhelming determination that she should never leave him. No remote question of that entered his brain. The difficulties were many, but he dismissed them with an impatient gesture of his unoccupied hand. Gilbert Penny would be heavily censorious; he had, Howat recognized, the moral prejudices of a solid, unimaginative blood. But, lately, his father had sunk to a place comparatively insignificant in his thoughts. This was partly due to the complete manner in which Isabel Penny had silenced the elder at breakfast. His mother, Howat gladly felt, would give him the sympathy of a wise, broad understanding. David and Caroline would interpose no serious objection. Felix Winscombe remained; a virile figure in spite of his years; a man of assured position and a bitter will.

He determined to speak on the day that Felix Winscombe returned from Annapolis; there would be

no concealment of what had occurred, and no hypocrisy. A decent regret at Winscombe's supreme
loss. The other would not relinquish Ludowika
without a struggle. Who would? It was conceivable that he would summon the assistance of the
law, conceivable but not probable; the situation had
its centre in a purely personal pride. Nothing essential could be won legally. A physical encounter
was far more likely. Howat thought of that coldly.
He had no chivalrous instinct to offer himself as a
sop to conventional honour. In any struggle, exchange of shots, he intended to be victorious . . .
He would have the naming of the conditions.

"It's beautiful here," Ludowika broke into his
speculations; "the great forests and Myrtle Forge.
I can almost picture myself directing servants like
your mother, getting supplies out of the store, and
watching the charcoal and iron brought down to the
Forge. The sound of the hammer has become a
part of my dreams. And you, Howat — I have
never before had a feeling like this for a man.
There's a little fear in it even. It must be stronger
than the other, than Europe; I want it to be."
They could see below them the lighted windows at
Myrtle Forge. The horses turned unguided into the
curving way across the lawn. A figure stood obsequiously at the door; it was, Howat saw with deep
automatic revulsion, the Italian servant. He wondered again impatiently at the persistently unpleasant impression the other made on him. Gilbert

Penny was waiting in the hall, and Howat told him fully the result of his investigation.

His father nodded, satisfied. "You are taking hold a great bit better," he was obviously pleased. "We must go over the whole iron situation with the Forsythes. It's time you and David stepped forward. I am getting bothered by new complications; the thing is spreading out so rapidly — steel and a thousand new methods and refinements. And the English opposition; I'm afraid you'll come into that."

Ludowika did not again appear that evening, and Howat sat informally before a blazing hearth with his mother, Gilbert Penny and Caroline. Myrtle had retired with a headache. Howat felt pleasantly settled, almost middle-aged; he smoked a pipe with the deliberate gestures of his father. He wondered at the loss of his old restlessness, his revolt from just such placid scenes as the present. Never, he had thought, would he be caught, bound, with invidious affections, desires. Howat, a black Penny! He had been subjugated by a force stronger than his rebellious spirit. Suddenly, recalling Ludowika's doubt, he wondered if he would be a subject to it always. All the elements of his captivity lay so entirely outside of him, beyond his power to measure or comprehend, that a feeling of helplessness came over him. He again had the sense of being swept twisting in an irresistible flood. But his confusion was dominated by one great assurance — nothing

108

should deprive him of Ludowika. An intoxicating
memory invaded him, touched every nerve with delight and a tyrannical hunger. His fibre seemed to
crumble, his knees turn to dust. Years ago he had
been poisoned by berries, and limpness almost like
this had gone softly, treacherously, through him.

VIII

THEY entered into a period of secret contentment and understanding. Ludowika
displayed a grave interest in the details
of the house and iron at Myrtle Forge; he explained
the processes that resulted in the wrought blooms
despatched by tons in the lumbering, mule-drawn
wagons. They explored the farm, where she listened approvingly to the changes he proposed making, kitchen gardens to be planted, the hedges of
roses and gravelled paths to be laid — for her. She
suggested an Italian walk, latticed above, with a
stone seat, and was indicating a corner that might
be transformed into a semblance of an angle of
Versailles, when, suddenly, she stopped, and clasped
his wrist.

"No! No!" she exclaimed, with surprising
energy. "We'll have no France, no court, here,
but only America; only you and myself, with no
past, no memories, but just the future." How that
was to be realized neither of them considered; they
avoided all practical issues, difficulties. They never
mentioned Felix Winscombe's name. However, a
long communication came from him for his wife.
She read it thoughtfully, in the drawing room, await-

ing dinner. No one else but Howat was present, and he was standing with his hand on her shoulder. "Felix hasn't been well," she remarked presently. "For the first time he has spoken to me of his age. The Maryland affair drags, and that has wearied him."

"What does he say about returning?" Howat bluntly asked.

"Shortly, he hopes; that is, in another ten days. He says there is a good ship, the *Lindamira*, by the middle of November." Howat said, "Excellent." Ludowika gazed at him swiftly. "It will be difficult." His face became grim, but he made no direct reply. A silence fell on the room through which vibrated the blows of the trip hammer at the Forge. The day was grey and definitely cold; a small cannon stove glowed in the counting house; but Ludowika kept mostly to her room. She sent him a note by the Italian, and Howat eyed the fellow bowing in the doorway. A flexibility that seemed entirely without bones. His eyes were jet slits, his lips shaven and mobile; a wig was repulsively saturated with scented grease. Yet it was not in actual details that he oppressed Howat; but by the vague suggestion of debasing commendations, of surreptitious understanding, insinuations. He seemed, absurdly, unreal, a symbol the intent of which Howat missed; he suppressed an insane movement to touch the Italian, discover if he was actually before him.

He reread Ludowika's note whenever he was not

actually employed in recording, until he was obliged
to conceal it in the Forge book.

Later Abner Forsythe arrived with David, and
there was a stir of preparing rooms and communication
with the farm. David's mother was dead, and
Abner conducted the wedding negotiations with the
Pennys. " I thought it would be the pretty little
one," he said at the table, with a Quaker disregard of
small niceties of feeling; " but, Gilbert, any girl of
yours would be more than the young men of the present
deserve." It was a difficult conversation for every
one but Ludowika and Abner Forsythe. A greater
ease appeared after supper. David and Caroline
disappeared in the direction of the clavichord, from
which sounded some scattered, perfunctory measures.
The two elder men returned, over a decanter of
French spirits, to the inevitable and engrossing subject
of iron and the Crown regulations; Myrtle sat
stiffly before the fireplace with Isabel Penny; and
Howat moved up and across the room, his gaze lying
on Ludowika, spread in an expanse of orange chiffon
and bold silver tracery on the small sofa.

She smiled at him once, but, for the most part, she
was lost in revery. Ludowika had a fan, to hold
against the fire; and her white fingers were playing
with its polished black sticks and glazed paper
printed with an ornamental bar of music. A faint
colour stained her cheeks as he watched her, and set
his heart tumultuously beating. He told himself
over and over, with an unabated sense of wonder,

that she was his. He longed for the moment when they could discard all pretence and be frankly, completely, together. That must happen after Felix Winscombe arrived. Meanwhile he was forced to content himself with a look, a quick or lingering contact of fingers, the crush of her body against his momentarily in a passage. They had returned once to the rock where he had first been intoxicated by her; in a strangling wave of emotion he had taken her into his arms; but she had broken away. The width of the stream and screen of trees had apparently disconcerted Ludowika, and she contrived to make him feel inexcusably young, awkward.

But usually he dominated her; there was a depth to his passion that achieved patience, the calmness of unassailable fortitude. She gazed at him often with a surprise that bordered on fear; again she would delight in his mastery, beg him to hold her forever safe against the past. He reassured her of his ability and determination to accomplish that; there was not the shadow of a doubt in his own mind. He was more troubled now than formerly; but he was eager for the climax to pass, impatient to claim his own.

As if a dam had been again thrown across the flood of his emotions he felt them mounting, growing more and more irrepressible. He slept in feverish snatches, with gaps in which he stared wide-eyed into the dark, trying to realize his coming joy, visualizing Ludowika, a brilliant apparition of flowing silk, on the night. He thought of the store house at the Furnace, of the rain beating on the roof, and Ludowika . . . God, if that old man would only return, go, leave them! The clouds vanished and left the nights emerald clear, the constellations glittered in frosty immensities of silence. He stood at the open window with his shoulders bare, revelling in the cold air that flowed over him, defying winter, death itself. The moon waned immutably.

David was now at Shadrach Furnace, living with the Heydricks, and the necessities that brought him to Myrtle Forge were endless. He was absolutely happy, and Howat watched him with mingled long-ing and envy. His affair, darker, more tragic in spite of a consummation that must be joyous, seemed infinitely more mature. Caroline was a nice enough girl, but Ludowika was supremely fascinating. David amused him:

" Caroline is a miracle. Of course there are pret-tier, and Mrs. Winscombe has more air; but none has Caroline's charming manner. Of course, you have noticed it. Even a thick-headed brother couldn't miss that. We have plans for you, too. And it's no good your looking glum; we'll glum you."

The amusement faded from Howat's countenance, and he listened sullenly to the end of the raillery. His temper was growing daily more uneven, the de-light had largely left his reflections. His passion had become too insistent for happy conjecturing; the visions of Ludowika now only tormented him.

114

Her eyes were like burning sapphires, her warm palms caressed his face; he was increasingly gaunt and shadowed. Once he gave a note for her to the Italian servant, loathing the hand that adroitly covered the folded sheet, the other's oblique smile; but she sent back word that she was suffering from a headache. He began to plan so that he would intercept her in unexpected places. She, too, was passionate in her admissions; but, somehow, some one always stumbled toward them, or they were summoned from beyond. He began to feel that this was not mere chance, but desired, deliberately courted, by Ludowika. Very well, he would end it all, as it were, with a shout when Felix Winscombe came back.

When Felix Winscombe came back!

He was, too, increasingly aware of his mother's scrutiny. Howat was certain that Isabel Penny had surmised a part of his feeling for Ludowika. He didn't greatly care; any one might know, he thought contemptuously. It had destroyed his sympathetic feeling for his mother, the only considerate bond that had existed with his family. Unconsciously he placed her on one side of a line, the other held only Ludowika and himself.

He explained this to her in a sere reach of the garden. It was afternoon, the sun low and a haze on the hills. Ludowika had on a scarlet wrap, curiously vivid against the withered, brown aspect of the faded flower stems. " You and me," he repeated. She gazed, without answering, at the bar-

115

rier of hills that closed in Myrtle Forge. From the thickets came the clear whistling of partridges, intensifying the unbroken tranquillity that surrounded the habitations. Howat was suddenly conscious of the pressure of vast, unguessed regions, primitive forces, illimitable wildernesses. It brought uppermost in him a corresponding zest in the sheer spaciousness of the land, a feeling always intensified by the thought of England. "The Province," he said disjointedly, " a place for men. Did you see those that followed the road this morning? Perhaps five with their women, some pack horses, kitchen tins and hide tents. The men wore buckskin, and furred caps, and the women's skirts were sewed leather. One was tramping along with a feeding baby. Well, God knows where they have been, how many days they have walked; their shoes were in shreds. And their faces, thin and serious, have looked steadily over rifles at death. The women, too. You'll only get them here, in a big country, a new —"

"They were terrible," Ludowika declared; " savage. I was glad when they were by. The baby at the woman's great breast!" she shuddered at the memory. "Like animals."

He gazed at her with a slight surprise; he had never heard her speak so bitterly. He saw her more clearly than ever before; as if her words had illuminated her extraordinary delicacy of being, had made visible all the infinite refinements of which she was the result. He had a recurrence of his sense of her

116

incongruity here, balanced on polished black pattens, against the darkening hills. The sun disappeared, there was a cool flare of yellow light, and a feeling of impending evening. The hills were indigo, the forest a dimmer gold, a wind moved audible in the dry leaves.

Ludowika gasped. "It's so — so huge," she said, "all the lonely miles. At times I can't bear to think of it." A faint dread invaded him. "Last night, when I couldn't sleep, a thing howled in the woods. And I got thinking of those naked men at the Forge, with their eyes rimmed in black, and — and —"

He disregarded the publicity of their position and put an arm about her shoulders, in an overwhelming impulse to calm and reassure her; but she slipped away. "I'll be all right again," she promised; "but I think it's more cheerful with the candles. We'll get your sister to play Belshazzar and pretend we're across the green from St. James."

A mood darker than any he had lately known settled over him. It was natural for Ludowika to be lonely, at first; but in a little she would grow to love the wild like himself. She must. The Province was to be her life. He was standing before the fire in the informal chamber beyond the dining room, watching his mother's vigorous hands deftly engaged in embroidery. There was no one present, and a sudden, totally desperate recklessness possessed him. Isabel Penny said:

"Mr. Winscombe will be here shortly."

117

"I wish it would be to-night," he declared. She raised her calm gaze with brows arched in inquiry. "There is something —" he broke off. "She belongs to me," he said in a low, harsh voice, " and not to that old man."

Mrs. Penny secured her needle, and put the colourful web aside. She was, as he had been sure she would be, entirely composed, admirable. Her questioning look grew keener. "I was afraid of that," she admitted simply; "after the first. It is very unpleasant and difficult. This is not London, and your father will make no allowances. You are not any easier to bend, Howat. With Mrs. Winscombe —" she paused, "I am not certain. But there is no doubt about the husband."

"She belongs to me," he reiterated sullenly.

"There is no need for you to make yourself offensively clear. I know something of details of that kind. I told you once that they might mean only a very little to — to certain women. I am not prepared to judge about that. But I know you, what bitter feeling you are capable of. You are a very pure man, Howat; and for that reason such an occurrence would tear you up and across. There is no use in begging you to be cautious, diplomatic. Mr. Winscombe, too, is very determined; he has many advantages — maturity, coldness, experience. He won't spare you, either. It's excessively unfortunate."

118

" I'll get it over as quickly as possible. I didn't
want the thing to happen, it wasn't from any choice;
it hit me like a bullet. Nothing else is of the slightest importance. I've gone over this again and
again; I'll tell him and let him try what he can.
Ludowika's gone from — from the fireworks and
fiddles and stinking courts; I've got her, and, by
God, I'll keep her!"

" Talk quietly; you can't shout yourself into this.
Are you certain that Mrs. Winscombe really finds
the courts — stinking? I remember, at first," she
stopped. Even in the midst of his passion he listened for what revelation she might make; but none
followed. She was silent for a minute. " They become a habit," she said finally; " love, loves, become
a habit. Only men brought up in the same atmosphere can understand. At first Felix Winscombe
will be infuriated with you for speaking, then he will
realize more, and the trouble will follow. Are you
certain that you have comprehended? It would be
stupid to mistake an episode, you would succeed
only in making yourself ridiculous."

He lifted up both his hands and closed them with
a quivering, relentless force.

" Truly," Isabel Penny remarked, " truly I be-
gin to be sorry for her. There is something she has
yet to learn about men. Nothing can be said; and
that is what your father will not penetrate. Howat,
I am even a little afraid . . . now. That, I believe,

119

is unusual for me. It's your blackness, like powder. The explosion can kill. Nothing may be said. Life drags us along by the hair."

Her questions about Ludowika joined to the memory of the latter's revulsion from the primitive conditions of the Province and added to the heaviness of his heart. He mentally denied his mother's suggestions, drove them from him, but they left a faint enduring sting, a vague unrest. His passion for Ludowika swelled, dominated, him; he forgot everything but his own, supreme desire. Nothing else stood before its flood; all thought of Ludowika's final happiness was lost with the other detritus. The tense closing of his hands had symbolized his feeling, his intent. He held her in a manner as nakedly primitive as the inchoate sexuality of the emotion that had engulfed him.

Ludowika did not appear for supper, and he was possessed by a misery of vague apprehensions. He must know something of her thoughts, have a token from her of some feeling like his own; and, waiting, he stopped the Italian on the stairs. The latter knew his purpose immediately, without a spoken word; and he followed Howat's brusque gesture to his room. He hastily wrote a note; and the latter brought him back a reply, only partly satisfactory, with an air of relish. For the first time the affair had the hateful appearance of an intrigue, like a court adventure. It was the Italian servant, Howat decided; and immediately he recognized why he dis-

120

liked the other — it was because he expressed an
aspect of slyness that lay over Ludowika and himself.
He put that from him, too; but it was like brushing
away cobwebs. His hunger for Ludowika increased
all the while; it became more burningly material, in-
satiable and concrete.

On the day following she clung to him, when opportunity offered, with a desperate energy of emotion. "You must hold me tighter," she told him.
Her mood rapidly changed, and she complained of
the eternal, pervasive fall of the forge hammer.
"It will drive me mad," she declared almost wildly.
"I can't bear to think of its going on and on, year
after year; listening to it —" He heard her with
sombre eyes. She had come to the counting house,
empty for the moment but for themselves, and stood
with her countenance shadowed by a frown. "If
the hammer stops," he replied, waving his hand
largely, "all this, the Pennys, stop, too. I'm afraid
that sound of beating out iron will be always
wrought through our lives. You will get accustomed
to it —"

Her expression grew petulant, resentful. "Do
you mean that we couldn't, perhaps, go to England,
if — if I wanted?" He moved closer to her, brushing the circumference of her skirt. "You asked me
to hold you, to keep you from the past; and I am
going to do it. London is all that you wish to forget; it must go completely out of your life . . . never
finger you again." A faint dread that deepened al-

most to antagonism was visible on her countenance. " I suppose to men talk like that seems a sign of strength, of possession ; but it doesn't impress women, really. You see, women give, or else — there is nothing."

" I had no thought of impressing you," he said simply ; " I only repeated what came into my mind, what I mean. It would be a mistake for me to take you to England, and make both of us miserable. Beside, there is more to tend here than I'll ever accomplish." She objected, " But other people, workmen, will do the actual labour. Surely you are not going to keep on with anything so vulgar —" she indicated the office and desks. Her features sharpened with contempt. " I'll not be a clerk," he told her gravely. " But I am responsible for a great deal. You should understand that for you showed it to me. Most of what I am now has been you." He reached out his hands to her in a wave of tenderness, but she evaded him. She stood irresolute for a moment and then abruptly turned and disappeared.

A white rim of new moon grew visible at the edge of dusk, and he stood gazing at it before he entered the dwelling. A dull unrest had become part of his inner tumult, a premonition falling over him like an advancing shadow. But above all his vague fears rose the knowledge that he would never let Ludowika go from him ; that was the root of his being. Now she could never leave him. It was natural, he assured himself again, that she should

122

feel doubts at first; everything here was so different from the life she had known; and women were variable. He would have to understand that, learn to accommodate himself to changing, surface moods, immovable underneath.

She had put on for supper, he saw, a daring dress; and her expression was that which he had first noted, indifferent, slightly scoffing. Her shoulders and arms gleamed under fragile gauze, her bodice was hardly more than a caress of silk. He watched her every movement, and got a sort of satisfaction from the knowledge that she grew increasingly disturbed at his unwavering scrutiny. His mother's attitude toward Mrs. Winscombe had not changed by a shade, an inflection; she was correctly cordial in her slightly distant manner.

In the ebb and flow of the evening Howat was left with Ludowika for a little, and he bent over her, kissing her sharply. She was coldly unresponsive; and he kissed her again, trying vainly to bring some warmth to her lips. She did not avoid him actually, but he felt that something in her, essential, slipped aside from his caress. His emotion changed to a mounting anger. "You will have to get over this now or later," he asserted. She said surprisingly, "Felix will be home this week." He stood with an arm half raised, his head turned, as he had been arrested by her period.

"Well?" he demanded stupidly. Her tone had been beyond his comprehension. "Felix," she went

on, apparently at random, " is very satisfactory."
Something of her intent penetrated his stunned faculties. He advanced toward her dark with rage.
" And if he is," he replied, " it will do him no good.
It will do you no good, if you think —" he broke off
from an accession of emotion. " What damned
thing are you thinking of ? "

" The Princess Amelia's stockings," she answered
pertly.

" You'll never put them on her again, like any
dirty chamber maid."

" Felix, the end of this week," she repeated.

" I'll kill him," Howat whispered; " if he lifts a
hand I'll shoot him through the head. This was
forced on me; some one else, responsible, can pay."
Her chin was up, her expression mocking. " Ridiculous, like any cloddish countryman." She walked
deliberately away, seated herself in a graceful eddy
of panniered silk.

A cold torment succeeded his rage; he had the feeling of being hopelessly trapped, stifling in his passion. He followed her. " Ludowika, this is horrible,
so soon. I am willing to think that I am to blame;
stupid; no experience. You will have to be patient
with me. Naturally everything, now —" he broke
off and wandered to a window, holding aside the
draperies, gazing out into the night. The sky was
so luminous that the barriers of surrounding hills
were printed clearly against starry space. The
forest swept about in a dark veil; nowhere could be

124

seen a glimpse of habitation. He heard the wavering cry of an owl.

The Province, immense, secretive! Paper lanterns strung in parks, hid music, provocative smiles only playing with the heart! It was tremendously unfortunate. Why must they suffer so unreasonably? Something, he was certain, had gone wrong; it lay both within them and outside; a force diverted, a purpose unaccomplished. It bent, broke, them like two twigs; they were no more than two bubbles, momentarily reflecting the sky, on a profound depth. A wind stirred, oppressed them, and they were gone. A great pity for Ludowika took its place in his feelings. He was sorry for himself. Suddenly the rustle of her skirts approached.

An infinitely seductive, warm arm crept about his neck; she abandoned herself to a ruthless embrace. "It's been wonderful, Howat; and — and it isn't over, yet. Nothing lasts, it's a mistake to demand too much. We must take what we may. Perhaps, even, later — in London. No, don't interrupt me. After all, I'm wiser than you are. I was swept away for a little. Impossibilities. I am what I am. I was always that, inside of me. If the longing I told you about had been stronger, it, and not the court, would have made me; but it was no more than a glimpse seen from a window, a thing far away. I'd never reach it. This, now, has been the best of me, all."

He had a mingled sense of the truth and futility of

125

her words. It was as if his passion stood apart from them, dominating them, lashing him with desire. Nothing she might say, no necessity nor effort, could free them. The uselessness of words smote him. She spoke again, an urgent flow of dulcet sound against his ear; but it was without meaning, lost in the drumming of his blood. The stir of feet approached, and he released her, moving to the fireplace. It was Caroline. She stopped awkwardly, advancing a needless explanation of a trivial errand from the doorway, and vanished.

His position at Myrtle Forge was fast becoming impossible. There would be an explosion now at any moment. He took the fire tongs and idly rearranged the wood on the hearth. The flames blazed more brightly, their reflection squirmed over the lacquer frames on the walls, gleamed richly on polished black walnut, and fell across the Turkey floor carpet. It even reached through the pale candle light and flickered on Ludowika's dull red gown, flowered and clouded with blue. She was turned away from him, against the window; her shoulders drooped in an attitude of dejection. The flames died away again.

IX

LUDOWIKA'S manner toward him became
self-possessed, even animated; and, Howat
thought, preoccupied. She was expectant,
with a slightly impatient air, as if she were looking
beyond his shoulder. The cause occurred to him in
a flash that ignited his anger like a ready-charged
explosive. She was waiting, desiring, the return of
her husband. Felix Winscombe, she thought, would
mean — escape. He used the word deliberately,
realizing that that now expressed her attitude toward the Province, toward him. It made no difference in his feeling for her, his determination that
nothing should take her from him. His power of
detachment vanished; he became utterly the instru-
ment of his passion.

He didn't press upon her small expressions of his
emotion; somehow, without struggle, she had made
them seem foolish; beyond that they were inadequate. He was conscious of the approach of a great
climax; his feeling was above the satisfaction of trivial caresses. Soon, he told himself, soon he would
absolutely possess her, for as long as they lived.
Ultimately she must be happy with him. He
thought the same things in a ceaseless round; he

walked almost without sight, discharging mechanically the routine of daily existence; answering inevitable queries in a perfunctory, dull voice. Myrtle Forge made a distant background of immaterial
colours and sounds for the slightly mocking figure
of Ludowika.

In mid-afternoon David arrived with a face stung
scarlet by beating wind, and a clatter of hoofs. He
immediately found Gilbert Penny, and the two men
sat together with grave faces, lowered voices.
Howat, who had left the counting house at the sound
of the hurried approach, caught a few words as he
drew near the others:

". . . a bad attack, crumpled him up. Coming
out from the city now." They were talking about
Felix Winscombe, who, it appeared, had been as-
saulted by a knife-like pain; and was returning
to Myrtle Forge. "Watlow saw no reason why it
should be dangerous," David continued; "he thinks
perhaps it came from unusual exertions, entertaining. A little rest, he says. He thinks the Winscombes will be able to sail on the *Lindamira* as they
planned."

Ludowika listened seriously to Gilbert Penny's
few, temperate words of preparation. "He has had
a pain like that before," she told them. "It always
passes away. Felix is really very strong, in spite
of his age. He won't ordinarily go to bed, but I'll
insist on that now, simply for rest." Felix Winscombe appeared at the supper hour. He was helped
128

out of Abner Forsythe's leather-hung chaise, and
assisted into the house. Howat saw him under the
hanging lamp in the hall; with a painful surprise he
realized that he was gazing at the haggard face of
an old man. Before he had never connected the
thought of definite age with Mr. Winscombe. The
man's satirical virility had forbidden any of the
patronage unconsciously extended to the aged.

A trace of his familiar, mocking smile remained,
but it was tremulous; it required, Howat saw, great
effort. An involuntary admiration possessed him
for the other's unquenchable courage. The latter
protested vehemently against being led to his room
by Ludowika; but she ignored his determination to
go into supper, swept him away with a firm arm
about his waist.

The house took on the slightly strange and dis-
ordered aspect of illness; voices were grave, low; in
the morning Howat learned that Felix Winscombe
had had another vicious attack in the night. Dr.
Watlow arrived, and demanded assistance. Howat
Penny, in the room where Ludowika's husband lay
exhausted in a bed canopied and draped in gay
India silk, followed Watlow's actions with a healthy
feeling of revulsion. The doctor bared Winscombe's spare chest, then filled a shallow, thick glass
with spirits; emptying the latter, he set fire to the
interior of the glass; and, when the blue flame had
expired, clapped the cupped interior over the prostrate man's heart. There was, it seemed, little else

that could be done; bleeding was judged for the once unexpeditious.

An effort at commonplace conversation was maintained at dinner. Ludowika openly discussed the arrangements for their return to London. Felix Winscombe had rallied from the night; his wife said that it was difficult to restrain him. The most comfortable provisions, she continued, had been made for their passage on the *Lindamira*. Howat heard her without resentment. He had no wish to contradict her needlessly even in thought; he was immovably fixed. Mr. Winscombe's debilitated return had completely upset his intentions. An entirely different proceeding would now be demanded, but with an identical end. What pity he felt for the eld r had no power to reach or alter his passion.

He returned to the counting house, and worked methodically through the afternoon, with an increasing sense of being involved in an irresistible movement. This gave him a feeling almost of tranquillity; from the beginning he had not been responsible. In the face of illness the Italian servant proved utterly undependable; he cringed, stricken with dread, from the spectacle of suffering. And when late in the day Mr. Winscombe, partially drugged with opium, grew consciously weaker, Howat's assistance was required.

Ludowika now remained in the room with her husband, and there was a discreet movement in and out by various members of the household. Isabel

130

Penny remained for an hour, Caroline took her place, Myrtle fluttered uncertainly in the doorway. Through the evening Felix Winscombe lay propped on pillows, his head covered by a black gros de Naples cap. His keen personality waned and revived on his long, yellow countenance. At one side wigs stood in a row on blocks, a brilliant, magenta coat lay in a huddle on a chair. At intervals he spoke, in a thinner, higher voice than customary, petulantly uneasy, or with a familiar, sardonic inflection. At the latter Ludowika would grow immensely cheered. She entirely ignored Howat on the occasions when he was in the room. He saw her mostly bent over leather boxes, into which disappeared her rich store of silk and gold brocades, shoes of purple morocco, soft white shifts. Howat watched her without an emotion visible on his sombre countenance.

Occasionally Mr. Winscombe's tenuous fingers dipped into a snuff box of black enamel and brilliants, and he lifted his hand languidly. The man's vitality, his sheer determination, were extraordinary. Even now he was far from impotence. He had, Howat had learned, completely dominated the Provincial Councils, forced a mutual compromise and agreement on them. He spoke of still more complicated affairs awaiting him in England. He damned the Italian's " white liver," and threatened to leave him in America. Dr. Watlow had been forced to return to the city.

Through the unaccustomed stir Howat was ceaselessly aware of his feeling for Ludowika; he thought
of it with a sense of shame; but it easily drowned all
other considerations. He continued to speculate
about their future together. Whatever his father
might conclude about his personal arrangements, the
elder would see that he was necessary to the future
of the Penny iron. They might live in one of the
outlying stone dwellings at the Forge . . . for the
present. He was glad that Gilbert Penny, that he,
was rich. Ludowika could continue to dress in rare
fabrics, to step in elaborate pattens over the common earth. That could not help but influence, as-
suage, her in the end. The Pennys' position in the
Province, too, was high; the most exclusive assem-
blies were open to them. He regarded his satisfaction in these details with something of Mr. Winscombe's bitter humour. In the past he had repudiated them with the utmost scorn. In the past —
dim shapes, scenes, that appeared to have occurred
years before, but which in reality reached to last
month, trooped through his mind. Youth had vanished like a form dropping behind a hill. He looked
back; it was gone; his feet hurried forward into the
unguessed future; anxiety joined him; the scent that
was Ludowika accompanied him, an illusive figure.
He reached toward it.

He was standing at the foot of the bed where
Felix Winscombe lay. The latter was restless, and
complained of pains in his arms, reaching down to

his fingers. Ludowika bent over him, her face
stamped with concern. She regarded Howat with a
new expression — narrowed eyes and a glimmer of
flawless teeth: a look he had never foreseen there;
but it was impotent before the thing that was. It
had, however, the effect of intensifying his desire, his
passion for her fragility of silk and flesh. He would
kiss her hate on her mouth.

She sat by the bedside, and Howat took a place
opposite her. Candles burned on a highboy, on
a table at his back; and their auriferous light
flowed in about the bedstead. The latter was
draped from the canopy to the bases of the posts in
a bright printing of pheasants and conventional
thickets — cobalt and ruby and orange; and across
a heavy counterpane half drawn up stalked a row of
panoplied Indians in clipped zephyr. It was a
nebulous enclosure with the shadows of the hangings
wavering on the coloured wool and cold linen, on the
long, seamed countenance of the prostrate man.

A clock in the hall struck slowly — it needed winding — ten blurred notes. Felix Winscombe took a
sip of water. A minute snapping sounded from the
hearth. A window stirred, and there was a dry
turning of leaves without; wind. One of the Indians, Howat saw, had his arm raised, flourishing a
blade; a stupid effigy of savage spleen. Beyond the
drapery Ludowika's face was dim and white. It
was like an ineffable May moon. Ludowika . . .
Penny. For the first time Howat thought of her

endowed with his name, and it gave him a deep thrill of delight. He repeated it with moving but soundless lips — Ludowika Penny.

Her husband lay with his eyes closed, his head bowed forward on his chest, as if in sleep. At irregular intervals small, involuntary contractions of pain twitched at his mouth. At times, too, he muttered noiselessly. Extraordinary. Ludowika and Felix Winscombe and himself, Howat Penny. A world peopled only by them; the silence of the room dropped into infinite space, bottomless time. A sudden dread of such vast emptiness seized Howat; he felt that he must say something, recreate about them the illusion of safe and familiar spaces and walls. It seemed that he was unable to speak; a leaden inhibition lay on his power of utterance. He made a harsh sound in his throat, loud and startling. Felix Winscombe raised his head, and Ludowika cried faintly. Then silence again folded them.

Howat fastened his thoughts on trivial and practical affairs — the furnishing of the house where he would take Ludowika, what David and himself intended to do with the iron, and then his last, long talk with his mother. She was astonishingly wise; she had seen far into Ludowika and himself, but even her vision had stopped short of encompassing the magnitude of his passion; she had not realized his new patience and determination. He found himself counting the gorgeous birds in the bed-hangings —

twenty-six, twenty-seven, twenty-eight, and stopped abruptly.

It had grown chilly in the room, and Ludowika had an India cashmere shawl about her shoulders. The sombre garnets and blues hid the tinsel gaiety of her gown and her bare shoulders. She appeared older than he had ever seen her before. Her face, carefully studied, showed no trace of beauty; her eyes were heavy, her lips dark; any efforts of animation were suspended. She showed completely the effect of her life in courts and a careless prodigality of hours and emotions. Howat, seeing all this, felt only a fresh accession of his hunger for her; she was far more compelling than when romantically viewed as a moon.

He sat with his chin propped on a palm; she was rigidly upright with her arms at her sides; Felix Winscombe moved higher on the pillows. His eyes glittered in a head like a modelling in clay; his arms stirred ceaselessly with weaving fingers. Howat could almost feel Ludowika's hatred striking at him across the bed. He smiled at her, and she faced him with an expression of stony unresponse. He thought luxuriantly of her in his arms, with the rain beating on the store house roof; he caught the odours of the damp, heaped merchandise, the distant clamour in the casting shed. He had a brutal impulse to lean forward and remind her of what had occurred, of the fact that she was his; he wanted to fling it

135

against her present detachment, to mock her with it. Then he would crush her against his heart. Felix Winscombe raised up on an elbow, distorting the row of sanguinary Indians.

Ludowika moved to the edge of the bed, and put a firm, graceful arm about him. A grey shadow of pain fell on Mr. Winscombe's features. The silence was absolute. He seemed to be waiting in an attitude of mingled dread and resolution. He whispered an unintelligible period, the pain on his face sharpened, and he released himself from Ludowika's support. She sank back on her chair, gazing at her husband with wide, concerned eyes.

Slowly the lines in his face deepened, and a fine, gleaming sweat started out on his brow. His face contorted in a spasm of voiceless suffering, and he drew a stiff hand down either arm. Howat watched him in a species of strained curiosity, with a suspension of breath. Something, he felt, should be done to relieve the oppression of agony gathering on Felix Winscombe's countenance, but a corresponding sense of complete helplessness settled like a leaden coffin about him. The other became unrecognizable; his face seemed to be set in an unnatural grin. His head drew back on a thin, corded neck, and a faint gasping for air stirred in the shadows. Even Howat felt the pain to be unendurable, and Ludowika, white as milk, had risen to her feet. She stood with a hand half raised beneath a fringed corner of the India shawl.

It was incredible that the sufferer's agony should increase, but it was apparent that it did remorselessly. All humanity was obliterated in an excruciating spasm over which streamed some meagre tears. Mr. Winscombe's arms raised and dropped; and, suddenly relaxed, he slipped down upon the pillows. Immediately the torment vanished from his countenance; it became peaceful, released. The familiar mockery of the mouth came back. The head, slightly turned, seemed to regard Ludowika with contentment and interrogation. Howat was conscious of a relief almost as marked as that on the face before him. He had gripped his hands until they ached. The tension in the room, too, seemed spent. He was about to address a reassuring period to Ludowika, when, at a glimpse of her expression, the words died on his lips.

He bent over the bed, with his hand on a ridged, still chest; he gazed down at flaccid eyes, a dropped chin. Felix Winscombe was dead.

Howat raised up slowly, facing the woman through the draperies. She was gazing in an incredulous, shocked surprise at the limp, prostrate body capped in black gros de Naples. A shuddering fear passed over her, and then her eyes met those of Howat Penny. Even separated from him by the bed she drew away as if from his touch. He saw that she had forgotten the dead man in a sharp realization of the portent of the living. She glanced about the room in the panic of a trapped

137

lark, an abject fright, searching for an escape.

He realized that there was none; Ludowika now belonged to him absolutely; he was as remorseless as the pain that had killed Felix Winscombe. Below the automatic sensations of the moment Howat was conscious of utter satisfaction. A miracle had given Ludowika to him; in the passing of a breath all his difficulty had been ended. She was alone with him in a province of forests and iron and stars. He would make her forget the gardens of fireworks and scraping violins; but forget or not she was his . . . Ludowika Penny.

II   THE FORGE

X

JASPER PENNY stood at a window of his bed room, his left arm carried in a black silk handkerchief, gazing down at the long, low roof of Myrtle Forge, built by his great, great grandfather Gilbert over a hundred and ten years before. It was February, and he could hear the ringing blows of axes, cutting the ice out of the forebay to liberate the water power for the completion of a forging of iron destined to be rolled into tracks for the slowly lengthening Columbia Steam Railway System. It was midday, a grey sky held a brighter, diffused radiance where the veiled sun hung without warmth, and the earth was everywhere frozen granite-like. He could see beyond the Forge shed heaped charcoal, and the black mass seemed no more dead than the ground or bare, brittle trees sweeping down and up to where, on encircling hills, they were lifted sharply against the cloudy monotony.

He was ordinarily impervious to the influence of weather, the more depressing aspects of nature; but now he was conscious of a dejection communicated, in part at least, he felt, by the bleak prospect without. Another, and infinitely more arresting, reason for this feeling had just stirred his thoughts — for

141

the first time he was conscious of the invidious, beginning weariness of accumulating years. He was hardly past forty, and he impatiently repudiated the possibility that he was actually declining; in fact he had not yet reached the zenith of his capabilities, physical or mental; yet his broken arm, slow in mending, the pain, had unquestionably depleted him more than a similar accident ten years ago. Not only this, but, during the forced inaction, his mind had definitely taken a different cast; considerations that had seemed to constitute the main business of existence had lately faded before preoccupations and feelings ignored until now.

Jasper Penny saw, objectively, not so much the surrounding circumstance as his own former acts and emotions; detached from his habitual being by hardly more than a month his past was posed before his critical judgment. Looked at in this manner his life appeared crowded with surprisingly meaningless gestures and words, his sheer youth an incomprehensible revolt. A greater part of that had been lately expressed by his mother, when he had returned to Myrtle Forge with an arm broken by a fall in a railroad coach travelling to Philadelphia. She had said, shaking her head with tightened lips:

"I warned you plenty against those train brigades. It isn't safe nor sensible with a good horse service convenient. But then you have always been a knowing, head-strong boy and man . . . A black Penny."

142

How she would get along without that last phrase he was at a loss to conjecture. From his first consciousness he recalled it, now a term of reproach and now extenuation. Only a few weeks before she had repeated it in precisely the same tone of mingled admonition and complaint that had greeted his most boyish mishaps. He had grown so accustomed to it, not only from Gilda Penny but from every one familiar with the Pennys and their history, that it had become part of his automatic entity. Jasper — a black Penny.

The course of his thoughts turned back to the earliest episodes remembered in that connection, to a time in which the especial quality had necessarily freest play. Now he characterized it as mere uninformed wildness; but he still recalled the tremendous impatience with which he had met the convenient enclosure of a practicable, organized society. Even at Myrtle Forge, where — in contrast to dwelling in the confines of a city — he had had a rare amount of actual freedom, a feeling of constriction had sent him day after day into the woods, hunting or merely idle along the upper reaches of still unsullied streams. Yet it had been an especial kind of wildness; he owed that recognition to his vanished youth. The term generally included champagne parties and the companionship of various but similar ladies of the circus or opera house. But nothing of that had then entered into his deeprooted rebellion. He had had merely a curious pas-

sion for complete independence, an innate turning
from street-bound affairs and men to the isolation
and physical accomplishment of arduous excursions on horses or foot. He had, then, avoided,
even dreaded, women. And that instinct, he told
himself, shifting his injured arm to a more comfortable position, had been admirably founded.

The ax blows ceased; from his position he could
just see the top of the great wheel that drove the
Forge trip hammer; and slowly the rim blurred, commencing to turn. The forebay was open. A pen-
nant of black smoke, lurid with flaming cinders,
twisted up in the motionless air. The hammer fell
once, experimentally, with a faint jar, and a grimy
figure shovelled charcoal into a barrow.

His mind soon returned to the point where it had
been deflected by the movement at the Forge; he
could even visualize his mature boyhood — a
straight, arrogant figure, black certainly, with up-
sloping brows and an outthrust chin. And that, he
thought, not without complacency, was not very far
from a description of himself at present. There
were, of course, the whiskers, severely trimmed on
his spare face, and showing, in certain lights, a glimmer of silver; but he was as upright, as comfortably
lean, now as then. He was still capable of prolonged physical exertion . . . It was ridiculous to
think of himself as definitely aging. Yet he was
past forty, and the years seemed to go far more
swiftly than at twenty-one.

144

Women! The silent pronouncement included the smallest plural possible — only two; but it seemed to Jasper Penny that they comprised all the variations, the faults and virtues, of their entire sex. With a certain, characteristic formality, propriety, he considered his wife first, now a year dead. He wondered if she had found the orthodox and concrete heaven in the frequent ecstatic contemplation of which so much of her life had been spent. It had been that fine superiority to the material that had first attracted him to her, a quality of shining enthusiasm, of reflected inspiration from a vision, however trite, of eternal hymning; and it had been that same essence which finally held them apart through the greater number of their married years. Phebe's health, slowly ebbing, had drawn her farther and farther from the known world in general and the affairs and being of her husband in particular; her last strength had gone in the hysteria of protracted religious emotion, during which she had become scarcely more to Jasper Penny than an attenuated, rapt invalid lingering in his house.

Her pale, still presence was usurped by a far different, animated and colourful, figure. He thought of Essie Scofield, of all that she paramountly held and expressed, with a reluctance that had lately, almost within the past week, grown to resemble resentment, if not actual irritation. Yet, however, casting back through the years, in his present remoteness, he was able to recreate her and

145

his emotions as they had first, irresistibly moved together. The absolute opposite of Phebe, already withdrawing into her religious, incorporeal region, Essie Scofield had immediately swept him into the whirlpool of her vivid, physical personality. Before her the memory of his wife faded into insignificance. But there was no mere retrospect in the considering of Essie; very much alive she presented, outside the Penny iron, the one serious preoccupation, complication, of his future.

At the time when he had first admitted, welcomed, her claim on him, he had felt a sudden energy in which he had recognized a play of the traits of a black Penny. Here was a satisfactory, if necessarily private, exercise of his inborn contempt for the evident hypocrisy, the cowardice, of perfunctory inhibitions and safe morals. That, however, had been speedily lost in his rocketing passion, flaring out of a quiet continence into giddy spaces of unrestraint. Essie, after a momentary surrender, had attempted retreat, expressing a doubt of the durability of their feeling; she had, in fact, made it painfully clear that she wished to escape from the uncomfortable volume of his fervour; but he had overborne her caution — her wisdom, he now expressed it.

That, more than anything else, brought before him the undeniable passage of time, the fact that he was rapidly accomplishing middle age — the total extinguishing of an emotion which he had

146

felt must outlast life. It had gone, and with it
his youth. Of course, he had recognized that he
was no longer thirty; he had been well aware of his
years, but only during the last few weeks had there
been the slight, perceptible dragging down . . . On
the black walnut dressing stand past the window lay
a letter he had received from Essie that morning;
it contained her usual appeal for an additional sum
of money — he gave her, formally, six thousand dollars a year; and the manner of the demand, for the
necessities of their daughter, showed his sharpened
perceptions that she had never really experienced the
blindness of a generous emotion. Eunice, the child,
was incontrovertible proof of that — no more than
an additional lever for her to swing.

His face darkened, and he moved his shoulder impatiently, as if to throw off a burden grown unendurable. But it was fastened immovably — his responsibility was as baldly apparent as the February noon, its greyness now blotted by a wind-driven,
metallic shift of snow.

He had been criminally negligent of Eunice.
This realization was accompanied by no corresponding warmth of parenthood; there was no quickening
of blood at the thought of his daughter, but only
a newborn condemnation of his neglected, proper
pride. He had, thoughtlessly, descended to a singularly low level of conduct. And it must abruptly
terminate. Jasper Penny had not seen Eunice for

147

seven, nine, months; he would remedy this at once, supervise advantages, a proper place, for her. Afterward Essie and himself could make a mutually satisfactory agreement.

XI

THROUGHOUT an excellent dinner, terrapin and bass, wild turkey with oysters and fruit preserved in white brandy, he maintained a sombre silence. His mother, on the right, her sister opposite — Phebe's place seemed scarcely emptier than when she had actually occupied it — held an intermittent verbal exchange patently keyed to Jasper Penny's mood. They were women with yellow-white, lace-capped hair, blanched eyebrows and lashes, and small, quick eyes on hardy, reddened faces. Gilda Penny was slightly the larger, more definite; Amity Merken had a timid, almost furtive, expression in the opulence of the Penny establishment, while Gilda was complacent; but otherwise the two women were identical. Their dresses were largely similar — Amity's a dun, Gilda Penny's grey, moire silk, high with a tight lace collar, and bands of jet trimming from shoulder to waist, there spreading over crinoline to the floor. Lace fell about their square, capable hands, and Gilda wore broad, locked bracelets checked in black and gold.

Sherry, in blue cut decanters stoppered with gilt, gave place to port. An épergne of glass and burnished ormolu, in the form of suporting oak leaves, with numerous sockets for candles, was set, filled with fruit, in the centre of the table; silver lustre plates were laid; but Jasper Penny heedlessly fingered the stem of a wine glass. He said suddenly, "I'm going to the city this afternoon."

"Is it safe yet?" his mother queried doubtfully. "Hadn't you better wait till to-morrow, when you can drive easily, or without stopping at a tavern?"

He looked up impatiently. "I shall go by the railroad," he stated decisively. "Can't you understand that, with the future of iron almost dependent on steam, it is the commonest foresight for me to patronize such customers as the Columbia Railway! I have no intention of adding to the ignorant prejudice against improved methods of travelling."

"There's your arm," she insisted with spirit.

"An untried engine. The Hecla works along smoothly at twenty miles an hour." Amity cast a glance of swift appeal at her sister, but Gilda Penny persisted. "Ungodly," was the term she selected. Jasper ignored her. He had decided to straighten the tangled affair of Eunice at once; he would see Essie that evening, arrive at an understanding about the child's future. It would be even more difficult to terminate his connection with Essie herself. That, he now recognised, was his main desire. The affair had actually died before Phebe; but its onerous consequences remained, blighting the future.

The future! It was that, he now discovered,

which occupied him, rather than the past. A new need had become apparent, a restless desire analogous to the urge of seeking youth. Jasper Penny was aware of a great dissatisfaction, a vast emptiness, in his existence; he had a feeling of waste growing out of the sense of hurrying years. Somehow, obscurely, he had been cheated. He almost envied the commonality of men, not, like himself, black Pennys, impatient of assuaging relationships and beliefs. Yet this, too, turned into another phase of his inheritance — his need was not material, concrete, it had no worldly, graspable implications, and his general contempt was not less but greater. He wished to bring a final justification to his isolation rather than lose himself in the wide, undistinguished surge of living.

"You'll stop at the Jannans?" his mother queried.

"I think not, probably Sanderson's Hotel. Stephen is giving a ball to-night for Graham and his wife. I have some important transactions." Not an echo of his affair with Essie Scofield had, he knew, penetrated to Myrtle Forge. It was a most fortunate accident. The vulgarity consequent upon discovery would have been unbearable. Stephen Jannan, his cousin, a lawyer of wide city connections, must have learned something of the truth; but Stephen, properly, had said nothing; a comfortable obscurity had hid him from gabbled scandal. Now, soon, it would all be over. Unconsciously he drew a deeper breath of relief, of prospective freedom.

The Hecla, a wooden barrelled engine with a tall, hinged stack, drew its brigade of canary-coloured chariot cars forward with a rapid bumping over inequal rails. Jasper Penny's seat, number nineteen, was fortunately in the centre, close by the stove, where a warmth hung that failed to reach to the doors. Lost in speculation the journey was both long and vague. Twilight deepened within the car, and two flickering candles were lit at either end, their pallid light serving only to cast thin, climbing shadows over the rocking, box-like interior. At irregular intervals the train stopped with a succession of subsiding crashes, and started again at the blowing of a horn; passengers would leave or enter; or it would prove to be merely a halt to take on cut and piled wood fuel for the engine.

Finally the train brigade reached the inclined plane leading to the river and city; the engine was detached, and the cars, fastened to a hemp cable, were lowered spasmodically to where a team of mules drew them through a gloomy, covered bridge echoing to the slow hoof falls and creaking of loose planks. Jasper Penny fastened the elaborate frogs of his heavily furred overcoat over his injured arm, and with a florid bandanna wiped the cinders from his silk hat.

The coaches rolled into the station shed, where he changed, taking a swaying Mulberry Street omnibus to Fourth, and Sanderson's Hotel. It was a

impudence of a cynically debased doll. She turned and surveyed Jasper Penny with a petulant, silent inquiry, and whatever gaiety was in progress abruptly terminated as he advanced into the room.

"You never let me know you'd be here," Essie complained; "but I suppose I ought to be glad to see you anyway — after four months without a line. Jasper, Mr. Daniel Culser." The younger of the men on the sofa, a stolidly handsome individual with hard, blue eyes, rose with an over-emphasized composure. "Mr. Penny, extremely pleased." Jasper Penny was irritated by the other's instant identification, and he nodded bluntly. "Lambert Babb and Myrtilla Lewis," Essie continued indifferently. Babb, an individual of inscrutable age, with ashen whiskers and a blinking, weak vision in a silvery face, was audibly delighted. Myrtilla Lewis smiled professionally over her expanse of bewildering silk plaid. "Wine in the cooler," Essie added, and Daniel Culser moved to where a silver bucket reposed by a tray of glasses and broken, sugared rusks. Jasper Penny refused the offered drink, and found a chair apart from the others. A moody silence enveloped him which he found impossible to break, and an increasing uneasiness spread over the room.

"Well," Essie Scofield commanded, "say something. You look as black as an Egyptian. What'll my friends think of you? I suppose it doesn't matter any more what it is to me; but you might play at being polite."

155

"Don't chip at a man like that," Myrtilla advised. "Mr. Penny has a right to talk or not." She smiled more warmly at him, and he saw that she had had too much champagne. The room reeked with the thin, acrid odour of the wine, and a sickly perfume of vanilla essence. Essie, as usual, had a glass of her favourite drink — orange juice and French brandy — on the floor beside her, the brandy bottle and fresh oranges conveniently near. His repulsion for her deepened until it seemed as if actual fingers were compressing his throat, stopping his breath. He wondered suddenly how far he was responsible for her possible degeneration. But he had not been the first; her admission of that fact had in the beginning attracted him to an uncommon frankness in her peculiar make-up. He was willing to assume his fault, to pay for it, whatever payment was possible, and escape . . . Not only from her, but from all that she embodied, from himself — what he had been — as much as anything else.

"You are an Ironmaster," Mr. Babb finally announced; "in fact, one of our greatest manufacturers. Now, Mr. Penny, what is your personal opinion of engine as against the public coach? Will the railroad survive the experimental stage, and are such gentlemen as yourself behind it?"

"I saw in the *Ledger* some days back," Daniel Culser added, "that your arm had been broken travelling by steam."

156

" One had nothing to do with the other," Jasper stated tersely, ignoring Babb's query, " but was entirely my own fault." The conversation lagged painfully again, during which Essie skilfully compounded another mixture of spirits and thick, yellow juice. She grew sullen with resentment at Jasper Penny's attitude, and exchanged enigmatic glances with Culser. The liquor brought a quick flush to her slightly pendulous cheeks, and she was enveloped in an increasing bravado. " Penny's a solemn old boy," she announced generally. Lambert Babb attempted to embrace Myrtilla, but, her gaze on the newcomer, she pushed him away. " You got to be a gentleman with me," she proclaimed with a patently unsteady dignity. " My grandfather was a French noble."

" What I'd like to know," Essie remarked, " is what's his granddaughter? "

" Better'n you! " Myrtilla heatedly asserted ; " one who'd appreciate a real man, and not be playing about private with a tailor's dummy." Daniel Culser's face grew noticeably pinker. " I'm going," Myrtilla continued, rising. " Mr. Penny, I'd be happy to meet you under more social conditions. Here I cannot remain for — for reasons. I might be tempted to —" Mr. Babb caught her arm under his, and, at an imperious gesture from Essie, piloted her from the room. Culser rose.

" Don't go, Dan," Essie Scofield told him defiantly. But Jasper Penny maintained a silence that forced the younger man to make a stiff exit. "Well," Essie demanded, flinging herself on the deserted sofa, "now you've spoiled my evening. Why did you come at all if you couldn't behave genteel?"

"Where, exactly, is Eunice?" he asked abruptly.

She glanced at him with an instant masking of her resentment. "I've told you a hundred times — in the house of a very respectable clergyman. My letter was clear enough; she's had bronchitis, and there's the doctor, and —"

"Just where is Eunice?" he repeated, interrupting her aggrieved recital.

"Where I put her," her voice grew shrill. "You haven't asked to see her for near a year, you haven't even pretended an interest in — in your own daughter. I've done the best I could; you know I don't like children around; but I have attended to as much of my duty as you. Now you come out and insist on being unpleasant all in an hour. Why didn't you write? I'd had her here for you. Come back in two or three days."

"To-morrow," he replied. "I am going to see her in the morning."

"You just ain't. I did the best I knew, but, if it isn't all roses, you'll blame everything on me. I will have Eunice fetched —"

"Where is she?" he asked still again, wearily.

Every instinct revolted against the degradation into which he had blindly walked. His youth had betrayed him, involving him, practically a different

158

man, in a payment which he realized had but commenced . . . To escape. He had first thought of that with the unconscious conviction that the mere wish carried its fulfilment. In fact, it would be immensely difficult; a man, he saw, could not sever himself so casually from the past; it reached without visible demarcation into the present, the future. All was a piece, one with another; and Essie Scofield was drawn in a vivid thread through the entire fabric of his being.

Yet the need, the longing forward, so newly come into his consciousness, persisted, grew — it had become the predominate design of his weaving. Through this he recognized a reassertion of his pride, the rigid pride of a black Penny, which, in the years immediately past, had been overwhelmed by a temporary inner confusion. Beyond forty men returned to their inheritance, their blood; this fact echoed vaguely among his memories of things heard; and he felt in himself its measure of truth. His distaste for a largely muddled, pandering society, for men huddled, he thought, like domestic animals, returned in choking waves. In the maculate atmosphere of flat wine and stale cologne he had a sharp recurrence of the scent of pines, lifting warmly in sunny space.

He produced a morocco bound note book, a gold pencil; and, with the latter poised, directed a close interrogation at Essie. Her face flushed with an ungovernable anger, and she pressed a hand over

159

her labouring heart. "Get her then; out Fourth Street, Camden; the Reverend Mr. Needles. But afterwards don't come complaining to me. You ought to have seen to her; you've got the money, the influence. And you have done nothing, beyond some stinking dollars . . . wouldn't even name her. Eunice Scofield, a child without —"

All that she had said was absolutely true, just.

"I suppose you'll even think I didn't give her the sums you sent; that damned Needles has been bleeding me, suspects something." She stopped from a lack of breath; her darkened face was purplish in the shadows. "I haven't been well, either — a fierce pain here, in my heart."

It was the brandy, he told her; she should leave the city, late wine parties, go back into the country. "Go back," she echoed bitterly. "Where? How?" He winced — the past reaching inexorably into the future. Jasper Penny made no attempt to ignore, forget, his responsibility; he admitted it to her; but at the same time the tyrannical hunger increased within him — the mingled desire for fresh paths and the nostalgia of the old freedom of spirit. But life, that had made him, had in the same degree created Essie; neither had been the result of the other; they had been swept together, descended blindly in company, submerged in the passion that he had thought must last forever, but which had burned to ashes, to nothing more than a vague sense of putrefaction in life.

160

" Thank you," he said formally, putting away the note book. " Something, of course, must be done; but what, I can only say after I have seen Eunice. I am, undoubtedly, more to blame than yourself."

" I suppose, in this holy strain, you'll end by giving her all and me nothing."

". . . what you are getting as long as you live? "

" That's little enough, when I hear how much you have, what all that iron is bringing you. Why, you could let me have twenty, thirty thousand, and never know it."

" If you are unable to get on, that too will be rectified."

" You are really not a bad old thing, Jasper," she pronounced, mollified. " At one time — do you re-member? — you said if ever the chance came you would marry me. Ah, you needn't fear, I wouldn't have you with all your iron, gold. I —" she stopped abruptly, uneasily. " Not a bad old thing," she repeated, moving to secure a half-full glass.

" Why do you call me old? " he asked curiously.

" I hadn't thought of it before," she admitted; " but, this evening, you looked so solemn, and there is grey in your hair, that all at once you seemed like an old gentleman. Now Dan Culser," she hesitated, and then swept on, " he's what you'd name young." At Daniel Culser's age, he told himself, he, Jasper Penny, could have walked the other blind; and now Essie Scofield was calling him old; she had noticed the grey in his hair. He rose to go, and she came

161

close to him, a clinging, soft thing of flesh faintly reeking with brandy. "I have a great deal to pay, where money goes I don't know, even a little would be a help." He left some gold in her hand, thankful to purchase, at that slight price, a momentary release.

Outside Cherry Street was blackly cold, a gas lamp at the corner shed a watery, contracted illumination. He made his way back toward the hotel, but a sudden reluctance to mount to his lonely chambers possessed him. Before the glimmering marble façade he took out his watch, a pale gold efflorescence in the gloom, and rang the hour in minute, clear notes. The third quarter past ten. He recalled the ball, but then commencing, at Stephen Jannan's; there it would be indescribably gay, a house flooded with the music of quadrilles, light, polite chatter; and he determined to proceed and have a cigar with Stephen.

He walked briskly up Mulberry Street to Sixth and there turned to the left. Jasper Penny soon passed the shrouded silence of Independence Square, with the new Corinthian doorway of the State House showing vaguely through the irregularly grouped ailanthus trees. Beyond, the brick wall with its marble coping and high iron fence reached, on the opposite side, to the Jannan corner. The length of the brick dwelling, with white arched windows and coursings faced the vague emptiness of Washington Square, closed for the winter.

Inside the hall was bright and filled with the pungent warmth of fat hearth coal. A servant, with a phrase of recognition, directed him above, to a room burdened with masculine greatcoats and silk hats. There an attendant told him that Mr. Jannan was below. Jasper Penny had no intention of becoming a participant in the ball, but neither did he propose to linger among wraps, listening to the supercilious chatter of young men in the extreme mode of bright blue coats, painfully tight black trousers with varnished pumps and expanses of ankle in grey silk. One, inspecting him through an eyeglass on a woven hair guard, expressed a pointed surprise at Jasper Penny's informal garb. " Christoval! " he ejaculated. " It approaches an insult to the da-da-darlings." Another commenced to sing a popular minstrel air:

" Blink — a — ho — dink! Ah! Ho!
" Roley Boley — Good morning Ladies all! "

Jasper Penny abruptly descended to a small room used for smoking. Young men, he thought impatiently, could no longer even curse respectably. They lisped like females at an embroidery frame. When he was young, younger, he corrected himself, he could have outdrunk, outridden . . . His train of thought was abruptly terminated by a group unexpectedly occupying the smoking room. He saw Stephen Jannan, his wife Liza, the newly married young Jannans, and a strange woman in glacé mus-

163

lin and a black Spanish lace shawl about her shoulders. Stephen greeted him cordially. "Jasper, just at the moment for a waltz with — with Susan." The stranger blushed painfully, made an involuntary movement backward, and Liza Jannan admonished her husband. "Do you know Miss Brundon, Jasper?" she asked.

Jasper Penny bowed, and Miss Brundon, with an evident effort, smiled, her shy, blue eyes held resolutely on his countenance. She at once slipped into the background, talking in a low, clear voice to Graham Jannan's wife; while the older men enveloped themselves in a fragrant veil of cigars. "Come, Mary, Susan," Mrs. Jannan directed, "out of this horrid, masculine odour." Accompanied by her son the women left, and Stephen turned to his cousin. "Thought, of course, you knew Susan Brundon," he remarked. "A school mistress, but superior, and a lady. Has a place on Spruce Street, by Raspberry Alley, for select younger girls; unique idea, and very successful, I believe."

Jasper Penny said comfortably, "Humm!" The other continued, "I want Graham to get out to Shadrach Furnace as soon as may be. That old stone house the foremen have occupied is nearly fixed for him. I am very well content, Jasper, to have him in the iron trade, with you practically at its head. No deliberate favours, remember, and I have told him to look for nothing. But, at the same time — you comprehend: folly not to push the boy

164

on fast as possible. No reason for us all to go through with the hardships of the first Gilbert and his times. Must have been fatiguing, the wilderness and English troubles and all that."

"Splendid, I should say," Jasper Penny replied. He repeated satirically the conversation he had heard above. "Makes me ill. You will remember there was a Howat, son of our original settler — now he must have been a lad! Married some widow or other; wild at first, but made iron in the end."

"A black Penny, Jasper; resembled you. Personally, I like it better now." Jasper Penny surveyed with approbation Stephen's full, handsome presence. Jannan was a successful, a big, man. Well, so was he too. But he thought with keen longing of the time when he was twenty-one, and free, free to roam self-sufficient. He thought of that Howat Penny of which they had spoken, black as he was black in the family tradition; he had seen Hesselius's portrait of the other; and, but for the tied hair and continental buff, it might have been a replica of himself. It was curious — that dark strain of Welsh blood, cropping out undiminished, concrete, after generations. The one to hold it before Howat had been burned in Mary's time, in the sixteenth century, dead almost three hundred years. Jasper had a sudden, vivid sense of familiarity with the Howat who had married some widow or other. His mind returned to his own, peculiar problem, to Essie Scofield, to the burden with which he had encumbered himself, the payment that faced him for — for his sheer youth. He said abruptly, belated:

"You fit the present formal ease of society, Stephen; you like it and it likes you. In a superficial way I have done well enough, but underneath —" his voice sank into silence. A profound, familiar dejection seized him; incongruously he thought of Miss Brundon's delicate shrinking from the mere contact of the amenities of speech. Supersensitive. "I must go," he announced, and refused Stephen Jannan's invitation for the night.

"Stay for some supper, anyhow," the other insisted, and, a hand on his arm, led him past the doors open upon the dancing.

Chandeliers, great coruscating pendants of glass prisms and candles, glittered above the expanse of whirling crinoline and blue coats, vermilion turbans, gilt feathers and flowered hair. The light fell on shoulders as white and elegantly sloping as alabaster vases, draped in rose and citron, in blanched illusion frosted and looped with silver; on bouquets of camellias swinging from jewelled chains against ruffled and belled skirts swaying about the revealed symmetry of lacy silk stockings and fragile slippers. "Ah, Jasper," Stephen Jannan said; "in our time, what! Do you remember your first Wellington boots? The gambling room and veranda at Saratoga? Tender eyes, old boy, and little tapering hands." Jasper Penny replied, "It seems my hair is grey." Silence fell on them as they

entered the dining room. A long table was burdened with elaborate pagodas of spun barley sugar
topped with sprigs of orange blossom, the moulded
creams of a Charlotte Polonaise, champagne jelly
valanced with lemon peel, pyramids of glazed fruits
on lacquered plates; with faintly iridescent Belleek
and fluted glass and ormolu; and, everywhere, the
pale multitudinous flames of candles and the fuller
radiance of astral lamps hung with lustres. Jasper
Penny idly tore open a bon bon wrapped in a verse
on fringed paper.

> "Viens! Viens! ange du ciel, je t'aime! je t'aime!
> Et te le dire ici, c'est le bonheur supreme."

Love and the great hour of life! He had missed
both; one, perhaps, with the other. His marriage
to Phebe, except for a brief flare at the beginning,
had been as empty as the affair with Essie Scofield.
God, how hollow living seemed! He had missed
something; or else existence was an ugly deception,
the false lure of an incomprehensible jest. The
music beat in faint, mocking waves on his hearing,
the lights of the supper shone in the gold bubbles
of his wine glass. He drained it hurriedly. Outside the night, lying cold on deserted squares, blurred
with gas lamps, was like a vain death after the idle
frivolity of Stephen Jannan's ball. In an instant,
in the shutting of a door, the blackness had claimed
him; the gaiety of warm flesh and laughter vanished.
Death . . . and he had literally nothing in his

hands, nothing in his heart. A duty, Eunice, remained. The sound of his footfalls on the bricks, thrown back from blank walls, resembled the embodied, stealthy following of the injustice he had wrought.

XII

THE following morning he made his way past the continuous produce arcade that held the centre of Market Street to the Camden Ferry. At the river the fish stall, with its circular green roof and cornucopias, reached almost to the gloomy ferry-house with its heavy odour of wet wood. The boat clattered through broken ice, by a trim packet ship, the *Susquehanna*, and into the narrow canal through Windmill Island. Camden was a depressing region of low, marshy land, its streets unpaved and without gas, the gutters full of frozen, stagnant water. He inquired the way to the Reverend Mr. Needles', passed a brick meeting house, and, turning into Fourth Street, isolated frame dwellings, coming at last to a dingy wooden house with broken panes in the upper windows and a collapsing veranda at the edge of a blackened, skeleton wood.

A tall, gaunt woman in a ravelled worsted shawl answered his summons, and informed him, interrupted by a prolonged coughing, that Mr. Needles was away on circuit. "I came for a child staying with you," Jasper Penny explained shortly, suppressing an involuntary repulsion at the degraded surroundings. "She's not well," the woman replied, with instant suspicion. "I don't just like to let a chancy person see her." He discarded all subterfuge. "I am her father," he stated. The other shifted to a whining self-defence. "And her in this sink!" she exclaimed, gazing at Jasper Penny's furred coat, his glossy hat and gloves and ebony cane.

"I did all for her I could, considering the small money I was promised, and then half the time I didn't get that, neither. The lady owes for three weeks right now. I suppose you'll have to come in," she concluded grudgingly. They entered a dark hall, clay cold. Beyond, in a slovenly kitchen hardly warmer, he found Eunice, his daughter; a curiously sluggish child with a pinched, hueless face and a meagre body in a man's worn flannel shirt and ragged skirt and stockings.

"Here's your father," Mrs. Needles ejaculated.

Eunice stood in the middle of the bare floor, staring with pallid, open mouth at the imposing figure of the man. She said nothing; and Jasper Penny found her silence more accusing than a shrill torrent of reproach. "She's kind of heavy like," Mrs. Needles explained. "I have come to take you away," Jasper Penny said. Then, turning to the woman: "Are those all the clothes she has?" She grew duskily red. "There are some others about, but I don't just know where, and then she spoils them so fast."

"That's a lie," the child announced, with a faint

170

patch of colour on either thin cheek. "Mr. Needles sold them." The man decided to ignore such issues; his sole wish now was to take Eunice away as speedily as possible. "Well," he directed impatiently, "get a shawl, something to wrap her in." He regretted vainly that he had not come for the child in a carriage. He paid without a question what the woman said was owing; and, with Eunice folded in a ragged plaid, prepared to depart. "I guess," the child decided, in a strangely mature voice, "we'd better take my medicine." She turned toward a mantel, Mrs. Needles made a quick movement in the same direction, but the small shape was before her. Jasper Penny took a bottle from the diminutive, cold hand. The label had been obliterated; but, impelled by a distrustful curiosity, he took out the cork.

Laudanum!

He was at the point of an indignant condemnation when the words perished without utterance — not the haggard woman before him, but himself, Jasper Penny, was entirely guilty. He, in reality, had given the drug to his daughter, placed her in this sorry and bitter poverty. "Come, Eunice," he said, taking her by the hand, his face grey and stony.

Once more in the city he walked with the child to the ferry and foot of Chestnut Street, where they found places in The Reaper, a stage brightly painted with snowy ships and drawn by four sorrel horses. His first concern was to purchase proper clothes for

171

his daughter; then he would face the problem of her happier disposal. They passed the columned façade of the Philadelphia Bank, the Custom House with its wide steps set back from the street, hedged dwellings, and the United States Hotel to Independence Square and Sixth Street, where he lifted the child from the stage. They stopped before an entrance between bowed windows which had above it the sign, The Misses Dunlop, Millinery.

Jasper Penny had had no idea that it would be so difficult to procure clothes for a girl of seven. At first he was told that the necessary garments could not be furnished, when discussion revealed the fact that a nearly complete, diminutive wardrobe, especially ordered from Paris and neglected by the customer, was to be had. In a surprisingly short while a sentimental saleswoman had apparelled Eunice in black velvet with rows of small bows and gold buckles and a lace collar, cambric pantaloon ruffles swinging about her ankles, a quilted pink satin bonnet tied, like those of her elders', with a bow under her right cheek, and a muff and tippet of ermine. Other articles — a frock of rose gros de chine, with a flounced skirt, a drab velvet bonnet turned in green smocked silk, and sheer underthings — he ordered delivered at Sanderson's Hotel.

The effect of what laudanum Eunice had taken faded, and her lethargy was replaced by an equally still, incredulous amazement. She followed Jasper Penny about with the mechanical rigidity of a minute

172

sleepwalker. They went into a jewelry store beyond, with a square low bow window and white trimming, where he purchased a ring with a ruby, and small gold bracelets with locks and chains. His restless desire was to clothe Eunice in money, to overwhelm her with gifts; yet, although an evident delight struggled through her stupefaction, he failed to get from the expenditure the release he sought. A leaden sense of blood guiltiness persisted in him. At Parkinson's, the confectioner opposite the State House, he bought her syllabubs, a frozen rose cordial and black cake. On leaving, he paused at the marble steps with a lantern on either side and awning drawn out over the pavement, considering the next move. It should be toys — a German doll, slate and coloured crayons and jumping figures. Then he took her back to his rooms at the Hotel.

Sitting in a stiff crimson chair opposite him, the doll clasped in straining fingers, and a flush of excitement on her sharp features, she presented an enormous difficulty. What, justly, was he to do with her? How could he provide for a reasonable happiness, a healthy, normal existence? He decided coldly that he would prevent Essie Scofield's influence from ever touching the child again. Essie, he knew, was utterly without any warmth of motherhood. She had solely and callously used their daughter to extort money from him. But, he admitted to himself, neither had he any feeling of parentage for the small, lonely figure before him:

173

nothing but a burning self-accusation, a lacerated pride. His act proceeded entirely from his head in place of his heart. For that very reason, Jasper Penny thought, he could give his daughter a greater measure of security. He would see Stephen Jannan to-morrow and with the lawyer's assistance get complete control of Eunice's future. He must alter his will.

None of this, however, assisted in solving the actual immediate necessity. There was, certainly, Myrtle Forge; his mother, however she might silently suffer, protest, would ultimately accede in his wishes. But it was a dreary place for a child, with only the companionship of old women. He was, for the greater part, away in the interest of his widely scattered activities, forges, furnaces, nail factories and rolling mills.

He felt in anticipation the censure of the Penny connections that would rise like a wall and shut Eunice from the companionship of the other children of the family, embittering her at what he had somewhere heard described as the formative period of growth. His home, he decided, for the present at least, was an undesirable place for his daughter.

It was, he discovered, past two, and he remorsefully summoned a servant. He gazed with bewilderment at the list of dinner dishes tended him; bear's meat, he felt, canvas back duck or terrapin, was not a diet proper to seven; but he solved the perplexity by ordering snipe, rolled and sugared cakes filled

174

with whipped cream and preserved strawberries, and a deep apple pandowdy. After this, and a block of nougat, Eunice discovered herself to be sleepy. As she lay with tossed arms and pale streaming hair under the feather coverlet of a great hotel bed he saw with a sharp uneasiness that, in a subtle but unmistakable accent, she resembled her mother, Essie Scofield.

XIII

HIS thoughts darkened with the falling day; he supposed them to be solely addressed to the problem of Eunice; but, in reality, they constantly evaded his will, following countless trivialities, and returned to his own, peculiar need. He made some small changes of dress for the evening, replacing brown with glazed black boots, and struggled, with one hand, through the ordeal of tying a formal neckcloth. He had purposely left behind his negro servant as a possible source of unguarded chatter. When Jasper Penny had finished he went in to Eunice and found her awake. The new clothes lay in their open boxes; and, lighting candles, he wondered if he had better have some one in to assist her. " Can you fix yourself up in these? " he asked, indicating the purchases.

" Oh, yes," she assured him gravely; " that is except the very backest buttons." She stood by the folded piles of shirred muslin, the elaborate velvets and silks and ribbons, obviously at a loss before such an unparalleled choice; and he was once more disturbed by the attenuation of her small body. But that could be soon remedied; she had suffered other, far greater, irremedial, oppressions; her very birth

had confronted her, in the puritanical self-righteous-
ness of his world, with an almost insuperable barrier
to happiness. Still back of that, even before the
birth of himself and Essie Scofield, back, back in the
unguessed past, Eunice had been shaped, condemned.
Her fate had only culminated in his own unbalanced
passion, in a desire that had blinded him like a
flash of ignited powder, leaving him with a sense of
utter void, of inexplicable need. "For what?" he
demanded unconsciously and bitterly aloud.

Eunice, startled, dropped the garment in her
hands. She gazed at him with a shrinking dread.
"Come," he told her gently, "that will be very
pretty; and, don't you think, the velvet bonnet with
green?" After supper he questioned her. "What
time do you usually go to bed?" She answered
promptly, "When it got too cold to stay up, at Mr.
Needles', but I wouldn't know here."

"We might go to the Circus," he suggested, half
doubtful of the propriety of such a course. However, they went. She clung tightly to his sleeve before the illuminated, high-pillared façade of Welches'
Circus, where Jasper took seats in a box. Eunice
was breathless before the gleaming white and gold
of the interior, the fabulous, glittering chandelier,
the crimson draperies and great curtain with its
equestrienne on a curvetting steed. The orchestra,
with a blare of trombones, announced the raising of
the curtain and appearance of Mr. John Mays, the
celebrated clown. He was followed by Chinese

177

sports, the Vision of Cupid and Zephyr, and the
songs, the programme stated, of Lowrie and Wil-
liams. These gentlemen, in superb yellow satin, emphasized harmoniously the fact that

> " And joy is but a flower,
>   The heart with sorrow meeting
>   Will wither 'neath its power."

Jasper Penny wondered abstractedly what was
to be done with the tense, excitable child at his side?
A voice from the wings announced: " Mouse and
Harebell, the Lilliputian ponies, with Infant Jockies,
the smallest schooled racers in existence."   And the
word " schooled " recalled to him the diffident woman
he had met at Stephen Jannan's, the night before.
Miss . . . Brundon. A place for the education of
younger girls. He could send Eunice there, for the
present at any rate; and decide later upon her ultimate situation. Miss Brundon had a sensitive, yes,
distinctly, a fine face. Her school, he remembered,
was at Raspberry Alley, far out Spruce Street, close
to Tenth. He drew a deep breath of relief at this
bridging of the immediate complications the child
presented.

The next morning, again in the Reaper coach,
they rolled west over Chestnut Street, past a theatre
with elevated statues of Comedy and Tragedy, the
Arcade with its outside stairs mounting across the
front, stone mansions set back in gardens with gravelled paths, and the Moorish bulk of Masonic Hall

half hid by stores. Beyond the Circus they proceeded on foot to a four square brick dwelling with weeping willows and an arched wood sign above the entrance painted with the designation, " Miss Brundon's Select Academy."

Jasper Penny found Miss Brundon in a small, bare, immaculate office. She was sitting at a table; and, as he entered, with Eunice dragging desperately at his hand, she half rose, with a quick, faint blush.

" Mr. Penny," she exclaimed, in a low, charming surprise. " I didn't expect, so soon, to have the pleasure . . . here, at my school." He firmly moved Eunice from her position at his back. " An unexpected pleasure for me," he replied. " I came to consult with you about this little girl — the daughter of a friend of mine. A friend, I may add, in difficult circumstances, and for whom I am prepared to do a great deal. I had hoped — Stephen Jannan told me about your exceptional establishment — that you could take her. She needs just the supervision that I am certain you offer."

" Of course," she replied immediately, " I'd be glad to have any one recommended by you. I do think my school is unusual. You see, there is almost no provision for the supervision of such young ladies. And I have been very fortunate in my girls; I try not to be snobbish, Mr. Penny; but, indeed, if a place like this is to be useful, some care is required. Probably you would like an assurance of their studies and deportment."

179

"No," he stopped her hastily; "it is quite enough to have seen you." A deeper, painful colour suffused her cheeks. He had, he thought, been inexcusably clumsy. He had unconsciously given voice to the conviction that Miss Brundon, like her establishment, was exceptional. She was, ordinarily, too pale for beauty; her countenance, with high cheek bones, was irregular; yet her eyes, tranquil blue, held a steady quality almost the radiance of an inward light. Her diffidence, it was clear, co-existed with a firm, inviolable spirit. He said, later:

"You will discover that there are many things Eunice requires, and I would be obliged if you would procure them without stint, and send the accounts to my Philadelphia office. The child has been in circumstances of considerable poverty; but I wish to give her whatever advantages money can bring. Yes — Eunice Scofield. And —" he hesitated, "in view of this . . ."

"I understand, oh, completely," Susan Brundon interrupted him warmly. "You don't wish your charity exposed; and not only on your own account, but from consideration for the susceptibilities of the parents, parent — a mother, I gather."

It had been, he thought, leaving, ridiculously simple. His meeting with Miss Brundon was a fortunate chance. A fine, delicate, unworldly woman; a fineness different from Phebe's, submerged in the pursuit of her own salvation. The former, he realized, was close to forty. If she had been sympathetic with a strange child such as Eunice how admirably she would attend any of her own. Unmarried. The blindness of men, their fatuous choice, suddenly surprised him.

He determined to proceed directly to Stephen Jannan, and put into motion at once the solving of his daughter's future. Never, he repeated, should Eunice fall again into the lax hands of Essie Scofield. Stephen would advise him shrewdly, taking advantage of the law, or skilfully overcoming its obstacles. He had unbounded faith in the power of money where Essie was concerned; at the same time he had no intention of laying himself open to endless extortion, threats, almost inevitable, ultimate scandal. What a bog he had strayed into, a quagmire reaching about him in every direction. He must discover firmer ground ahead, release from the act of that other man, his youth. The memory of the serene purity of Miss Brundon's office recurred to him like a breath from the open spaces where he had first known the deep pleasure of an utter freedom of spirit.

Jasper Penny, revolving the complications of his position, made his way directly over the uneven sidewalk of Spruce Street to Fourth; there, passing the high, narrow residences of Society Hill, he proceeded to Stephen's office, beyond Chestnut. It was in a square brick edifice of an earlier period, with a broad marble step and door and wide windows coped in scoured white stone. The lawyer's private chamber was bare, with snowy panelling and mahogany,

181

the high sombre shelves of a calf-bound law library, a ponderous cabriolet table, sturdy, rush-seated Dutch chairs, and a Franklin stove with slender brass capitols and shining hod.

"A chair, Jasper," Stephen Jannan directed. "You ought to know them, they came out of Myrtle Forge — some of old Gilbert's. Your mother gave them to me when she did over the house in this new French fancy." Jasper Penny was momentarily at a loss for an adequate opening of the subject that had brought him there. Finally he plunged directly into his purpose. "You must know, Stephen," he said, "that I am decidedly obligated to a Mrs. Scofield." Jannan nodded shortly. "The thing dragged on for a number of years, but is quite dead now; in fact, it has been for a considerable number of months. That, in itself, doesn't bother me; it is comparatively simple; but there is a child, a girl, Stephen."

"I didn't know that," the other acknowledged. "It is an ugly difficulty. Do you wish to legitimatize your — the child? There is marriage of course."

"I have no intention of marrying Essie Scofield," Jasper Penny said coldly. "And I am almost certain she wouldn't consent if I had. I am quite willing to assume a proper responsibility; but there is a limit to my conception of that. There was never any serious question of marriage; there is none now.

182

I simply wish to get complete control of Eunice; by adoption, perhaps; she is seven years old."

"There are no laws of adoption, as such, in Pennsylvania," Jannan told him. "The only State with that provision is Louisiana; there, by an act of Legislature, the thing can be legalized. I could arrange it through correspondence, a certain residence within the State. It would be cumbersome and expensive, but possible." He paused, frowning. "Devilish awkward," he muttered; "make a stench in a family such as ours. However," he added, "a contract practically to the same effect can be drawn. This, with her consent, would be entirely binding on Mrs. Scofield. If the child can write it would be well to have her signature on the deed. Bring them here; she should have counsel."

"After that, I suppose, the name could be arranged."

"Exactly. The child, of course, would have no legal status as your heir. Anything she got would have to be willed direct." The other nodded. It was all far more simple than he had hoped. He almost saw a definite lightening of the future. "Is the girl with her mother now?" Jannan queried.

"I took her away yesterday," Jasper Penny replied negligently. "We went to the Circus, and at present she is at Miss Brundon's Academy." He was surprised by the sudden concern on his cousin's handsome, florid countenance. "By heaven, Jasper," the lawyer exclaimed, " am I to understand that you took a — well, an illegitimate child, to Miss Brundon, left her in the School? It's — it's incredible."

" Why not? "

" If such a thing were known it would ruin Susan Brundon over night. Haven't you a conception of how this is regarded? She would be stripped of pupils as if the place reeked of malignant fever. A most beastly egotistical and selfish act."

" Never thought of that," Jasper Penny admitted. He saw again the fine, sensitive face of Miss Brundon, presiding over the establishment that was like an emanation of her diffident and courageous spirit; the last person alive he would harm. And people were exactly as Stephen had said, particularly women. They would destroy Susan Brundon ruthlessly, without a moment's hesitation. He thought of her as suffering incalculably, betrayed by his implied lie; he saw her eyes stricken with pain, her hands twisting together . . . He rose sharply.

" A blind, infernal fool! " he ejaculated, grasping his hat. " I'm glad I saw you when I did. Put it right at once. Obliged, Stephen; come to you later about changing my will and the rest."

He was in such haste to remove the danger of Eunice from Susan Brundon that not until he again stood at the door of the Academy did he realize what a difficult explanation lay before him. Unconsciously he had reached a point where he would do his utmost to avoid hurting her. Already she occupied an unusual elevation in his thoughts, an unworldly plane bathed in a white radiance.

She was not in the office, but soon appeared, with a questioning gaze; and, he felt, an appealing lessening of her reserve. He hesitated, casting vainly about for an acceptable expression of his errand. Another lie, he thought, acutely distressed, must be necessary. "I am extremely sorry, Miss Brundon," he told her, "but unexpected developments in the last hour make it necessary for me to remove Eunice from your school."

A slow flush invaded her countenance lifted to meet his troubled gaze. "Mr. Penny!" she exclaimed, in a faint dismay. "Oh, I hope it is because of nothing — nothing derogatory you have heard. Please tell me directly —"

"Absolutely no," he replied, his voice carrying a vibrating reassurance. "You are entirely without the need of recommendation, far beyond any unfavourable report. I am profoundly disturbed by causing you inconvenience, and I only hope to offer you sufficient apology; but I shall have to take Eunice away with me, at once."

"Perhaps her mother can't bear separation."

"It is not that," he said grimly, a tangible hurt sharpening within; "but something that cannot be gone into, with you." She turned away immediately. "I will send for her," she replied. They stood facing but mutually avoiding each other's gaze while Eunice was being fetched. "Her things have already come from the hotel," Miss Brundon proceeded. "Where shall I send them?" Eunice broke in with a shrill protest. "Do I have to go? I don't want to." Her face was scarlet with revolt. "I can walk up and down the room with a book on my head, while another little girl had to be all done with a board to her back."

Jasper Penny wondered if he would see Miss Brundon again soon. The last was an afterthought bred by the realization that he could not permit her to depart absolutely from his life. There was a great deal that he, a rich and influential man of practical affairs, might do for her. He was certain that Susan Brundon needed exactly the assistance he could give; probably people robbed her, traded callously on her unsuspicious nature. Yet, when the moment came to leave, he could think of nothing to say beyond the banality of looking for her at the Jannans'.

"I go out very little," she told him; "the work here absorbs me; and, unfortunately, my eyes are not strong. They require constant rest." He expressed regret once more for any disturbance he might have caused; and, after hesitating awkwardly, left with Eunice hanging fretfully at his hand. What, in God's name, was he to do with the child? He walked slowly, his face half lost in the fur of his overcoat, oblivious, in his concentration on the difficulties of her situation, of Eunice progressing dis-

186

contentedly at his side. A petulant complaint rose
at intervals to an audible sob. Looking down, as
the sobs threatened to become a continuous crying,
he saw the top of the velvet bonnet and her diminutive hands in scarlet knitted mitts. He would have
to stop dragging her from place to place; a suitable
position for the present was all he hoped for now.
There must be other institutions, larger and farther
away, to which Eunice could be sent. He had a
vague memory of such a place somewhere on the
Delaware, was it at Burlington?

But he could not continue living with his daughter
at Sanderson's Hotel. Jasper Penny decided that
he would take her that afternoon to the house of the
head machinist of his nail works at Jaffa, the town
that, its beginning growing largely out of the Penny
industries, lay a scant mile from Myrtle Forge.
Speever was a superior man; his wife, a robust Cor-
nish woman in a crisp apron, would give Eunice an
energetic and proper care.

A thin, flexible mantle of snow lay over the drab
earth, sweeping up to a Grecian marble edifice, making more dreary the bulk of the Eastern Peniten-
tiary and foundation of Girard College, and emphasizing the winter desertion of the reaches of the
Fairmount Water Works. She soon grew absorbed
in the various aspects of their transportation —
the echo of the whip cracking over the mules that
drew the coaches across the covered viaduct, the
labouring stationary engine and their slow ascent

187

beyond. They saw, lining the river, a cemetery elevated starkly against the sky; and followed a canal by a broken, black flood between snowy banks.

Past a town with impressive residences and manufactories with low spreading veils of smoke, they came on a confusion of canals and canal boats, lock dams and bridges, mules and raffish crews with tanned faces and brightly coloured jackets and boots. Again crossing the river and a shallow, tranquil valley, the train brigade rolled into the main street of Jaffa. It was a town of small brick dwellings, spaced in orderly yards, echoing to the diminished clamour of the Penny Rolling Mills on the outskirts. Beyond the walls, starkly red against the snow, the blackened main street, the river was spotted with ice.

Edgar Speever's wife accepted Eunice with an immediate and unquestioning capability, and Jasper Penny turned away with a momentary but immense relief. In a few days, after the deed for the possession of the child had been executed, he could place her more permanently. He walked out to the miscellaneous group of buildings and cluttered yards that held his inherited activity; and in the small single-roomed building of the main office discussed with his superintendent the changes, improvements of process, then under way. The old nail machines, propelled by the feet and hands of an operator, and producing but one nail at a time, had been replaced by a high power engine, self-heading machinery.

188

The superintendent complained of the pig from the new hot blast furnaces. "Impure," he declared. "And this new stone coal firing, too, makes but poor stuff. It'll never touch the old charcoal forging. Hammered bar's at ninety, and I'm glad to get it then. The puddling furnaces will do something with the grey pig; we have eight in blast now, turning out the railroad and heavier bars. This year will see forty-five hundred tons of iron worked, and close to four thousand kegs of nails."

Jasper Penny listened attentively; it was his intention soon to dispense entirely with all the time-honoured methods of iron manufacture. Water power, with its unequal flow, any large employment of charcoal, growing increasingly expensive with the rapid diminishment of the forests, must give place to the steam blast machine and anthracite. If his manager was unable to change, develop, with the changing times he would find another, more scientific.

Outside the early twilight made more grey the dingy sheds and buildings, the heaped slag; the long brick rectangle of the rolling mill, with its triple imposed, ventilated roof and the high, smoking stacks of the puddling furnaces, rising four from either length, gave out an undiminished, deafening uproar, the clamour of the bars falling out from the rollers, the spatter of hammers and dull dragging of heavy weights. The engine of the nail works rent all other sound with an unaccustomed, harsh blast. . . . Jasper Penny was conscious of a deep, invol-

189

untary relief when he reached the comparative tranquillity, the secession of vexatious problems, accomplished by Myrtle Forge.

XIV

THERE was, as always, an elaborate, steaming supper, with his mother, in a pelisse of black silk ruching, and Amity Merken at their places. He noted that an empty chair had been put, as customary, at the opposite end of the table, and with a trace of impatience ordered its removal. He wondered momentarily at his petty act; and then his thoughts returned to Susan Brundon. Jasper Penny saw her blue gaze lifted to his face, the hesitating smile; he felt again the pervading influence of her delicate yet essentially unshrinking spirit. She would possess an enormous steadfastness of purpose, he decided; a potentiality of immovable self-sacrifice. Yet she was the gentlest person alive. An unusual and resplendent combination of traits, rare possibilities.

She had told him that she seldom went about — her school absorbed her, and her eyes needed care, rest. He must ask Stephen Jannan further about her. They were sitting, Jasper Penny, his mother and her sister, in the parlour; a large, square chamber hung with dark maroon paper and long, many tasselled and corniced window curtains in sombre green plush. A white wedgewood mantel with ornaments in olive and blue, above a brass-fretted closed stove, supported a high mirror, against which were ranged a pair of tall astral lamps shining in green and red spars of light through their pendants, a French clock — a crystal ball in a miniature Ionic pavilion of gilt — and artificial bouquets of coloured wax under glass domes. A thick carpet of purplish black velvet pile covered the floor from wall to wall; stiff Adam chairs and settee with wheelbacks of black and gold were upholstered in dusky ruby and indigo. Ebony tables of framed, inlaid onyx held tortoise shell and lacquer ornaments, an inlaid tulip-wood music-box, volumes in elaborately tooled morocco, and a globe where, apparently, metallic fish were suspended in a translucent, green gloom.

The light from the multiple candelabras of ormolu and cut lustres streamed from the walls over Jasper Penny, sunk forward in profound absorption, and his mother's busy, fat hands working with gay worsteds. At her side a low stand of rubbed Chinese vermilion held her spilling yarns. Her face was placid, dryly pinkish and full. An irreproachable, domestic female. Herself the daughter of a successful Pennsylvania German Ironmaster, her wealth had doubled the Penny successes. There had been other children; Jasper could only faintly remember two, mostly in the form of infantile whimpering.

The inevitable termination of the evening was reached by the appearance of a pitcher of steaming, spiced mulled wine. A cupful was formally presented to Amity Merken; Gilda Penny sipped hers with an audible satisfaction, and Jasper Penny absently drank the fragrant compound of cinnamon bark and lemon, cloves, sugar and claret. A measure of that, before retiring, could not but be beneficial to Susan Brundon, fatigued by the duties of her Academy. He thought of the sharper breath of the brandy and oranges compounded by Essie Scofield. A thin odour of foxglove clung to the memory of his wife.

XV

JASPER PENNY supplemented Jannan's letter to Essie Scofield, asking for an appointment with his client at the law office, with a short communication laying before her the condition in which he had found Eunice, his knowledge of her neglect to provide their daughter with the funds he had sent for that purpose, and definite plans for his complete control of the child. At the despatch of this he felt that his duty, where Essie as a formal parent resided, was ended. It was now only a question of an agreement on terms. He got no reply, other than a notification from Stephen Jannan that a meeting had been arranged for the following week. And, at eleven o'clock, on a clear, thin blue winter morning, he mounted, with Eunice, to the entrance of Jannan's offices on Fourth Street.

Essie Scofield, in widespread mulberry silk with tight sleeves and broad steel buttons, a close brimmed blue bonnet filled with lilacs and tied with an old rose ribbon, was more compelling than Jasper Penny had remembered her for, actually, years. A coffee-coloured India shawl, with a deep fringe and trace of a lining checkered in cherry and black slipping from her shoulders, toned her appearance to a potential dignity.

"Eunice," she exclaimed, as the child entered, "do come here at my side!" A small, cold mouth was silently raised for a straining embrace. Stephen Jannan proceeded at once, addressing Essie Scofield. "Mr. Penny informs me that he has written you explaining our purpose. I have already instructed you of the law in such a connexion, and there remains only your signatures to these papers. I begged you, if you will remember, to come with counsel, but since you have not done that it will be best for you to read this deed, which is quite clear in its intent."

Essie gazed dramatically at the paper the lawyer tended her. "It means," she said, "that I am to lose Eunice, and because I cannot offer her any advantages beyond those of a slim purse. I am a most unfortunate creature." Jasper Penny scraped his chair back impatiently, but Stephen enforced his silence with a gesture. "While my client understands that no monetary consideration can compensate for the breaking of ties of affection," Stephen Jannan went on smoothly, "and while he offers none in payment to that end, still we feel that some material recognition should be due you. Have you anything to say, suggest, at this point?"

Essie Scofield's arm was about Eunice's waist. "I am to be parted from my little daughter," she exclaimed; "and my tears are to be stopped with

195

gold — an affectionate breast, a heart-wrung appeal, stilled by a bribe. That is the price paid by a trusting, an unsuspicious, female. Long ago, when a mere girl, dazzled by —"

"We won't go into that," Jannan interrupted, "but confine ourselves to the immediate development. By signing the paper in question, and accepting a sum of money, you surrender all claim to this child, known as Eunice Scofield."

"How will that affect my — my position in other ways?" she demanded, in a suddenly shrewd, suspicious tone. "Not at all," the lawyer assured her. She sobbed once, emotionally; and Eunice regarded her with a wide, unsparing curiosity. "A stranger to me," she gasped, with a paper white face and fluttering eyelids. Jasper Penny ejaculated sharply, "How much, Essie?" In a moment, he judged, familiar with a potential hysteria, she might faint, scream; there were clerks, people, in the next rooms. On the brink of collapse she hesitated, twisting her purple kid gloves.

"Ten thousand dollars," she said.

Stephen Jannan glanced swiftly at his cousin, and the latter nodded. "That is satisfactory," Jannan announced. "A mere formality — witnesses." Essie Scofield traced her signature in round, unformed characters; Jasper Penny followed with a hasty, small script; and Eunice, seated at the impressive table, printed her name slowly, blotting it

196

with a trailing sleeve. The lawyer swung back the door of a heavy safe, and took out a package of white bills of exchange on the Bank of Pennsylvania. Essie counted the notes independently, thrust the money into a steel-beaded reticule with silk cords, and rose, gathering together her cashmere shawl. She ignored Eunice totally in the veiled gaze she directed at Jasper Penny. "It is better," she told him, "if you write first when you expect to visit me. Really, the last time, with some friends there, you were impossible." He bowed stiffly. "Don't let a sense of duty bring you," she concluded boldly. "I get on surprisingly well as it is, as it is," she reiterated, and, he thought, her voice bore almost a threat.

When she had gone the two men sat gazing in a common perplexity at the child. Stephen Jannan's lips were compressed, Jasper Penny's face was slightly drawn as if by pain. Eunice was investigating a thick stick of vermilion sealing wax and a steel die. "Well?" Jannan queried, nodding toward the table. "I thought something of Burlington," Penny replied, "but decided to place her in New York. Want to give her all the chance possible. I intend, at what seems the proper time, to secure her my own name." He stopped the objection clouding his cousin's countenance. "We won't argue that, please. Now about the will; the provision must be explicit and generous. There, at

197

least, I am able to meet a just requirement." Jasper Penny's will was produced, a codicil projected, appended, and witnesses recalled.

"I wanted to inquire about Miss Brundon," Jasper said finally, the business despatched. "She seems to me very fragile for the conducting of an Academy. Is there no family, men, to support her? And her institution — does it continue to progress well?"

"Very." Jannan replied to the last question first. "Her children come from the best families in the city; and, under my advice, her charges are high. She has a brother, I believe, a cotton merchant of New Orleans, and quite prosperous. But he has a large family, and Susan will not permit him to deprive it of a dollar for her benefit. As you say, she is not strong; but in spite of that she needs no man's patronage. The finest qualities, Jasper, the most elevated spirit. A little too conscientious, perhaps; and, although she is thirty-nine, curiously ignorant of the world; but rare . . . rare. It almost seems as if there were a conspiracy to keep ugly truths away from her."

Truths, Jasper Penny thought bitterly, such as had just been revealed in Stephen's office. There was, it seemed, nothing he could do for Susan Brundon. He envied the lawyer his position of familiar adviser, the ease with which the other spoke her name: Susan. He rose, fumbling with a jade seal. "Come, Eunice," he said, the lines deepening about his mouth and eyes. Stephen Jannan assisted him into the heavy, furred coat. "Well, Jasper," he remarked sympathetically, "if we could but look ahead, if we were older in our youth, yes, and younger in our increasing age, the world would be a different place." He held out to Eunice a newly minted Brazilian goldpiece. "Good-bye," he addressed her; "command me if I can be of any use." She clutched the gold tightly, and Jasper Penny led her out into the winter street. "We must have dinner," he said gravely. "With some yellow rock candy," she added, "and syllabubs."

XVI

H E returned to Myrtle Forge from New York
with a mingled sense of pleasure and the
feeling that his place was unsupportably
empty. The loneliness of which he had been increasingly conscious seemed to have its focus in his house.
The following morning he walked restlessly down the
short, steep descent to the Forge, lying on its swift
water diverted from Canary Creek. Unlike a great
many iron families of increasing prosperity, the
Pennys had not erected the unsightly buildings of
their manufacturing about the scene of their initial
activity and mansion. Jasper's father, Daniel
Barnes Penny, under whose hand their success had
largely multiplied, had grouped their first rolling mill
and small nail works by the canal at Jaffa, preserv-
ing the pastoral aspect of Myrtle Forge, with its
farmland and small, ancient, stone buildings.

Jasper had only made some unimportant changes
at the Forge itself — the pigs were subjected to the
working of two hearths now, the chafery, where the
greater part of the sulphur was burned out, and the
finery. The old system of bellows had been replaced
by a wood cylinder, compressing air by piston into
a chamber from which the blast was regulated. A

blacksmith's shed had been added in the course of time, and a brick coke oven. He stopped at the Forge shed, filled with ruddy light and shadow, the ringing of hammers, and silently watched the malleable metal on the anvil. Flakes of glowing iron fell, changing from ruby to blue and black.

The Penny iron! The Forge had been operated continuously since seventeen twenty-seven, hammering out the foundation of his, Jasper's, position. He had taken a not inconsiderable place in the succession of the men of his family; in him the Pennys had reached their greatest importance, wealth. But after him . . . what? He was, now, the last Penny man. The foothold Gilbert had cut out of the wild, which Howat and Casimir — an outlandish name obviously traceable to his mother, the foreign widow — had, in turn, increased for Daniel and Jasper, would be dissipated. His great, great aunt, Caroline, marrying a solid Quaker, had contributed, too, to the family stamina; while her granddaughter, wedding a Jannan, had increased the social prestige and connections of the family. The Jannans, bankers and lawyers, had already converted the greater part of their iron inheritance into more speculative finance; and the burden of the industry rested on Jasper Penny's shoulders.

At his death the name, the long and faithful labour, the tangible monument of their endurance and rectitude, except for the tenuous, momentary fact of Eunice, would be overthrown, forgot. He was conscious of a strong inner protest against such oblivion. He had, of course, often before lamented the fact that he had no son; but suddenly his loss became a hundred times more poignant, regrettable. Jasper Penny caught again the remembered, oppressive odour of foxglove, the aromatic reek of brandy and oranges; one, in its implications, as sterile as the other. He was possessed by an overwhelming sense of essential failure, a recurrence of the dark mood that had enveloped him in leaving the Jannans' ball.

Yet, he thought again, he was still in the midstride of his life, his powers. His health was unimpaired; his presence bore none of the slackening aspect of increasing years. These feelings occupied him, speeding in a single cutter sleigh over the crisp snow of the road leading from his home to Shadrach Furnace, where Graham Jannan and his young wife had been newly installed in the foremens' dwelling. There was a slight uneasiness about Graham's lungs, in consequence of which he had been taken out of the banking house of an uncle, Jannan and Provost, and set at the more robust task of picking up the management of an iron furnace.

It was early afternoon; the sky was as dryly powdered with unbroken blue as was the earth with white. The silver bells and scarlet pompons of the harness crackled in the still, intense cold; and a blanched vapour hung about the horse's head. Jasper Penny,

202

enveloped in voluminous buffalo robes and fur, gazed
with an increased interest at the familiar, flowing
scene; nearby the forest had been cut, and suave,
rolling fields stretched to a far mauve haze of trees;
the ultramarine smoke of farmhouse chimneys everywhere climbed into the pale wash of sunlight; orderly
fence succeeded fence. How rapidly, and prosperous, the country was growing! Even he could remember wide reaches of wild that were now cultivated. The game, quail and wild turkey and deer,
was fast disappearing. The country was growing
amazingly, too, extending through the Louisiana
Purchase, State by State, to Mexico and the Texan
border. The era of the greatness of the United
States had hardly begun, while it was more than
probable that the greatness, the power, of the Penny
family faced an imminent destruction. His revolt
at this, joining the more personal sense of the emptiness of his existence, filled him with a bitter energy,
a determination to conquer, somehow, the obdurate
facts hemming him in.

The sleigh dropped over a rise into a shallow fold
of hills, with a collection of structures on a slope,
and a number of solid, small grey stone dwellings.
He glanced subconsciously at the stack of Shadrach
Furnace, and saw that it was in blast — a colourless,
lively flame, with a thin, white smoke like crumpled
muslin, playing about its base. The metallic ring of
a smithy rose at a crossing of roads, and, from the

cast house, drifted the refrain of a German song. He turned in by the comparatively long, low façade of the house where the Jannans were living.

A negro led the horse and sleigh back to a stable; and, briskly sounding the polished iron doorknocker, he let himself into the dining room, a chamber with a wide, pot-hung fireplace and plain mahogany consul tables with wood chairs brightly painted with archaic flowers and scrolls in gold. Standing at the far side of the room, delicately outlined against a low, deeply embrasured window, was Susan Brundon.

A slow tide of colour rose to her ordinarily pale cheeks, corresponding with a formless gladness permeating his own being. She wore ruffled lavender, with a clear lace pelerine caught at her breast by a knot of straw-coloured ribbon and sprig of rose geranium. "Mr. Penny," she said, with a little gasp of surprise; but her gaze was unwavering, candid.

"Why not?" he replied lightly. "I have a small interest in Shadrach. You are surprising — so far from that absorbing Academy."

"It's my eyes again," she explained. "I am obliged to rest. There is a very good assistant at the school; and Mary sweetly thought the country would do me good."

"It is really miraculous," Mary Jannan stated, entering from the kitchen; "she'll almost never. Weren't we lucky?" She was a small woman with smooth brown hair and an air of quiet capability. "And it's splendid to see you," she continued to

Jasper Penny. "Don't for a minute think you'll get off before to-morrow, perhaps not then. Graham is out, chop-chopping wood. Actually — the suave Graham." She indicated a high row of pegs for Jasper Penny's furs. "Everything is terribly primitive. Most of the furniture was so sound that we couldn't bring ourselves to discard it all, however old-fashioned. Little by little." Graham Jannan entered, a tall, thin young man with crisp, pale yellow hair and a clean shaven, sanguine countenance with challenging light blue eyes. He greeted the older man with a firm, cold hand clasp. "I suppose you've come out to discover what I have learned about iron. Well, I know now that a sow is not necessarily a lady, and that some blooms have no bouquet. Good rum has, though, after sleighing."

Upon alternately burning his fingers and throat with a steaming glass of St. Croix, Jasper Penny and Graham Jannan proceeded to the Furnace where, in the cast house, they watched the preparations for a flow of metal. The head founder, McQuatty, bearded to the eyes and swathed in a hide apron, stood at the Ironmaster's side. "The charcoal you'd get's not worth a bawbee," he complained; "soft stuff would hardly run lead. And where they'd cut six thousand cords of wood will no longer show more than four. Shadrach ought to put out twenty-eight tons of pig in a week; and you see the statements."

"Stone coal," Jasper Penny replied; "and a hot blast." He turned to describe the latter to Jannan.

" It'll come," the founder agreed, " and the quality will go." He went forward to tap the clay-sealed hearth. The liquid iron poured into the channels of its sand bed, sputtering and slowly fading to dingy grey. " I'd like you to take hold of this," Jasper Penny told the younger man; " great changes, improvements, are just over the hill. I'll miss them — a link between the old and the new. But you would see it all. The railroad will bring about an iron age; and then, perhaps, steel. I look for trouble, too — this damned States Rights. The South has been uneasy since the Carolina Nullification Act. It will be a time for action." He gazed keenly at Graham Jannan. A promising young man, he thought, with a considerable asset in his wife. A woman, the right woman, could make a tremendous difference in a man's capabilities.

He elaborated this thought fantastically at dinner, sitting opposite Susan Brundon. Mary Jannan wore orange crêpe, with black loops of ball fringe and purple silk dahlias; and, beside her, Miss Brundon's dress was noticeably simple. She volunteered little, but, when directly addressed, answered in a gentle, hesitating voice that veiled the directness, the conviction, of her replies. The right woman, Jasper Penny repeated silently. Ten, fifteen, years ago, when he had been free, he would have acted immediately on the feeling that Susan Brundon was exactly the wife he wanted. But no such person had appeared at that momentous period in his life.

However, then he had been a totally different being; perhaps the appreciation of Miss Brundon, her actual reality, lay for him entirely in his own perceptions. But if she would not have been the woman for him then, by heaven, she was now! He expressed this unaware of its wide implications, unconscious of the effect it would instantly have. The thing silently uttered bred an enormously increased need, the absolute determination that she was necessary to his most perfunctory being. The thought of her alone, he discovered, had been sufficient to give him a new energy, a sense of rare satisfaction.

Shortly expressed, he wanted to marry her; he had not, he told himself oddly, ever been married. The word had a significance which heretofore he had completely missed. A strange emotion stirred into being, a longing thrown out from his new desire, the late-born feeling of dissatisfaction; it was a wish for something in Susan Brundon which he experienced but could not name. Roughly stated it was a hunger to surround her with security, comfort, to fortify the, at best, doubtful position of life in death for her. Yet he acknowledged to himself that this regard for her safety was mostly the result of his own inner, blind striving. Her happiness had magically become his. Beyond that he was unable to penetrate.

After supper they gathered in the chamber beyond the dining room. Here Jasper Penny found an incongruous mingling of old and new furniture. There

207

was a high, waxed walnut desk and cabinet, severely
simple, and before it a chair with a back of elaborately carved and gilded tulips tufted in plum-coloured velvet. The thick carpet was a deep rose, and
the drapery of the mantel and windows garnet. A
painted hood of brilliant Chinese colours had been
fastened before what was evidently an open hearth,
for which a coal stove was substituted. On the middle of the floor was an oriental hassock in silver brocade; while a corner held a spinet-piano decorated in
roseate cupids, flower sprays and gold leaf. Again,
an old clock in Spanish mahogany, with a rudely
painted glass door, had been left on the wall.

Mary Jannan, at the piano, wove a delicate succession of arpeggios. She sang, in a small and
graceful voice, a cavatina, *Tanti Palpiti*. Then,
" Ah, que les amours . . . de beaux heurs." Jasper
Penny listened with an unconscious, approving pretence of understanding. But when, in the course of
her repertoire, she reached *Sweet Sister Fay*, and
The Horn of My Loved One I Hear, his pleasure
became active. Susan Brundon, on the hassock,
lifted her sensitive face to the mild candle light,
and its still pallor gave him a shock of delight. Her
hands were folded in the voluminous sweep of her
crinoline; the ribbons at her breast rose and fell
softly.

Jasper Penny and Graham were smoking long,
fragrant cigars that the former had produced from a
lacquered case, and Jannan had the ingredients of

the hot punch at his elbow. It amused the young man to persuade Susan Brundon to take a sip from his glass; and they all laughed at her subsequent gasping. Jasper Penny was astoundingly happy; his being radiated a warmth and contentment more potent than that of the St. Croix rum. It was accompanied by an extraordinary lightness of spirit, a feeling of the desirability of life. The memory of his greying hair had left him; not, it was true, to be replaced by the surging emotions of youth, but by a deep satisfaction.

Susan Brundon, Susan . . . the right woman. He marvelled again at the brightness of spirit that shone in her — like a flame through a fine paper lantern. Susan, at Myrtle Forge. His thought became concrete; he knew now, definitely, that he had determined to marry her. His peace of mind increased. There was no need for hurry, the mere idea was irradiating; yet there must be no unnecessary delay. Incontrovertibly he had passed forty. The best period in a man's life. They would go to the West Indies, he decided. A ring with a square emerald, and roses of pearls. It was, almost immediately, time to retire. His room, narrow with a sloping wall, had a small window giving on a flawless rectangle of snow like the purity of Susan Brundon.

As he lay in bed, staring wakefully against the dark, another memory crept into his thoughts — the echo of a small, querulous voice, " yellow rock candy and syllabubs." Eunice! A sudden consternation seized him as he realized the necessity of telling Susan fully about his daughter. No escape, evasion, was possible. If she discovered the existence, the history, of the child afterward — he lingered over the happiness that term implied — it would destroy her. This, he told himself, was not merely melodrama; he was thinking of her delicate spirituality, so completely shielded from the bald fatality of facts. An increasing dread seized him at the thought of the hurt his revelation would inflict on her. The interweaving of life in life, consequence on consequence, the unbroken intricacy of the whole fabric of existence, realized anew, filled him with bitter rebellion. The blind commitment of a vanished youth, potent after years, still hung in a dark cloud over Susan Brundon. He was conscious of the past like an insuperable lead weight dragging at his attempted progress. The secret errors of all the pasts that had made him rose in a haggard, shadowy troop about his bed, perpetuated, multiplied, against his aspirations of tranquil release.

Yet, he told himself, dressing in the bright flood of morning, if nothing perished but the mere, shredding flesh, one quality persisted equally with the other — the symbol of Essie Scofield was no more actual than Susan. He had breakfast early, with Graham Jannan; and, in a reviving optimism, arranged for the Jannans to bring Miss Brundon to Myrtle Forge for a night before her departure. He whirled away, in a sparkling veil of flung snow crystals, before the women appeared.

Susan Brundon would, naturally, shrink from what he must tell her; but he was suddenly confident of his ability to convince her of the superior importance of the actuality of what they together might make of the future. He was accustomed to the bending of circumstance to his will; in the end he would prove stronger than any hesitancy she might, perhaps, reveal. His desire to have her had grown to such proportions that he could not, for an instant, think of existence without her as an intimate part. He even mentally determined when he should go to the city, the jeweller's, for the square emerald and flowered pearls. He would do over the rooms where he had lived in the thin formality of his marriage with Phebe, settle an amount on Essie . . . shredding flesh. It would do the living woman no more injury than the dead. Oranges and brandy, satin and gold and ease.

He wrote, through Stephen Jannan, to Essie Scofield that afternoon, stating the generous terms of his final arrangement with her, making it plain that all personal contact between them had reached an end. Hereafter she must exclusively address any unavoidable communications to Mr. Jannan. She disregarded this in a direct, inevitably complaining, laborious scrawl. However, he could read through it her obvious relief at complete independence. She would, she thought, stay where she was for a little

. . . a period of perfunctory sentimentality followed. He destroyed the letter, turning with deep pleasure to the message from Graham Jannan that he would bring Susan Brundon and Mary to Myrtle Forge the following day.

His mother, with Amity Merken like a timid and reduced replica at her back, greeted the Jannans and Miss Brundon at the door. Jasper Penny came forward from the smoking room, to the right of the main entrance; where the men retired for an appetizer of gin and bitters. The older man was garbed with exact care. His whiskers were closely trimmed on either side of his severe mouth and shapely, dominant chin; and his sombre eyes, under their brows drawn up toward the temples, held an unusual raillery. Amity Merken, he learned, had desired to stay away from the supper table; but, to her distress, he forced her into a chair set by himself. Susan sat at the other end of the table, in the place that had been Phebe's. He gazed at her with a satisfaction without surprise; for it seemed to him that the woman beyond him had always occupied the fore of his existence. She wore pale grey, the opening at her neck filled with soft lace and pinned with a garnet brooch, and a deep-fringed, white silk shawl. The conversation was ambling, but, to Jasper Penny, pitched in a key of utter delight. He said little through supper; and, at its end, with Graham Jannan, immediately followed the others into the parlour.

212

There Mary Jannan repeated her songs, French, English and Italian; and Jasper Penny listened with a poignant, emotional response. Graham and his wife had arranged to sleigh back to Shadrach Furnace that evening; but Susan Brundon was to stay at Myrtle Forge, and take the train from Jaffa tomorrow. The Jannans, finally, departed; and Jasper Penny, showing Susan through the chambers of the lower floor, succeeded in delaying her, seated, in the smoking room.

XVII

NOW that the moment which he had so carefully planned had arrived he was curiously reluctant to precipitate Susan and himself into the future. The lamps on a mantel, hooded in alabaster, cast a diffused radiance over Susan's silvery dress, on her countenance faintly flushed above the white folds of the shawl. "What is that sound?" she suddenly queried. "I heard it all through supper and before. It seems to live in the walls, the very air, here."

"The trip hammer of Myrtle Forge," he replied gravely. "I suppose it might, fancifully, be called the beating of the Penny heart; it does pound through every associated stone; and I have a notion that when it stops we shall stop too. The Penny men have all been faithful to it, and it has been faithful to us, given us a hold in a new country, a hold of wrought iron."

"How beautiful," she murmured; "how strong and safe!"

"It pleases me that you feel that," he plunged directly into his purpose; "for I intend to offer you all the strength and safety it contains." Her hands fluttered to her cheeks; a sudden fear touched
214

her, yet her eyes found his unwaveringly. " If that were all," he continued, standing above her, " if I had only to tell you of the iron, if the metal were flawless, I'd be overwhelmed with gladness. But almost no iron is perfect, the longest refining leaves bubbles, faults. Men are like that, too . . . Susan." She grew troubled, sensitively following his mood; her hands were now pressed to her breast, her lips parted. She was so bewilderingly pure, in her dim-lit, pearly haze of silk, that he paused with an involuntary contraction of pain at what must follow.

" The child, Eunice," he struggled on; " I couldn't leave her at the Academy because it might injure you. I had brought her in a most blind egotism; and so I took her away. She is my daughter."

He saw that at first she totally missed the implication of his words. " But," she stammered, " I was told you had no . . . how would that —? " Then she stopped as sharply as if a hand had compressed her throat. A vivid mantle of colour rose in her face; she made a motion of rising, of flight, but sank back weakly. " It is criminally indelicate to speak to you of this," he said, " but it was absolutely necessary. I want to marry you; in that circumstance a lie would be fatal, later or sooner."

She attempted to speak, her lips quivered, but only a low gasp was audible. It was worse, even, than he had feared. Now, however, that he had told her, he felt happier, more confident. Surely, after a little, she would forgive, forget. " I want

to marry you," he repeated, torn with pity at her
fragility, her visible suffering. " All that might
hurt you has been put out of my life, out of our
future. The way is open before us, the refining. I
would do anything to spare you, believe that; but
the truth, now, best."

" Always," she said in a faint voice. " I am trying to — to realize. Oh! I suppose such things do
occur; but the child herself, you — don't see how
that, so near —" she broke off, gazing wide-eyed out
of her misery. He was conscious of the dull, regular
beat of the Forge hammer. God, how the imperfec-
tions persisted! But, he told himself savagely, in
the end the metal was steadfast. He would, certainly, overcome her natural revulsion from what she
had just heard. The colour had left her cheeks,
violet shadows gathered about her eyes; she seemed
more unsubstantial than ever. He would repay
again and again the suffering he had brought her.
Having declared himself he was almost tranquil;
there was a total absence of the impetuous emotion-
alism of youth, the blind tyranny of desire. His
feeling was deeper, and accompanied by a far more
involved philosophy of self-recognition. At the same
time, while acutely conscious of his absolute need of
Susan Brundon, he was at a loss to discover its essence, shape. Before he had known her he had been
obsessed by a distaste for his existence; he had desperately wanted something without definition . . .
And Susan was that desire, delicate, clear-eyed

216

Susan. Yet, still, the heart of her escaped him.

Jasper Penny had told himself that his new dissatisfaction was merely the result of his accumulating years; but, beyond the fact that such an increase might have brought him different and keener perceptions, that explanation was entirely inadequate. He wanted a quality beyond his experience, beyond, he realized, any material condition — Susan Brundon, yes; but it was no comparatively simple urge of sex, the natural selection of the general animal creation. There was no question of passionate importunities; those, here, would be worse than futile; all that he desired was beyond words, moving in obedience to a principle of which he had not caught the slightest glimpse. Yet, confident of his ultimate victory, he maintained the dominating presence of a black Penny.

Susan Brundon had sunk back into the depths of her capacious chair; she seemed utterly exhausted, as if she had been subjected to a prolonged brutal strain. But still her eyes sought him steady in their hurt regard. "There is so much that I can give you," he blundered, immediately conscious of the sterility of his phrase. "I mean better things — peace and attention and — and understanding. I won't attempt any of the terms usual, commonplace, at such moments, you must take them, where they are worthy, for granted. I only tell you a lamentable fact, and ask you to marry me, promise you the tenderest care —"

" I know that," she replied, with obvious difficulty, hesitation. " I'll not thank you. It is terribly difficult for me. I'd like to answer you as you wish, I mean reply to — to your request. But the other, the child, dragged about; there was such a distrust, a wariness, in her face."

" There is no good in thinking of that alone," he stated, with a return of his customary decision. " No one can walk backwards into the future. Try to consider only the immediate question, what I have asked you — will you marry me? "

" Is that all you have to explain? " she asked. " Is there, now, no one else that counts? " The edge of a cold dread entered his hopes. " If you refer to the child's mother," he said stiffly, " she is amply well taken care of, you need waste no sentimental thoughts on her."

" Ah! " Susan exclaimed, shrinking. Her hands closed tightly on the wide silk of her skirt. The fear deepened within him; it would be impossible to explain Essie to the woman before him. Essie, falsely draped in conventional attributes, defied him to utter the simple truth. He raged silently at his impotence, the inhibition that prevented the expression of what might be said for himself. Essie Scofield had, like every one else, lived in the terms of her being, attracting to herself what essentially she was; it was neither bad nor good, but inevitable. His contact with her had been the result of mutual qualities, qualities that were no longer valid. Yet to say that

218

would place him in a damnable light, give him the aspect of the meanest opportunist. Susan breathed, " That poor woman." It was precisely what he had expected, feared — the adventitious illusion! He had an impulse to describe to her, even at the price of his own condemnation, the condition in which he had found Eunice; but that too perished silently. Jasper Penny grew restive under the unusual restraint of his position.

" Do you mind — no more at present." Susan Brundon said. " I am upset; please, another time; if it is necessary. I feel that I couldn't answer anything now. I must go up; no, your mother will show me." She rose, and he realized that she would listen no further. There was an astonishing strength of purpose behind her deprecating presence. She was more determined than himself. He watched her walk evenly from the room, heard the low stir of voices beyond, with a feeling that he had been perhaps fatally clumsy. All that he had said had been wrong, brutally selfish. He had deliberately invited failure; he should have been patient, waited; given her a chance to know and, if possible, value him, come to depend on him, on his judgment, his ability in her welfare. But, in place of making himself a necessity, he had launched at once into facts which she must find hideous. She had said, " another time, if necessary." His mouth drew into a set line — there would be another and another, until he had persuaded, gained, her.

He lit a cigar, and walked discontentedly up and across the room. The sound of the Forge hammer again crept into his consciousness: the Penny iron — the fibre, the actuality, of the Penny men! He repeated this arrogantly; but the declaration no longer brought reassurance; the certainty even of the iron faded from him; he had failed there, too, digging a pit of oblivion for all that their generations of toil had accomplished. The past inexorably woven into the pattern of the future! Eunice, so soon wary, distrustful, Susan had seen that immediately, would perpetuate all that he wished dead — Essie and himself bound together, projected in an undesirable immortality through endless lives striving, like himself, to escape from old chains.

If he failed with Susan his existence would have been an unmitigated evil; the iron, his petty, material triumphs, would rust, but the other go on and on. His thoughts became a maze of pity for Eunice, infinite regret of the past, a bitter energy of hope for what might follow.

He turned with pride to his forging — long-wrought charcoal iron; the world would know no better. Still, with his penetration of the future, he realized that the old, careful processes were doomed. He had difficulty in assembling enough adequate workmen to fill the increasing contracts for bar iron and rails now; and the demand, with the extension of steam railways, would grow resistlessly. More wholesale methods of production were being utilized daily; he was one of the foremost adherents of "improvement"; but suddenly he felt a poignant regret at the inevitable passing of the old order of great Ironmasters, the principalities of furnaces and forges. He was still, he felt, such a master of his men and miles of forests and clearings, lime pits and ore banks, coal holes, mills, coke ovens, hearths and manufactories. He might still drive to Virginia through a continuous line of his interests; his domination over his labourers, in all their personal and industrial implications, was patriarchal; he commanded, through their allegiance and his entire grasp on every iota of their living, their day's journey; but, he told himself, he was practically the last of his kind.

New and different industrial combinations were locking together in great agglomerations of widely-separated activities; the human was superseded by the industrial machine, where men were efficient, subservient cogs in a cold and successful automaton of business. A system of general credit was springing up; the old, old payments in kind, in iron or even meal and apparel, or gold, had given place to reciprocal understandings of deferred indebtedness. The actual thousands of earlier commerce were replaced by theoretical millions. His own realty, his personal property, because of such understandings, were outside computation. They were, he knew, reckoned in surprising figures; but in a wide-spread panic, forced liquidation, the greater part of his

221

wealth would break like straw. It was the same with the entire country.

His thoughts returned to Susan, to the longing for the peace, the inviolable security, she would bring to the centre, the heart, of his life. No material catastrophe could shape, deplete, her richness of spirit. Fragile as she was, with her need of rest, her diffidence and pallor, she yet seemed to Jasper Penny the most — the only — secure thing in the world. She defied, he murmured, death itself. Wonderful.

He moved slowly to his sombre bed room, with its dark velour hangings and ponderous black walnut furniture, precisely scrolled with gilt. The interior absorbed the light of a single lamp, robbing it of radiance. A clock deliberately struck the hour with an audible whirring of the spring. Jasper Penny took out from a drawer a tall, narrow ledger, its calf binding powdering in a yellow dust, with a blurring label, "Forgebook. Myrtle Forge, 1750." He sat, opening it on the arm of an old Windsor reading chair he had insisted on retaining among the recent upholstery, and studied the entries, some written in a small script with ornamental capitals and red lined day headings, others in an abrupt manner with heavy down strokes. The latter, he knew, had been made by his great grandfather, Howat.

"Jonas Rupp charged with three pair of woollen stockings . . . shoes for Minnie." Howat had been young when Minnie's shoes were new; twenty some-

thing — five or six. He must have married not long
after. Howat — like himself — a black Penny.
The special interest Jasper Penny felt for this particular ancestor grew so vivid that he almost felt
the other's presence in the room at his shoulder.
He consciously repressed the desire to turn suddenly
and surprise the shadowy and yet clear figure in the
gloom. The features of the youth so long gone, and
yet, too, he felt, the replica of his own young years,
were plain; the dark eyes, slanted brows, the impatient mouth.

His community of sympathy with the other, who
was still, in a measure, himself, was inexplicable; for
obviously Howat had escaped Jasper's blundering —
an early marriage, a son, the son whose name, like
his mother's, made such an exotic note in a long,
sound succession of Isabels and Carolines and Gil-
berts, was a far different tale from his own. Yet it
persisted. It seemed to him that the silence of the
room grew strained, there was the peculiar tension
of a muteness desperately striving for utterance.
He waited, listened, in a rigidity of which he was
suddenly ashamed; ridiculous. He relaxed; the
memory of his own youth flooded back, rapt him in
visions, scents, sounds. The premonitory whirring
of the clock spring sounded once more, followed by
the slow, increasing strokes . . . Again. His body
wavered, on the verge of sleep, and he straightened
himself sharply; then he rose and, putting back the
Forgebook, undressed.

Susan, at breakfast, her shoulders wrapped in a serious-toned pelerine, said little. Jasper Penny instinctively excluded her from a trivial conversation. She was, he decided, paler than usual, the shadows under her eyes were indigo. He was filled with self-condemnation. Mrs. Penny, gazing at her with a beady discernment, asked if her rest had been interrupted. " I am always an indifferent sleeper," Susan Brundon replied evasively. He followed her into the carriage that was to take her to the station at Jaffa; and, ignoring her slight gasp of protest, grasped the reins held by the negro coachman. However, they proceeded over the short distance to the town without speech. He was torn between a wish to spare her and the desire to urge his own purpose. But more immediately he wanted to make secure the near hour of his seeing her again. He asked, finally, " Will you be at the Jannans' this week, or are visitors received at the Academy? "

" No," she replied to the first; " and I have very little time between classes. You see, they fill the whole day, tasks and pleasures. It is difficult for me to — to talk on a generality of themes with callers."

" I have no intention of being diffuse," he replied pointedly. " I could confine my entire conversation to one request —"

" Please," she interrupted pitiably. " I am utterly wretched now. The simplest gentility —" she paused, but her wish was clear. He restrained himself with difficulty. Drifting slowly across the scattered roofs of the town was the leaden smoke of his mills and fires; as they drove into the main street the thin crash of his iron was audible. Men everywhere bowed to him with marked respect. But the woman at his side sat erect, drawn away from him, unmoved by all that, to the world, he was. There was an appalling quality in her aloofness from what, materially, he might advance in extenuation; the things so generally potent here were no more than slag. He searched within for what might bend, influence, her, for whatever he might have of value in her eyes. He found nothing. It was a novel and painful experience; and it bred in him a certain anger; he became merely stubborn. He declared to himself, with an oath, that he would gain her; and he pulled up his horses viciously at the station rack. This, too, hurt her; she exclaimed faintly at the brutally drawn bits. A man hurried forward to take her bag, and then, in a blowing of horn, a harsh exhaust of steam, she was gone. A last, hurried impression of her delicate profile on a small pane of glass accompanied him back to Myrtle Forge. There his mother regarded him with an open concern. "Something's on your mind," she declared. "I passed your door at midnight, and there was light under it. I've often told you about sitting up late."

"I'm getting along," he replied lightly. "You

225

fail to do justice to the weight of my increasing majority. But, in a little, you'll be astonished at my renewed youth." He became serious in speaking, conscious of the new life Susan would, must, bring into his existence.

XVIII

SINCE he had declared himself so decidedly
and at once, no hesitation was possible; he
must, he was aware, move remorselessly forward in assault. To sweep Susan Brundon into his
desire, overwhelm her defences — he called them
prejudices but immediately after withdrew that term
— offered the greatest, the only promise of success.
An obliterating snow fell for the following thirty
hours, and a week went by in the readjustment to
ordinary conditions of living and travel. But at
the end of that period Jasper Penny left Myrtle
Forge for the city, with a determined, an almost
confident, mouth, and a bright, hard gaze. Late
afternoon, he decided, would be the best time for his
appearance at the Academy. And the western sky
was a luminous, bright red when he passed under
the stripped, uneasy branches of the willow trees to
the school door.

Miss Brundon's office, rigorous as the corridor of
a hospital, had a table and uncompromising wooden
chairs on a rectangle of bluish-pink carpet; a glowing, round stove held a place on a square of gleaming, embossed zinc, while the remaining surfaces were
scrubbed oak flooring and white calcimine. A large

geographer's globe, a sphere of pale, glazed yellow traced in violet and thin vermilion and cobalt, rested on an involuted mahogany stand; and a pile of text books covered in gay muslin made a single, decisive note of colour.

She kept him waiting, he felt uneasily, a long while; perhaps she had a class; but he felt that that was not the reason for her delay. When she finally appeared in soft brown merino, with a deep fichu of old, dark lace, and black ribbons, she courageously held out a delightfully cool, smooth hand. " At first," she said directly, " I thought it would be better not to see you at all. Yet that wasn't genteel; and I felt, too, that I must speak to you. Even at the danger, perhaps, of trespassing into your privacy."

" I have given you the absolute right to do that," he told her. " It will only bring me pleasure, to — to suppose I interest you enough —"

" Ah, but you do," she cried with clasping fingers. " It has made my work here very difficult; the quiet has gone before echoes that I think every child must hear, echoes from spaces and things that appall me. Here, you see, I have lived so apart from others, perhaps selfishly, that I had grown accustomed to a false sense of peace. Only lessons and little questions, little hands. It seems now that I have been outside of life itself, in a cowardly seclusion. Yet it had always been that way; I didn't know." Her face was deeply troubled, the clear depths of her eyes held a new questioning doubt.

228

" It's because of that, mainly, I ask you to marry me," he replied, standing before the table at which, unconsciously, she had taken her place; " it is because of your astonishing purity. You are so beautiful; and this quiet, peace — you must have it all your life; it is the air, the garden air, for you to flower in. I can give it to you, miles of it, farther than you can see. All that you care for heaped about you. But not that only," he insisted, " for I realized that no one lives to whom such things are less; I can give you something more, not to be talked about; whatever my life has been it has at least brought me to your feet. I have learned, for you, that there is a thing men must have, God knows exactly what — a craving to be satisfied, a — a reaching. And that itself, the knowledge of such need, is not without value. Because of it I again, and shall again, if necessary, ask you to marry me."

She replied in a low voice. " You must marry the child's mother." For the first time she avoided him; bright blood burned in her cheeks; a hand on the edge of the table was straining, white. A sudden feeling of helplessness came over him, with, behind it, the ever-present edge of anger, of impatience. He took a step forward, as if to crush, by sheer insistence, her opposition; but he stopped. He lost entirely the sense of her fragile physical being; she seemed only a spirit, shining and high, and insuperably lovely. Then all feeling was lost but the realization that he could not — in any true sense —

live without her. " Susan," he said, leaning forward, " you must marry me. Do you care for me at all? "

Her breast rose and fell under the delicate contour of her wool gown. " The child's mother," she repeated, " you should marry her. How can you do differently? What can it matter if I care about you? " She raised a miserable face. " How can I? " she asked.

He could think of no other answer than to repeat his supreme necessity for her. He struggled to tell her that this was an altogether different man from Essie Scofield's companion; but his words were unconvincing, limited by the inhibition of custom. A transparent dusk deepened in the room accompanied by a pause only broken by the faint explosions of the soft coal. The power of persuasion, of speech, appeared to have left him. There must be some convincing thing to say, some last, all-powerful, argument. It eluded him. The exasperation returned, spreading through his being.

" Surely," she said laboriously, " there is only one course for you, for us all."

" I'll never marry Essie Scofield! " he declared bluntly. His voice was unexpectedly loud, unpleasant; and it surprised him only less than Susan Brundon. She drew back, and the colour sank from her cheeks; an increasing fear of him was visible. " In the first place," he continued, " Essie probably wouldn't hear of it. And if I managed that it would be only to make a private hell for us both. It would not, it couldn't, last a month. There is nothing magical in marriage itself, there's no general salvation in it, nothing to change a man or woman. Why, by heaven, that's what you have taught me, that is the heart of my wanting you. You must feel it to understand." He circled the table and laid a hand on the back of her chair. "Susan."

Her head was bowed, and he could see only her smooth, dark bands of hair and the whiteness of her neck. "Susan," he said again. "A second wrong will not cure the first. If one was inexcusable the other would be fatal. Married — to some one else, with yourself always before me — surely you must see the impossibility of that. And am I to come to nothing, eternally fail, because of the past? Isn't there any escape, any hope, any possibility? You don't realize how very much will go down with me. I am a man in the middle of life, and haven't the time, the elasticity, of youth. A few more years to the descent. But, with you, they could be splendidly useful, happy; happy, I think, for us both. I know that a great many people would say as you have, but it is wrong in every aspect, absolutely hopeless. Essie's values are totally different from yours; she has her own necessities; one measure will not do for all women."

She rose and stood facing him, very near, her crinoline swaying against him, and said blindly, "You shall marry her."

231

"I'll be damned if I do," Jasper Penny asserted. "I will marry you, you," he whispered, with his lips against the fineness of her ear. Her hands were on his shoulders; but she neither drew herself into his embrace nor repulsed him. He wanted to crush her softness in his arms, to kiss her still face into acquiescence. The quality, the kind, of his need made it impossible. She slipped back without a sound into her chair, drooping forward over the table.

A sharp pity invaded him, holding him back from her, silencing the flow of his reasoning and appeal. It defeated, in the stirring tenderness of its consideration, his purpose. He could not continue tormenting her, racking her delicate, taut sensibilities by a hard insistence. He withdrew quietly, to where his hat and stick rested on a chair, and gathered them up. Still she didn't move, raise her head, break the low fumbling of the soft coal. He could no longer distinguish her clearly, she was blurring in a dusk deeping so imperceptibly that it seemed a gradual failing of his vision. The geographer's globe appeared to sway slightly, like a balloon tied to a string; the gay muslin of the piled text books had lost their designs. Suddenly the room without motion, the approaching night, the desirable presence of the woman growing more immaterial, more shadowlike to elude his reaching hands, presented a symbol, an epitome, of himself. Day fading swiftly into dark; dissolving the realities of table and flesh and

232

floor; leaving only the hunger, the insuperable inner necessity and sense of loss.

"Good-bye," he breathed. Jasper Penny saw that she raised her head, he caught the glimmering pallor of her face. But she said nothing, and sank back into the crumpled position on the table. He went out, closing the door of the office, shutting her into the loneliness of her resolve, her insistence.

In the familiar rooms at Sanderson's Hotel he revolved again and again all that she had said. For a little he even endeavoured to inspect calmly the possibility of a marriage with Essie Scofield. Steeped in Susan's spirit he thought of it as a reparation, to Eunice, perhaps to Essie, but more certainly to an essence within himself. But immediately he saw the futility of such a course; the inexorable logic of existence could not be so easily placated, its rhyming of cause and effect defeated. All that he had told Susan Brundon recurred strengthened to an immovable conviction. The thought of marrying Essie was intolerable, farcical; to the woman herself it would mean utter boredom. Such a thing must lead inevitably to a greater misfortune than any of the past. Susan, in her resplendent ignorance of facts, failed to realize the impossibility of what she upheld. No, no, it was out of the question.

He wondered if he had progressed in the other, his supreme, wish. And he felt, with a stirring of blood, that he had. Susan cared for him; her action had made that plain. That was a tremendous advantage; with another he would have thought it conclusive; but not — not quite with Susan Brundon. He had a deep regard for her determination, so surprising in the midst of her fragility. Yet, if pity had not prevented him, this afternoon, in her office, he might have forced her to a sharper realization of a more earthly need, the ache for sympathy, consolation, the imperative cry of self. That was his greatest difficulty, to overcome her lifelong habit of thinking of others before herself. Such, he knew, was the root of her appeal for Essie, rather than a cold, dogmatic conception. Self-effacement.

At this a restive state followed; personally he had no confidence in the sacrifice of individual aims and happiness. Any course of that sort, he told himself, in the management of his practical affairs, would have resulted in his failure. There were a hundred men in the country plotting for his overthrow, anxious to take his position, scheming to undersell him, to discover the secret of the quality of his iron rails. Others he had deliberately, necessarily, ruined. No good would have been served by his stepping aside, allowing smaller men to flourish and annoy him, cut down his production by inconsiderable sales. He, and his family, had built a great, yes, and beneficial, industry by ruthlessly beating out a broad and broader way for their progress. It was needful to gaze fixedly at the end desirable and move in the straightest line possible.

Susan stopped by the way. A thousand little acts

234

of alleviation, at best temporary, interrupted her living. Children, not hers, dragged at her skirt. How much better for her to have a child of her own. Their child! A great deal that had been vague in his thoughts became concrete at that last period; not only the possible succession of the iron, but the comprehension that a child now, before the increasing sterility of multiplying years, would be an image of all his inmost craving and which must else be lost.

Eunice was different. Pity, mingled with a rigid sense of his duty and a faint accent of parenthood, comprehended his feeling for her. He stated this to himself clearly, admitting what delinquency it carried. It was, simply, an incontrovertible fact; and it was his habit to meet such things squarely. A black Penny, he had no impulse to see existence in imposed sentimental or formally moral conceptions. From all this he returned with a feeling of delight to his personal longing for Susan Brundon; he saw her bowed over the table in an exhaustion almost an attitude of surrender. A slender, pliable figure in soft merino and lace. He saw her beyond the candles of Graham Jannan's supper table, a rose geranium at her breast. The motto of the bon bon partially returned:

> ". . . ange du ciel . . . je t'aime!
> ". . . le bon heur supreme!"

XIX

IN the morning he walked over to Stephen Jannan's office on Fourth Street. The day was unexpectedly warm, and a mist rose about the wet bricks of the city. He proceeded directly into Stephen's private enclosure. " I was about to write you," the latter stated. " It's well enough for you to direct Mrs. Scofield to confine her pleas to me, and comparatively simple to picture her drawing a quarterly sum in an orderly manner; but how you are going to realize that happy conception is increasingly beyond me. I have to point out to her daily — a great nuisance it is — that she cannot have her income before it is due. Heaven knows what she has done with the other money in so short a while. She hasn't moved, apparently increased her establishment; at your direction the bills were settled, and heaven knows she had no reluctance in presenting all that were permissible and a number doubtful. There is, of course, one probability."

Jasper Penny's thoughts returned to the stony, handsome youth he had seen in the company of Essie's friends, to the insinuations of the woman who had been removed protesting her superiority and warning him against a " tailor's dummy." Well, it was no longer his affair what Essie did with her

money, what in her affections remained unimpaired.
Rather it was reassuring that she had so promptly
found solace; it enlarged his own feeling of freedom. " It got worse, yesterday," Stephen Jannan
continued; " she came to the office, insisted on seeing
me. Luckily I was busy with a mastership that
kept me over three hours. But she left, I was told,
with the air of one soon to return. She was brandied
with purpose. There is no end, Jasper, to what I
am prepared to do for you; but, my dear fellow,
neither of us can have this. She wept. My young
gentlemen were pierced with sympathetic curiosity.
You must realize, Jasper, that you are not a spar-
row, to float unnoticed from ledge to ledge."

An angry impotence seized Jasper Penny. He
was tempted to have Stephen Jannan turn over to
Essie, at once, a conclusive sum of money. That
would put an end to any communication between
them, provide her with the power of self-gratification
which for Essie Scofield spelled forgetfulness . . .
For a little, he was obliged, wearily, to add. Together with such a young man as he had seen in her
house her capacity for expenditure would be limitless. She would come back to him with fresh demands, perhaps at an inconceivably awkward time,
in a calculated hysteria — he had cause to know —
surprisingly loud and convincing. Susan must be
absolutely secured against that possibility. He
could not help but think of the latter as yielding in
the end, married to him.

237

He gazed at Stephen Jannan in a sombre perplexity. "A nuisance," the other nodded. "Only time, I suppose, and the most rigid adherence to your statements will convince the lady of what she may expect. In the meanwhile, frankly, we had better put it in some other hands; not so much on my account as your own — the sympathetic young gentlemen, you see. That can be easily arranged."

Jasper Penny was not thinking of the material Essie, the present, concrete problem; but he was once more absorbed in the manner in which her influence followed, apparently shaped, his existence. He was again appalled by the vitality of the past; the phrase itself was an error, there was no past. All that had gone, that was to come, met ceaselessly in the present, a confusion of hope and regret. It was evident that he would have to see Essie again, and explain that what she had from him depended entirely on her reciprocal attitude. This could only be satisfactory in person. He would go to her at once, to-day. An enormous reluctance to enter her house again possessed him. The mere act had the aspect of an acknowledgment of her continued potency, her influence over him. He put it off as long as possible, and it was past five when he finally walked slowly toward her door.

She was in; and he saw, on the hall stand, a silk hat and overcoat cut in an extreme of current fashion. The servant preceded him above, toward the room usual for casual gatherings; and he heard a sudden low murmur, expostulation, follow the announcement of his name. Essie Scofield appeared at the top of the stairs. "Come up," she said in a hesitating, sullen voice. He mounted without reply. As he had expected Daniel Culser was present, and rose to greet him negligently, from a lounging attitude on the sofa. His coat, cut back to the knees, was relentlessly tapered, the collar enormously rolled and revered, and a white Marseilles waistcoat bore black spots as large as a Bolivian half dollar; while a black scarf, it was called the Du Casses, fell in an avalanche of ruffles. He moved toward the door, fitting his coat carefully about his slim waist. "I'm away, Essie," he proclaimed.

"When will you come again, Daniel?" she asked with an oppressive humility. She gazed at Jasper Penny with a momentary delay; then, with an utter disregard of his presence, laid her hands on the younger man's shoulders. "Soon," she begged. Obviously ill at ease he abruptly released himself. "I don't care," she cried defiantly; "I'll tell the whole world you are the sweetest man in it. Jasper's nothing to me nor I to him. And I'm not afraid of him, of what he might threaten, either. Stay, Daniel, and you'll see. I will look out for us, Dan."

Her unexpected frankness was inevitably followed by an awkward silence. Daniel Culser finally cursed below his breath, avoiding Jasper's cold inquiring gaze. "I'm glad I said it," Essie proceeded; "now he knows how things are." She went up again to the younger, and laid a clinging arm about his shoulders. " I'm mad about you, Daniel, you know it; there's nothing I wouldn't do for you, give you if I could. Isn't he beautiful? " she fatulously demanded of Jasper Penny.

" You are making a fool of yourself and me," the subject of her adulation roughly declared. He removed her arm so forcibly that the scarlet print of his fingers was visible on her soft, dead white skin. " Probably you have gone and spoiled everything. And remember what I said. I am a man of my word."

Jasper Penny dryly thought that the term man was singularly inappropriate in any connection with the meticulously garbed figure before him. Essie would have a difficult time with that stony youth. She regarded him with eyes of idolatry, drawing her fingers over the sleeve impatiently held aside from her touch. " I'm going," he stated once more, impolitely; but she barred him at the door. " I want you to stay," she cried excitedly; " hear what I am going to say, what I am going to do for you." She advanced toward Jasper Penny. " I asked that Jannan for more money because I had given Daniel all I had, and I wanted still more, to give him. I'll demand things all my life for him; everything I have is his." She gasped, at the verge of an emotional outburst. Her heart pounded unsteadily beneath an adventitious lace covering; her face was leaden with startling daubs of vermilion paint. " Give me

240

a great deal of money, now, at once . . . so that I can go to Daniel with my hands full."

"That is why I came here," Jasper Penny replied; "to tell you that you must not use up your income at once, on the first week, almost, of its payment; because you will be able to get no more until another instalment is due. I haven't the slightest interest in where your money goes, it is absolutely your own; but I cannot have you after it every second day. The administration will be put in a different quarter, rigidly dispensed; and any continued inopportunities will only result in difficulties for yourself."

She cursed him in a gasping, spent breath. Essie looked ill, he thought. Daniel Culser, listening at the door, made a movement to leave, but the woman prevented him, hanging about his neck. "No! No!" she exclaimed. "It will be all right, I can get it . . . more. Be patient." Jasper Penny walked stiffly to the exit, where he paused at the point of repeating his warning. Essie Scofield was lifting a quivering, tear-drenched face to the vexation of the fashionable youth. He was attempting to repulse her, but she held him with a desperation of feeling. The elder descended the stairs without further speech.

Outside, the warmth of the day had continued into dusk. The mist had thickened, above which, in a momentary rift, he could see the stars swimming in removed constellations. He was wrapped in an utter loathing of the scene through which he had passed, his undeniable part in it. It was all hideous beyond words. His late need, his sense of void and illimitable longing, tormented him ceaselessly. He was sick with rebellion against life, an affair of cunning traps and mud and fog. Above the obscured and huddled odium of the city the distances were clear, serene. Above the degradation . . . Susan. A tyrannical desire to see her possessed him, an absolute necessity for the purification of her mere presence. Unconsciously he quickened his step, charged with purpose; but he couldn't go to the Academy now; it was six o'clock. He must delay an hour at least. Habit prompted him to a supper which he left untried on its plates, the lighting of a cigar, quickly cold, forgot. At seven he hurried resolutely over the dark streets with the dim luminosity of occasional gas lamps floating on the unstirring white gloom. The bricks under foot were soggy, and the curved sign above her entrance, the bare willows, dropped a pattering moisture.

She saw him immediately, not in the familiar office, but in a hall laid with cold matting and nearly filled by a stairway, lit with a lamp at the further end. " I am sorry," she told him; " I have no place to take you. The rhetoric mistress is correcting papers there," she indicated the shut door. He made no immediate answer, content to gaze at her sensitive, appealing countenance. " It is so warm," she said finally, colouring at his intentness, " and I

242

have been indoors all day. I might get my things. We could, perhaps . . . a walk," she spoke rapidly, her head bent from him. She drew back, then hesitated. "Very well," he replied. Susan disappeared, but she quickly returned, in a little violet bonnet bound and tied with black, and a dark azure velvet cloak furred at her wrists and throat. She held a muff doubtfully; but, in the end, took it with her.

Outside, the mist and night enveloped them in a close, damp veil. They turned silently to the right, passing the narrow mouth of Currant Alley, and Quince Street beyond. The bricks became precarious, and gave place to a walk of boards; the corners about a broad, muddy way were built up; but farther on the dwellings were scattered — lighted windows showed dimly behind bare catalpas, iron fences enclosed orderly patches between sodden flats, gas lamps grew fewer.

A deep, all-pervading contentment surrounded Jasper Penny, an unreasoning, happy warmth. He said nothing, his stick now striking on the boards, now sinking into earth, and gazed down at Susan, her face hid by the rim of her bonnet. This companionship was the best, all, that life had to offer. He felt no need to importune her about the future, their marriage; curiously it seemed as though they had been married, and were walking in the security, the peace, of a valid and enduring bond. There was no necessity for talk, laborious explanation, periods infinitely more empty than this silence. They walked as close to each other as her skirt would permit; and at times her muff, swinging on a wrist, would brush softly against him. How strangely different the actual values of existence were from the emphasized, trite moments and emotions. In the middle of his life, at the point of his greatest capability for experience, his most transcendent happiness came from the present, the deliberate, unquestioning walk with Susan, the aimless progress through an invisible city and under a masked clear heaven of stars. No remembered thrill compared with it, reached the same height, achieved a similar dignity of consummation.

The way became more uneven; low clustered sheds rose out of the darkness against a deeper black beyond, and they came to the river. The bank was marshy, but a track of pounded oyster shells, visible against the mud, led to a wharf extending into the solid, voiceless flow of the water. Jasper Penny stood with Susan gazing into the blanketing gloom. A wan, disintegrated radiance shone from a riding light in the rigging of a vessel, and a passing warm blur flattened over the wet deck as a lantern was carried forward. No other lights, and no movement, rose from the river; no sound was audible at their back. The city, from the evidence of Jasper Penny's sensibilities, did not exist; it had fallen out of his consciousness; suddenly its bricked miles, its involved life stilled or hectic, stealthy in the dark, seemed a thing temporary, adventitious; he had an extraordinary feeling of sharing in a permanence, a continuity, outlasting stone, iron, human tradition. He had been swept, he thought, into a movement where centuries were but the fretful ticking of seconds. "Outside death," he said fantastically, unconsciously aloud. A remarkable sentence recurred to him, the most profound, he told himself, ever written: "Before he was I am." Its vast implications easily evaded his finite mind, just as the essence of his present rapture — it was no less — lay beyond his grasp. He lingered over it; gave it up . . . returned to Susan.

"Wonderful," she said gravely, with a comprehensive wave of her muff. And her simplicity thrilled him the more with the knowledge that she shared his feeling. She drew up the fur collar of her cloak, shivered; and, in the wordless harmony that pervaded them, they turned and retraced their way.

The rhetoric mistress had left the office with a low turned lamp, and Jasper Penny stopped, taking the furred wrap from Susan's shoulders. She slowly untied the velvet strings of her bonnet, and laid it on the table. She extended her hands toward him, and, taking their cool slightness, he drew her to him. She rested with the fragrance of her cheek against his face, with her hands pressed to his breast. They stood motionless; he closed his eyes, and she was gone. He was confused in the dimness empty except for himself, and fumbled with his gloves. Susan's wrap lay limply over a chair; the damp bonnet ribbons trailed toward the floor. He looked slowly about, noting every object — a pile of folded yellow papers, the stove, the globe bearing a quiver of light on its varnished surface.

The willow trees and board above the entrance were dripping ceaselessly; the lights of the city, increasing at its centre, like the discs of floating sunflowers. If he slept he was unaware of it, the magic joy so equally penetrated his waking and subconscious hours, the feeling of an elevation higher than years and mountains was so strong. The morning, he found, was again cold, and clear. He must go out to Jaffa, where new blast machines demanded attention; but, the day after —

His thoughts were broken by a sharp rap on the outer door. Mr. Stephen Jannan was below, and demanded to see him immediately. Stephen's appearance at the hotel at that early hour, he recognized, was unusual. But a glance at his cousin's serious aspect showed him at once that the reason was urgent. Stephen Jannan, as customary, was particularly garbed; and yet he had an expression of haste, disturbance. He said at once, in the bedroom where Jasper Penny was folding his scarf,

"That young waster, Culser, Daniel Culser, was shot and killed in Mrs. Scofield's house last evening."

The ends of the scarf fell neglected over the soft,

cambric frills of his shirt. Jasper Penny swallowed dryly. " At what time? " he asked.

" He was seen in the Old White Bear Tavern at about seven, then apparently he went back to the woman's. The servant said he found the body at something past nine, and that there had been no other caller but yourself."

His hearer expressed a deep, involuntary relief. " I was there late in the afternoon," he acknowledged; " but I left around six." Stephen Jannan, too, showed a sudden relaxation. " I have already sent a message to the Mayor," he continued; " confident that you would clear yourself without delay. Mrs. Scofield's history is, of course, known to the police. You have only to establish your alibi; she, Essie Scofield, can't be found for the moment. She may have taken an early stage out of the city; but it is probable that she has only moved into another police district. Just where were you, Jasper? "

The latter said stupidly, " Walking with Susan Brundon."

A swiftly augmented concern gathered on Stephen Jannan's countenance. " You were walking with Susan," he repeated increduously. " Yes," Jasper asserted, with a sharp inner dread. " You don't know, but I want to marry her." Stephen Jannan faced him with an exclamation of anger. " You want to marry her, and, in consequence, drag her, Susan, into the dirtiest affair the city is like to know

247

for years. Susan Brundon, with her Academy; all she has, all her labour, destroyed, ruined, pulled to pieces by slanderous tongues! By God, Jasper, what a beast you look! The most delicate woman alive, the one farthest from just this sort of muck, being sworn in the Mayor's office, testifying in an obscene murder case, before the Sheriff and Constable, and heaven knows what police and vilely curious!"

A sickening feeling of utter destruction seized on Jasper Penny, a dropping of his entire being from the heights of yesterday to the last degradation. He felt the blood leave his heart and pound dizzily in his brain, and then recede, followed by an icy coldness, a wavering of the commonplace objects of the room. He raised his fingers to his collar, stared with burning eyes at Stephen Jannan. "Everything spoiled," the latter said again; "her pupils will positively be taken from her at once by all the nice females. Her name will be pronounced, smiled over, in every despicable quarter of the city, printed in the daily sheets. I — I can't forgive you for this. Susan, our especial joy!"

Jasper Penny saw in a flash, as vivid and remorseless as a stab of lightning, that this was all true. The fatality of the past, sweeping forward in a black, strangling tide, had overtaken not only himself but Susan, too; Susan, in soft merino, in an azure velvet cloak; her face against his. "I shall go away at once," he said hoarsely. "I'll never appear, and they can think what they will. Then there will be no necessity for her to come forward. She shall be spared that, no matter what it costs."

" Romantic and youthful folly," Jannan declared; " loud-sounding and useless. How little you understand Susan — immediately it is known Culser was killed between seven and nine, whether you stay or go, she will come forward with the truth, free you from any suspicion. I tell you every detail will be canvassed, familiar to the boys on the street. A man important as yourself, with all your industries and money, and such salacity, together with Susan Brundon, will make a pretty story. If I had a chance, Jasper, I'm almost certain I'd sacrifice you without a quiver. How could you? Susan Brundon! Never telling her —"

" On the contrary, she knew everything. I am not so low as you seem to think."

" That has no importance now!" Stephen Jannan exclaimed impatiently. " All that matters is to make it as easy as possible for her. I have, I think, enough position, influence, to keep the dregs out. But there will be enough present, even then. Damnable insinuations, winks, cross-questioning."

His excitement faded before the exigencies of the unavoidable situation; he became cold, logical, legal. Jasper Penny listened, standing, to his instructions, the exact forecasting of every move probable at the hearing in the Mayor's chamber. " After that," Stephen added, " we can face the problem of Susan's future. She thinks tremendously of her school. It will fall to pieces in her hands. There can be no question of material assistance; refused her own brother.

" Now, understand — stay in these rooms until I send for you. See no one. I'll get on, go to Susan. The thing itself should be short; her character will assist you there. What a mess you have made of living, Jasper."

XX

IN the silence of the sitting room Jasper Penny heard diverse and yet mingled inner voices: Essie's younger, exuberant periods, her joy at presents of gold and jewelled trifles; changing, rising shrilly, to her last imploring sobs, her frantic embrace of the man that, beyond any doubt, she had herself killed. Running through this were the strains of a quadrille, the light sliding of dancing feet, and the sound of a low, diffident voice, Susan Brundon at the Jannans' ball. The voice continued, in a different surrounding, and woven about it was the thin complaint of a child, of Eunice, taken against her will from the Academy. These three, Essie and Susan and Eunice, combined, now one rising above the other, yet inexplicably, always, the same. Back of them were other, less poignant, echoes, flashes of place, impressions of associated heat or cold, darkness or light:

He saw the features of Howat Penny, in the canvas by Gustavus Hesselius, regarding him out of a lost youth; he recalled, and again experienced, the sense of Howat's nearness; integral with himself; merging into his own youth, no less surely lost, yet enduring. His mother joined the immaterial com-

pany, accents, rigid with pride in him. And penetrating, binding, all was the dull beat of the trip
hammer at Myrtle Forge. He had mechanically finished dressing, and stood absently twisting the drapery at a window. A fine tracery of lines had suddenly appeared about his eyes; the cold rays of the
winter sun, streaming over his erect figure, accentu-
ated the patches of grey plentiful in his hair.

He saw, on the street below, a parade of firemen,
in scarlet tunics and brass helmets, dragging a glittering engine. The men walked evenly abreast, at
cross ropes. A leader blew a brilliant fanfare on
an embossed, silver horn. Women passed, foreshort-
ened into circular bells of colour, draped with gay
pelerines and rich India shawls. He saw all and
nothing. The horn of the firemen sounded without
meaning on his distracted hearing. The flood of his
suffering rose darkly, oppressing his heart, choking
his breath. Perhaps if, as he had desired, he had
gone away, Susan would be spared. But Stephen
was right; nothing could keep her from the pronouncement of the words that would free him and
bind herself in intolerable ill. Her uprightness was
terrible. It would take her fearful but determined
into the pits of any hell. His hands slowly clenched,
his muscles tightened, in a spasm of anguish. God,
why hadn't he recognized the desperation in Essie's
quivering face! It would have been already too late,
he added in thought; it went back, back —

A knock sounded discreetly on the **door**; and,

opening it, he saw a young man, remembered as a law student in Stephen's office. " They are ready for you, sir, at the City Hall," he stated, in an over-emphasized, professional calm.

XXI

THE restrained curiosity and inaudible comments which greeted his passage through the lower floor of the hotel gave place to a livelier interest when he was readily recognized on the street. The news of the murder had, evidently, already become city property. He was indicated to individuals unaware of his identity, with a rapid sketch of the crime, of fabulous ascribed possessions, and hinted oriental indulgence. He strode on rapidly, his shoulders squared, his expression contemptuous, challenging; but within he was possessed by an apprehension increasing at every step. It was not, fortunately, far from Sanderson's Hotel to the City Hall; west on Chestnut Street they reached their destination at the following corner. The loungers from the trees before the State House had gathered, with an increasing mob aware of the hearing within, at the entrance to the municipal offices. The windows on either side of the marble steps were crowded with faces, ribald or blank or censorious, and Jasper Penny had to force his way into the building. He tried to recall if there was another, more private, ingress, through which Susan might be taken; but his thoughts evaded every dis-

cipline; they whirled in a feverish course about the
sole fact of the public degradation he had brought
on Susan Brundon. They passed the doors of civic
departments, he saw their signs — Water, City
Treasurer, and then entered the Mayor's chamber.

The latter was seated at a table facing the room
with his back to a wide window, opening on the
blank brick wall of the Philosophical Society building; and at one side the High Constable of the district in which the murder had been committed was
conversing with the Sheriff. Beside them, Jasper
Penny saw, there were only some clerks present and
three policemen. The Mayor spoke equably to the
Ironmaster, directed a chair placed for his con-
venience, and resumed the inspection of a number of
reports. He had a gaunt, tight-lipped face framed
in luxuriant whiskers, a severely moral aspect oddly
contradicted by trousers of tremendous sporting
plaid, a waistcoat of green buckskin cassimere, while
his silk hat held a rakish, forward angle. The Constable and Sheriff punctuated their converse by prodigious and dexterous spitting into a dangerously
far receptacle, and the clerks and police murmured
together. The Mayor, finally glancing at a watch
enamelled, Jasper Penny saw, with a fay of the bal-
let, spoke to the room in general. "Ten and past.
Well! Well! Where are the others? Who is to
come still, Hoffernan?"

"Mr. Jannan, sir; and a witness," a clerk answered. The other gazed at the paper before him.

"Susan Brundon," he read in a loud, uncompromising tone. Jasper Penny's eyes narrowed belligerently; he would see that these pothouse politicians gave Susan every consideration possible. He was, with Stephen, a far from negligible force in the city elections. "School mistress," the Mayor read on. "Never heard of her or her school. Ah —" Stephen Jannan had entered with Susan.

Jasper rose as she came forward, and the Mayor had the grace to remove his hat. She wore, he saw, the familiar dress of wool, with a sober, fringed black silk mantle, black gloves and an inconspicuous bonnet. She met his harried gaze, and smiled; but beneath her greeting he was aware of a supreme tension. There was, however, no perceptible nervousness in the manner of her accepting an indicated place; she sat with her hands quietly folded in her lap, the mantle drooping back over the chair. Stephen Jannan, facing the Mayor, made a concise statement in a cold, deliberate voice. "I now propose to show your honour," he finished, "that, between the hours in which Daniel Culser is said to have been shot to death, my client was peacefully in the company of Miss Brundon, strolling in an opposite quarter of the city."

"Hoffernan," the Mayor pronounced, waving toward the seated woman. The clerk advanced with a Bible; and, rising, Susan followed the words of the oath in a low, clear voice. To Jasper Penny the occasion seemed intolerably prolonged, filled with needless detail. Never had Susan Brundon appeared more utterly desirable, never had his need to protect, shield, her been stronger. He — protect her, he added bitterly; rather he had betrayed her, dragged her immaculate sweetness down into the foul atmosphere of a criminal hearing. His attention, fastening on the trivialities of the interior, removed him in a species of self-hypnotism from the actualities of the scene. He heard, as if from a distance, the questioning of the Mayor, "At what time, exactly, did you say? How did you know that?" Susan said, "I saw the clock at the back of the hall. I noticed it because I wondered if the younger children had retired."

"You say you walked with Mr. Penny — where? . . . How long did you remain at the river? No way of knowing. Seemed surprisingly short, I'll venture." Why didn't Stephen put an end to such ill-timed jocularity? "And Mr. Penny had spoken to you of his — his relations with Mrs. Scofield, the woman in whose house Culser was killed. Did he refer to her on this particular evening, standing by the river's brink?" Susan replied in the negative. "Did he seem ill at ease, worried about anything? Was he hurried in manner?"

To all of this Susan Brundon answered no, in a voice that constantly grew lower, but which never faltered, hesitated. The Mayor turned aside for a whispered consultation with the High Constable. The former nodded. "Have you any — shall we say — proprietary interest in Mr. Penny's affairs?" Her reply was hardly audible in the room stilled for what might be revealed. "No," she breathed, her gloved fingers interlacing. Jasper Penny's lips were drawn in a hard line; Stephen gazed fixedly at the floor. The Mayor gesticulated affably toward the lawyer. "That'll do," he declared. "Pleasure, Mr. Penny, to have you so completely cleared. I shall have to demand your assistance further, though — knowledge of Mrs. Scofield. And, in the case of her apprehension and trial, you will, of course, be called. Communication will be made through Mr. Jannan. No doubt in our mind now of the facts." A policeman opened the door and a surge of the curious pressed in. "Take her away," Jasper Penny whispered to Jannan; "this is damnable."

Susan rose, gathering up her mantle, and moved to Stephen Jannan's side. He offered his arm with a formal courtesy, and together they made their way out through the corridor. Jasper, lost in a moody abstraction, waited until they had vanished; and then, with a lowered head, walked rapidly over Chestnut Street in the direction of the terminus of the railroad for Jaffa. A brigade of cars was made up; he took a place and was immediately dragged on and over the viaduct to the plane and waiting engine beyond. He could see, from the demeanour of the loungers on the Jaffa platform, that the news of the murder, his connection with it, had preceded him.

258

To-morrow's papers would provide them with full accounts, the name of Susan Brundon among the maculate details. . . . The meanest cast boy in his works would regard him, the knowledge of Essie, with a leer.

His mother was at the main door of Myrtle Forge, pale but composed. "Take Mr. Penny's overcoat," she brusquely directed a servant. He had never seen a more delectable supper than the one awaiting him; and he tasted most of what found its way to his plate — he owed that to the maternal solicitude secretly regarding him, hastily masked as he met his mother's gaze. Sitting later in accustomed formality the dulness of a species of relief folded him. The minor sounds of his home, the deliberate loudness of an old clock, the minute warring of his mother's bone needles, her sister's fits of coughing, painfully restrained, soothed his harried being; subjected to an intolerable strain his overwrought nerves had suddenly relaxed; he sank back in a loose, almost somnolent, state. A mental indolence possessed him; the keen incentives of life appeared far, unimportant, his late rebellions and desires inexplicable. Even the iron was a heavy load; the necessity of constantly meeting new conditions with new processes, of uprooting month by month most with which the years had made him familiar, seemed beyond his power.

A faint dread crept into his consciousness; he roused himself sharply, straightened his shoulders, glanced about to see if his tacit surrender had been noticed — this lassitude creeping over him, the indifference, was, at last, the edge of the authentic shadow of age, of decay; it was the deadening of the sensibilities preceding death. He banished it immediately, and all his desire, his need, his sense of the horror of the past day, surged back, reanimated him, sent the blood strongly to its furthest confines. But, none the less, a vague, disturbing memory of the other lingered at the back of his perceptions; he had a fresh realization of the necessity for him to make haste, to take at once — before the hateful anodyne of time had betrayed his vigour — what life still, and so fully, held.

His desire for Susan increased to an intensity robbing it of a greater part of the early joy; it had, now, a fretful aspect drawing him into long and painfully minute rehearsals of his every contact with her, and of the disgraceful publicity brought upon her by his past. At the usual hour the hot wine appeared; the glassful was pressed on Amity Merken; his mother drank hers with the familiar, audible satisfaction. An old custom, an old compound, brought from Germany many years ago, binding, in its petty immortality, distant times, places, beings. He saw that his mother was noticeably less able than she had been the week before; her hands fumbled at her knitting, shook holding the glass. Her lined face quivered as she said good night. He bent and kissed a hot, dry brow, conscious of the

260

blanched skull under her fading colour, her ebbing warmth. He had done this, too — hastened her death; she must have suffered inordinately in her prideful affection. She said nothing, beyond the repeated admonition that he must not sit up into the night.

The next day he forced himself to read to the end the report of the murder in the *Gazette*. The references to Susan Brundon were as scant as, evidently, Stephen Jannan could arrange; but her name, her Academy, were invested with an odious publicity. Jasper Penny saw again that he was a person of moment; his part in the affair gave it a greatly augmented importance. Yet now the worst, he told himself, was at an end; the publicity would recede; after a decent interval he could see Susan.

This mood was interrupted by an imperative communication from Stephen — he must be in the other's office at eleven o'clock to-morrow. Nothing more definite was said; but Jasper Penny was not wholly surprised to see Essie Scofield huddled in a chair at the lawyer's table. She had made an attempt at the bravado of apparel, but it had evidently failed midway; her hair hung loosely about a damp brow, the strings of her bonnet were in disarray, a shawl partially hid a bodice wrongly fastened. Her face was apathetic, with leaden shadows and dark lips ceaselessly twisting, now drawn into a petulant line, now drooping in childish impotence. She glanced at him fleetly as he entered, but said nothing. Robbed of the pretensions of pride, stripped of feminine subterfuge, she was appalling. He involuntarily recalled the Essie who had swept him into a riot of emotion — a vivid and palpitating creature radiating the exuberance of careless health and youth. She could not, he calculated, be beyond thirty-seven now. He abruptly ceased his speculation, turned from her, with a feeling of impropriety. Stephen Jannan said shortly:

"Al Schimpf will be here. It seemed to me he was the best man to retain. It's obvious that I can't defend her. You will, of course, require everything possible done." Essie Scofield shivered. "I don't want to go into court," she articulated, "and answer all the dreadful questions." There was a stir without, and a hugely fat man in a black cape fastened with a silver chain and velvet collar entered. Al Schimpf's face was so burdened with rolling chins that he disregarded the customary fashion of whiskers, but a grizzled moustache lay above his well-formed lips, and an imperial divided his heavy, aggressive chin. He was, evidently, fully informed of the case before him; for, after saluting Jannan and Jasper Penny, he seated himself directly before Essie Scofield, fastening upon her an unwavering, glacial gaze.

"Now, pay attention," he proceeded at once. "I'll go over a few facts — this Daniel Culser, you were in love with him; no length you wouldn't go, lost your senses completely; and he — all he cared about was the money he could wring out of you. As soon as you were paid the sums that Mr. Penny allowed you, this Culser got it from you; he took every cent and wanted more. Said he would leave you unless you got hold of something really worth while. Then, of course, you carried on, promised to get him more and more; said you could force a fortune from Mr. Penny, anything to keep the young man. Hey?" he demanded suddenly.

The woman looked up with a haggard wonder, an irrepressible shudder; her hands raised and fell, and she nodded dumbly.

"Then, while Culser was in the house, Mr. Penny unexpectedly turned up and said — perhaps before Daniel himself — that you could expect nothing more, and made it plain that he was not to be intimidated. Daniel Culser was for leaving you, didn't intend to hang around for a bloody little quarterly; and, when you realized that he meant, or you thought he meant, what he said, you went crazy and shot him. . . . What!" He got no response from her now; she cowered away from him, hiding behind an updrawn shoulder, a fold of the shawl. "But listen to this," Al Schimpf shot at her, leaning forward, "here's what happened, and you must remember every fact:

"The fellow had been around the house day after day. You had encouraged him at first; but then you got frightened; he beat you — hear that? — struck you with his fist, and threatened worse if you

263

didn't go through old Penny's pocket for him. He even hinted at something you might do together, and then get away with a mint. Culser was at it when Mr. Penny called, and took it up when he left, at about six o'clock. He said he wanted money bad, debts were hounding him; and he was going to get it out of Penny, out of you. There's where you said you would warn Jasper Penny; and remember how he struck you, in the back, because you turned, and it hurts yet — there up by the left shoulder, the left shoulder, the left! Then, he had been drinking in your house and at a tavern, he threatened to kill you if you didn't do what he wanted. You honestly thought he'd do it, and snatched a pistol out of a table drawer, and . . . Do you understand? That's what happened, and it's all you know. Said he would kill you, apparently commenced then, and you acted in self-protection. Now, repeat that."

She gazed at him in a trembling confusion. " But," she objected, " he was only — he said. Oh! I was afraid I'd lose him." The lawyer moved closer to her, his unwinking, grey-green eyes like slate. " He said he'd kill you," he reiterated; " remember that, if you don't want to hang. He struck you; where? " After a long pause she replied haltingly, " In the back." Al Schimpf nodded, " Good. And he said you both were to get away with a mint. He told you it would be easy; the old man would gladly buy silence; and, by heaven, if he didn't —"

Jasper Penny stonily watched the intolerable degradation of the woman bullied into the safety of a lie. This was worse than anything that had gone before; he fell deeper and deeper into a strangling, humiliating self-loathing. Stephen Jannan's handsome countenance was fixed and pale; one hand lay on the table, empty and still. In the silence between Schimpf's insistent periods Jasper Penny could hear Essie's sobbing inspirations; he was unable to keep his gaze from her countenance, jelly-like and robbed of every trace of human dignity. He wondered vaguely at an absence of any sense of responsibility for what Essie Scofield had become; he felt that an attitude of self-accusation, of profound regret for the way they had taken together, should rest upon him; but the thought, the effort, were perfunctory, obviously insincere. If now he had a different, perhaps deeper, sense of responsibility, he had known nothing of it in the first months of his contact with her. . . . A different man, he reiterated; and one as faithfully representative as he was to-day. But totally another; men changed, evolved, progressed. Jasper Penny was convinced that it was a progression; but in a broad manner beyond all hope of his comprehension, and entirely outside dogmatic good and evil. The germ of it must have been in him from the first; his burning necessity for Susan, he told himself, had been born in him, laid dormant until, yes — it had been stirred into activity by Essie Scofield, by the revulsion which had followed that natural development.

He was suddenly conscious that Al Schimpf had ceased domineering Essie. The lawyer swung about, facing them with an expression of commonplace satisfaction. "It's all in fine order," he declared. "I want, if possible, to study our jury through a preliminary case or so. We shall, of course, surrender our client at once, without making any difficulty about moving her from one police district to another. I can produce a witness to the fact that this Culser openly said that he expected shortly to come into more money. And he had dishonoured debts all about. You will have to appear, Mr. Penny; no way out of that, but our defence should go like a song. Now, Mrs. Scofield, I have a carriage outside."

When they had gone Jasper Penny and Jannan sat in a lengthening silence. Stephen's hand moved among the papers on the table; the other drew a deep breath. "I regret this tremendously for you," Stephen Jannan said at last. He spoke with feeling; his momentary anger at the entanglement of Susan vanished. "But it will pass, Jasper. You are too solid a man to be hurt permanently by private scandal. And you have no concrete political position to invite mud slinging. Yes, it will drop out of mind, and your iron will continue to support enterprise, extension."

"But Susan," Jasper Penny demanded, "what about her? Where is she?"

"With Graham at Shadrach. She was badly torn, and I insisted on her retreating for a week or more. There is a very capable assistant at the Academy. It's too early to speak conclusively, but I am afraid that Susan's usefulness is ended there. Have you seen the cheaper sheets? Every one, of course, is buying them. Rotten! The assistant, I understand, is anxious to procure the school, and I am considering allowing her the capital. Something might be arranged paying Susan an income . . . If she would accept; confoundly difficult to come about."

"I am going to marry her," Jasper Penny asserted once more.

"What was the initial trouble?" the other asked, tersely.

"Essie." Stephen frowned.

"She would hit on that," he agreed; "stand until the last gasp of some fantastic conception of right."

Jasper explained:

"She thinks I ought to marry Essie, mostly on account of the child. She likes me, too, Stephen; I think I may tell you that. Well, I'll keep at her and at her. In the end she will get tired of refusal." The other shook his head doubtfully. "I've known Susan a good many years, and I have never seen her lose an ideal, or even an idea, yet."

Jasper Penny rose. "Meanwhile I'll have to go through with this trial. Thank God, Susan has no part in it." He warmly gripped Stephen's palm. "You're worth something in a life, immovable. Thank you, Stephen."

XXII

IT was early in April, an insidiously warm morning with the ailanthus trees in bud before the State House, when Jasper Penny left the court room where Essie had been freed. Provision had been made for her — she had had a severe collapse during the trial — and a feeling almost of renewed liberty of spirit permeated Jasper, as, with his overcoat on an arm, he turned to the left and walked over the street in the blandly expanding mildness. A train left shortly for Jaffa, and he was bound directly home, to Myrtle Forge, anxious to steep himself in the echo of the trip hammer mingled with the poignant harmony of spring sounds drifting from the farm and woods. He was possessed by a sharpened hunger for all the — now recognized — beauty of the place of his allegiance and birth, the serenity of the acres Gilbert Penny had beaten out of the wild of the Province. He was astonishingly conscious of himself as a part of the whole Penny succession, proud of Gilbert, of Howat, who had always so engaged his fancy, of Casimir, and Daniel, his own father. Theirs was a good heritage; their part of the earth, the ring of their iron, his particular characteristic of a black Penny, formed a really splendid entity.

The low, horizontal branches of the beech tree on

268

the lawn, older than the dwelling, opposed a pleasant variety on the long façade, built of stone with an appearance of dark pinkish malleability masking its obduracy. His mother was awaiting him on the narrow portico, and he at once told her of Essie's release. They stood together, gazing out across the turf, faintly emerald, over the public road, at the grey, solid group of farm buildings beyond. The farmer's daughter, in a white slip, emerged against the barnyard, and called the chickens in a high, musical note, scattering grain to a hysterical feathery mob. The air was still with approaching twilight; the sun slipped below the western trees and shadows gathered under the lilac bushes; the sky was April green.

"Your father has been dead twelve years," Gilda Penny said unexpectedly. He looked down and saw that she was decrepit, an old woman. Her mouth had sunken, her ears projected in dry folds from her scant strands of hair. He recalled Daniel Barnes Penny; the earliest memories of his mother, a vigorous, brown-faced woman with alert, black eyes, quick-stepping, dictatorial in the sphere of her house and dependents. One after the other, like the sun, they were slipping out of the sight of Myrtle Forge; vanished and remained; passed from falling hand to hand the unextinguished flame of life. Gilda Penny was merging fast into the formless dark. She clung with pathetically tense fingers to his arm as they turned into the house.

He had ordered a carriage immediately after an early supper; and, informing his coachman of his wish to proceed alone, drove quickly away through the dusk. He was going to Shadrach Furnace, to meet Susan for the first time since the unhappy occasion in the Mayor's chamber. He had decided, stifling his increasing impatience, not to see her until Essie's trial was over. Susan had been at Graham Jannan's house for nine weeks. Her sight, he had learned, had almost completely failed in a general exhaustion; but, with rigorous care, she had nearly recovered. The Academy had been sold to the assistant mistress; and there was an expressed uncertainty about Susan's near future. It had, however, no existence in Jasper Penny's thoughts, plans — she must marry him; any other course would now be absurd. The track from Myrtle Forge to the Furnace was bound into his every thought and association; its familiarity, he mused, had been born in him; his horses, too, took correctly, without pressure, every turning of the way. The road mounted, and then dropped between rounded hills to the clustering buildings, where lighted, pale yellow windows floated on the dusk, crowned by the wide-flung radiance of the Furnace stack. The air was potent in the valley with the indeterminate scent of budding earth — the premonitory fragrance of blossoms; and, hardly less delicate, stars flowered whitely in blue space.

He paused for a moment before entering Graham

Jannan's house, saturated with the pastoral tranquillity, listening to the flutter of wings under the eaves. Then he went in. They had finished supper, but were lingering at the table, with the candles guttering in an air from the open door. His greeting was simple and glad, and without restraint. Susan wore a dress like a white vapour, sprigged with pale buds, her throat and arms bare. She smiled the familiar, hesitating smile, met his questioning gaze with her undeviating courage. Jasper Penny took a chair opposite her. Little was said. Peace deepened about his spirit.

Graham, he saw, had a new ruddiness of health; he laid a shawl tenderly about his wife's shoulders; and Jasper remembered that a birth was imminent. Later he drifted with Susan to the door, and they passed out into the obscurity beyond. Even now he was reluctant to speak, to break with importunities the serene mood. "All the iron making," she spoke at last, "lovely. I have stood night after night in the cast house watching the metal pour out in its glorious colours. And, when I wake, I go to my window and see the reflections of the blast on the trees, on the first leaves. The charcoal burners come down like giants out of the mythology of the forest. And, when I first came, there was a raccoon hunt, with a great stirring of lanterns and barking dogs in the dark . . . all lovely."

"It is yours," he said, bending over her. "You can come here at your will. A house built. And

Myrtle Forge, too; whatever I have, am." He paused; but, without reply, continued more rapidly. "It's over, the — the misery of the past weeks; the mistakes are dead; they are paid, Susan. Now we may take what is left and make it as beautiful as possible. After suffering, reparation, happiness, is every one's due. And I am certain I can make you happy."

A longer pause followed, in which he regarded her with an increasing anxiety. Her face was turned away, her progress grew slower until they stood by the shadowy bulk of a small stone structure. The door was open, and it seemed to him that she looked within. "A store house," he explained. Nothing was visible in the interior gloom but some obscure shapes, bales, piled against the walls, and the scant tracery of a rude stair leading up to a greater blackness above. She stopped, as if arrested by his period, laying a hand on the door frame.

"Why don't you answer me, Susan?" he proceeded. "You know that I want to marry you; surely it is all right now. Everything possible has been done. A great deal of life remains." Her answer was so low that it almost escaped him; the faintest breath of pain, of longing and regret. "I can't," she whispered; "not with her, the child. I can't."

"That," he replied gently, "is a mistaken idea of responsibility, a needless sacrifice. I could never urge you into an injustice, a wrong; at last I have got above that; what I want is the most reasonable thing imaginable, the best, in every conceivable way, for yourself and — any other. You are harming, depriving, no one. You are taking nothing but your own, what has been yours, and only yours, from the first moment I saw, no — from my birth. What has happened brought me in a straight road to you, the long road I have never, really, left."

"I can't," she said still again. "I want to, Jasper. Oh, with a heart full of longing; I am so tired that I would almost give the rest of my life for another secure hour with you. And I would pay that to give you what you want, what you should have. But something stronger than I am, more than all this, holds me; I can't forget that miserable woman, nor her child and yours, so thin and suspicious. I am not good enough to be her mother myself, even if I felt I had the right. Inside of me I am quite wicked, selfish. I want my own. But not with the other woman outside. She'd be looking in at the windows, Jasper, looking in at my heart. I would hear her." She leaned against her arm, her face hid, her shoulders trembling.

The musty odour of the stores floated out and enveloped him. He was suddenly annoyed. Susan herself lost some of her beauty, her radiance. He muttered that she was merely stubborn, blind to reality, to necessity. His attitude hardened, and he commenced to argue in a low, insistent voice. She

273

made no reply, but remained supported in the doorway, a vague form against the inner dark.

"You must change your mind," he asserted; "you can't be eternally so foolish. There is absolutely no question of my marrying Essie Scofield."

"I don't want you to, really," she admitted in an agonized whisper. "I shall never again ask you to do that. Ah, God, how low I am."

He saw, in an unsparing flash of comprehension, that it was useless. She would never marry him as long as the past stayed embodied, actual, to peer into their beings. A return of his familiar irritability, spleen, possessed him. "You are too pure for this world," he said brutally. She turned and stood facing him, meeting his scorn with an uplifted countenance. A shifting reflection from the Furnace stack fell over her in a wan veil, over the vaporous, sprigged white of her dress, her bare throat and arms, her cheeks wet with tears. Out of it her eyes, wide with pain, steadily met his angry scrutiny. Out of it she smiled at him before the reflection died.

III   THE METAL

XXIII

IN the warm, subdued light of a double lamp
with apricot glass shades Howat Penny was
turning over the pages, stiff with dry paste, of
an album filled with opera programmes. The date
of the brief, precisely penned label on the black
cover was 1883–84; it was the first of a number of
such thick, recording volumes he had gathered; and
the operas, the casts, were of absorbing interest.
At once a memento of the heroic period of American
music and of his first manhood, the faded crudely
embellished strips of paper, bearing names, lyric
tenors and sopranos of limpid, bird-like song long
ago lost in rosy and nebulous clouds of fable and
cherished affection, roused remembered pleasures
sharper than any calm actuality of to-day. He
paused with a quiet exclamation, the single glass
adroitly held in his left, astigmatic, eye fastened on
the announcement of a famous evening, a famous
name. His sense of the leaf before him blurred in
the vivid memory of Patti, singing Martha in the
campaign brought by Mapleson in the old Academy
of Music against the forces of the new Metropolitan
Opera House. He had been one of a conservative
number that had supported the established opera,

declaring heatedly that the Diva and Mapleson were an unapproachable musical combination, before which the shoddier magnificence of its rival, erected practically in a few summer months, would speedily fade.

Nevertheless, he recalled, the widely heralded performance had been coolly received. Patti, although she had not perceptibly failed in voice, had been unable to inspire the customary enthusiasm; and the scene at the evening's end, planned to express her overwhelming triumph and superiority, when the horses had been taken from her carriage and it had been dragged by hand to the portal of the Windsor Hotel, had been no better than perfunctory. The wily Mapleson had arranged that beforehand, Howat Penny realized, with a faint, reminiscent smile on his severe lips — the "enthusiastic mob" had been coldly recruited, at a price, from the choristers. Another memory of Patti, and of that same performance, flooded back — the dinner given her in the Brunswick. He saw again the room where, on a divan, she had received her hosts, the seventy or more men of fashion grouped in irreproachable black and white, with her suave manager, the inevitable tea rose in his lapel, on a knee before Adelina, kissing her hand. The dinner had been laid in the ball room, lit with a multitude of wax candles. The features, appearance, of the more prominent men, of Mahun Stetson and Daly and William Steinway, were clear still. The original plan had been to in-

278

clude ladies at the dinner, but the latter, affecting outrage at the Diva's affair with the Marquis de Caux, had refused to lend their countenance to the singer's occasion. His smile broadened — this was so characteristic of New York in the eighties. How different it had been; but it was no better, he added silently, now.

It was mid-August, and the air floating in through an open door was ladened with the richness of ultra-luxuriant vegetation, the persistent, metallic whirring of locusts, the mechanical repetition of katydids. One of the owls that inhabited the old willow tree before the house cried softly . . . How different! He straightened up from the book open on his knees, and the glass fell with a small clatter over his formal, starched linen, swinging for an instant on its narrow ribbon. The unwavering lamp light was deflected in green points through the emeralds of his studs.

The thought of bygone, gala nights of opera fastened on him with a peculiar significance — suddenly they seemed symbolic of his lost youth. Such tides of impassioned song, such poignant, lyric passion, such tragic sacrifice and death, were all in the extravagant key of youth. The very convention of opera, the glorified unreality of its language, the romantic impossibility of its colour, the sparkling dress like the sparkling voices and blue gardens and gilded halls, were the authentic expression of the resplendent vagaries of early years.

The winter of eighty three and four; his first season of New York music. The autumn before he had returned from the five years spent in Europe, in Paris practically, with Bundy Provost, related to him by a marriage in the past generation, through the Jannans. He had gone abroad immediately after his graduation as a lawyer; and in the indolent culture of the five Parisian years, he now realized, he had permanently lost all hold on his profession. At his return he had drifted imperceptibly into an existence of polite pleasure. It had been different with Bundy; he had gone into the banking house of Provost, lately established in New York; and, with the extraordinary pertinacity and acumen sometimes developed by worldly and rich young men, he had steadily risen to a place of financial importance. An opening had, of course, been offered to Howat Penny when he had definitely decided not to settle in Philadelphia, where the Pennys had always been associated, and pursue the law. And, at first, he had occupied a desk in the Provost counting rooms. But he had soon grown discontented, he disliked routine and a clerk's condition; and, after two years of annoyed effort, withdrew to lead a more congenial existence on a secure, adequate income.

"It was a mistake," he said aloud, in a decided, clearly modulated voice, gazing blankly into the warm stillness of the room. It had come partly from his innate impatience with any inferior state whatever, and part from the old inability to identify himself with the practicalities of existence. He had always viewed with distaste the apparently necessary compromises of successful living; the struggle for money, commercial supremacy, seemed unendurably ugly; the jargon and subterfuges of financial competition beneath his exacting standard of personal dignity. That had been his expression at the time — permeated by an impatient sense of superiority; but now he felt that there was something essential lacking in himself. An absence of proper balance. Solely concerned with the appearance, the insignificant surface, of such efforts as Bundy Provost's, their moving, masculine spirit had evaded him. Yes, it had been a mistake. He had missed the greatest pleasure of all, that of accumulating power and influence, of virile achievement.

Well, it was over now; he was old; his life, his chance, had gone; and all that remained were memories of Patti smiling disdainfully in the flare of oil torches about her carriage; the only concrete record of so many years the scrap books such as that on his knees.

It had been an error; yet there had been, within him, no choice, no intimation of a different, more desirable, consummation. Bundy had gone one way and himself another in obedience to forces beyond their understanding or control. They had done, briefly, what they were. There was no individual blame to attach, no applause; spare moralizing to append. He returned to the pages before him, to the

281

memories of the radiant Ambre and Marimon, the sylvan echoes of Campanini singing Elvino.

Now his recovered glass was intent on a programme of the rapidly successful Metropolitan forces, of the new German Opera, with Seidl-Krauss singing Elizabeth, and Brandt in *Fidelio*. Even here, after so long, he vibrated again to the exquisite beauty of Lenore's constancy and love. Then Dr. Damrosch dead, the sonorous funeral in the Opera House . . . That had been changed with the rest; the baignoires were gone, the tiers of boxes newly curved; gone the chandeliers and Turkey red carpet and gold threaded brocade that had seemed the final expression of luxury. Lehmann in the premier of *Tristan und Isolde*, with the vast restrained enthusiasm and tensity when, at the end of the third act, Niemann bared his wounded breast. Eames' rise; but that, and what followed, were in successive books. He closed the one under his hand.

As the years drew nearer the present their features became larger, more indistinct, their music grew louder, dissonant. He had retired further and further from an opera, a life, with which he was increasingly out of harmony. Or rather, he added, life moved away from the aging. It was as if the surrounding affair became objective; as if, once a participant in a cast — a production, however, less than grand — he had been conducted to a seat somewhere in the midst of a great, shadowy audience, from which he looked out of the gloom at the brilliant, removed spectacle. The final fact that had taken him from the setting of so many of his years had been the increasing expense of a discriminating existence in New York. Again his distaste for anything short of absolute nicety had dictated the form and conditions of his living. When the situation of his rooms had definitely declined, and the cost of possible locations — he could not endure a club — became prohibitive; when his once adequate, unaugmented income assumed the limitations of a mere sufficiency; and when, too, the old, familiar figures, the swells of his own period and acquaintance had vanished one by one with their vanishing halls of assembly — he had retreated to the traditional place of his family. He had gone back to the home of the Pennys in America.

Not, however, to Myrtle Forge itself, the true centre of his inheritance. The house there had been uninhabited since his father's early years; it was a closed and melancholy memento; he had reanimated a comfortable stone dwelling at Shadrach Furnace; its solid grey façade drawn out by two happy additions to the original, small square. It had been, traditionally, at first, the house of the head furnacemen; sometime after that, perhaps a hundred years, Graham Jannan, newly married, had lived there while occupied with the active manufacture of iron; and three summers back he, Howat Penny, the last Penny now, had returned to the vicinity of Jaffa.

XXIV

THE room in which he sat had two windows, set in the deep recesses of heavy stone walls, and three doors, two leading into opposite rooms and the third opening without. The double lamp stood on a low, gate-legged table of fibrous, time-blackened oak, together with an orderly array of periodicals — the white, typographical page of the *Saturday Review* under the dull rose of *The Living Age* and chocolate-coloured bulk of the *Unpopular, Gil Blas*, the mid-week *Boston Transcript* and yesterday's *New York Evening Post*. The table bore, in addition, a green morocco case of dominoes; a mahogany box that, in a recess, mysteriously maintained a visible cigarette; a study of Beethoven, in French; an outspread volume by Anatole France, *Jacques Tournebroche*, in a handsome paper cover; a set of copper ash trays; and a dull red figurine, holding within its few inches the deathless spirit of a heroic age. An angle of the wall before him was filled by a white panelled fireplace, the mantel close against the ceiling; and on the other side of a doorway, through which he could see Rudolph noiselessly preparing the dinner table, was a swan-like sofa, in olive wood and pale yellow satin,

from the Venice of the *ottocento*. At his right, beyond a window, mounted a tall, austere secretary in
waxed walnut; and behind him, under the white chair
rail, bookcases extended across the width of the
room. Gustavus Hesselius' portrait of the first
Howat Penny hung on a yellow painted wall, his
gilt-braided major's facings still vivid, his dark, perceptible scorn undimmed. There were, too, framed
in oak, a large photograph of Tamagno, as Othello,
with a scrawled, cordial message; another of a graceful woman in the Page's costume of *Les Huguenots*,
signed "Sempre . . . Scalchi"; a water colour
drawing by Jan Beers; and a Victorian lithograph
in powdery foliage and brick of *The Penny Rolling
Mills. Jaffa.* A black-blue rug, from Myrtle
Forge, partly covered the broad, oak boards of the
floor; and there was a comfortable variety of chairs
— sturdy, painted Dutch, winged Windsors and a
slatted Hunterstown rocker.

Howat Penny's gaze wandered over the familiar
furnishing, come to him surviving the generations of
his family, or carefully procured for his individual
dictates. A sense of tranquillity, of haven, deepened
about him. "Rudolph," he inquired, "has Honduras gone for Miss Jannan?"

The man stopped in the doorway, answering in
the affirmative. He was slight, almost fragile, with
close, dark hair that stood up across his forehead,
and dry, high-coloured cheeks. Rudolph hesitated,
with a handful of silver; and then returned to his

task. Mariana would be along immediately, Howat
Penny thought. He put the album aside and rose,
moving toward the door that led without. He was a
slender, erect figure, with little to indicate his age
except the almost complete silvering of his hair —
it had, evidently, been black — and a rigidity of body
only apparent to a sharp scrutiny.

A porch followed that length of the house, and
doubled the end, where he stood peering into the
gathering dusk. The old willow tree, inhabited by
the owls, spread a delicate, blurred silhouette across
a darkened vista of shorn wheat fields, filled, in the
hollows, with woods; and a lamp glimmered from a
farm house on a hill to the left. His lawn dropped
to the public road, the hedged enclosure swimming
with fireflies; and beyond he saw the wavering light
shafts of his small motor returning from the insignificant flag station on the railroad, a mile distant.

The noise of the engine increased, sliding into a
lower gear on the short curve of the driveway; and
he met Mariana Jannan at the entrance directly into
the dining room. She insisted, to his renewed discomfort, on kissing him. " It's wonderful here, after
the city," she proclaimed; " and I've had to be in
town three sweltering days. I'll dress right away."

Honduras, his coloured man, as indispensable outside as Rudolph was in, followed with her bag up the
narrow flight of steps to the floor above. He waited
through, he thought, a reasonable interval, and then

286

called. An indistinguishable reply floated down, mingled with the filling of a tub; and another half hour passed before Mariana appeared in white chiffon, securing a broad girdle of silver oak leaves about her slight waist. " Do you mind? " she turned before him; and, with an impatience half assumed and half actual, he fastened the last hooks of her dress. " As you know," he reminded her, " I don't attempt cocktails. Will you have a gin and bitters? "

She wouldn't, frankly; and they embarked on dinner in a pleasant, unstrained silence. Mariana was, he realized, the only person alive for whom he had a genuine warmth of affection. She was a first cousin; her Aunt Elizabeth had married James Penny, his father; but his fondness for her had no root in that fact. It didn't, for example, extend to her brother Kingsfrere. He speculated again on the reason for her marked effect. Mariana was not lovely, as had been the charmers of his own day; her features, with the exception of her eyes, were unremarkable. And her eyes, variably blue, were only arresting because of their extraordinary intensity of vision, their unquenchable and impertinent curiosity. A girl absolutely different from all his cherished mental images; but, for Howat Penny, always potent, always arousing a response from his supercritical being, stirring his aesthetic heart. Everything he possessed — his pictures, the albums, the moderate income, although she had little need of that — had been willed to her.

It would be hers then just as it was, practically, now. And he was aware that her feeling generously equalled his own.

His speculation, penetrating deeper than customary, rewarded him with the thought that she was unusual in the courage of her emotions. That was it — the courage of her emotions! There was a total lack of any penurious trait, any ulterior thought of appraising herself against a possible advantageous barter. She was never concerned with a conscious prudery in the arrangement of her skirt. Mariana was aristocratic in the correct sense of the term; a sense, he realized, now almost lost. And he rated aristocracy of bearing higher than any other condition or fact.

He wondered a little at her patent pleasure in visiting him, an old man, so frequently. Hardly a month passed but that, announced by telegram, she did not appear and stay over night, or for a part of the week. She would recount minutely the current gaiety of her polite existence. He knew the names of her associates, a number of them had been exhibited to him at Shadrach; the location of their country places; and what men temporarily monopolized her interest. None of the latter had been serious. He was, selfishly, glad of that; and waited uneasily through her every visit until she assured him that her affections had not been possessed. However, this condition, he knew, must soon come to an

288

end; Mariana was instinct with sex; and a short while before he had sent his acknowledgment of her twenty-sixth birthday.

She sat occupied with salad against the cavernous depths of a fireplace that, between the kitchen door and a built-in cupboard, filled the side of the dining room. The long mantel above her head was ladened with the grey sheen of pewter, and two uncommonly large, fluted bowls of blue Stiegel glass. In the centre of the table linen, the Sheffield and crystal and pictorial Staffordshire, was a vivid expanse of rose geraniums. She broke off a flower and pinned it with the diamond bar on her breast. " Howat," she said, " to-morrow's Saturday, and I've asked two people out until Sunday night. Eliza Provost and a young man. Do you mind? "

" Tell Rudolph," he replied. It was not until after dinner, when they were playing sniff, that he realized that she omitted the young man's name. He intended to ask it, but, his mind and hand hovering over an ivory domino, he forgot. " Twenty," he announced, reaching for the scoring pad. " Oh, hell, Howat! " she protested. " That's the game, almost." She emptied her coffee cup, and speculatively fingered one of the thin cigars in the box at his hand. " It's the customary thing in Peru," she observed, pinching the end from the cigar and lighting it. He watched her absently, veiled in the fragrant, bluish smoke. Automatically his thoughts

289

returned to the women that, at a breath of scandal, had refused to attend the dinner to Patti. So much changed; the years fled like birds in a mist.

"I feel like a politician," she told him. "Eliza Provost would pat me on the back. She's talking from a soap box on the street corners now, winging men for such trifles as forced birth. I'm fond of Eliza; she's got a splendid crust. I wish you'd get excited about my rights; but your interest really goes no further than a hat from Camille Marchais. You are deleterious, Howat. Isn't that a lovely word! Which was the first double?" He blocked and won the game. "Fifty-five," she announced; "and ninety-five before. I owe you a dollar and a half."

She paid the debt promptly from a flexible gold mesh bag on the table; then stooped and wandered among his books. Howat Penny turned to yesterday's *Evening Post*, and Mariana settled beyond the lamp. Outside the locusts were desperately shrill, and the heavy ticking of an old clock grew audible. "I don't like George Moore!" she exclaimed. He raised surprised, inquiring eyebrows. "He is such a taster," she added, but particularized no more. She sat, with the scarlet bound book clouded in the white chiffon of her lap, gazing at the wall. Her lips were parted, and a brighter colour rose in her cheeks. Her attitude, her expression, vaguely disturbed him; he had never seen her more warmly, dangerously, alive. A new reluctance stopped the question forming in his mind; she seemed to have retreated from him. "Moore is a very great artist," he said instead.

"That's little to me," she replied flippantly, rising. "I think I'll go up; and I almost think I will kiss you again." He grumbled a protest, and watched her trail from the room, the silver girdle and chiffon emphasizing her thin, vigorous body, the lamplight falling on her bare, sharp shoulders. Howat Penny had early acquired a habit of long hours, and it was past one when he put aside his papers, stood for a moment on the porch. The fireflies were gone, the locusts seemed farther away, and the soft, heavy flight of an owl rose from the warm grass.

Below, on the right, he could vaguely see the broken bulk of what had been Shadrach Furnace, the ruined shape of the past. The Pennys no longer made iron. His father had marked the last casting. They no longer listened to the beat of the trip hammer, but to the light rhythm of a conductor's baton; they heard, in place of ringing metal, a tenor's grace notes. Soon they would hear nothing. They went out, for all time, with himself. It was fitting that the last, true to their peculiar inheritance, should be a black Penny. He, Howat, was that — the ancient Welsh blood finally gathered in a cup of life before it was spilled.

Old influences quickened within him; but, attenuated, they were no more than regrets. They came

late to trouble his remnant of living. He was like
the Furnace, a sign of what had been; yet, he
thought in self-extenuation, he had brought no dis-
honour, no dragging of the tradition through the
muck of a public scandal. Not that . . . nor anything else. Now, when it was absurd, he was resentful of the part he had played in life; like a minor,
cracked voice, he extended a former figure with a
saving touch of humour, importuning the director
because he had not been cast in the great rôles. The
night mist came up and brushed him; he was conscious of a sudden chill, an aching of the wrists.
"Cracked," he repeated, aloud, and retreated into
the house; where, Rudolph gone up, he put out the
lights and stiffly retired.

XXV

THEY accomplished little the following morning. Mariana, in a scant brown linen skirt, a sheer waist through which were visible precarious incidentals and narrow black ribbon, and the confoundedest green stockings he had ever seen, lounged indolently in a canvas swing. The heat increased in a reddish haze through which the sun poured like molten copper. "You'd better come inside," he said from the doorway; "the house, shut up, is quite comfortable." Within the damp of the old, stone walls made a comparative coolness. The shades were drawn down, and they sat in an untimely twilight.

"When I think of how energetic Eliza will be," Mariana asserted, "I am already overwhelmed. But you never look hot, Howat; you are always beautiful." His flannels and straw-coloured silk coat were crisply ironed; his hair, his scarf and lustrous yellow shoes, precise. "Howat," she continued almost anxiously, "you put a lot on, well — good form. You think that the way a man knots his tie is tremendously significant —"

"Perhaps," he returned cautiously. "A good many years have shown me that the right man usually wears the right things."

" Couldn't that be just the smallest bit unfair?
Aren't there, after all, droves of the right men in
rubber collars? I don't know any," she added
hastily; " that is, not exactly the same. But it seems
to me that you have lived so exclusively in a certain atmosphere that you might have got blinded
to — to other things."

" Perhaps," he said again, complacently. " I can
only judge by my own feeling and experience. Now
Mapleson, never was a finer conductor of opera —
you didn't catch him in a pink tie in the evening.
And some of those others, who failed in a couple of
weeks, I give you my word, dress shirts with forget-
menots."

She regarded him with a frowning, half closed
vision. " It sounds wrong," she commented. " It's
been your life, of course." He grew resentful under
her scrutiny, the implied criticism. A sudden suspicion entered his mind, connected with her expression last evening, the young man whose name he had
omitted to ask. His reluctance to question her returned. But if Mariana had attached herself to
some rowdy, by heaven, he would . . . He fixed the
glass in his eye, and, pretending to be occupied with
a periodical, studied her. He realized that he would,
could, do nothing. She was a woman of determination, and, her father dead, a very adequate income
of her own. His fondness for Mariana resided principally in a wish to see her free from the multitudinous snares that he designated in a group as common.

294

He was fearful of her entanglement in the cheap implications of the undistinguished democracy more prevalent every year. All that was notable, charming, in her, he felt, would be obliterated by trite connection; he had no more patience for the conventional fulfilment of her life than he had for the thought of women voting. Howat Penny saw Mariana complete, fine, in herself, as the *Orpheo* of Christopher Gluck was fine and complete. He preferred the contained artistry of such music to the cruder, more popular and moral, sounds.

Early in the afternoon she went to her room, although Honduras had no occasion to go to the station for considerably more than an hour, explaining that she must dress. Howat Penny sat with his palms on his white flannelled knees, revolving, now, himself in the light of his aspirations for Mariana. He wondered if, in the absence of any sympathy for the mass of sentiment and living, he was blind, too, to her greatest possibilities; if, in short, he was a vicious influence. Perhaps, as the old were said to do, he had hardened into a narrow and erroneous conception of values. Such doubts were both disturbing and unusual; ordinarily he never hesitated in the exact expression of his vigorously held opinions and prejudices; he seldom relaxed the critical elevation of his standards. He was, he thought contemptuously, growing soft; senility was diluting his fibre, blurring his inner vision.

Nothing of this was visible as he rose on Mariana's

295

reappearance; there was not a line relaxed; his handsome, dark profile was as pridefully clear as if it
had been stamped on a bronze coin. Mariana wore,
simply, blue, with an amber veiling of tulle about
her shoulders, and a short skirt that gave her a
marked youthful aspect. She seemed ill at ease; and
avoided his gaze, hurrying out to meet the motor as
it noisily turned sharply in at the door. Howat
Penny heard Eliza Provost's short, impatient enun-
ciation, and a rapid, masculine utterance. Eliza
entered, a girl with a decided, evenly pale face
and brown eyes, in a severe black linen suit and a
small hat, and extended a direct hand, a slightly
smiling greeting. Mariana followed, for a moment
filling the doorway. "We'll go up, Eliza," she said,
moving with the other to the stair, a few feet distant.
A man followed into the house, and Mariana half
turned on the bottom step. "Howat," she proceeded hurriedly, "this is James Polder." Then she
ascended with Eliza Provost.

An expression of amazement, deepening almost to
dismay, was momentarily visible on Howat Penny's
countenance. His face felt hot, and there was an
uncomfortable pressure in his throat, such as might
come from shock. Surely Mariana wouldn't . . .
without warning him —! He was conscious of the
necessity, facing a tall, spare young man with an
intent expression, of a polite phrase; and he articulated an adequate something in a noticeably disturbed tone. But, of course, he had made a mistake.

296

James Polder's intensity increased, concentrated in a gaze at once belligerent and eager. He said:

"Then Miss Jannan didn't tell you. It was a mistake. It may be I am not exactly desirable here," his voice sharpened, and he retreated a step toward the door.

"No," Howat Penny replied; "she didn't." He found himself studying a face at once youthful and lined, a good jaw contradicted by a mouth already traced with discontent, and yellow-brown eyes kindling with a surprising energy of resentment. "You are Byron Polder's son?" he said in a manner that carried its own affirmation. "Eunice Scofield's grandson."

"Eunice Penny's," the other interjected. "Your own grandfather saw to that." His hand rested in the doorway, and he stopped Honduras, carrying in the guests' bags. Howat Penny's poise rapidly returned. "Go right up, Honduras," he directed; "the Windmill room, I think. I had never seen you," he said to James Polder, as if in apology. "But your father has been pointed out to me." He waved the younger man into the room beyond, and moved forward the cigarettes.

James Polder took one with an evident relief in the commonplace act. He struck a match and lit the cigarette with elaborate care. "Will you sit for a little?" the elder proceeded. "Or perhaps you'd rather change at once. I've no doubt it was sticky in the city."

"Thank you; perhaps I'd better — the last."
Rudolph appeared, and conducted the young man
above. Howat Penny sat suddenly, his lips folded
in a stubborn line. Mariana had behaved out-
rageously; she must be familiar with the whole,
miserable, past episode; she had given him some very
bad moments. He had a personal bitterness toward
that old, unhappy affair, the dereliction of his dead
grandfather — it had been, he had always felt,
largely responsible for his own course in life; it had,
before his birth even, formed his limitations, as it
had those of his father.

The latter had been the child of a dangerously
late marriage, a marriage from which time and
delay had stripped both material potency and sus-
taining illusion. Jasper Penny had been nearing
fifty when his son was born; and that act of deliberate sacrifice on the part of his wife, entering middle age, had imposed an inordinate amount of
suffering on her last years. Their child, it was
true, had been of normal stature, and lived to within
a short space of a half century. But then he had
utterly collapsed, died in three days from what had
first appeared a slight cold; and, throughout his
maturity, he had been a man of feverish mind. His
disastrous, blind struggle against the great, newly
discovered iron deposits of the Middle West was characteristic of his ill balance. And, in his own, Howat
Penny's, successive turn, the latter told himself

298

again, he had paid part of the price of his grand-father's indulgence.

It was incorporated in the Penny knowledge that Susan Brundon had refused to marry Jasper while the other woman was alive. The latter had died, some years after the disgraceful publicity of the murder and trial; the wedding had then taken place; but it seemed to Howat Penny to have been almost perfunctory. Yes, he had paid too, in the negative philosophy, the critical sterility, of his existence. He recognized this in one of the disconcerting flashes of perception that lately illuminated him as if from without. Some essential proportion had been disturbed. He looked up, at a slight sound, and saw Mariana standing before him. His expression, he knew, was severe; he had been quite upset.

"I can see," she proceeded slowly, "that I have been very wicked. I didn't realize, Howat, that it might affect you; how real all that old stir might be. I am tremendously sorry; you must know that I am awfully fond of you. It was pure, young selfishness. I was afraid that if I spoke first you wouldn't let him come. And it was important — I must see him and talk to him and think about it. You can realize mother and Kingsfrere!"

"Where did you meet him?" he demanded shortly.

"With Eliza, at a meeting," she went on more rapidly. "He's terribly brilliant, and a steel man. Isn't it funny? The Pennys were steel, too; or iron, and that's the same. I wish you could be nice to him or just decent, until — until I know."

"Mariana!" he exclaimed, rising. "You don't mean that you are really —. That you —"

"Perhaps, Howat," she answered gravely. "I have only seen him twice; and he has said nothing; but, you see, I am an experienced young woman. No other man has made the same impression."

"That," he declared coldly, "is unthinkable. You can't know all the facts."

"I do; but, somehow, I don't care."

"Everything about him is impossible — his history, family . . . Why, Eunice Scofield, well, Penny, married a man from behind a counter, a fellow who sold womens' gloves; yes, and more than half Jew. And this man's mother was Delia Mullen, a daughter of the dirty ward leader. All this aside from — from his bad blood."

"It's partly yours, you know," she said quietly. "After all, there are other places I can see him." She turned away. "Eliza Provost is insane," he muttered. "No," Mariana returned, "only superior to narrow little prejudices. She can see life, people, as they are. Jim Polder is one of the most promising men in the steel mills. He is going up and up. That is enough for Eliza, it is enough for me; and if it won't do for my family —" she made an opening gesture with her fingers. Her expression had hardened; she gazed at him with bright, contemptuous eyes. In a moment the affectionate bonds between them seemed to have dissolved. His feeling was one of mingled anger and concern; but he endeavoured to regain his self-control, conscious that a hasty word more might do irreparable harm.

"Of course, I can't have you meeting him about the streets," he stated. "It is better here, if necessary. I am very much displeased," a note of complaint appeared, and she immediately returned to him, laid a hand on his shoulder. "Nothing is certain," she assured him. "I wanted to be sure, that is all. I don't want to make a mess out of things."

It was a part of the very quality of emotional courage he had so lately defined, extolled; a part of her disdain for ordinary prudence and conventional approbation. A direct dislike for this James Polder invaded him, a determined attitude of hyper-criticism. When the younger man reappeared Howat Penny found justification for this attitude. The details of Polder's apparel, although acceptable in the main, were without nicety. His shoes were a crude tan, and his necktie from the outer limbo. His hands, too, had a grimy surface and the nails were broken, unkempt.

But it was evident that all the criticism was not to be limited to his own. James Polder regarded the single glass with a scoffing lip, as if it were the appendage of a ludicrous Anglomania. He glanced with indifference at Howat Penny's pictures, books, the collected emblems of his cultivated years. His brows raised at the photograph of Scalchi in the

301

Page's trunks — as if, the elder thought, she had been a " pony " in the *Black Crook* — and was visibly amused at the great Mapleson, posed in a dignified attitude by a broken column. An irrepressible and biting scorn, Howat Penny saw, was, perhaps, the young man's strongest attribute. He had violent opinions expressed in sudden, sharp movements, gestures with his shoulders, swift frowns and fragmentary sentences.

Howat Penny had never seen a more ill-ordered youth, and he experienced an increasing difficulty in keeping a marked asperity from his speech and conduct. Eliza Provost shortly came down, and the three strolled out into the ruddy light of late afternoon. Howat Penny consumed a long time dressing for the evening; and, in the end, irritably summoned Rudolph. " I can't get these damned studs in," he complained; " whatever do you suppose women use for starch now? " Rudolph dexterously fixed the emeralds, then held the black silk waistcoat. " And coats won't hang for a bawbee," he went on. " Gentlemen like Gary Dilkes used to go regularly to London, spring and fall, for their things. No doubt then about a man of breeding. You didn't see the other kind around. Wouldn't have 'em." Rudolph murmured consolingly. " Sat in the pit but never got into the boxes," his voice grew thin, querulous. " I'm moving along, Rudolph," he admitted suddenly; " the manners, and, by thunder, the music too, don't suit me any more. Give me the old Acad-

302

emy days in Irving Place." He hummed a bar from
Ernani.

Through dinner he maintained a severe silence,
listening with a frowning disapproval to Eliza
Provost's tranquil, subversive utterances. Howat
Penny couldn't think what her father was about,
permitting her to harangue loafers by the streets
and saloons. She was, in a cold way — she had
Peter Jannan Provost's curious grey colouring —
a handsome piece of a girl, too. " A fine figger,"
he told himself.

Later, Mariana and James Polder had gone out
on the porch, he faced with reluctance the task
of furnishing her with entertainment; but, to his
extreme relief, she procured a leather portfolio,
and addressed herself to a sheaf of papers. But
that, in itself, was a peculiar way for a young
woman to spend an evening. She would have done
it, he felt, if he had been half his actual age. God
help the man with a fancy for her! Charming
visions were woven on his memory from the fading
skeins of the past — a ride in a dilapidated, public
fiacre after a masked ball in Paris . . . at dawn.
Confetti tangled in coppery hair, a wilful mouth,
fragrantly painted, and phantomlike swans on a
black lake. His silk hat had been telescoped in the
process of smacking a Frenchman's eye. Perhaps,
they had told each other, there would be cards later
in the day, an affair of honour. He forgot what,
exactly, had happened; but there had been no duel.

He looked up with a sudden concern, as if his thoughts might have been clear to Eliza Provost, in irreproachable evening dress and shell rimmed glasses, intent on statistical pages. Mariana and James Polder appeared; the former, Howat Penny thought, disturbed. Polder's intense countenance was sombre, his brow corrugated. Mariana, accompanied by Eliza, soon after went up; and left the two men facing each other across a neutral silence. "You manufacture steel, I believe," the elder finally stated.

"The Company does," Polder replied more exactly. "I've been in the open hearth since I left school," he went on; "it was born in me, I've never thought of anything else." His tone grew sharp, as if it might occur to the other to contradict the legitimacy of his pursuit. "I have done well enough, too," he said pridefully. "Most of them come on from college. I went from shovelling slag in the pit, the crane, to second helper and melter; they gave me the furnace after a year and now I am foreman. It will be better still if a reorganization goes through. Not many men have a chance at the superintendent's office under thirty-five."

"That is very admirable," Howat Penny said formally. He wondered, privately, at the far channel into which the original Penny ability had flowed. There could be no doubt, however objectionable, that James Polder was the present repository of the family tradition. He had had it from the source; and
304

the iron had not, apparently, been corroded by tainted blood. He was forced to admit that a coarser strain had, perhaps, lent it endurance. All this failed to detract from his initial dislike of young Polder. There was a lack of breeding in the manner in which he sat in his chair, thrust forward on its edge, in his arrogant proclamation of ability, success. James Polder was anxious, he realized, to impress him, Howat Penny, with the fact that he was not negligible. Such things were utterly unimportant to him. He was unable to justify, or even explain to himself, his standards of judgment. They were not founded on admirable conduct, on achievement, what was known as solid worth; but on vague accents, intuitive attitudes of mind visible in a hundred trivial, even absurd, signs. The "right things" were more indispensable to him than the sublimest attributes.

On the following morning Mariana, Eliza and Polder disappeared in his car — it seemed that the latter was an accomplished mechanic in addition to his other qualities — and Howat Penny faced the disagreeable possibilities of the near future. Mariana would, he knew, meet this fellow promiscuously if necessary. As she had indicated, it was impossible to conceive of him in Charlotte Jannan's house. The latter was a rigidly correct woman. She would, too, and properly, be nasty if she learned that such meetings had taken place at Shadrach. The only thing to do was to bring Mariana to what he designated as her senses. And, at the start, he had a conviction that he might fail.

She did not accompany Eliza Provost and Polder, when, late Sunday afternoon, they departed; but sat absorbed in thought through the evening meal. He found his affection for her increasing to an annoying degree; he was almost humble in his anxiety not to wound her.

"Life is so messy," she said with sudden violence. "You can't think, Howat, how I hate myself; the horridest things go round and round through my mind. We're all wrong — I'm more like you than I admitted — born snobs. I mean the kind who look down on people different from themselves. I can't help being on — on edge. I can tell you this, though, I care more for Jim Polder than for any other man I've ever met. I'm mad about him; and yet, somehow, I can't quite think of marrying him. He's asked me already. But I knew he would."

"You must wait," he temporized; "such things clear up after a little."

"And if they don't?" she demanded. "What if they are choked by a hundred cowardly or selfish thoughts? It can be too late so terribly soon, Howat. You must know that. You see, I can't decide what really is the most valuable, what should be held tight on to, or let go. There are two me's, it seems — one what I want and the other what I am. I want Jim and I'm Mariana Jannan. All that about Eunice or Essie, or whatever her name was, doesn't matter a bawbee, as you say. I hate it because I think at times it makes him unhappy. Really, I believe I am fonder of him because of it. We owe him something — the superior Jannans and Pennys. Why, Howat, he's your own blood, and you looked at him as if he were a grocer's assistant. And I watched hatefully for the little expressions that seemed common. Of course, out in those mills, he would pick up a lot that wouldn't touch us; and, after all, he could drop them."

"If you have any thought of reforming him," he commented dryly, "you might as well see a wedding stationer."

"I could influence him," she insisted; "I'd at least count for as much as those shovellers and furnace men."

"But not," he proceeded relentlessly, "against the Essie Scofield you dismissed so easily. I don't doubt for a minute the unhappiness you spoke of; it would be a part of his inheritance; and you'd never charm it out of him. Damn it, Mariana," he burst out, "he's inferior! That's all, inferior." Anger and resentment destroyed his caution, his planned logic, restraint. "I can see what your life would be, if you can't. You would live in a no-man's land; and all the clergymen in the world couldn't make you one."

"It wouldn't be the clergymen, Howat," she said simply. "And you mustn't think I am only a silly with her first young man. I have kissed them before,

Howat; yes, and liked it. I am not happy with Jim; it's something else, like tearing silk. He is so confident and so helpless; he's drinking now, too."

"I suppose that is an added attraction," he commented. She chose to ignore this. "I half promised him," she continued, "to take dinner with his family. He will be in the city next week. I said I thought you'd bring me."

"Well, I won't," he replied in a startled energy. "Mariana, you're out of your head. Go to Byron Polder's house! Me!" In his excitement he dropped a lighted cigarette on the Chinese rug. "I have no one else," she told him. "Perhaps I'll marry Jim, and go away . . . I thought you might want to be with me, at the last."

He fumbled for his glass, fixed it in his eye, and then dropped it out, clearing his throat sharply. He rose and crossed the room, and looked out through the open door at the night. The stars were hazy, and there was a constant reflection of lightning on the horizon. Howat Penny swore silently at his increasing softness, his betrayal by his years. Yet it might be a good thing for her to see the Polder family assembled, Byron — he was a pretentious looking fool — at one end of the table and Delia Mullen Polder at the other. There were more children, too. But if it became necessary, heaven knew how he would explain all this to Charlotte. "I believe," he said, apparently innocently, "that they live in the north end of the city."

308

"It won't damage you," she replied indirectly. Already, he thought with poignant regret, a part of the old Mariana had gone; her voice was older, darker with maturity.

XXVI

HOWAT PENNY arrived in town late on the day when he was to dine with Mariana at the Polders. He entered a taxicab, and was carried smoothly through the thick, hot air; open electric cars, ladened with damp, pallid salespeople, passed with a harsh ringing; and the foliage in Rittenhouse Square hung dusty and limp and still. The houses beyond, on Nineteenth Street, where the Jannans' winter dwelling stood, were closed and blankly boarded. The small, provisional entrance before which he stopped opened, and a servant, out of livery, appeared. "Shall I tell the driver to return, sir?" he queried; "the telephone is disconnected." He issued instructions, and, with Howat Penny's bag, followed him into the darkened house.

The windows of a general chamber on the second floor had been thrown open; and there he found Mariana's brother. Kingsfrere Jannan was a young man with a broad white face, shadowed in pasty green, and leaden eyes. His countenance, Howat knew, masked a keen and avaricious temperament. He did uncommonly well at auction bridge in the clubs. Kingsfrere, in a grey morning coat with white linen gaiters and a relentless collar, nodded and lounged from the room; and Mariana soon appeared. "Perhaps, Howat," she said, "it would be better if you didn't dress. I have an idea the Polder men don't."

At the stubborn expression which possessed him she exclaimed sharply, "If you tell me that the Colonel or Gary Dilkes were always formally dressed at dinner I think I'll scream." Nevertheless, he had no intention of relinquishing a habit of years for the Polders, or the north end of the city; and when, later, he came down into the hall, where the man stood with his silk hat and cape, Mariana put an arm about his shoulders. "I wish every one could be as beautiful as yourself," she told him. They passed the Square, bathed in dusk and the beginning shimmer of arc lights, went through the flattened and faintly thunderous arch of a railway, and turned into a broad asphalt street, on which wide, glistening bulk windows gave place to sombre shops with lurid, flame-streaked vistas, and continuous residences beyond. Howat Penny gazed curiously at the tall, narrow dwellings, often a continuous, similar façade from street corner to corner, then diversified in elaborate, individual design. All, however, had deep stone steps leading to the sidewalk, thronged with figures in airy white dresses, coatless men smoking contentedly; there was a constant light vibration of laughing voices and subdued calling, and the fainter strains of mechanical music, the

311

beat of popular marches and attenuated voices of celebrated singers.

The motor turned suddenly in to the curb, and they got out. The house before them, like its fellows, was entered from a high flight of red sandstone steps, and was built of a smooth, soapy green stone, with red coursings, an elaborate cornice and tiled Italian roof. No one was sitting outside, although there was a pile of circular, grass-woven cushions; and Howat sharply rang the bell. A maid in aproned black admitted them into a narrow hall, from which stairs mounted with a carved rail terminating in a newel post supporting an almost life-sized bronze nymph, whose flowing hair was encircled by a wreath of electrically lit flowers, and who held a dully shining sheaf of jonquils. There was no other illumination, and Howat Penny discovered in the obscurity a high mirror bristling with elk horns, on which hung various hats and outer garments. He stood helpless, apparently, in an attitude he found impossible to deny himself, waiting to be relieved of his coverings, when Mariana whispered angrily, "Don't be so rotten, Howat."

Finally the maid secured his cape, and he was conscious of a stir at the head of the stairs. Immediately after, a shrill, subdued voice carried to where he stood. "I told you," it said violently, ". . . dress suit." There was an answering murmur, in which he could distinguish James Polder's impatient tones. The latter descended, and flooded

312

the hall with light from a globe in the ceiling. He was garbed in blue serge and flannels. "Isabella," he stated directly, belligerently even, "thinks we ought to change our clothes; but we never do, and I wouldn't hear of — of lying for effect." Howat Penny's dislike for him pleasantly increased. Mariana, in rose crêpe with a soft, dull gold girdle and long, trumpet-like sleeves of flowered gauze, smiled at him warmly. "It is a harmless pose of Howat's," she explained: "a concession to the ghosts of the past." She patted the elder on the shoulder.

Above, James Polder ushered them into a room hung with crimson and gilt stamped paper, an elaborately fretted cherry mantel about the asbestos rectangle of an artificial hearth, and a multitude of chairs and divans shrouded in linen. There was an upright, ebonized piano draped in a fringed, Roman scarf and holding a towering jar of roses, a great, carved easel with a painstaking, smooth oil painting of a dark man in an attitude of fixed dignity, and an expensively cased talking machine. The original, evidently, of the portrait, and a small, rotund woman in mauve brocade, advanced to meet them. Young Polder said, "My mother and father. This is Miss Jannan and Mr. Howat Penny."

The latter saw that Mrs. Byron Polder was distinctly nervous; she twisted the diamonds that occupied a not inconsiderable portion of her short fingers, and smiled rigidly. "I am very pleased to meet you, Miss Jannan," she proceeded; "and Mr. Penny too." She held out a hand, then half withdrew it; but Mariana captured it in her direct palm. "Thank you," she replied. Byron Polder had a more confident poise; in reality there was a perceptible chill in his manner. He was a handsome man, with a cleanly-shaven face, introspective brown eyes and a petulant, drooping mouth. "You have succeeded in finding your way to my house," he pronounced enigmatically, gazing at Howat Penny.

It was, Howat thought, just such an ill-bred utterance as he had looked for from Byron Polder; and he made no effort to mitigate it. He was conscious of, and resolutely ignored, Mariana's veiled entreaty. "You don't know my girls," Mrs. Polder continued rapidly. "Here is Isabella, and Kate will be along for dinner." A tall, bony woman of, perhaps, thirty-five, in an appalling complication of ribbons and silk, moved forward with a conventional sentence. In her, Howat's appraisements went on, virginity had been perpetuated in a captious obsession. They stood awkwardly silent until James Polder exclaimed, "Good heavens, this isn't a wax works! Why don't we sit down?" The older woman glanced with a consuming anxiety at Isabella, and nodded violently toward an exit. "It's a quarter after seven," she said in a swift aside. Isabella, correctly disposed on a chair of muffled and mysterious line, resolutely ignored the appeal.

"I didn't suppose you'd be in the city," she ad-

314

dressed Mariana; " I read in the paper that you had gone to Watch Hill with Mrs. Ledyard B. Starr."

" You can see that I'm back," Mariana smiled. " The family, of course, are at Andalusia, but we have all been in town the past days. I am really staying with Howat at Shadrach."

" The former location of Shadrach Furnace, I believe," Byron Polder stated. " Now in ruins." Howat Penny accurately gathered that the other inferred the collapse not only of the Furnace. He secured the single glass in his eye and looked deliberately around. Isabella watched him with a tense interest. Mrs. Polder gave a short, perturbed giggle. " Just like George Arliss," she told her son. James Polder, on the edge of a chair, was twitching with repressed uneasiness; he frowned antagonistically and then gazed appealingly at Mariana. " I have been introduced to your cousin, Miss Provost," Isabella again took up her social thread. " A dear friend of mine, a talented actress, gave a recitation at Miss Provost's request, for suffrage."

" Eliza's splendid," Mariana pronounced.

" Peter Jannan Provost's daughter," Byron Polder added fully. But his voice indicated that even more, darkly unfavourable, might be revealed. " Miss Provost has been under arrest." Damn the solemn ass, Howat Penny thought. " She's been in the jug twice now," Mariana went on cheerfully; " Kingsfrere had to put up a bond the last time." Mrs. Polder was rapidly regaining her ease. " Wasn't her mamma scared?" she inquired. "I'd go on if Isabella was taken up."

"Imagine Isabella!" Jim Polder exploded. "It's quite the thing," that individual asserted. "Isabella," her mother declared, "it is twenty-five past seven. I wish you'd go out and see where dinner is." She rose with an expression of mingled surprise and pain. "Really, mother," she said, "that is an extraordinary request." Her brother snorted. There was a sudden muffled clamour of chimes from below, and Mrs. Polder gave a sigh of relief. "I didn't want it spoiled," she explained, descending; "Jim would be wild after all his eagerness to have things nice."

The dining room, resembling all the interior, was long and narrow, and had a high ceiling in varnished light wood. Byron Polder faced his wife at the opposite end of the table. Howat Penny sat beside Mariana, with Jim Polder across; Isabella was on her mother's right; and a waiting place was filled by a dark, surprisingly beautiful girl. "This is Kate," Mrs. Polder said proudly. Howat thought he had not seen such a handsome female for years. She wore a ruffled, transparent crêpe de Chine waist that clung in frank curves to full, graceful shoulders; her hair was a lustrous, black coil, and she had sultry, topaz eyes and a mouth drooping like her father's, but more warmly bowed. Kate Polder met the direct pleasure of his inspection with a privately conveyed admission that she understood and subscribed to it.

Here, at last, was a girl up to the standard of old days, the divinity of Scalchi herself. She would have created a sensation in Delmonico's, the real Delmonico's. Gary and the Colonel —

"We think they're elegant," Mrs. Polder's voice broke in on his revery. He looked up and saw a great fish on a huge platter before his host, a fish in surprising semblance to life, had it not been for the rosettes of lemon, the green bed, which surrounded it. "Gracious, no," she answered Mariana's query; "we don't do it home. Mr. Polder has them sent from a Rathskeller down town. He'll make a meal off one." The latter was plainly chagrined at this light thrown on his petty appetites. He assumed an air of complete detachment in the portioning of the dish; but, at the same time, managed to supply himself liberally. The conversation was sporadic. Howat Penny found the dinner lavish, and divided his attention between it and Kate Polder. James and Mariana addressed general remarks to the table at succeeding intervals. Mr. Polder gloomed, and Isabella went through the gestures, the accents, of the occasion with utter correctness. Howat studied Mariana, but he was unable to discover her thoughts; she was smiling and cordial; and apologized for losing her slipper. "I always do," she explained. James Polder hastily rose, and came around to assist her. The dinner was at an end, and she stood with a slim, silken foot outheld for him to replace the fragile object of search.

317

They reassembled above, and Mrs. Polder suggested music. " My son says you are very fond of good music," she addressed Howat Penny. " I can tell you it is a lovely taste. We have the prettiest records that come. Isabella, put on *Hark, Hark, the Lark*." She obediently rose, and, revolving the handle of the talking machine, fixed the grooved, rubber disk and needle. Howat listened with a stony countenance to the ensuing strains. Such instruments were his particular detestation. Mrs. Polder waved her hand dreamily. " Now," she said, " the *Sextette*, and *The End of a Perfect Day*. No, Mr. Penny would like to hear *Salome*, I'm sure, with all those cymbals and creepy Eastern tunes." An orgy of sound followed, applauded — perversely, he was certain — by Mariana. James, he saw, was as uneasy as himself; but for a totally different reason. He gazed at Mariana with a fierce devotion patent to the most casual eye; his expression was tormented with concern and longing.

" When do you return to Harrisburg? " Byron Polder inquired. " My son," he went on to Howat Penny, " is a practical iron man. I say iron, although that is no longer the phrase, because of natural associations. The present system of the manufacture of steel, as you doubtless know, evolved from the old Ironmasters, of whose blood James has a generous share. We look to him to re-establish, er — a departed importance. I need say no more." His women's anxiety at this trend of speech became pain-

ful. " Play a right lively piece," Mrs. Polder interjected, and an intolerable cacophony of banjoes followed, making conversation futile.

The evening, Howat Penny felt, was a considerable
success; by heaven, Mariana would never get herself
into this! Byron Polder's innuendoes must have
annoyed her nicely. When the mechanical disturbance ceased, Mrs. Polder said, " I believe that's the
bell." Evidently she had been correct, for, immediately after, a young woman with bright gold hair,
and a mobile, pink countenance unceremoniously entered the room. " Oh! " she exclaimed, in an instinctively statuesque surprise; " I didn't know you
were entertaining company."

" Come right in, Harriet," Mrs. Polder heartily
proclaimed. " Miss Jannan, Mr. Penny, this is Isabella's friend, Harriet de Barry, a near neighbour
and a sweet girl. She's an actress, too; under-
studies Vivian Blane; and is better, lots say, than the
lead."

Harriet de Barry made a comprehensive gesture.
" I wanted to say good-bye to you all," she announced. " I am going on tour. Leave at midnight.
Just had a wire from Mrs. Blane." There were
polite Polder exclamations, regret, congratulations;
through which the son of the house moodily gazed
at the carpet. " Haven't you anything to say to
Hatty? " his mother demanded. " And after all the
passes she sent you." Howat Penny saw Mariana's
gaze rest swiftly on the latest comer's obvious good

looks; and the scrutiny, he was certain, held a cold feminine appraisal. As they descended to leave Mariana lingered on the stairs with Jim. The latter closed the door of the public motor with a low, intense mutter; and, moving away, Howat Penny lit a cigarette with a breath of audible relief.

" I don't know which I detest most," Mariana declared viciously, " you or myself."

" You might include that fish," he added plaintively. She gazed at him in cold contempt, with an ugly, protruding lip. Nothing else was said until they were in the opened room at the Jannans. Mariana flung herself on a broad divan, with her narrowed gaze fixed on the points of her slippers. " Comfortable, isn't it," she addressed him; " this feeling of superiority?" He placidly nodded, inwardly highly pleased. " I wish I'd married Jim the first week I knew him, without trying to be so dam' admirable. Howat, what is it that makes people what they are, and aren't?" It was, he told her, difficult to express; but it had to do with inherited associations. " Mrs. Polder is as kind as possible," she asserted; " and I could see that you were absorbed in Kate."

" Really, Mariana," he protested, " at times you are a little rough. She is a very fine girl; in fact, reminds me of Scalchi. Old Byron, though, what — a regular catafalque!" A blundering step mounted to the stair; Kingsfrere entered and stood wavering and concerned, the collar wilted and a gaiter missing. " Ought to do something about the front door," he asserted; " frightful condition, no paint; and full of splinters. Very plump splinters," he specified, examining a hand. Mariana surveyed him coolly, thoroughly. " Sweet, isn't he? " she re-marked. " Kingsfrere Gilbert Todd Jannan."

" That's absolutely all," that individual assured her. " Except if you want to add Sturgeon; some do. Hullow, Howat! Grand old boy, Howat," he told her. " But if he says I'm drunk, I will tell you one of Bundy's stories about him. This — this ele-gant deception tremendous noise with the song birds." He sat abruptly on a providentially con-venient chair. There, limply, he hiccoughed. " Sweet," Mariana repeated. Kingsfrere finally rose, and, with a friendly wave, wandered from the room.

" It was good of you to take me, Howat," she told him wearily. " Although, now, I can see that you went willingly enough. You thought it would cure me. But of what, Howat — of love? Of a feeling that, perhaps, I'd found a reason for living? "

A decidedly uncomfortable feeling, doubt, invaded him. He had an unjustified sense of meddling, of blundering into a paramount situation to which he lacked the key. He had done nothing debatable, he assured himself; Mariana's inherent, well — preju-dices, couldn't be charged to him. In the room where he was to sleep the uneasiness followed him. She was his greatest, his only concern. Howat Penny reviewed his desire for her, his preference for a Mariana untouched by the common surge of living. He recalled the discontent, the feeling of sterility, that had lately possessed him; the suspicion that his life had been in vain. All his philosophy, his accumulated convictions, were involved; and, tie in hand, he sat endeavouring to pierce the confusion of his ideas.

He was conscious of a slow change gathering within him; and, in itself, that consciousness was disturbing. It had a vaguely dark, chill aspect. He shivered, in the room super-heated by summer; his blood ran thinner and cold. Howat Penny had a sudden, startling sense of his utter loneliness; there was absolutely no one, now, to whom he could turn for the understanding born of long and intimately affectionate association. Mariana was lost to him in her own poignant affair . . . No children. So many, so much, dead. His countenance, however, grew firm with the determination that age should not find him a coward. He had always been bitterly contemptuous of the men that, surfeiting their appetites, showed at the impotent last a cheap repentance. But he had done nothing pointedly wrong; he had — the inversion repeated itself — done nothing.

XXVII

AT Shadrach his customary decision returned; he went about, or sat reading, well-ordered, cool-appearing, dogmatic. He learned from the *Evening Post* that Mariana was at Warrenton. She had carefully described to him the Virginia country life, the gaiety and hard riding of the transplanted English colonies; and he pictured her at the successive horse shows, in the brilliant groups under the Doric columns of the porticoes. Then, he saw, she had gone north; he found her picture in a realistic Egyptian costume with bare, painted legs at an extravagant ball. He studied her countenance, magnifying it with a reading glass; but he saw nothing beyond a surface enjoyment of the moment.

Then, to his utter surprise, on an evening after dinner, when he was seated in the settling dusk of the porch, intent on the grey movements of his familiar owls, a quick step mounted the path, and James Polder appeared.

"I wanted to ask about Miss Jannan," the latter stated frankly and at once. Howat Penny cleared his throat sharply. "I believe she is well," he stated formally. "You will find it cooler here." It struck him that the young man was not deficient

323

in that particular. More, of still greater directness, followed. "I suppose you know," Polder
stated, "that I want to marry her . . . and she
won't."

"I had gathered something of the sort," the
other admitted. "It's natural, in a way." Polder
proceeded gloomily: "I'd take her away from so
much. And, yet, look here — you can shut me up
if you like — what's it all about? Can you tell me
that?" Howat Penny couldn't. "I'm not to blame
for that old mess any more than you. And it's not
my fault if something of — of which you think so
much came to me by the back door. I've always
wanted what Mariana is," he burst out, "and I
have never been satisfied with what I could get.
And when I saw her, hell — what's the use!

"Any one in Harrisburg will tell you I am a
good man," he reiterated, at a slightly different angle. "When you kick through out of that racket
of hunkies and steel you've done something. Soon
I'll be getting five or six thousand." He paused, and
the other said dryly, "Admirable." The phrase
seemed to him inadequate; it sounded in his ear as
unpleasantly as a false note. Yet he was powerless
to alter it, change its brusque accent. The personal tone of Polder's revelations was inherently distasteful to him. He said, rising, "If you will ex-
cuse me I'll tell Rudolph you will be here."

"But I won't," Polder replied; "there's a train
back at eleven. I have to be at the mills for the

324

day shift to-morrow. I came out because I had to talk a little about Mariana." He had deserted the more formal address. " And I wanted to tell some one connected with her that I have gimp of my own. I know why she won't marry me, and it's a small reason; it would be small in —"

" Hold up," Howat Penny interrupted, incensed. " Am I to understand that you came here to com‹ plain about Miss Jannan's conduct? That won't do, you know."

" It's a small reason," the other insisted hotly. " Hardly more than the idiotic fact that I'm not in the Social Register. I am ashamed of her, and I said so. It was so little that I told her I wouldn't argue. She could go to the devil."

" Really," the other observed, " really, I shall have to ask you to control your language or leave."

" I wonder if she will? " the surprising James Polder sombrely speculated. " I wonder if I am? But there are other women, with better hearts."

" Are we to construe this as a threat? " Howat asked in a delicately balanced tone.

" For God's sake," he begged, " can't you be human ! " The other suddenly recalled Mariana's imploring anger at the Polders. " Don't be so rotten, Howat." The confusion of his valuations, his habitual attitudes of thought, returned. His gaze strayed to the obscured ruin of Shadrach Furnace, at once a monument of departed vigour and present disintegration. Perhaps, just as the energy had expired in the Furnace, it had seeped from him. It might be that he was only a sere husk, a dry bundle of inhibitions, insensible to the green humanity of life.

"I couldn't go on my knees to anything," the younger took up his burden. "Wrong or not it is the way I'm made. I'd not hang about where I wasn't wánted. Although you mightn't think it. And I am sorry I came here. I do things like that all the time; I mean I do, say, exactly the opposite of what I plan. You'll think I am a braying ass, of course."

"Stop for a breath," Howat Penny recommended; "a breath, and a cigarette." He extended his case; and, in place of taking a cigarette, Polder examined the case resentfully. "There is it," he declared; "correct, like all the rest of you. And it's only old leather. But mine would be different. I could sink and Mariana wouldn't put out a hand just on account of that. It's wrong," he insisted. Expressed in that manner it did seem to Howat Penny a small reason for the withholding of any paramount salvation. Yet, he told himself, he had no intention, desire, to undertake the weight of any reformation. A futile effort, he added, with his vague consciousness of implacable destiny, his dim sense of man moved from without, in locked progression. Polder was young, rebellious; but he could grow older; he would grow older and comprehend; or else beat himself to death on obdurate cir-

326

cumstance. What concerned Howat was the hope that Mariana would be no further involved in either process. She too had this to learn — that, in the end, blood was stronger than will; the dead were terribly potent. He had, even, no inclination to say any of this to the man frowning in the dusk at his side. It would be useless, a mere preaching. An expression, too, of a slight but actual sympathy for James Polder would be misleading. In the main Howat was entirely careless of what might happen to the other; it was only where, unfortunately, he touched Mariana that he entered into the elder's world. He would sacrifice him for Mariana in an instant. Polder rose.

"I must leave," he announced. Howat Penny expressed no regret, and the other hesitated awkwardly. "It's no use!" he finally exclaimed. "I can't reach you; as if one of us spoke Patagonian. Hellish, it seems to me." He turned and disappeared, as violently as he had come, over the obscurity of the lawn. A reddish, misshapen moon hung low in the sky, and gave the aging man an extraordinarily vivid impression of dead planets, unthinkable wastes of time, illimitable systems and spaces. James Polder's passionate resentment, his own emotion, were no more articulate than the thin whirring of the locusts. He went quickly into the house, to the warm glow of his lamp, the memories of his pictures, the figurine in baked clay with Hermes' wand of victory.

XXVIII

THE heat dragged through the remainder of August and filled September with steaming days and heavy nights, followed by driving grey storms and premonitory, chill dawns. A period of sunny tranquillity succeeded, but crimson blots of sumach, the warmer tone of maples, made it evident that summer had lapsed. Honduras mulched the strawberries, and set new teeth in his lawn rakes. The days passed without feature, or word from Mariana, and Howat Penny fell into an almost slumberous monotony of existence. It was not unpleasant; occupied with small duties, intent on his papers, or wandering in a past that seemed to grow clearer, rather than fade, as time multiplied, he maintained his erect, carefully ordered existence. Then, among his mail, he found a large, formal-appearing envelope which he opened with a mild curiosity. His attitude of detachment was soon dispelled.

Mrs. Corinne de Barry desired the pleasure of his attendance at the wedding of her daughter, Harriet, to James Polder. Details, a church and hour, were appended. The headlong young man, he thought, with a smile. Mariana was well out of that. He had been wise in saying nothing to Charlotte; the thing had expired naturally. But, irrationally, he thought of Polder with a trace of contempt — a man who had, unquestionably, possessed Mariana Jannan's regard marrying the pink-faced understudy to a second-rate emotional actress! In a way it made him cross; the fellow should have shown a — a greater appreciation, delicacy. "Commonplace," he said decisively, aloud. The following day Mariana herself appeared, with a touch of sable and a small, wickedly becoming hat.

He was at lunch; and, without delay, she took the place smilingly laid for her by Rudolph. It was characteristic that she made no pretence of concealing the reason that had brought her to Shadrach. "Jim's going to marry that Harriet de Barry," she said at once, nicely casual. "I had a card," he informed her. "It's to be on the thirtieth," Mariana proceeded, "at eight o'clock and in church. Of course you are going."

"Not at all of course," he replied energetically. "And you'll stay away for the plainest decency."

"We will go together," she proceeded calmly. "I want to see Jim married, happy." She gazed at him with narrowed eyes.

"Mariana," he told her, "that's a shameful lie. It is cold, feminine curiosity. It's worse — the only vulgar thing I can remember your considering. I won't hear of it." He debated the wisdom of recounting James Polder's last visit to Shadrach and decided in the negative. " Let the young man depart with his Harriet in peace."

" It's sickening, isn't it? " she queried. " And yet it is so like Jim. He had a very objectional idea of his dignity; he was sensitive in a way that made me impatient. He couldn't forget himself, you see. That helped to make it difficult for me; I wasn't used to it; his feelings were always being damaged."

Howat Penny nodded. " You'll recall I emphasized that." Mariana looked worn by her gaiety, he decided, white; for the first time in his memory she seemed older than her actual years. Her friends, he knew, her existence, bore the general appellation, fast; Howat had no share in the condemnatory aspect of the term, but he realized that it had a literal application. Their pace was feverish, and Mariana plainly showed its effects. Her voice, already noted as more mature, had, he was sure, hardened. She dabbled her lips thickly with a rouge stick. " Mariana," he said querulously, " I wish you'd stop this puppet dance you're leading. I wish you would marry."

" I tried to," she coolly replied, " but you spoiled my young dream of happiness."

" That isn't true," he asserted sharply, perturbed. " Anything that happened, or didn't happen, was only the result of yourself, of what you are. I am extremely anxious to have you settled, and your legs out of the Sunday papers. I — I am opposed to your present existence; it's gone on too long. I believe I'd rather see you orating on the streets, like Eliza Provost. And, by thunder, I never thought I should come to that! Champagne and those damnable syncopated tunes played by hysterical niggers make a poor jig." He spoke impetuously, unconscious of any reversal of previous judgments, opinions.

"You are so difficult to please, Howat," she said wearily; "you were aghast at the thought of my marrying James, and now you are complaining of the natural alternative. The truth is," she added brutally, "you are old-fashioned; you think life goes on just as it did when the Academy of Music was the centre of your world. And nothing is the same." She rose, and, with a lighted cigarette and half-shut eyes, fell into a rhythmic step of sensuous abandon. "You see," she remarked, pausing. An increasing dread for her filled his heart. He felt, in response to her challenge, a sudden bewilderment in the world of to-day. Things, Howat Penny told himself, were marching to the devil. He said this irritably, loud, and she laughed. " I'm going in by an early train," she proceeded. "We have left the country. Will you stop for me on the thirtieth? Early, Howat, so we can be sure of a good place."

His helplessness included the subject of her remarks; he would, he realized, be at James Polder's wedding, but he persisted in his opinion. " A low piece of business," Howat declared. When she had gone he felt that he had not penetrated her actual attitude toward Polder's deflection. He had not for a moment got beneath her casual manner, her lightness, pretended or actual. He wished vehemently that he were back again in the past he comprehended, among the familiar figures that had thronged the notable dinner to Patti, the women who had floated so graciously through the poetry of departed waltzes. He got out his albums once more, scrutinized through his polished glass the programmes of evenings famous in song. But he went to bed a full two hours earlier than customary; his feet positively dragged up the stairs; above he sat strangely exhausted, breathing heavily for, apparently, no reason whatever.

He retraced, with Mariana, the course over the broad, asphalt way into the north end of the city early on the evening of the thirtieth. They found the church easily, by reason of a striped canvas tunnel stretched out to the curb; and a young man with plastered hair and a gardenia led them, Mariana on his arm, to a place on the centre aisle. The church had a high nave newly vaulted in maple, and stained glass windows draped with smilax, garish in colour against electric lights. Above the altar a great illuminated cross maintained an unsteady flickering; and — it was unseasonably cold — heating steam pipes gave out an expanding racket.

The pews through the centre filled rapidly; there was a low, excited chatter of voices, and a spreading tropical expanse of the dyed feathers and iridescent foliage of womens' hats. An overpowering scent of mingled perfumes rose and filled the interior. The strains of an organ grew audible, contesting with the rattle of the steam pipes. Howat Penny was detached, critical. Mariana, in a dull, black satin wrap of innumerable soft folds and wide paisley collar slipping from a sheath-like bodice of gleaming, cut steel beading, was silent, incurious. He turned to her, to point out an extravagant figure, but he said nothing. She was, evidently, in no mood for the enjoyment of the ridiculous. This disturbed him; he had not thought that she would be so — so concerned. He suppressed an impatient exclamation, and returned to the scrutiny of the culminating ceremony.

Here was a sphere, vastly larger than his own, to the habits and prejudices of which he was complete stranger. It was as James Polder had said — as if one or the other spoke Patagonian. He had no wish to acquire the language about him; a positive antagonism to his surrounding possessed him, beyond reason. He thought — how different Mariana is from all this, and was annoyed again at her serious bearing. Then he was surprised by his presence there at all; confound the girl, why didn't she play with her own kind! Yet only the other day the glimpse she had given him of her natural associates had filled him with dread. His mind, striving to encompass the problem of Mariana's existence, failed to overcome the walls built about him by time, by habit. He gave it up. The louder pealing of the organ announced immediate developments.

There was a stir in the front of the church, a clergyman in white vestment advanced; and, at a sudden murmurous interest, a twisting of heads, the wedding procession moved slowly up the aisle. The ushers, painstakingly adopting various lengths of stride to the requirements of the organ, passed in pairs; then followed an equal number of young women, among whom he instantly recognized the handsome presence of Kate Polder, in drooping blue bonnets, with prodigious panniers of celestial-hued silk, carrying white enamelled shepherd's crooks from which depended loops of artificial buttercups. An open space ensued, in the centre of which advanced a child with starched white skirts springing out in a lacy wheel about spare, bare knees, her pale yellow hair tied in an overwhelming blue bow; and holding outstretched, in a species of intense and quivering agony, a white velvet cushion to which were pinned two gold wedding bands.

After that, Howat Penny thought, the prospective bride could furnish only the diminished spectacle of an anti-climax. Led by the virginal presence of Isabella Polder she floated forward in a foam of white tulle and dragging satin attached below her bare, full shoulders. A floating veil, pinned with a wreath of orange blossoms, manifestly wax, covered the metallic gold of her hair. Her countenance was unper-

334

turbed, statuesque, and pink. As the sentimental clamour of the organ died the steam pipes took up, with renewed vigour, their utilitarian noise. " Why don't they turn them off? " Mariana exclaimed in his ear. Personally he enjoyed such an accompaniment to what he designated as the performance.

He cast the participants in their inevitable rôles — the bride as prima donna, James Polder the heroic tenor. Mrs. Corinne de Barry, a thin, concerned figure in glistening lavender, supported a lamenting mezzo, the bulky, masculine figure at her side, with an imposing diamond on a hand like two bricks, was beautifully basso —

His train of thought was abruptly upset by James Polder's familiar, staccato utterance. The precipitant young man! It stamped out all Howat Penny's humorous condescension; his sensitive ear was conscious of a note, almost, of desperation. He avoided looking at Mariana. Damn it, the thing unexpectedly cut at him like a knife. James Polder said, " I will." The clear, studied tones of Harriet de Barry, understudy to Vivian Blane, were spoiled by the crackling of steam. Howat moved uneasily; he had an absurd sense of guilt; he hated the whole proceeding. What was that Polder, whose voice persisted so darkly in his hearing, about, getting himself into such a snarl? He recalled what the younger had said on his porch —" women with better hearts." He had implored him, Howat Penny, to be " more human." The memory, too, of the

335

shaken tone of that request bothered him. Now it
appeared that he might have been, well, more human.
He composed himself, facing such sentimental illusions, into a savage indifference to what remained
of the ceremony; he ignored the passage of Polder,
with Harriet Polder on his arm; the relief of the
unspeakable child carrying the white velvet cushion
no longer in the manner of a hot plate; the united
bridesmaids and ushers. "Thank heaven, that's
over!" he ejaculated in the deeply-comfortable
space of the Jannan's motor laundalet. "But it
isn't," Mariana said briefly. She sat silent, with
her head turned from him, through the remainder of
the short drive about Rittenhouse Square. Then
she went abruptly to her room.

Charlotte Jannan and her oldest child, Sophie
Lewis, were above in the living room. The former
was handsome in a rigid way; her countenance,
squarely and harshly formed, with grey hair exactly
waved and pinned, had an expression of cold firm-
ness; her voice was assertive and final. Sophie, apparently midway in appearance between Kingsfrere
and Mariana, was gracefully proportioned, and gave
an impression of illusive beauty by means of a mystery of veils, such as were caught up on her hat now.
They were discussing, he discovered, the family.

"It's an outrage, Howat," Charlotte told him,
"you never married, and that the name will go.
Here's Mariana at twenty-seven, almost, and nothing in sight; and Sophie flatly refuses, after only

one, to have another child. I wish now I'd had a
dozen. It is really the duty of the proper people.
And Eliza Provost won't hear of a man! I tell
Sophie it's their own fault when they complain about
society to-day. It's the fault of this charity work
and athletics, too; both extremely levelling. Hundreds of women wind bandages or go to the hunt
races and gabble about votes for no reason under
heaven but superior associates."

"Howat will feelingly curse the present with you,"
Sophie said rising. "I must go. Borrow the motor, if you don't mind. I saw in the paper a Polder
was married." Howat Penny lit a cigarette, admirably stolid. "A name I never repeat," Charlotte Jannan said when her daughter had left. He
heard again the echo of James Polder's intense
voice, "I will." Something of his dislike for him,
he discovered, had evaporated. Howat thought of
Mariana, in her room — alone with what feelings?
He realized that Charlotte would never have forgiven
her for any excursion in that direction. He himself
had been, was, entirely opposed to such a connection. However, he could now dismiss it into the
past that held a multitude of similarly futile imagin-
ings.

Charlotte, he inferred, had no elasticity; it was a
quality the absence of which he had not before noted.
She was a little narrow in her complacency. Her
patent satisfaction in Sophie was a shade too — too
worldly. Sam Lewis was, of course, irreproachably

337

situated; but he was, at the same time, thick-witted, an indolent appendage for his name. Suddenly he felt poignantly sorry for Mariana; in a way she seemed to have been trapped by life. James Polder resembled her in that he had been caught in an ugly net of circumstance. A great deal had been upset since his day, when the boxes and pit had been so conveniently separated; old boundaries no longer defined, limited, their content; social demarcations were being obliterated by a growing disaffection. It was very unfortunate, for, as he was seeing, unhappiness ensued. It was bound to. An irritability seized him at being dragged into such useless conjecturing; into, at his age, confusing complications; and he greeted with relief the long, low front of his dwelling at Shadrach, its old grey stone a seeming outcropping of the old green turf, the aged, surrounding trees.

XXIX

MARIANA, however, followed him almost immediately. She stood before him in an informal, belted black wool sweater, a ridiculously inadequate skirt, and the solid shoes he detested on women. But he soon forgot her garb.

"Howat," she told him, "I have made a cowardly and terrible mistake. I was meant to marry Jimmy, and I didn't. Perhaps I have ruined his life. Mine will be nothing without him." They were in the middle room, and a fire of hickory was burning in the panelled hearth. She dropped on a chair, and sat gazing into the singing flames. Here it's all to do over, he thought, with a feeling of weariness. "He may get along very well with his Harriet," he remarked, resentful of his dissipated contentment.

"You know he won't," she replied sharply. "He loves me; and I love him, Howat. I never knew how much, or how little anything else mattered, until I was in my room, after his wedding. It wasn't a wedding, really," she declared. "All that doesn't make one. He'll find it out, too. Jimmy will be desperate, and I'm afraid he will drink harder. He told me they were getting frightfully strict about that at the Works. And there's that reorganization; it will embitter him if he isn't made superintendent. He has worked splendidly for it. That woman he — he went off with is a squash," she said vindictively. " She will be in bed when he goes away in the morning, and in crêpe de Chine negligee when he gets back. Perhaps it won't last," she added thoughtfully.

The sense of future security generated in Howat Penny by the marriage abruptly departed. He fumbled with his glass, directed it at Mariana. " What do you mean by that? " he demanded. " I would go to him like a shot, if he needed me," she coolly returned. The dreadful part of it was that he was sure she would. " Nonsense," he asserted, hiding his concern; " there will be no fence climbing." All this came from the letting down of conversational bars, the confounded books he found about on tables. Words, like everything else, had lost their meanings. In his day a bad woman was bad, a good, likewise, good; but the Lord couldn't tell them apart now. It was the dancing, too. Might as well be married to a man, he thought.

Mariana was haggard, the paint on her face crudely — paint. He saw that there were tears in her eyes, and he turned away confused, rose. The slot in his cigarette box refused to open, and he shook it violently, then put it back with a clatter. " Tell Rudolph you're here," he said disjointedly; and, miserable, left the room. Dressing he stood at a window; the west held a narrow strip of crimson light under a windy mass of cloud. The ruin of Shadrach Furnace was sombre. Within, the room was almost bare. There was a large, high-posted bed without drapings, a vermilion lacquered table, dark with age, supporting a glass lamp at its side; a set of drawers with old brass handles; a pair of stiff Adam chairs with wheel backs; and a modern mahogany dressing case, variously and conveniently divided, a clear mirror in the door.

The day failed rapidly, and he lit a pair of small lamps on the set of drawers. The sun sank in no time at all. Mariana, crying. The girl ought to go to her mother, and not come out to him, an old man, with her intimate troubles. " A name I never repeat," Charlotte had said. That was just like her. Small sympathy there, and no more understanding. He knotted his tie hurriedly, askew; and gathered the ends once more. It tired him a little to dress in the evening; often he longed to stay relaxed, pondering, until Rudolph called him to dinner. But every day something automatic, tyrannical, dragged him up to his room, encased him in rigid linen, formal black. Mariana, against the fireplace, ate listlessly; and, later, he beat her with shameful ease at sniff.

" You can't do that," he pointed out with asperity, when she thoughtlessly joined unequal numbers. " Why not? " she asked. She must be addled. " It's against the rule." Mariana said, " I'm tired

341

of rules." She always had put away the dominoes, but to-night she ignored them, and he returned the pieces to their morocco case. She relapsed into silence and a chair; and he sat with gaze fixed on the hickory in the fireplace, burning to impalpable, white ash.

What a procession of logs had been there reduced to dust, warming generations of men now cold. The thought of all those lapsed winters and lives soothed him; the clamour of living seemed to retreat, to leave him in a grey tranquillity. His head sank forward, and his narrow, dark hands rested in absolute immobility on the arms of his chair. He roused suddenly to discover that Mariana had gone up, and that there were only some fitful, rosy embers of fire left. In November it had been his custom to go into town for the winter; and it was time for him to make such arrangement; but, all at once, he was overwhelmingly reluctant to face the change, the stir, of moving. The city seemed intolerably noisy, oppressive; the thought of the hurrying, indifferent crowds disconcerted him. At Shadrach it was quiet, familiar, spacious. He had had enough of excursions, strange faces, problems. . . . He would speak to Rudolph. Stay.

XXX

THE countryside, it appeared to Howat
Penny, flamed with autumn and faded in a
day. Throughout the night he heard the
crisp sliding of dead leaves over the roof, the lash
of the wind swung impotently about the rectangular,
stone block of his dwelling. At the closing of shutters the December gales only penetrated to him in
a thin, distant complaint. The burning hickory
curtained the middle room with a ruddy warmth.
It was a period of extreme peace; he slept for long
hours in a deep chair, or sat lost in a simulation of
sleep, living again in the past. The present was
increasingly immaterial, unimportant; old contro-
versies occupied him, long since stilled; and among
the memories of opera, of Eames as a splendid girl,
forgotten rôles, were other, vaguer associations, impressions which seemed to linger from actual happenings, but persistently evaded definition. At
times, his eyes closed, the glow of his fireplace burned
hotter, more lurid, and was filled with faintly clamorous sounds; at times there was, woven through his
half-wakeful dreaming, a monotonous beat . . .
such as the fall of a hammer. He saw, too, strange
and yet familiar faces — a girl in silk like an ex-

travagant tea rose; a countenance seamed and glistening with pain floated in shadow; and then another mocked and mocked him. Once he heard the drumming of rain, close above; and the illusion was so strong that he made his way to the door; a black void was glistening with cold and relentless stars. . . . Now he was standing by a dark, hurrying river, nothing else was visible; and yet he was thrilled by a sense of utter rapture.

He developed a feeling of the impermanence of life, his hold upon it no stronger than the tenuous cord of a balloon straining impatiently in great, unknown currents. The future lost all significance, reality; there were only memories; the vista behind was long and clear, but the door to to-morrow was shut. Looking into his mirror the reflection was far removed; it was hollow-cheeked and silvered, unfamiliar. He half expected to see a different face, not less lean, but more arrogant, with a sharply defined chin. The actual, blurred visage accorded ill with his trains of thought; it was out of place among the troops of gala youth.

A wired letter, a customary present of cigarettes, came from Mariana on Christmas, gifts from Charlotte and Bundy Provost. There was champagne at his place for dinner; and he sealed crisp money in envelopes inscribed Rudolph, Honduras, and the names of the cook and maid. He drank the wine solemnly; the visions were gone; and he saw himself as an old man lingering out of his time, alone.

There was, however, little sentimental melancholy in the realization; he held an upright pride, the inextinguishable accent of a black Penny. His disdain for the commonality of life still dictated his prejudices. He informed Rudolph again that the present opera was without song; and again Rudolph gravely echoed the faith that melody was the heart of music.

The winds grew even higher, shriller; the falls of snow vanished before drenching, brown rains, and the afternoons perceptibly lengthened. There was arbutus on the slopes, robins, before he recognized that April was accomplished. A farmer ploughed the vegetable garden behind the house; and Honduras dragged the cedar bean poles from their resting place. Mariana soon appeared.

"I wouldn't miss the spring at Shadrach for a hundred years of hibiscus," she told him. He gathered that she had been south. She brought him great pleasure, beat him with annoying frequency at sniff, and was more companionable than ever before. She had, he thought, forgot James Polder; and he was careful to avoid the least reference to the latter. Mariana was a sensible girl; birth once more had told.

She was better looking than he had remembered her, more tranquil; a distinguished woman. It was incredible that a man approximately her equal had not appeared. Then, without warning — they were seated on the porch gazing through the tender green

foliage of the willow at the vivid young wheat beyond
— she said:

"Howat, I am certain that things are going badly
with Jimmy. He wrote to me willingly in the winter, but twice since then he hasn't answered a letter."

He suppressed a sharp, recurrent concern. "It's
that Harriet," he told her, capitally diffident.
"You are stupid to keep it up. What chance would
he have had answering her letters married to you?"

"This is different," she replied confidently. He
saw that he had been wrong — nothing had
changed, lessened. Howat swore silently. That
damnable episode might well spoil her entire existence. But he wisely avoided argument, comment.
A warm current of air, fragrant with apple blossoms,
caught the ribbon-like smoke of his cigarette and
dissipated it. She smiled with half-closed eyes at
the new flowering of earth. Her expression grew
serious, firm. "I think we'd better go out to Harrisburg," she remarked, elaborately casual, "and see
Jimmy for ourselves."

He protested vehemently, but — from experience
in that quarter — with a conviction of futility.
"She'll laugh at you," he told Mariana. "Haven't
you any proper pride?" She shook her head.
"Not a scrap. It's just that quality in Jim that
annoyed me, and spoiled everything. I'd cook for
them if it would do any good." Irritation mastered
him. "This is shameful, Mariana," he declared.
"Don't your position, your antecedents, stand for

346

anything? If I had Jasper Penny here I would tell him what I thought of his confounded behaviour!" He rose, and walked the length of the porch and back.

"The first part of next week?" she queried. "I won't go a mile," he stated, in sheer bravado. "Then," said Mariana, "I must do it alone." He muttered a period in which the term hussy was solely audible. "Which of us?" she asked, calmly. "Actually," he exploded, "I feel sorry for that Harriet. I sympathize with her. She got the precious James fair enough, and the decent thing for you is to keep away."

"But I'm not decent either," Mariana continued. "If you could know what is in my head you'd recognize that. I seem to have no good qualities. I don't want them, Howat," her voice intensified; "I want Jim."

He was completely silenced by this desire persisting in spite of every established obstacle. It summoned an increasing response at the core of his being. Such an attitude was, more remotely, his own; but in him it had been purely negative, an inhibition rather than a challenge; he had kept out of life instead of actively defying it. In him the family inheritance of blackness was subsiding with the rest.

Howat maintained until the moment of their departure his protest, his perverse community with Harriet Polder. "You'll find a happy house," he

347

predicted, " and come home like a fool. I hope you do. It ought to help make you more reasonable. She will tell James to give you a comfortable chair, and apologize for not asking you to dinner." She gazed through the car window without replying. He realized that he had never seen Mariana more becomingly dressed — she wore a rough, silver-coloured suit with a short jacket, a pale green straw hat, like the new willow leaves, across the blueness of her eyes, and an innumerably ruffled and flounced waist of thinnest batiste. A square, deep emerald hung from a platinum chain about her neck; and a hand, stripped of its thick white glove, showed an oppressive, prismatic glitter of diamonds.

The morning was filled with dense, low, grey cloud, under which the river on their left flowed without a glimmer of brightness. Howat was aware of an increasing sulphurous pall, and suddenly the train was passing an apparently endless confusion of great, corrugated iron sheds, rows of towering, smoking stacks, enormous, black cylinders, systems of tracks over which shrilling locomotives hauled carloads of broken slag, or bumped strings of trucks, with reckless energy, in and out of the grimy interiors. The overpowering magnitude of the steel works — Howat Penny needed no assurance of its purpose — exceeded every preconception.

Shut between the river and an abrupt hillside, where scattered dwellings and sparse trees and ground were coated with a soft monotony of rose-

348

brown dust, the mills were jumbled in mile-long perspectives. Above the immediate noise of the train
he could hear the sullen, blended roar of an infinity
of strident sounds — the screaming of whistles, a
choked, drumming thunder, rushing blasts of air, the
shattering impact of steel rails, raw steam, and a
multitudinous clangour of metal and jolting wheels
and connective power. He passed rusting mountains
straddled by giant gantries, the towering lifts of
mammoth cranes, banks of chalk-white stone, dizzy
super-structures mounted by spasmodic skips.

As the train proceeded with scarcely abated speed,
and the vast operation continued without a break,
mill on mill, file after file of stacks, Howat Penny's
senses were crushed by the spectacle of such incredible labour. Suddenly a column of fire, deep orange
at the core, raying through paler yellow to a palpitating white brilliancy, shot up through the torn vapours, the massed and shuddering smoke, to the
clouds, and was sharply withdrawn in a coppery
smother pierced by a rapid, lance-like thrust of steel-
blue flame.

These stupendous miles were, to-day, the furnaces
and forges that Gilbert Penny had built and operated in the pastoral clearings of the Province.
Howat recalled the single, diminutive shed of Myrtle
Forge, the slender stream, the wheel, its sole power;
the solitary stack of Shadrach Furnace, recreated in
his vision, opposed its insignificant bulk against the
living greenery of overwhelming forests. Now the

forests were gone, obliterated by the mills that had grown out of Gilbert's energy and determination, his pioneer courage. His spirit, the indomitable will of a handful of men, a small, isolated colony, had swept forward in a resistless tide, multiplying invention, improvement, with success until, as Howat had seen, their flares reached to the clouds, their industry spread in iron cities. James Polder had a part in this. Here, under the ringing walls of the steel mills, he got a fresh comprehension of the bitter, restless virility of the younger man.

Out of the station Mariana furnished the driver of a public motor with James Polder's address, and they twisted through congested streets, past the domed Capitol, rising from intense green sod, flanked by involved groups of sculpture, to a quieter reach lying parallel with the river. They discovered Polder's house occupying a corner, one of a short row of yellow brick with a scrap of lawn bound by a low wall, and a porch continuous across the face of the dwellings.

The door opened after a long interval, and a woman with bare arms and a spotted kitchen apron admitted them to an interior faintly permeated with the odours of cooking. There were redly varnished chairs, upright piano, a heavily framed saccharine print of loves and a flushed, sleeping divinity; a table scarred by burning cigarettes, holding cerise knitting on needles one of which was broken, glasses with dregs of beer, a photograph in a tarnished sil-

350

ver frame of Harriet de Barry Polder with undraped shoulders and an exploited dimple, and a copy of a technical journal. A fretful, shrill barking rose at their heels; and Howat Penny swung his stick at a diminutive, silky white dog with matted, pinkish eyes, obsessed by an impotent fury.

An indolent voice drifted from above. "Cherette!" And a low, masculine protest was audible. Mariana Jannan's face was inscrutable. The woman continued audibly, "How can I — like this? You will have to see what it is." A moment later James Polder, drawing on a coat, descended the stairs. He saw Mariana at once, and stood arrested with one foot on the floor, and a hand clutching the rail. A sudden pallor invaded his countenance and Howat turned away, inspecting the print. But he could not close his hearing to the suppressed eagerness, the stammering joy, of Polder's surprise.

"And you, too," he said to the elder, with a crushing grip. Howat immediately recognized that the other was marked by an obvious ill health; his eyes were hung with shadows, like smudges of the iron dust, and his palm was hot and wet. "Harriet," he called up the stair, "here's Miss Jannan and Mr. Howat Penny to see us." A complete silence above, then a sharp rustle, replied to his announcement. "Harriet will be right down," he continued; "fixing herself up a little first. Have trouble finding us? Second Street is high for a foreman, but we're moving out against the future."

The dog maintained a stridulous barking; and James Polder carried her, in an ecsatsy of snarling ill-temper, out. "Cherette doesn't appreciate callers," he stated, with an expression that contradicted the mildness of his words. His gaze, Howat thought, rested on Mariana with the intensity of a fanatic Arab at the apparition of Mohammed. And Mariana smiled back with a penetrating comprehension and sympathy. The proceeding made Howat Penny extremely uncomfortable; it was — was barefaced. He hoped desperately that something more appropriately casual would meet the appearance of Harriet. Mariana said:

"You haven't been well." Polder replied that it was nothing. "I get a night shift," he explained, "and I've never learned to sleep through the day. We're working under unusual pressure, too; inhuman contracts, success." He smiled without gaiety. "You didn't answer my letter," the outrageous Mariana proceeded. Howat withered mentally at her cool daring, and Polder, now flushed, avoided her gaze. The necessity of answer was bridged by the descent of his wife. Her face, as always, brightly coloured, was framed in an instinctively effective twist of gold hair; and she wore an elaborately braided, white cloth skirt, a magenta georgette crêpe waist, with a deep, boyish collar, drawn tightly across her full, soft body.

"Isn't it fierce," she demanded cheerfully, "with Jim out as many nights as he's in bed?" She produced a pasteboard package of popular cigarettes and offered them to Howat Penny and Mariana. "Sorry, I can't smoke any others," she explained, striking a match. "I heard you saying he doesn't look right," she addressed Mariana. "And it's certainly the truth. Who would with what he does? I tell him our life is all broke up. One night stands used to get me, but they're a metropolitan run compared with this. Honest to God," she told them good naturedly, "I've threatened to leave him already. I'd rather see him a property man with me on the road."

"It must be a little wearing," Mariana agreed; "but then, you know, your husband is a steel man. This is his life." Howat Penny could see the cordiality ebbing from the other woman's countenance. Positively, Mariana ought to be . . . "I can get that," Harriet Polder informed her. "We are only hanging on till Jim's made superintendent. Then we'll be regular inhabitants. Any other small thing?" At the sharpening note of her voice James Polder hurriedly proceeded with general facts. "You'll want to see the Works, as much as I can show you. Hardly any of the public are let through now. It will interest you, sir, to see what the Penny iron trade has become. I can take you down this afternoon. Harriet will find us some lunch." The latter moved in a sensuous deliberation, followed by a thin, acidulous trail of smoke, into inner rooms. "When do you have to go back?" Polder asked

353

" This evening," Howat told him; " we just stopped to —"

" To see how you were," Mariana interrupted him baldly, studying the younger man with a concerned frown. " You ought to rest, you know," she decided. " That's possible," he returned. " I thought of asking for a couple of weeks. I hurried back right after I was married. They are coming to me." She enigmatically regarded Howat Penny; he saw that she was about to speak impetuously; but, to his great relief, she stopped. " It's been pretty hard on Harriet," he said instead. " After the stage and audiences, and all that." Mariana's expression was cold. Confound her, why didn't she help the fellow! Howat Penny fidgeted with his stick. What a stew Polder had gotten himself into. This was worse, even, than the marriage threatened.

Lunch was a spasmodic affair of cutlets hardening in grease, blue boiled potatoes, sandy spinach and blanched ragged bread. There was more beer; but Jim, his wife proceeded, liked whiskey and water with his meals. The former glanced uneasily at Mariana, tranquilly cutting up her cutlet. The diamonds on her narrow, delicate hand flashed, the emerald at her throat was superb. Their surroundings were doubly depressing contrasted with her fastidious dress and person. Before her composure Harriet Polder seemed over-florid; a woman of trite phrases, commonplace, theatrical attitudes and emotions. As lunch progressed the latter relapsed into a sulky silence; she glanced surreptitiously at Mariana's apparel; and consumed cigarettes with a straining assumption of easy indifference.

Howat Penny was acutely uncomfortable, and Polder scowled at his plate. The whiskey and water shook in a tense, unsteady hand. He rose from the table with a violent relief. He proposed almost immediately that they go over to the Works, and Mariana turned pleasantly to his wife. " Shall you get a hat? " The other hesitated, then asserted defiantly, " I've always said I wouldn't go into that rackety place, and I won't now. It's bad enough to have it tramped back over things." Mariana extended a hand. " Then good-bye," she proceeded. " I think we won't get back here. We're tremendously obliged for the lunch. It has been interesting to see where Jim lives." Harriet Polder's cheeks were darker than pink as they moved out to the sidewalk. " Jim," she called, with an unmistakably proprietary sounding of the familiar diminution; " don't forget my cigarettes, and a half pound of liver for Cherette."

XXXI

JAMES POLDER conducted them to the river, sweeping away in a wide curve beneath solid, grey stone bridges into a region of towering hills. They turned to the left, and, walking on a high embankment, passed blocks of individually pretentious dwellings, edifices of carved granite, alternating with the simpler brick faces of an older period. A narrow, whitely dusty sweep of green park was followed by a speedy degeneration of the riverside; the houses shrunk to rows of wood marked by the grime of steel mills. Soon after they reached a forbidding fence; and, passing a watchman's inspection, entered into a clamorous region of sheds, tracks and confusing levels such as Howat Penny had viewed from the train.

"I'm in the open hearth," Polder told them, leading the way over a narrow boardwalk, still skirting the broad expanse of the river. "It's a process, really, but the whole mill is called after it. We make steel from iron scrap; that's our specialty in the Medial Works; and our stuff's as good as the best. The bigger concerns mostly use pig. Turn in here." They were facing the towering end of an iron shed, and mounted a steep ascent to gain the upper entrance. The multiplication of noises beat in an in-

creasing volume about Howat Penny. Below him a
locomotive screeched with a freight of slag; beyond
was a heap of massive, broken moulds; and a train
of small trucks held empty iron boxes beside an
enormous bank of iron scrap dominated by a huge
crane swinging a circular magnet that dispassion-
ately picked up ton loads and bore them to the
waiting cars.

Inside he gazed through a long vista under a roof
lost in tenebrious shadow. On one side were ranged
the furnaces, a continuous bank of brick bound in
iron; each furnace with five doors, closed with black
slides in which a round opening emitted an intolerable, dazzling white glare. But few men, Howat
thought, were visible in proportion to the magnitude
of the work; deliberately engaged, with leather
shields hanging from their wrists and blue spectacles
pushed up on their grimy brows.

A crane advanced with the shrill racket of an electric gong, its operator caged in midair, and herculean grappling chains swinging. A grinding truck,
filling the width of floor, moved forward to where
Howat stood. It was, Polder told him, the charging
machine. An iron beam projected opposite the furnace doors, and it was locked into one of the charging boxes, filled with scrap metal, standing on the
rails against the furnaces. A man behind him
dragged forward a lever, the slide which covered a
door rose ponderously on a blinding, incandescent
core, and the beam thrust forward into the blaze,

turning round and round in the emptying of the box. It was withdrawn, the slide dropped, and the machine retreated, its complex movements controlled by a single engineer at crackling switches where the power leaped in points of light like violets.

At another furnace, an opened door, where the heat poured out in a constricting blast, workmen were shovelling in powdery white stone; moving up with their heads averted, and quickly retreating with shielding arms. "That's dolomite," James Polder's explanations went rapidly forward. "They are banking up the furnace. The other, in the bins, is ferro manganese." He procured a pair of spectacles; and, with a protected gaze, Howat looked into a furnace, an appalling space of apparently bubbling milk over which played sheets of ignited gases. The skin on his forehead shrivelled like scorching paper.

"I particularly wanted you to see a heat tapped," Polder told Mariana. "And they're making a test at number four." They followed him to where a small ladle of metal had been dipped out of a furnace. It was poured, with a red-gold shower of sparks, into a mould, then dropped in a trough of water. The miniature ingot, broken under the wide sweep of a sledge, was examined by a lean, grizzled workman — "the melter"— who nodded. "We must get back of the furnace," Polder continued, indicating a narrow opening between brick walls through the unstopped chinks of which seethed the scorifying blaze.

Howat Penny stood at a railing, looking down into an apparent confusion of slag and cars, pits and gigantic ladles and upright moulds set upon circular bases. A crane rumbled forward, grappled a hundred-ton ladle, a fabulous iron pot, and petulantly deposited it under a channel extending out from the base of the furnace where they had been stationed. A workman steadied himself below their level and picked with a long iron bar at a plugged opening. It was, James Polder went on, the most dangerous moment of the process —" sometimes the furnace blows out." The labour of tapping was prolonged until Howat was conscious of an oppressive tension. Workmen had gathered, waiting, in the pit. More appeared along the railing above. This was, he felt, the supreme, the dramatic, height of steel making. The men suddenly seemed puny, insignificant, before the stupendous, volcanic energy they had evoked. The tapping stopped. Polder commenced, " It will be rammed out from the front —"

A stunning white flare filled the far roof with a dazzling illumination; and, in a dull explosion, a terrific billowing of heat, a cataract of liquid steel burst out through lambent orange and blue flames. It poured, searing the vision, into the ladle, over which rosy clouds accumulated in a bank drifting through the great space of the shed. Nothing, Howat thought, could contain, control, the appalling expansion, the furious volume, of seething white metal. He was obliged to turn away, blinded by

sheets of complementary green hanging before his
eyes.

The uproar subsided, the flooding steel became
bluer, a solid stream curving into the black depths of
the ladle. Vapours of green and sulphur and lilac
shivered into the denser ruby smoke and rising silver
spray. Polder called a warning into Mariana's ear,
they drew back as a lump of coal was heaved up from
the pit, into the ladle. A dull vermilion blaze followed, and Howat Penny partly heard an explanation —" recarburizing." He could now see the steel
bubbling up to the rim of the container. Men,
Polder said shortly, had fallen in . . . Utterly unthinkable. With a sudorific heat that drove them
still farther back the slag boiling on the steel flowed
in a gold cascade over a great lip into a second
receptacle below. That was soon filled, and gorgeous streams and pools widened across the riven
ground. The steel itself escaped in a milky incan-
descence. "A wild heat," James Polder told them,
pleased. "The bottom of a furnace may drop
out. I was almost caught in the pit at Cambria."
The crane chains swung forward, picked up the ladle
of molten metal, and shifted it through the air to a
position over a circular group of moulds. There, a
valve opened, the steel poured into a central pipe.
"Bottom-filled," Polder concluded, assisting Mariana over the precarious flooring; "the metal rises
into the ingot forms."

They descended again, by the blackened brick, box-like office of the superintendent, to the level of the pit, retraced the way over the boardwalk. They passed a cavernous interior, filled with a continuous crashing, where a great sheet of flushing steel was propelled over a system of rollers through a black, dripping compression. "I can take you to the Senate," James Polder told them, once more outside; "or the Engineers' Society. Dinner will be ready at the club."

He conducted them into the serious interior of a large, solidly constructed dwelling that had been transformed into a club. The dining room was already filling but they secured a small table against the wall. Across the floor ten or twelve men were gathered in a circle. Some, Howat thought, were surprisingly young for the evident authority in their manner, pronouncements; others were grey, weather-worn, men with immobile faces often lost, in the middle of a gay period, in a sudden gravity of thought, silent calculation. He saw the smooth, deft hands of draughtsmen, and scarred, powerful hands that, like James Polder's, had laboured through apprenticeship in pit and mill shop.

He recognized that Polder was more drawn than he had first observed. He was sapped by the crushing entity of the steel works, the enormous heat and energy and strain of the open hearth. If the younger did not lay off he would, unquestionably, break. Nevertheless, Howat was totally unprepared for the amazing suggestion quietly advanced by

361

Mariana. " Jimmy," she said, " couldn't you come to Shadrach for those two weeks? You'd find the quiet there wonderful. And any doctor will advise you to leave your family for a proper rest. I'm certain Howat would be as nice as possible."

A sudden, patent longing leaped to James Polder's countenance. Actually he stuttered with a surprised delight. Damn it, there was nothing for him, Howat, to do but stare like a helpless idiot. He ought to say something, second Mariana's impudent invitation, at once. She ignored him, gazing intently at the younger man. He, too, meeting Mariana's eyes, had apparently totally forgot the unimportant presence of Howat Penny. And he had been married to his Harriet for a scant half year! Howat Penny thought mechanically of the Polders' depressing house, the odours of old cooking and cheap cigarettes, the feverish yapping of the silky animal, Cherette, with matted, pinkish eyes. The precipitant, prideful, young fool! Why hadn't he held onto the merest memory, the most distant chance in the world, of Mariana, rather than fling himself, his injured self-opinion, into this stew?

" Don't say it can't be managed," she persisted. " Anything may. It's absolutely necessary; you can get a prescription — two weeks of green valley and robins and country eggs. Howat will take your money from you at penny sniff, and I'll — I'll come out for dinner."

" Harriet thought of going back to the family,"
362

he replied; " but it might —" he turned at last to Howat Penny. " Would you have me? " he asked directly. What, in thunder, choice of reply did he have? Howat couldn't point out the shamelessness of such an arrangement. Harriet, it seemed, was not to be considered; just as if she were a merely disinterested connection. He issued a belated period to the effect that Shadrach was spacious and Rudolph a capable attendant. It was, he saw, sufficient. " We can write," said Mariana. She endeavoured to caress Howat's hand, but he indignantly frustrated her.

" I'll have to get back to the hearth," James Polder announced regretfully. " It's been wonderful," he told Mariana Jannan. Howat scraped his chair at the baldness of Polder's pleasure. " Your work is tremendous, Jim," she replied; " the only stirring thing I have ever known in a particularly silly world. But you mustn't let it run you, too, into steel rails. President Polder," she smiled brilliantly at him. " Why not? " queried James, the sanguine, at once defiant, haggard and intense.

XXXII

THE following day Howat Penny was both
weary and irritable. Mariana declared,
remorsefully, that she had selfishly dragged
him away from Shadrach; and proposed countless
trivial amends, which he fretfully blocked. He had
no intention of affording her such a ready escape
from a sense, he hoped, of error and responsibility.
Before dinner, however, he found himself walking
with her over the deep green sod that reached to
the public road below. A mock orange hedge enclosed his lawn, bounding the cross roads, the upper
course leading to Myrtle Forge; and beyond they
passed, on the left, the collapsed stone walls and
fallen shingles of what, evidently, had been a small
blacksmith's shed. Farther along they came to the
sturdy shell of an old, single-room building, erected,
perhaps, when Shadrach Furnace was new, with
weeds climbing through the rotten floor, and a fragment of steps, rising to the mouldering peak of a
loft, still clinging to a wall.

Without definite purpose they turned from the
public way into an overgrown path, banked with
matted blackberry bushes, and were soon facing the
remains of the Furnace. It had been solidly con-

364

structed of unmasoned stone, bound by iron rods, and its bulk was largely unaffected by time. The hearth had fallen in, choked by luxuriant greenery; but the blank sides mounted to meet the walled path reaching out to its top from the abrupt hill against which it had been placed. Before it foundations could still be traced; and above, a rectangle of windowless stone walls survived, roofless and desolate. An abandoned road turned up the hill, and they followed it to where they could gaze into the upper ruin and the Furnace top below. Everywhere nature had marked or twisted aside cut stone and wood with its living greenery. Farther down a pathlike level followed the side of the hill, ending abruptly in a walled fall, and a confusion of broken beams, iron braces, and section of a large, wheel-like circumference. Out beyond were other crumbling remains of old activity — a stone span across the dried course of a water way, and a wide bank, showing through a hardy vegetation the grey-brown inequalities of slag.

The stillness, broken only by the querulous melody of a robin, and a beginning, faint piping of frogs, was amazingly profound after the roaring energy of the Medial Works. The decay of Shadrach Furnace showed absolute against the crashing miles of industry on the broad river. A breath of honeysuckle lifted to Howat Penny; the sky was primrose. Mariana moved closer to him and took his arm. They said nothing.

A warm light was spilling across the darkening grass from the lower windows of his dwelling, blurring in a dusk under the high leafage of aged maples. The white roses were already in bud on the vine climbing the lattices at his door, and Mariana fixed one in his buttonhole. "Howat," she said, "it isn't as if you were doing it just for Jim, but for a man, any man, really sick. I'll not even ask you to think of it for me. He can sit on the porch and converse with your owls, and poke about over the hills."

Howat considered the advisability of attempting to extract a promise from her that she would stay away from Shadrach if James Polder was there. He considered it — very momentarily. The possibility, he asserted to himself, was without any alleviating circumstance. What, in heaven's name, would Charlotte think if, as it well might, the knowledge came to her that Mariana and a Polder — that name she never repeated — a married Polder without his wife, were poking over the hills together at Shadrach? She would have him, Howat, examined for lunacy. Mariana demanded too much. He told her this with the dessert.

"It's only the commonest charity," she repeated. Her attack rapidly veered. "Howat," she asked, "do you really dislike Jimmy?" Certainly, he asserted, he — he disapproved of him . . . altogether. A headstrong young donkey who had made a shocking mess of his life. He would have to make the best of a bad affair for which no one was to blame but himself. "It is terrific," she agreed, almost cheerfully; and he had a vague sense of having, somehow, delivered himself into her hands. "Perhaps something can still be done," she said, frowning, increasing the dangers of his position. He managed, by a stubborn silence, to check further conversation in that direction; hoping, vainly, that James Polder couldn't come, that Harriet, sensibly, would insist on his accompanying her, or that Byron would solemnly intervene.

Mariana, later displaying a letter, dispelled his wishes. "It's been arranged quite easily," she told him. "Harriet will go home. I'd like to be here when he arrives, but I can't. You'll be a dear, Howat, won't you?" she begged. "I'm certain James will give you no trouble. And do send him to bed early." At this he grew satirical, and she laughed in an unaccustomed, nervous manner that upset him surprisingly. Honduras drove her to the station the next morning; and, three days later, deposited James Polder on the worn stone threshold under the climbing rose.

After dinner the younger man faced him squarely across the apricot glow of the lamp in the middle room. "This is the third time I've come here without an invitation from you," he said directly. "It was Mariana this last. I shut my mouth on what I'd once have crammed down your throat, and came like any puppy. It wasn't on account of my health, there are miles of quiet country; it wasn't —" he hesitated, then went on —" altogether because of Mariana. I wanted to watch you closer; I want to find out what you are like inside, so I might understand some — some other things better. I can get out if it's a rank failure."

Howat issued a polite, general dissent. " Now, right there," Polder stated; " you don't want me; you'd rather I was a thousand miles away, dead. Well — why don't you say so? " He had not the least conception of a decent reticence of address, Howat Penny thought, resentfully, at the discomfort aroused by the young man's sharp attack.

" Certain amenities," he observed coldly, " have been accepted as desirable, as obligations for —" he hesitated, casting about for a phrase that would not too conspicuously exclude James Polder. " Say it," the latter burst out rudely, " gentlemen. And you all stand about with one thing to say and another in your head."

" A degree of perception is always admirable," Howat Penny instructed him. " That's a nasty one," Polder acknowledged; " but I got into it myself. I can see that." His hand, seared with labour, was pressed on the table; and the elder realized that, since he had witnessed a heat tapped, he was not so censorious of the broken nails, the lines of indelible black. He caught James Polder's gaze, and turned from its intense questioning. Young cheeks

368

had no business to be so gaunt. Polder picked up
the figurine in red clay, studied it with a troubled
brow, and replaced it with a gesture of hopeless-
ness. "Possibly," Howat Penny unexpectedly remarked, "possibly you find beauty in a piece of open
hearth steel."

"It's useful," Polder declared; "it has a tensile
strength. I know what it will do. This," he indicated the fragment of a grace razed over twenty-
three hundred years before, "is good for nothing
that I see." Now, Howat told himself, it was merely
a question of tensile strength. His old enthusiasms,
his passionate admiration for the operas of Christopher Gluck, the enthusiasms and admirations of
his kind, were being pushed aside for things of more
obvious practicality. The very term that had distinguished his world, men of breeding, had been discarded. Individuals like James Polder, blunt of
speech, contemptuous, labour scarred, were paramount to-day.

His thoughts, he realized, were a part of the
questioning thrust on him by the intrusion of Mariana's unfortunate affair into his old age. She was
always dragging him to a perplexing spectacle for
which he had neither energy nor inclination. But
he'd be damned if he would allow the importunities
of the young man beyond the table to complicate
further his difficulties, and he retired abruptly behind the *Saturday Review*. "You'd better get
along up," he said brusquely, after a little.

Breakfast at an end, they settled into a not uncomfortable, mutual silence. They smoked; James Polder unfolded newspapers which he neglected to read; Howat went through the periodicals with audible expressions of displeasure. He wondered when Mariana would appear. Mariana made a fool of him, that was evident; however, he would put his foot on any philandering about Shadrach. He could be as blunt as James Polder when the occasion demanded. After lunch the latter fell asleep in his chair on the porch, pallidly insensible of the sparkling flood of afternoon. Howat rose and went into the house. It was indecent to see a countenance so wearily unguarded, shorn of all protective aggression. Mariana walked in unannounced.

" Why didn't you telephone for Honduras? " he complained. " Always some infernal difference in what you do." She frowned. " Suddenly," she admitted, " I wasn't in a hurry to get here. I almost went back. Idiotic."

" Sensible, it seems to me," he commented. " That Polder is asleep on the porch." She nodded, " Splendid. And you needn't try to look fierce. I can see through you and out the back." He lit a cigarette angrily. " Going to stay for the night? " he demanded. " Several," she replied coolly. " Three can play sniff."

" Look here, Mariana," he proclaimed, " I won't have any nonsense, do you understand? "

370

"We can keep a photograph of Harriet on the table."

James Polder entered, and put a temporary end to his determined speech. When the former saw Mariana his shameless pleasure, Howat thought, was beyond credence. Positively neither of them paid any more attention to him than they did to Rudolph. His irritation gave place to a deeper realization that an impossible situation threatened. There was nothing, obviously, that he could do to-day; but he would speak seriously to Mariana to-morrow; one or both of them would have to leave Shadrach. This determination took the present weight from his conscience; and, pottering about small concerns of his own, he ignored them comfortably.

They appeared late, dirty and hot, for dinner; and it was eight o'clock before Mariana came down in a gown like a white-petalled flower. She wore no rings, but about her throat was a necklace of old-fashioned seed pearls in loops and rosettes. "It's family," she told them; "it belonged to Caroline Penny. And she married a Quaker, too; a David Forsythe." She stopped suddenly, and Howat Penny recalled the tradition that Caroline Penny, Gilbert's daughter, had appropriated her sister Myrtle's suitor. Mariana favoured him with a fleet glance, the quiver of a reprehensible wink. He glared back at her choking with suppressed wrath. "I have a wonderful idea for to-morrow," she proceeded tranquilly; "we'll take

371

lunch, and leave Honduras, and go to Myrtle Forge for the day."

Her design was unfolded so rapidly, her directions to Rudolph so explicit, that he had no opportunity to oppose his plan of sending her away in the morning; and his impotence committed him to her suggestion. She could go in the evening almost as well. After dinner he rattled the dominoes significantly, but Mariana, smiling at him absently, went through the room and out upon the porch. Polder, with an obscure sentence, followed her. A soft rain sounded on the porch roof; but there was no wind; the night was warm.

Howat glanced at his watch, after a period of restful ease, and saw that it was past ten. He moved resolutely outside. Mariana was banked with cushions in the canvas swing, and Polder sat with his body extended, his hands clasped behind his head, in a gloomy revery. The night, apparently, had robbed her countenance of any bloom; more than once in the past year Howat had seen her stamped with the premonitory scarring of time. Polder rose as he approached, and Mariana struggled upright.

" Good night," she said ungraciously, to them both, and flickered away through the dark. James Polder was savagely biting his lips; his hands, the elder saw, were clenched. " Your wife," Howat proceeded, " how is she? " Polder gazed at him stonily, without

372

reply. " I asked after your wife," Howat repeated irritably. " No," the other at last said, " you reminded me of her. I suppose you are right." He turned and walked abruptly from the porch, into the slowly dropping rain.

XXXIII

THE road to Myrtle Forge mounted between rolling cultivated fields, the scattered, stone ruins of walls erected in the earliest iron days; and, after a pastoral course, came to the Forge dwelling, its shuttered bulk set in a tangle of bushes and rank grass. An ancient beech tree swept the ground with smooth, grey limbs, surrounded by long-accumulated dead leaves. James Polder shut off the motor by the low, stone wall that supported the lawn from the roadway; he crossed to the farm, where the house keys were kept, and Howat and Mariana moved slowly forward. A porch, added, the former said, in Jasper Penny's time, extended at the left; and they stood on the broken flooring and gazed down at a featureless tangle once a garden and the gnarled remainder of a small apple orchard beyond.

Polder soon returned, and they proceeded to a door on the further side, where the kitchen angle partly enclosed a flagging of broad stones. Inside, the house, empty of furnishing, was a place of echoes muffled in dust; the insidious, dank odours of corrupting wood and plaster; walls with melancholy, superimposed, stripping papers; older, sombrely blistered paint and panelled wainscoting varnished

374

in an imitation, yellow graining. It was without a relic of past dignity. Mariana was unable to discover a souvenir of the generations of Pennys that had filled the rooms with the stir of their living. Once more outside they sat on the stone threshold of an office-like structure back of the main dwelling and indulged in cigarettes.

The disturbing tension of last night, Howat thought comfortably, had vanished. Mariana was flippant, James Polder enveloped in indolent ease. "The Forge," Howat Penny told them, "was below." A path descended across a steep face of sparse grass; and, at the bottom, Polder's interest revived. "It stood there," he indicated a fallen shed beyond a masoned channel, choked with the broken stones of its walls and tangled shrubbery. "You don't suppose a joke that size was the great Gilbert's plant. Here's the drop for the water power; yes, and the iron pinions of the overshot wheel." He climbed down a precarious wall, and stood perhaps twelve feet below them. Securing a rough bolt, he brought it up for their inspection. "Look at that forging," he cried; "after it has lain around for a century and a half. Like silk. Charcoal iron, and it was hammered, too. Metal isn't half worked any more. We could turn that into steel at almost nothing a ton." He showed them in the mouldering shed the foundation of the anvil, traced the probable shafting of the trip hammer, marked the location of the hearths. "Three," he decided; "and a cold trickle of air. A

375

nigger pumping a bellows, probably. No, they could get that from the wheel," he drew an explanatory diagram in the blackened dust.

With the lunch basket on the running board of the motor they ate sitting on the low boundary wall of the lawn. The heat increased through the late May noon, and Howat remained while Mariana and James Polder wandered in the direction of the orchard. Finally the sun forced the former to move; and he, too, proceeded in a desultory manner, entering the shade of a grove of old maples. The trees, their earliest red leafage already emerald, followed the dry channel cut back from Canary Creek to the Forge, and he soon emerged at the broad, flashing course of the stream. A flat rock jutted into the hurrying water by an overthrown dam, its sun-heated expanse now in shadow; and he stayed, listening to the gurgling flow. Far above him a hawk wheeled in ambient space; a mill whistle sounded remotely from Jaffa.

The thought of Mariana hovered at the back of his lulled being; all he desired, he told himself, was her complete happiness. He might even have become reconciled to James Polder. His first, unfavourable opinion of the latter, he realized, had been modified by — by time. He had judged Polder solely in the light of an old standard. The fellow was painfully honest; good stuff there, iron . . . the iron of the Pennys. But the other strain had betrayed him. A cursed shame. The material of the present, moulded, perhaps, into seemingly new forms, was always that

376

of the past. This Polder was Essie Scofield and Jasper . . . Byron. He, Howat Penny, was Penny and Jannan and Penny — Daniel, James, Casimir, and Howat once more, the older Howat who had married the widow of Felix Winscombe. Black again. He wondered what the blackness, not spent like his own, had brought the other. A headstrong, dark youth with the characteristic sloping eyebrows and slender, vigorous, carriage. The traditional rebellious spirit had involved Jasper in disgrace; it had thinned his own blood.

Footfalls approached through the trees, and the others joined him. James Polder extended himself on the rock, and Mariana sat with her hands clasped about her slim knees. A silence intensified by the whispering stream enveloped them. The hawk circled above, and Howat had an extraordinary sense of the familiarity of the bird hanging in limitless space, of the warm stone and water choking in a smooth eddy. He had, as a boy, fished there. But his brain momentarily swam with a poignant, un-recognizable emotion, different from the sensation of childhood. He rose, confused and giddy. With old age, he muttered.

Mariana followed. "It's all over," she announced, decisively. "We'll drive back and leave to-day." She sighed. "That's gone already," James Polder showed her the sun slipping toward the western hills. She moved up to him, laid her hand on his arm. Howat Penny went ahead. He must speak to her after dinner. As the motor slowly gathered momentum he turned and looked back at the dark, pinkish dwelling in its tangle of grass and bushes run wild. Dusk appeared to have already gathered over it, although the sun still shone elsewhere in lengthening dusty gold bars; the wide-spread beech was sombre against blank shutters, the chimneys broken and cold.

XXXIV

A LETTER for James Polder was at Shadrach, and he opened it immediately, glancing over its scrawled sheet. Howat saw a curious expression overspread the other's countenance. He called, "Mariana!" in a sharp tone. She appeared from the foot of the steps. "Harriet never went home," he told her; "this is from Pittsburgh. She's back on the stage." A premonitory dread filled Howat Penny. Mariana stood quietly, her gaze lifted to Polder. "She never went home," he repeated; "but writes that suddenly she — she didn't want to, and couldn't stand Harrisburg another week. She saw some one and had a part, that ought to be good, offered to her; and, so —"

"Is that all, Jim?"

"No," he replied; "there is more, absolutely unjustified. I think I'd like you to read it. It would be best." Mariana took the letter, and followed its irregular course. "It's true enough," she said quietly, at the end. "But I don't in the least mind, Jim. She had a perfect right to something of the sort. That is — I'm not annoyed about what she says of me, but it will upset you terribly. And it has been my fault, from the first." He protested vehemently, but she stopped him with a gesture; then walked to the door opening on the porch; where, her

379

head up, she stood gazing out into the serene, failing light.

James Polder followed her, and Howat heard the screen softly close. He was about to light a cigarette, but, his hand shaking, he laid it on the table. He put up his glass, without purpose, and then let it drop. Rudolph was placing the silver for dinner; old forks faintly marked with a crest that Isabel Howat had brought to her husband. A recurrence of the afternoon's sense of the continuity of all living flowed over him, whispering with old voices, old longing and sorrow and regret, mingled dim features, and the broken clasping of hands. He saw Mariana sweeping in a pale current — a remote, eternal passion winding through the transient body of life. She smiled, her subdued, mocking gaiety infinitely appealing, and vanished.

They came in to dinner without changing the informal garb of the day. James Polder was silent, disturbed, but Mariana was serenely commonplace. Her voice, clear and high, went unimportantly on; until, turning to Howat Penny, she said without the changing of a tone. " I want James to take me back to Harrisburg with him, but he won't." Howat endeavoured to meet this insanity with the silence usually opposed to Mariana's frequent wildness of statement. His knife scraped sharply against a plate; but, in the main, he successfully preserved an unmoved countenance. " Now that Harriet has surrendered him," she persisted, " I don't see why I can't

380

be considered. It is the commonest sense — Jim can't live alone, properly, in that house; I can't exist properly without him. You see, Howat, how reasonable it seems." What he did perceive was that his attitude of inattention must be sharply deserted.

"Your words, Mariana," he said coldly, "'proper' and 'reasonable,' in the connection you have used them, would be ridiculous if they weren't disgraceful. I have been patient with a certain amount of rash talk, yes — and conduct, but this must be the end. I had intended to have you leave Shadrach this morning, then later. Either that or I'll be forced to make my excuses to James Polder." He glanced with a veiled anxiety at the latter but could read nothing from the lowered, pinched countenance.

"We could leave together if you are tired of us," Mariana continued. "It's James, really, who is making all the trouble. He has some stupid idea about nobility of conduct and my best good. But the real truth is that he's afraid, for me, of course, and so he won't listen."

"Won't you show her that it is impossible?" the younger man cried at Howat Penny. "I can't take advantage of her heavenly courage. She doesn't realize the weight of opinion. It would make —"

"Stuff," she interrupted. "You'd make steel, and I would make an occasional dessert. You must be told, Jimmy, that the afternoon calling you have confused with life really isn't done any more. You

381

have been brought up in rather a deadly way. You ought to be saved from yourself. I am a very mature person, and I am advising you calmly."

The dinner had come to an end; a decanter, in old-fashioned blue and gold cutting, of brandy, a silver basket of oranges, the coffee cups and glasses, were all that remained; and James Polder played with the cut fruit, the half-full cordial glass before him. " I am going to be brutally frank, Jimmy," she said again. " You know that is a habit of mine, too. You are a very brilliant young man, but you are not omnipotent — you require stiffening, like a collar. And I would be a splendid laundress for you. Harriet is a long shot too lenient. I might not be so comfortable to live with, but I'd be bracing. I'd have you in that dirty little superintendent's box in no time."

He made no reply; and, obviously tormented, automatically squeezed a half orange into his goblet. Then he took a sip of brandy.

" Together, James," Mariana asserted. " we would go up like a kite. By yourself — forgive me — you haven't enough patience, enough balance; you wouldn't fly steadily. You might break all your sticks on the ground." He moodily emptied what remained of his brandy into the goblet and orange juice, and pushed it impatiently away. " I'd rather do that," he answered, " than try to carry you with me on such a flight."

Howat Penny was conscious of a diminution of his

382

fears. He had entirely underrated James Polder; the latter was an immense sight steadier than Mariana. His thoughts strayed momentarily to Harriet, back again in her public orbit. He could imagine that she had found Harrisburg insuperably dull, the hours with only Cherette empty after the emotional debauches of the plays elected by Vivian Blane. Yes, this young Polder would stand admirably firm. Mariana frowned at the cobalt smoke of her cigarette. " I am in a very bad temper," she told them. " No one for a minute thinks of what my feeling may be. You are both entirely concerned with your own nice sense of virtue."

" Not at all, but of your future," Howat Penny asserted.

Her lower lip assumed the contempt of which it was pre-eminently capable. She made no immediate reply. James Polder's fingers absently clasped the goblet before him; he drew it toward his plate, tipped the thick liquid it contained. " Just what do you recommend me to do? " Mariana challenged Howat. " Go through with a lifeful of winters like the last! Marry another Sam Lewis! I am not celebrated for reliability; it is only with Jimmy —" she broke off. Howat Penny recalled her callous expression, photographed in Egyptian dress at a period ball, her description of the hard riding and reckless parties of the transplanted English colonies in the south.

Polder lifted the goblet to his lips, but set it back

untasted. Howat looked away from Mariana's scornful interrogation, unable to reply. Finally, "I am old, as you once reminded me," he stated; "I'm out of my time, don't understand. I can only remember, and remembering isn't any longer of use. The men I knew, the kind, I hope, I was, would ruin themselves a hundred times before compromising a woman. Polder appears to understand that. And women I had the privilege of meeting sacrificed themselves with a smile for what you dismiss as mere stupidity. God knows which is right. They looked the loveliest of creatures then. There was a standard, we thought high . . . Things a man couldn't do. But I don't know — it seems so long ago." He stopped to watch James Polder take a sip of the mixture in his hand. The latter tasted it slowly, and then emptied the goblet. His face was blank, with eyes nearly closed.

"I could carry Jimmy up in my hands," Mariana said. "Don't," she added vaguely, as he squeezed out the remaining half of his orange and poured fresh brandy into it. "It's curious," he told her; "not at all bad."

They moved out of the dining room, and Mariana and Polder continued to the porch. Howat stood with a hand resting on the mahogany cigarette box; he had the feeling of a man unexpectedly left by a train thundering into the distance. It would not stop, back, for him now; he was dropped. He sank relaxed into an accustomed chair; his brain surrendered its troubling; the waking somnolence settled over him. He was conscious of his surrounding, recognized its actuality; yet, at the same time, it seemed immaterial, like the setting of a dream. He roused himself after a little and smoked, nodding his head to emphasize the points of his thought.

This Polder had shown the instinct of breeding; while Mariana was — just what she was he couldn't for the life of him determine. A hussy, he decided temporarily. After all, his own time, when black and white had been distinguishable, was best. Howat Penny relinquished, with a sigh, the effort to penetrate to-day; he was content to be left behind; out of the grinding rush, the dizzy speed, of progression. His day, when black had been black, was immeasurably superior; the women had been more charming, the men erect, clothed in proper garb and pride. Where, now, could be seen such an audience as Dr. Damrosch had gathered for his first season of German opera? Not, certainly, at the performance he had heard with Mariana two, no — three, winters ago. A vulgarized performance in the spirit of a boulevard café. The whole present air, he told himself, was wrong.

He looked at his watch, and was surprised to see that it was past ten. Not a sound came from the porch; and he determined to go outside, exercise the discretion which Mariana had cast to the winds. However, he didn't stir; he could not summon the energy necessary for the combating of their impetuous youth. He unfolded a paper, but it drooped on his knees, slid, finally, to the floor. Then Mariana appeared, walked swiftly, without a word, through the room, and vanished upstairs. Not even a civil period at the end of the evening. After another, long wait James Polder entered. The latter stood uneasily by the table, with a furrowed brow, a ridiculous, twitching mouth.

Polder went out into the dining room; where, through the doorway, Howat Penny could see him hovering over the silver basket of oranges, placed upon the sideboard. " If you don't mind," he called back, and there were a rattle of knives, a thin ring of glass. The light was dim beyond, and he stood in the doorway with the brandy decanter and orange juice. He drained the mixture and leaned, absorbed, against the woodwork. " This is a hell of a world!" he exclaimed suddenly. " Everything worth having is fenced off. A woman won't understand. Does any one suppose that I don't want Mariana! It's the responsibility. She's right — I am afraid of it. And she laughed at me. Nothing cowardly in her," his voice deepened.

" It is ignorance," Howat stated.

" I thought so, for a minute; you are wrong. She's had more experience than we'd get in a thousand years. The life she knows would fix that. She talked me into a tangled foolishness in five minutes; made me look like a whiskered hypocrite. Nothing I said sounded real, and yet I must be right. Suppose Harriet should turn nasty, suppose — oh, a thousand things."

" It isn't arguable," Howat Penny agreed.

This afforded the other no consolation. " What is she to do? " he demanded. " Mariana won't settle quietly against a wall. She told you that. She's full of — of a sort of energy that must be at something. Mariana hasn't the anchor of most women — respectability."

" Am I to gather that that is no longer considered admirable? " the elder inquired. " If you gather anything you are lucky," Polder replied gloomily. " I'm not sure about my own name. Good-night," he disappeared abruptly.

Above, Howat slowly made his preparations for retiring, infinitely weary. Waking problems fell from him like a leaden weight into the sea of unconsciousness. He was relieved, at breakfast, to see Mariana come down in a hat, with the jacket of her suit on an arm. He waited for her to indicate the train by which she was leaving, so that he could tell Honduras to have the motor ready; but she sat around in a dragging silence. Polder walked up and down the room in which they were gathered. Howat wished he would stop his clattering movement. An expression of ill-nature deepened in Mariana; she looked her ugliest; and James Polder was perceptibly fogged from a lack of sleep. Finally he said:

" Look here, we can't go on like this." He stopped in front of Mariana, with a quivering face.

She raised her eyebrows. "Come outside," he begged. "What's the use?" she replied; but, at the same time, she rose. "Don't get desperate, Howat," she said over her shoulder. "Even I can't do any more; I can only take my shamelessness back to Andalusia." Polder held open the screen door; and as, without her jacket, she went out, Howat Penny had a final glimpse of the man bending at her side. Like two fish in a net, he thought ungraciously. He was worn out by their infernal flopping. With a determined movement of his shoulders, a fixing of his glass, he turned to the accumulation of his papers.

Later he heard the changing gears of a motor. He thought for a moment that it was Honduras at his own car; then he recognized the stroke of a far heavier engine. The powerful, ungraceful bulk of an English machine was stopping at his door. Immediately after he distinguished the slightly harsh, dominating voice of Peter Provost. The latter entered, followed by Kingsfrere Jannan. Peter Provost, a member of the New York family and connection of the Jannans, had, since the elder Jannan's death, charge of the family's interest in the banking firm of Provost, Jannan and Provost. He occupied, Howat knew, a position of general advisor to Charlotte and her children. He was a large man who had never lost the hardness of a famous university career in the football field, with a handsome, cold countenance and spiked, grey moustache. He shook

388

hands with Howat Penny, and plunged directly into his present purpose.

"Kingsfrere," he said, "has heard some cheap stuff in the city, principally about that young Polder married last fall. Personally, I laughed at it, but Charlotte seemed upset. This Polder's wife, an actress, has left her husband, and gone back to the stage because — so Byron asserted; you know Byron — Mariana had broken up their home."

"Old Polder said just that," Kingsfrere affirmed. "And that wasn't all — he added that Mariana was out here with the fellow."

Provost laughed.

"Well," Howat Penny replied, "James Polder is staying at Shadrach. He was asked here because his health was threatening. He had two weeks leave; and, although I wasn't really anxious, I said he might recuperate with me."

"And Mariana?" Provost inquired.

"Came out day before yesterday, late; leaving this morning."

Howat Penny was conscious of a growing anger. There was no reason for his submitting to an interrogation by Peter Provost; he didn't have to justify his actions, the selection of his guests; and he had no intention of explaining his attitude toward Mariana. But Provost, it became evident, had no inclination to be intrusive. It was, he made that clear, wholly Charlotte. But Kingsfrere Jannan was increasingly impatient. "Where is Polder?" he demanded. Howat surveyed him with neither favour nor reply. Suddenly he understood the feeling of both men — they considered that he was too old to have any grip or comprehension of life. They were quietly but obviously relegating him to the back of the scene. His anger mounted; he was about to make a sharp reply, when he paused. There was a possibility that they were right; he was, undoubtedly, old; and he had been unable to influence, turn, Mariana, in the slightest degree. He didn't approve of her present, head-strong course . . . only a few hours ago he had voluntarily, gladly, relinquished all effort to comprehend it.

"Perhaps," Provost suggested, "since we are here we'd better talk to him. I suppose they're out about the place. You could send Rudolph." Howat replied that he would find them himself. He wanted, now, to prepare James Polder for any incidental unpleasantness. The latter, he knew, had a hasty temper, a short store of patience. After all, he had acted very well in a difficult situation. It had been Mariana. Howat Penny was aware of a growing sympathy for young Polder. His was a more engaging person than Kingsfrere's pasty presence and sharp reputation at cards. He got his hat, and went out over the thick, smooth sod, into the slumberous, blue radiance of the early summer noon.

He found Mariana and James Polder sitting on a bank by the Furnace. "Peter Provost's here with Kingsfrere," he told them quietly. "They want to see . . . James, about some nonsense bantered around town." Polder rose quickly, instantly antagonistic. " At the house? " he demanded, already moving away. Mariana stopped him with a hand on his shoulder. " Don't pay any attention to what they may say, Jimmy," she commanded. " It isn't Peter Provost's affair, and Kingsfrere in a fatherly pose is a scream." They moved forward together. " I'll see them," she added cuttingly.

" I will attend to this," James Polder told her. " I don't want any woman explaining my actions. They haven't a whisper on me. I'm glad enough of an opportunity to talk to a man."

" If you lose your temper —" Howat commenced, but Mariana impatiently interrupted him. " Why shouldn't Jim lose his temper? " she demanded. " I would. Personally, I'd be glad if he did, although it mightn't be fortunate for Kingsfrere. He's a good deal of a dumpling. But I will be furious if you look guilty. Tell them we're mad about each other and that I am waiting for the smallest encouragement to go with you."

Howat Penny left Mariana at the door, and went in with Polder. Provost was seated, with an open paper; Kingsfrere studying the photograph of Scalchi. " This," said Howat generally, " is my guest, James Polder." Peter Provost extended his square, powerful hand; but the other, Jannan, made no movement. " Well? " Polder demanded aggressively. Howat Penny proceeded through the room to the

391

porch, where he met Mariana. They walked to the further end and found chairs. "What makes me sick," Mariana proceeded, "is the way men calmly take everything into their own hands; as if women were still tied up, naughty bundles. Jim will have all the fun, and he has only said 'no' in horrified tones."

Again he could think of no adequate reply. He listened in vain for the sound of raised voices within. "What, in heaven's name, brought them?" Howat told her what he had heard. "I'm glad I did break up that mess they called a home," she asserted. "It was rotten with stale beer and half pounds of liver for that disgusting animal!"

The heat increased in waves; a wagon passing on the road below was enveloped in a cloud of dust. "I wish they'd hurry," Mariana said sharply. Howat Penny thought he heard Kingsfrere speaking in abrupt periods. Then a chair scraped, and Peter Provost's deliberate voice became audible. It was, however, impossible to distinguish his words; but suddenly Polder exclaimed, "Say something I can pound into you." Mariana rose, her hands clenched. "Go back to your mouldy little life!" James Polder continued. "I'm not surprised Miss Jannan wants to get out of it. I am sorry I hesitated. It seemed to me I couldn't offer her anything good enough; but that was before I'd listened to you. . . . And if you in particular come worming about me again I'll smash your flat face." The screen

392

door was wrenched violently open, and James Polder strode up to Mariana. "Suppose we get out of this slag pit," he said, his chest labouring; "I can't breathe here."

"I am ready, Jimmy," she replied quietly; "perhaps Howat will look up a train and let Honduras drive us to the station." She laid her hand on his arm. "Now we can forget them," she said. They turned, and, together, vanished into the house. Howat Penny followed them slowly. He found Peter Provost apparently undisturbed. "Nothing to be done," the latter commented. "I saw that immediately he turned up. Kingsfrere made a short effort, but it wasn't conspicuously successful; I imagine it rather worse than failed. God knows what's getting into these young women, Howat — Eliza and the rest of 'em — it's a gamble they don't. All right, Kingsfrere." Jannan lingered with a dark mutter, but the other unceremoniously drove him into the waiting car.

Mariana soon descended, with Polder carrying two bags. "One seven," Howat told them. In the extraordinary situation he found nothing adequate to say. Mariana might have been going unremarkably to Charlotte and her home; she was absolutely contained. James Polder had a dazed expression; without his companion, Howat thought, he would blunder into the walls. He stood, holding the bags until told to put them down. Honduras was soon at the door. Mariana moved forward, and mechanically Howat Penny made his customary pretence of avoiding her kiss. The warm fragrance of her lips remained long after she had gone.

A pervasive stillness settled upon Shadrach; outside the sunlight lay on the hills in a thick, yellow veil; the cool interior held only the familiar crepitation of the old clock above. Now, he told himself, he could read the papers peacefully; but he sat with empty hands. Mariana had gone. "Outrageous conduct," he said aloud, without conviction. His voice sounded thin, unfamiliar. His dreams of her continued superiority to the commonplace, of her fine aloofness like the elevation of the strains of *Orfeo*, had been utterly destroyed. He could not imagine a greater descent than the one which had overtaken her. As he rehearsed its details they seemed increasingly disgraceful. He could not forgive James Polder for his relapse, his shocking failure to maintain the standards, the obligations, bred into himself, Howat Penny, by so many years, and by blood. It was that miserable old business of Jasper's once more, blighting the present, betraying Mariana.

This wheeled in his brain throughout summer. He had, as he expected, no word from her. Charlotte, too, sent no line; he was isolated in the increasing and waning heat, in a sea of greenery growing heavy and grey with dust, then swept by rain, and touched with the scarlet finality of frost. Rudolph lit again the hickory fires in the middle hearth; the

394

days shortened rapidly; sitting before the glow of the logs he could see, through a western window, the afternoon expiring in a sullen red flame. The leaves streamed sibilantly by the eaves and accumulated in dry, russet heaps in angles and hollows; they burned in crackling fires, filling the air with a drifting haze rich with suggestion and memories. He saw the first snow on a leaden morning when the flexible and bald white covering, devoid of charm, held the significance of barrenness, death. All day this chilling similitude lingered in his mind. He walked about the house slowly, unpleasantly conscious of the striking of his feet on the wood floors.

At Christmas a revival of spirit overtook him; a long letter came from Mariana, Bundy Provost sent him a tall silver tankard, with a lid, for his night table. Howat, polishing his glass with a maroon bandanna, read Mariana's letter in the yellow light of the lamp and burning logs.

"I have been to see a new steel process," she wrote; "the Duplex, with immense tilting furnaces and the Bessemer blast. I know a great deal about iron now; far more than a Howat Penny who should be an authority. Jim is frightfully busy, but lately he has been able to sleep after the night shift, which makes it better for every one. He is one of the best men here, and that comes from the Works, and the reorganization is slowly but surely progressing, and we are progressing with it. I am not a particle lonely, with only one servant; really don't want another, and make a great deal more than desserts. You have no idea how absorbing it is to have a lot of things that must be done. The days simply fade. You mustn't worry about me, Howat; I always hated polite affairs and parties and people; even when I was young as possible I was more than anything else a Hell in the Corner."

He smiled, recognizing an old flippant phrase, and let his hand drop while he recalled Mariana — turning to him to hook her gown, constructing annoying towers with the dominoes, reprehensible and amusing. He resumed reading:

" It would be wonderful if — no, it is wonderful! But Howat, I can tell only you this, I wish oranges had never been invented." He drew his mouth into a compressed line. James was drinking. He remembered when the other first made the concoction of orange juice and brandy; he saw him clearly, leaning in the doorway to the dining room, with the emptied goblet, and a curious, introspective expression on his mobile countenance. " He ought to be hung!" he exclaimed sharply. The fellow should see himself as a mat for Mariana's feet. But that wasn't life, he realized; existence seemed to become more and more heedless of the proprieties, of the simplest concessions to duty. He saw the world as a ship which, admirably navigated a score or more years ago, had jammed its rudder. No one could predict what rocks the unmanageable sphere might be driving for.

396

The significance born by that sentence robbed the remainder of the letter of pleasure. He read that Mariana had ordered the customary gift of cigarettes, and hoped they would last him longer than everybody knew they would. The implied affection of all the paragraphs was visible in the last words. He put the letter carefully away. The cigarettes were sufficient for a considerable time beyond customary. Something of his appetite had gone; the periods of half wakeful slumber in his chair drew out through whole evenings. The actual world retreated; his memories, as bright as ever, became a little confused; the years, figures, mingled incongruously; famous arias were transposed to operas in which they had not been sung.

Winter retreated, but the latter part of March and April were bitterly cold; no leaves appeared; the ground remained barren; he seldom got out.

The albums of programmes were brought from their place on the low shelves, but now, more than often, they were barely opened, scanned. Then, on an evening when belated snow was sifting through the cracks of the solid shutters, he came on an oblong package, wrapped in strong paper. He opened it, in a momentary revival of interest, of life. It was a tall ledger, bound in crumbling calf, with stained and wrinkled leaves. Howat had not seen it for twenty years, but he recalled immediately that it was a forge book kept in Gilbert Penny's day; then Myrtle Forge had been new, that other Howat

alive. He opened it carefully, powdered his knees
with leather dust, and studied the faded entries;
what flourishing, pale violet initials, what rubicund
lines and endings!

There were two handwritings, listing commonplace
transactions now invested by time with an accumulated, poignant significance, one smooth and clerkly,
the other abrupt, with heavy, impatient strokes.
Youth, probably, held at an unwelcome task; and,
more than likely, Howat . . . October, in seventeen
fifty. Years of virility, of struggle and conquest,
of iron — iron, James Polder had shown him, still
uncorrupted, better than the metal of to-day — and
iron-like men. The ledger slipped to the floor, tearing the spongy leather and crumbling the sere leaves.
He recovered it, dismayed at the damage wrought.
A sheet apparently had come loose, and he bent forward with difficulty, a swimming head. Howat made
an attempt to find its place, when he discovered that
it was not a part of the volume. It was, he saw, a
note, obliterated by creases but with some lines still
legible, hurriedly scrawled, by a woman:

"You must be more careful. . . . Your mother.
So hot-headed, Howat. I can't do what you ask.
I have a headache now thinking about Felix and you
and myself. No one must find out." What followed was lost, then came a signature that, with the
aid of a reading glass, he barely deciphered —"Ludowika."

That was the name of the woman, a widow, Gil-

bert's son had married. Her first husband, Felix
Winscombe, had died at Myrtle Forge during a diplomatic mission from England. . . . An old man
with a young wife! His confusion, slowly resolv-
ing into a comprehension of what the note implied,
filled him with an increasing revolt. The earlier
Howat, too, like Jasper, in the tangle of an intrigue
— not a public scandal and shame, as had been the
later, but no less offensive. In a flare of anger
Howat Penny crumpled the paper and flung it into
the fire. There it instantly blackened, burst into
flame and wavered, a shuddering cinder, up the chim-
ney. He put the ledger, loosely wrapped in its covering, on the table, and sat breathing rapidly, curiously disturbed. The old fault, projected so unexpectedly out of the faithless burial of the past,
struck at him with the weight of a personal affront.

The heat subsided in the hearth, with the nightly
ebbing of steam in the radiator; the hickory, disintegrating into blocks, faded from cherry red to pulsating, and finally dead, ash. Lost in the bitterness
of his thoughts he made no movement to replenish
the fire.

He wondered if the explored histories of other
families would show such scarring records as his own.
Were there everywhere, back of each heart, puddles,
sloughs, masked in the deceiving probity maintained
for public view? And now — Mariana! Yet, somehow, her affair did not appear as ugly as these
others. Stated coldly, in conventional terms, it was

little different. Why, in plain words she had . . .
but Mariana evaded plain words, her challenging
courage forbade them. Here was more than could
be arraigned, convicted, by a stereotyped judgment.
Or perhaps this was only his affection for her, blinding him to the truth.

The first Howat and Jasper, striking contemptuously across the barriers of social morals, lived in
Mariana, alone with James Polder in illegitimate circumstance, and in himself — an old man without family, without the supporting memory of actual achievement; the negative decay of a negative existence.
His mind, confronted by a painful complexity of un-
answerable problems, failed utterly. He was conscious of his impotence chilling his blood, deadening
his nerves. Thin tears fell over his hollow cheeks;
and he rose shakily, fiercely dragging at his bandanna.

But he discovered that his hand was numb with
cold. The fire lay black and dead. The shrilling
wind, ladened with snow, wrenched at the shutters.
The room was bitter. He must get up to bed . . .
warm blankets. A chill touched him with an icy
breath. It overtook him midway on the stair, and
he clung to the railing, appalled at its violence in his
fragile being. He got, finally, to his room, to the
edge of his bed, where he sat waiting for the assault
to subside. He wanted Rudolph, but the effort to
move to the door, call, appeared insuperable. The

chill left him; and blundering, hideously delayed, he wrapped himself in the bed covering.

Not all the wool in the world, he thought, would be sufficient to drive the cold from his body. He fell into a temporary exhaustion of sleep; but was waked later by sharp and oppressive pains in his chest, deepening when he breathed. The suffering must be mastered, and he lay with gripping hands, striving by force of will to overcome what he thought of as the brutal play of small, sharp knives. He conquered, it seemed; the pain grew less; but it had left an increasing difficulty in his breathing; it was a labour to absorb sufficient air even for his small, aged demands. Sleep deserted him; and he waited through seeming years for the delayed appearance of dawn. He had hoped that the new day would be sunny, warm; it was overcast, he could see the snow drifted in the lower window panes.

Rudolph usually knocked at the door at half past eight; but, apparently, to-day he had forgot. Howat Penny's watch lay on the table, at his hand, yet it was far distant; he couldn't face the heavy effort of its inspection. At last the man came in with his even morning greeting. Howat was so exhausted that he could make no reply; and Rudolph moved silently to the bedside. His expression, for an instant, was deeply concerned. " I have a cold, or something of the sort," the other said. He raised his head, but sank back, with a thin, audible inspira-

401

tion. "It would be best, sir, to have the doctor from Jaffa," the servant suggested. Howat, in the midst of protest, closed his eyes; the pain had returned. When he had again defeated it Rudolph was gone.

The room blurred, lost its walls, became formless space; out of which, to his pleasurable surprise, he saw the carefully garbed figure of Colonel Mapleson walking toward him. He never forgot that tea rose! Confound him — probably another benefit for one of his indigent song birds. As Howat was about to speak the Colonel disappeared. It was Scalchi, in street dress, a yellow fur about her throat, warm, seductive. He had sent the divine Page the bouquet in paper lace. But she too vanished. He heard the strains of an orchestra; lingering he had missed the overture, and it might be the first duet — with Geister in superb voice. He was waiting for Mariana, that was it . . . always late. Then her hand was under his arm. But it was the doctor from Jaffa.

Rudolph was at the foot of the bed, and the two men moved aside, conversed impolitely in hushed tones. I'm sick, he thought lucidly. One word reached him — oxygen. It all melted away again, into a black lake with ghostly swans, a painted mouth and showering confetti; one of the supreme waltzes that Johann Strauss alone could compose. Later a woman in a folded linen cap was seated beside him, a chimera. But she laid cool fingers on his wrist, held a brownish, distasteful mixture to his lips. A draught of egg nog was better, although it wasn't

402

as persuasive as some he had had: Bundy Provost's, for example.

Bundy was a galliard youth, but he was clear as ice underneath. He wouldn't have let them put that thing over his, Howat's, face. He tried to turn aside, but a cap of darkness descended upon him. Afterward his breathing was easier. A blue iron tank was standing nearby, and the nurse was removing a rubber mask attached to a flexible tube. The latter led from a glass bottle, with a crystal pipe into the tank; the bottle held water; and the water was troubled with subsiding, clear bubbles. More of the dark, unpleasant mixture, more egg nog. Why did they trouble and trouble him — already he was late getting to Irving Place.

The opera, as he had feared, had commenced; and it was at once strange and familiar. The chorus and orchestra were singing in a deep ground tone; the stage was set with a row of great, seething furnaces; glaring white bars of light cut through vaporous, yellow gases and showered steel sparks where coppery figures were labouring obscurely in a flaming heat that rolled out over the audience. There was a shrilling of violins, and then a deafening blare of brass, an appalling volume of sound pouring out like boiling metal. . . . But here was Rudolph; the performance was at an end; it was time to go home.

"I took the liberty of searching for — for Miss Jannan's address," the other told him. Well, and why not! "Mr. Provost and Mrs. Jannan are away

403

for a week." Howat hoped that Kingsfrere would not turn up with his flat face. He was conscious of smiling at a memory the exact shape of which escaped him — something humorous that had happened to the pasty youth. A refreshing air came in at the open windows, and he struggled for a full, satisfying breath. The relief of what he dimly recognized as oxygen followed. The nurse moved to the door and Mariana entered.

"Howat," she exclaimed, sitting beside him, "how silly of you! A cold now with winter done. The snow is running away. And these soda-watery tanks." He felt a warmth communicated by her actual presence. "It's just my breathing," he told her; "it gets stopped up. A damned nuisance! Did Honduras meet you?"

She assured him that she had been correctly received, and vanished to remove her hat. Mariana must not sit in here, with the windows open, he told the nurse; but then, he added, it was no good giving Mariana advice. She wouldn't listen to it, except to do the opposite. She came back, in one of her eternal knitted things, this one like a ripe banana, and sat in the nurse's place. There was a great deal he wanted to know, in a few minutes, when he felt less oppressed. The night came swiftly, lit by his familiar lamps; Rudolph moved about in the orderly disposition of fresh white laundry. A coat needed pressing. It would do to-morrow. The doc-

404

tor hurt him with a little scraping stab at the bottom of his ear.

"Mariana," he at last made the effort of speech, questioning: "I have been bothered about your — your temporary arrangement. That Harriet, you know . . . make trouble."

"Why, Howat," she replied, admirably detached; "you don't read the important sheets of the papers! Harriet has made a tremendous success with what was supposed to be a small part. A New York manager has engaged her in letters of fire, for an unthinkable amount. James and I sent her our obscure compliments, but we were virtuously rebuked by a legal gentleman. Harriet, it seems, is going to cast us off."

Of all that she had said only the word obscure remained in his mind; and it roused in him an echo of his old, dogmatic pride. "Mariana," he demanded, "didn't the reorganization come about; isn't James Polder superintendent?"

She hesitated, then replied in a low, steady voice. "Yes, Howat, it did; but they didn't move Jim up. An older, they said steadier, man was chosen." It was the oranges, he told himself, the oranges and brandy; the cursed young fool. "You must come away, Mariana," he continued more faintly; "fair trial, failure — something to yourself, our family."

"Leave Jimmy because he wasn't made superintendent!" she replied in an abstracted impatience.

Then, " I wonder about a smaller plant ? Won't you understand, Howat," she leaned softly over him; " I need Jim as badly as he needs me; perhaps more. If I had any superior illusions they have all gone. I can't tell us apart. Of course, I'd like him to get on, but principally for himself. Jim, every bit of him, the drinking and tempers, and tenderness you would never suspect, is my — oxygen. I can see that you want to know if I am happy; but I can't tell you, Howat. Perhaps that's the answer, and I am — I have a feeling of being a part of something outside personal happiness, something that has tied Jim and me together and gone on about a larger affair. You see, Howat, I wasn't consulted," she added in a more familiar impudence; " whether I was pleased or not didn't appear to matter. In a position like that it's silly to talk about happiness as if it were like the thrill at your first ball."

He drifted away from her through the nebulous haze deepening about him. An occasional, objective buzzing penetrated to his removed place; but all the while he realized that he was getting farther and farther from such interruptions of an effort to distinguish a vaguely familiar, veiled shape. He saw, at last, that it was Howat, a black Penny. It was at once himself and that other Howat, yes, and Jasper. All three unremarkably merged into one. And the acts of the first, a dark young man with an erect, impatient carriage, a countenance and gaze of vigorous scorn, accumulated in a later figure,

406

hardly less upright, slender, but touched with grey
— a man in the middle of life. He paid with an an-
guished spirit for what had taken place; and at last
an old man lingered with empty hands, the husk of a
passion that had burned out all vitality.

Mariana, too, had been drawn into the wide implications of this mingled past and present. But now,
clearly, he recognized in her the meeting of spirit and
flesh that had been denied to him. That was life,
he thought, that was happiness. In the absence of
such consummation he had come to nothing. In
Jasper, in Susan Brundon who had married him over
late, the two had warred.

Life took the spirit to itself, mysteriously; wove
the gold thread into its design of scarlet and earth
and green, or else . . . a hearth soon cold, the walls
of a Furnace crumbled and broken, a ruin covered
from memory by growing leafage and grass throb-
bing with the song of robins, the shrilling of frogs in
the meadow.

The doctor and nurse, Rudolph and Mariana,
moved about him in a far, low stir. At times they
approached on a lighter flood of oxygen. Mariana
wiped his lips — an immaterial red stain. But
what was that confounded opera the name of which
he had forgot? It would be in his albums; in the
first, probably. Downstairs. He had a sudden
view of Mariana's face as she returned with the
volume. An expression of piercing concern overwhelmed the reassuring smile she had for him.

Howat understood at last, he was dying. An instinctive shuddering seized him; not in fear of the obliterating fact; but from a physical revulsion bred by his long years of delicate habit.

Yet it wouldn't do to expose Mariana to the terrors; and, after a sharp, inward struggle, he said almost fretfully, " Further on." She turned the pages slowly; but no one could read without a decent light. He moved his head, in an infinity of labour, toward the clear, grey opening of the window, and saw a pattern of flying geese wavering across the tranquil sky.

THE END